P9-CNC-901

WITHDRAWN

CONCORD FREE
CONCORD
MA
PUBLIC LIBRARY

MAR 2 8 2011

ANTHEM FOR DOOMED YOUTH

ALSO BY CAROLA DUNN

THE DAISY DALRYMPLE MYSTERIES

Death at Wentwater Court
The Winter Garden Mystery
Requiem for a Mezzo
Murder on the Flying Scotsman
Damsel in Distress
Dead in the Water
Styx and Stones
Rattle His Bones
To Davy Jones Below
The Case of the Murdered Muckraker
Mistletoe and Murder
Die Laughing
A Mourning Wedding
Fall of a Philanderer
Gunpowder Plot
The Bloody Tower
Black Ship
Sheer Folly

CORNISH MYSTERIES

Manna from Hades
A Colourful Death

ANTHEM FOR DOOMED YOUTH

A Daisy Dalrymple

Mystery

CAROLA DUNN

MINOTAUR BOOKS

NEW YORK

This is a work of fiction. All of the characters, organizations, and events portrayed in this novel are either products of the author's imagination or are used fictitiously.

ANTHEM FOR DOOMED YOUTH. Copyright © 2011 by Carola Dunn. All rights reserved. Printed in the United States of America. For information, address St. Martin's Press, 175 Fifth Avenue, New York, N.Y. 10010.

www.minotaurbooks.com

Library of Congress Cataloging-in-Publication Data

Dunn, Carola.
    Anthem for doomed youth : a Daisy Dalrymple mystery / Carola Dunn.—1st ed.
            p. cm.
        ISBN 978-0-312-38776-1 (alk. paper)
    1. Dalrymple, Daisy (Fictitious character)—Fiction. 2. Police spouses—Fiction. 3. Murder—Investigation—Fiction. 4. Nineteen twenties—Fiction.
5. England—Fiction. I. Title.
        PR6054.U537A85 2011
        823'.914—dc22

                                                            2010041086

First Edition: April 2011

10 9 8 7 6 5 4 3 2 1

To all victims of war

ACKNOWLEDGMENTS

My thanks to librarians Ruth Stickley, Kate Hanlon, and Heather Lees of Saffron Walden Library, for their patience in answering my endless questions about the town and its history. Thanks to Martin Hugall, retired teacher, for his help with the history of Friends' School, Saffron Walden; and to Heidi Thomas McGann and Karl Gibbs for assistance with regard to Saffron Walden Friends' Meeting. Thanks to fellow FSSW Old Scholars Frances Rothwell, Jane Heydecker, and Jon North for their memories of how we spent our Sunday afternoons. And thanks to Carole Rainbird, who didn't attend the school but lives near enough and was kind enough to take me there and patient enough to put up with my taking of photos and asking of questions.

Thanks to an Anonymous Librarian (by request) of Oregon Health Sciences University library for information about prostheses in the 1920s. Thanks to Jill Reay for help with translating English into Geordie. Thanks to Fergus McMullen for permission to use the name of McMullen & Sons' Hertford Brewery "so long as the beer was not the cause of death." And last but far from least, thanks to Mark Ropkins, gardener at the Bridge End Garden, for leading me to the centre of the maze (and out again) so that I could see what it was like.

All errors, omissions, or artistic alterations in these matters and others are entirely my own. All characters associated with the school and the brewery are products of my imagination. Though I have used the names of the then headmaster and headmistress, anything they may do or say as a result of meeting Daisy is, of course, pure fiction.

Anthem for Doomed Youth

What passing-bells for these who die as cattle?
Only the monstrous anger of the guns.
Only the stuttering rifles' rapid rattle
Can patter out their hasty orisons.
No mockeries for them from prayers or bells;
Nor any voice of mourning save the choirs,—
The shrill, demented choirs of wailing shells;
And bugles calling for them from sad shires.

What candles may be held to speed them all?
Not in the hands of boys, but in their eyes
Shall shine the holy glimmers of good-byes.
The pallor of girls' brows shall be their pall;
Their flowers the tenderness of silent minds,
And each slow dusk a drawing-down of blinds.

—Wilfred Owen

ANTHEM FOR DOOMED YOUTH

ONE

"*Ring a* ring o' roses," sang Daisy for the fifth time. "A pocket full of posies. Atishoo, atishoo, we all fall down." She subsided thankfully into the rocking chair while Oliver and Miranda flung themselves on the floor and rolled around squealing. Actually, Oliver had anticipated the dénouement as usual and dropped at the first "atishoo."

"Now that's enough of that, twins," said Nurse severely. "I'm afraid we're getting a little overexcited, Mummy. It'll end in tears, you mark my words."

"Now that they're so active, they need the exercise, and it's rained too hard to go out in the garden for days."

"Not proper June weather at all!" She sounded as if it was Daisy's fault.

Nana, who was even more apt to get overexcited than the toddlers and had had to be tied to a table-leg, whined mournfully.

"Nana play," Miranda commanded, going over to the little dog and hugging her. Nana frantically licked her face.

"Now come away at once, Miss Miranda! You'll get germs."

"Nonsense," said Daisy. "I was kissed by dogs every day of

my childhood and here I am, healthy as a horse." She looked round as the door opened. "What is it, Elsie?"

The parlourmaid bobbed a sketchy curtsy. "It's Sergeant Tring on the telephone, madam. The master would like a word with you."

"Thank you. I'll come down. I'll be back in a minute, babies."

"Mama go," Miranda observed dispassionately.

"Mama!" her brother shrieked.

"I'll be right back, Oliver. I've got to go and talk to Daddy."

"Dada!" Oliver rushed after her and had to be detached from her leg by Bertha, the nurserymaid.

Hastily closing the door, Daisy heard Nurse Gilpin mutter, "I knew it. It never does to spoil them."

She hurried downstairs, filled with foreboding. When Alec rang up in the middle of the day, it invariably meant a disruption of their plans. Not that plans were ever anything but tentative when one's husband was a detective chief inspector at Scotland Yard, liable to be called to the outer reaches of the kingdom at a moment's notice.

She picked up the "daffodil" stand, sat down on the chair by the hall table, and put the receiver to her ear. "Tom?"

"Afternoon, Mrs. Fletcher. How's my godson?"

"Screaming for Dada. Healthy lungs! But I assume he won't be seeing him for a while?"

"The chief'll have to tell you about that. Can you hold on half a mo, please, he's on another telephone."

"Of course. How is Mrs. Tring?"

"Blooming." DS Tring adored his wife, a large woman though not as large as Tom. That didn't stop his having a wonderful way with female servants when he needed to extract information. "And Miss Miranda?"

"Likewise. Her vocabulary grows by leaps and bounds. Not quite up to yours yet."

"I'll have to look to my laurels."

Daisy pictured his luxuriant moustache twitching as he

2

grinned. "Belinda's pretty good, too. It's her school sports day on Saturday. Oh no, don't tell me—"

"There's no way of knowing, Mrs. Fletcher. Here's the chief."

"Alec? Darling, you're not going to miss Bel's sports day, are you?"

"I hope not. If we haven't made an arrest by then, I might be able to sneak away for the afternoon. Epping can't be more than forty miles from Saffron Walden."

"You're only going to Epping? I was afraid it might be Northumberland."

"You always are, love. I can't think why."

"Because it's so far away. But Epping—You'll come home for the night, then?"

"Yes, but don't wait dinner for me."

"Don't half the murderers in London bury bodies in Epping Forest?"

"It's often been considered a convenient spot." Alec sounded amused.

"If that's where you're going, don't forget to take Wellington boots. It's still belting down."

"The forecast's for a clearing trend tonight. Let's hope they're right for once."

Daisy jumped to the obvious conclusion. "So you *are* going to dig up a body in Epping Forest?"

"Three of them. For a start. I'm only telling you because there's no conceivable way you can get yourself mixed up in this case."

"Of course not! But do be careful, darling. I'd hate for the fourth body to be you."

"No fear of that, love. I must run."

"Should I tell Mrs. Dobson to leave something out for you?"

"No, I'll pick up a bite to eat somewhere. Coming, Tom!" He said good-bye and rang off.

Daisy hung up. Three bodies! Assuming they had all been killed by the same person—a madman? Or perhaps a member of an East End gang? There would be a lot of pressure on the police to arrest someone before another murder followed. Not that Alec didn't always clear up his cases as quickly as possible.

Still, today was Wednesday. It didn't seem likely that he would be finished by Saturday, or even free to take an afternoon off. Poor Belinda! Though happy at school, she was so looking forward to seeing them. She would have to make do with her stepmother. Luckily she was used to Daddy disappearing at unpredictable intervals. She had been a detective's daughter much longer than Daisy had been a detective's wife. The twins had yet to learn.

But if Daisy had married a man considered suitable by her mother, the Dowager Lady Dalrymple, no doubt he would have gone off huntin', shootin', and fishin' all over the country, and spent much of the rest of his time stridin' across his acres taking potshots at rabbits and pigeons.

She went back to the nursery. The twins rushed to her, jabbering. They really needed more exercise, but a glance at the window showed no sign of the promised clearing. A nice noisy game would do. One look at Nurse Gilpin's face told her that was a battle she didn't want to fight.

"We'll play something quieter now. Bertha, would you untie Nana, please?"

"Yes'm." The nursemaid went to help Miranda, who got there first.

Daisy sat cross-legged on the floor, to Mrs. Gilpin's manifest disapproval—but then, she disapproved of practically everything Daisy did in her nursery. "Oliver, come and sit with Mummy."

Oliver promptly scrambled up into the rocking chair and sat there looking pleased with himself, babbling nonsense syllables. But when both Miranda and Nana sat neatly and expectantly on the floor in front of Daisy, he clambered down and joined them.

"Clap handies all together," warbled Daisy, suiting action to the words. "Clap hands away. This is the way we exercise upon a rainy day."

Escaping central London just before the start of the rush-hour, the police car crossed the industrial wasteland of the Lea Valley, bleaker than ever in still-pouring rain. The contrast with the lush green of Epping Forest was startling. The rain brightened the varied shades of the fresh foliage and washed the dust and soot of the nearby city off the grass.

The driver was a uniformed constable, PC Stock, a pal of Ernie Piper's. A Londoner, he knew the lanes, footpaths, and bridle paths of the Forest like the back of his hand, according to Piper. He had grown up in Walthamstow and misspent many happy hours of his youth playing truant in the woods and streams.

Alec had no intention of wandering about in the rain looking for the informal burial ground. The Essex detective from whom he was taking over the case, disgruntled no doubt, had given the vaguest of directions: "Broad Wood, towards the middle, you can't miss it." Broad Wood appeared on the map to cover nearly two hundred acres, with no defined boundaries. With Stock's assistance, they had a better chance of finding the right spot without fighting through thickets of brambles and hawthorn and holly on the way.

Tom, sitting next to Alec in the back seat, said with a gusty sigh, "Me and the missus used to come out here weekends and bank holidays when we were courting."

"Not in weather like this, I bet, Sarge," said Piper from the front seat.

"It was always sunny back then, lad."

"Back before the Ice Age, that'd be?"

"Don't you let the missus hear you say that if you ever want to taste her steak and kidney pud again!"

"Oh, Sarge, please, Sarge, you're not going to tell on me, are you?"

"Watch it, laddie. Too cheeky by half, you are."

He was lucky to have a team so well attuned to each other,

Alec thought. Besides being pleasant to work with, it made them work together more efficiently. Ernie Piper, neat in his blue serge, was shaping up nicely and might be encouraged to take his sergeant's exams soon. Tring, an awe-inspiring mountain in tan and yellow checks, didn't aspire to rise above his present rank. He was extremely good at what he did but not sufficiently imaginative to take the lead in a major case.

And it sounded as if they had a major case on their hands. Three bodies—though as yet he had no reason to believe they were associated in anything but proximity.

Stock turned into a narrow lane, not much more than a cart-track, no different, as far as Alec could tell from half a dozen they had passed. It was gravelled but not paved, with grass growing down the middle between the ruts. Stock took a right-hand branch. "This should do it, sir. Yes, look, there's a bloke waiting for us."

A constable in a shiny uniform cape stood on the verge waving at them. Stock pulled up beside him with rather more verve than strictly necessary, splashing mud on the man's already muddy boots.

He didn't even glance down, apparently already too sodden to notice. He stepped over to the rear window and stooped to look in as Alec rolled it down a couple of inches.

"DCI Fletcher," he announced himself. "Which way from here?"

With a sloppy salute, the man said in the flat tones of Essex, "PC Elliot, sir. Sorry, sir, this is as close as you can drive. You'll 'ave to walk from here." Rain dripped from his helmet and must be dripping down the back of his neck, if not streaming down the sides, too.

Stock twisted to say over his shoulder, "There's a ride—a bridleway—just a hundred yards farther on, sir. It's wide enough to drive, easy."

"Curves off in the wrong direction. 'Sides, like as not you'd get stuck in the mud. And the brook's up. There's a footpath here, sir. I'll show you the way."

"We'll walk," said Alec, closing the window and opening the door. He settled his trilby more firmly on his head, turned up the collar of his mac, and started to get out.

"Hold on, Chief!" Ernie Piper was behind the car already, reaching into the boot for their umbrellas and Wellingtons. "You don't want to get out till you've got these on. Knee-deep in mud before we even get into the Forest." A thoroughgoing city-dweller, he sounded disgusted, and had come prepared, having put on his boots while still in the car. He squelched round to hand Alec his.

Pulling them on, Alec said, "Stock, we'll go ahead. You'd better drive on a little and pull the car off the road, out of the way, though I don't imagine this road sees much traffic in this sort of weather."

"You don't want me to stay with the car, sir?"

"No, you can follow us, if you think you can find the way."

"I'll find you, sir, don't you worry."

The footpath was less muddy than the lane, being carpeted with last year's fallen leaves on top of a thick mulch of the leaves of centuries. Epping Forest had been a Royal hunting preserve, never set to the plough, though local villagers had always been allowed to coppice the trees. When the City of London took it over in the middle of the nineteenth century, the coppicing had been stopped. As a result the older hornbeams, beeches, and oaks were strange creatures with short, thick boles sprouting branches like Struwwelpeter's hair.

Between these had grown up an underlayer of their offspring mixed with hawthorn, holly, and service tree. A carpet of bluebells suggested that the sky had come down to earth, leaving a grey gloom above. Squirrels dashed up trees to chitter at the invaders, but the birds were too busy feeding nestlings to fall silent as they passed, in spite of the warning screech of a jay.

On fine weekends and holidays, well served by omnibuses and several tube stations, the Forest swarmed with escapees from the city. These tended to stick to the established trails and clearings, leaving much of the rest a practically impenetrable tangle of vegetation.

Squishing along the footpath on the heels of the local constable, Alec eyed the dripping jungle on either side with deep misgivings.

"Strewth!" said Tom, behind him. "How did anyone manage to lug three bodies off the beaten path through that lot?"

"And find enough clear ground to bury 'em!" Piper added from the rear.

"I imagine it was a dog that found the first grave, Elliot?" Alec asked.

"That's what I heard, sir. A Mr. Webster's Jack Russell."

"It'd take a Jack Russell to get in there," Tom muttered.

"Presumably Webster went to see what his dog had found," Alec pointed out, "and the local coppers, too. The site must be accessible, though perhaps not to someone of your size."

"That's all right, Chief. I'll stay on the path and you can tell me all about it later."

"There's plenty of room, sir," said Elliot. Tom sighed. "It's not in the thickest part—stands to reason or they couldn't've buried them—and a lot got trampled down when we was searching."

Alec echoed Tom's sigh. It was inevitable, nothing more than he had expected, but he wondered how many clues had disappeared into the leaf-mould. The local detectives who so resented the Yard being called in seldom considered the difficulties of coming to a case where evidence had already been mishandled or lost, witnesses antagonised, suspects alarmed.

The path they were on at one point ran near the swollen stream Elliot had warned of. Brown and turbulent it raced down the slope towards the Lea.

"Good job your pal didn't try to drive us through that," Tom remarked to Piper. "We'd've been stuck for a month of Sundays, if it didn't wash us down to the Thames."

"Don't like the look of it myself," Piper agreed.

Constable Stock caught up with them in time to hear this.

"It'll go down fast soon as this rain stops," he said, sounding a bit resentful.

"It's not coming down as hard," Tom said peaceably.

What could be seen of the sky through the trees was now light grey instead of dark grey. Leaves still dripped and occasional cascades descended on them, but as they emerged into a grassy glade, it was obvious that the worst was over.

A wide ride, more cart-track than bridleway, entered the clearing at an angle to their path. Muddy ruts filled with water suggested that it was occasionally used by vehicles. The ruts crossed the clearing and ran into the woods opposite. The footpath petered out, as if, having brought its followers to the glade, it abandoned them to decide for themselves which way to go.

"That way." Elliot pointed at a caped constable standing on the edge of what looked like an unbroken wall of greenery.

They altered course to trudge in his direction.

"Blimey," said Tom, at Alec's side, "I'd've left the perishing dog to find its own way home."

"It can't be as bad as it looks from here. Someone had already lugged three bodies through, remember."

" 'Less they came from the other side," Piper suggested.

"Nah," said Elliot, "Inspector Gant reckons it'd be impossible."

"Ah," said Tom, at his most inscrutable.

They reached the cross-track. Alec stopped to study the ruts.

"Horse and cart," said Tom, "not a motor vehicle. The most recent, at any rate."

"Yes, a heavy one. And we won't get much more than that after all this rain."

"You reckon it's how the bodies were brought here, Chief?" Piper asked.

"More likely than that someone carried 'em one by one over his shoulder from the lane," Tom responded. "That's quite a way."

"But let's not jump to conclusions. The cart may have nothing to do with the case. We don't even know whether the three burials took place at or near the same time. The report I was given was singularly uninformative."

"They didn't, sir," said Elliot. "What I heard is, the doc says the one the dog found is not too old, maybe a week or thereabouts. Then the one they found when they started searching, that's more like a few months. After that, they started looking for more and they found a sort of dip, like, where the ground had settled, but they hadn't hardly started digging—just enough to be sure there really was a body, when the chief constable heard about it and called in the Yard, sir, so they stopped."

The mild irritation Alec had been feeling about the inadequate report blossomed into fury. This was essential information that he should have been given by the detective in charge, not by a uniformed constable who happened to know. Naturally DI Gant was annoyed at having the case taken from him, but such unprofessional conduct was inexcusable. At least, he'd better have an excellent excuse, such as having dropped dead on the spot.

Elliot was not to blame. With difficulty keeping his voice even, Alec thanked the man. Tom, well acquainted with both protocol and his chief, shot him a shrewd glance, but the constable just looked pleased with himself.

"Piper, follow the tracks in both directions. See if there's anything else they can tell us, and get any measurements you can."

"Right, Chief."

The stretch of grass from the ruts to the waiting constable showed nothing more than the trampling of a great many police boots. Beyond him the trampling continued, with broken branches and crushed shrubs thoroughly obliterating any marks the murderer might have left.

With a sigh, Alec acknowledged to himself that the past few days of torrential rain probably had destroyed anything useful long before Detective Inspector Gant arrived on the scene.

They followed the trail, winding between trees for twenty yards or so. It ended at a fallen beech, one of the once-coppiced monsters, stretched out like a stranded giant squid. It couldn't have been downed more than a year or two ago because some branches were still putting out new growth, reaching upwards. Where the shallow root system had torn out of the earth, the soil was disturbed. Seeds of many different plants had sprouted, grasses, bracken, rosebay willowherb, and some small shrubs.

Amid this evidence of vigorous life gaped three ominous trenches.

TWO

Shortly before eleven, Alec telephoned from Epping police station to say he was about to leave for home. Daisy waited up for him, of course. And of course Mrs. Dobson had left a hefty snack for him, regardless of his instructions.

Sitting with him in the dining room while he ravenously disposed of a beef and horseradish sandwich, Daisy shared his Thermos flask of cocoa. She was dying to know what had kept him so late, but she refrained from asking. For once, her discretion was rewarded.

Alec sat back, nursing his mug of cocoa in both hands. "We were out at the site till it got too dark," he said. "The local man, the detective from Chelmsford, left as soon as he heard we'd been called in, and he took all but a couple of constables with him, including their spades and shovels. Not merely to Epping, but all the way to HQ in Chelmsford. I had to send to the Yard for some of our own people and equipment, and you know how happy that's going to make the super."

Daisy had had her own clashes with Superintendent Crane. One never could tell what would set off an explosion, and Alec had not always been on her side. It was a subject better avoided.

Suddenly she realised the implications of the need for digging tools. "There were more than three bodies?" she asked, aghast.

"No, no! Or at least, we didn't find any more. DI Gant's men had only dug down far enough to be sure there was a third body. Thank heaven they weren't buried very deep."

"If they had been, they probably wouldn't have been found. All the same, it must have been quite a job to bury three victims! Do you think there was more than one murderer? Or perhaps he had an accomplice."

"It's much too soon for any theories. But the local medico says one—the one that was found first—has been there for no longer than a week, one for several months, and one for at least a year."

"Ugh!"

"It was rather ugh. The two later ones, anyway. Not much left of the first, poor beggar, what with foxes and badgers and—"

"Darling, must you?"

"You asked. They left most of the bones, luckily, or we might never have realised he was there. The murderer must have covered over their diggings each time he brought a new victim." He yawned. "Come on, time for bed. I'll have to be up early."

"You must be awfully tired."

"Not *too* tired," he said with a grin, and kissed her. "Chief inspectors don't have to do the actual digging."

"How lucky I married a chief inspector!"

At an ungodly hour in the morning, Daisy got up in time to go downstairs in her dressing-gown to bid him good-bye. The sun was shining with the promise of a perfect June day.

"Better take your umbrella anyway," she said. "You never can tell. Do you think there's the slightest chance of clearing up the case in time to go to Belinda's sports day?"

"Very little."

"I'd better write and warn her, then if you can it'll be a nice surprise, instead of a nasty one when you don't turn up."

"You'll go anyway?" he asked a trifle anxiously. There were still occasional moments when he couldn't quite believe she loved Belinda like a daughter, not a stepdaughter.

"Darling, of course. I wouldn't let her down for the world. I'll stay the weekend, as we planned, and take her out to lunch on Sunday. Melanie and Sakari are going, too, so we'll have a lovely hen-party."

Alec laughed. "In fact, I'd be thoroughly in the way."

"Well, now you come to mention it . . ." she teased. "No, never! We'd just do different things if you were there." She stood on tiptoe to kiss him.

He put on his hat and opened the front door, then turned and said thoughtfully, "One curious circumstance you might want to ponder, but you must promise not to mention it to another soul."

"I promise."

"The most recent body had a piece of paper safety-pinned to the jacket, and the other two have safety-pins in the same position, though the paper's disintegrated. It's a bit tattered but as far as we can make out, it says, *Justice! Revenge!* with exclamation marks included."

"I'll think about it. Written, or one of those with cut-out words stuck on?"

"Cut-out letters, pasted in two semicircles, to form a circle. It's pinned over his heart, and he was shot right through the centre."

"Good gracious! I wonder what it means?"

"So do we. And you, as a writer, seem to pick up almost as many odd bits of information as do we coppers. Perhaps it will ring a bell with you if it doesn't with us."

"Not immediately, but I'll let it stew in the back of my mind."

"If ever I heard a mixed metaphor, that was one!"

"I'm always careful when I'm writing an article. Are all three of them men?"

"They are. And that's all you're getting out of me. I'll ring if I'm going to be late again."

Daisy stood on the front porch to watch him go down the steps, across the street, and down the path through the communal garden—it would have been a typical London Square if it hadn't been a Circle. Since she had learnt to drive and the Met had acquired more police cars, he often left their Austin Chummy for her use. The Hampstead tube station was only a couple of minutes' walk and took him direct to Charing Cross, a few minutes' walk from New Scotland Yard.

But she didn't want to drive alone all the way to Saffron Walden, she decided. She'd ring up Sakari later and beg a lift.

Alec turned at the fountain and waved to her. She waved back, then hurried into the house and closed the door. This wasn't the sort of neighbourhood where women stood on doorsteps in their dressing-gowns gossiping. Fortunately, having discovered Daisy was the daughter of the late Viscount Dalrymple, the neighbours tended to make allowances for the peculiarities of the aristocracy. All except the Bennetts, at the bottom: they had undoubtedly trained their field glasses on the Fletchers since the moment the front door opened.

Daisy enjoyed living in Constable Circle, but the nosy, gossipy Bennetts were definitely a fly in the ointment.

After breakfast she went to the kitchen for her daily consultation with Mrs. Dobson, to settle the everlasting question about what to have for dinner when they didn't know whether Alec would be eating at home or not, and if so, at what time. They sat at the kitchen table with a cup of tea each, a procedure that would have shocked Daisy's aristocratic mother quite as much as it had shocked her middle-class mother-in-law.

Then she took Oliver, Miranda, and Nana for a walk on Hampstead Heath. Mrs. Gilpin insisted on going, too; more, Daisy suspected, because she enjoyed the cachet of being nurse to twins than because she still thought Daisy incompetent to look after her own children for an hour. At least, now that the children were walking part of the way, Bertha was left behind to get on with the endless mountains of ironing. Once they were safely away from the road, Nana was let off the lead and the twins lifted down from their double pushchair. Nurse sat down on the nearest bench with this symbol of her pride parked beside her, while Daisy walked on and the dog and the twins ran and tumbled on the grass about her.

And all the time she was turning over in the back of her mind the strange target found on the body of the murdered man. It must represent a target, obviously, but what was the significance of the words pasted round the edge? *Justice! Revenge!*

"Mama, carry!"

Daisy picked up Miranda and turned back. Oliver clutched her skirt, whining. Nurse, whose eagle eye had never ceased to watch, came to meet them. Mrs. Gilpin could be a frightful wet blanket, but Daisy was very much aware she could never manage without her.

They returned to the house, where Nurse Gilpin dealt efficiently with the children and the pushchair. Daisy settled with a cup of coffee on the chair in the hall, and dialled Sakari's number.

The Prasads' butler, acquainted with Mrs. Fletcher, admitted that Mrs. Prasad might indeed possibly be available to speak upon the telephone.

"Daisy?"

"Good morning, Sakari."

"My dear Daisy, good morning to you." Sakari's rich voice, with its precise accent, conveyed as usual a hint of amusement. "I trust you have not rung to tell me you are unable to attend the coming ordeal. I count on your support."

"Darling, when it comes to sports, it's no good relying on me. I was always a hopeless duffer. I could never remember the score and the rules were all Greek to me."

"Then perhaps I shall be able to assist." She chuckled. "I have been taking Greek classes for some weeks." The Indian woman was an inveterate taker of classes and attender of lectures on all subjects under the sun.

"How brave! The alphabet's impossible, for a start!" Daisy's school for young ladies had not considered it wise to tax female brains with Latin and Greek.

"Indeed not. Compared to Hindi, the alphabet is very similar to your own. Unfortunately, I do not believe it will be of any assistance when we are watching our children run up and down the school field."

"I don't think they'll actually be playing games, just running races, so it shouldn't be too difficult to understand."

"I am much relieved. But you are not going to desert us, are you?"

"No. Alec almost certainly won't be able to go, though. I could drive myself—or go by train, I suppose—but I wondered whether you might have room for me in your car?"

"But yes, of course! As long as you do not intend to bring with you the twins and the nanny and the nurserymaid and the dog?"

"Belinda would love to see the twins, but it's just too complicated."

"Good. Melanie comes with me, but neither of our husbands is free, so there will be plenty of room. What fun! I will pick up Melanie first, as she lives so close to me, and then we will come to Hampstead for you." They arranged a time. Sakari went on, "I am so glad that Elizabeth and Belinda are at school with Deva. She would not have settled so happily, I think, without friends from home."

Daisy was touched. Sakari seldom alluded to the difficulty of being a dark-skinned person in a pale-skinned, prejudiced society. Before Daisy met them, Melanie, in her unassuming way, had done her best to introduce the Prasads into her own circle in St. John's Wood, with middling success. Important as he might be in diplomatic circles, the fact that Mr. Prasad was a high official at the India Office—one of a very few native Indians—and cousin of a maharajah bore little weight in suburbia.

"We are so glad," Daisy said, "that you found the Friends'

School to be a welcoming place for Deva and that Belinda chose to go, too."

"We do not tell relatives at home that boys and girls share lessons and eat together. It would be considered very shocking."

"It's not exactly commonplace here. Neither Alec nor I would have thought of sending her to a Friends' School, let alone a co-educational one, but it suits her very well. What's more, she's getting a much better education than I did. The children are actually encouraged to think for themselves! Her last letter was full of some science experiment she'd done in Mr. Tesler's laboratory. We never did any science."

"You should come to a few lectures with me. You could write articles about them."

"That's a good idea. I'll think about it. If only I knew in advance when Alec's going to be away in the evening."

"Is he involved in something complicated and exciting now? Or has he merely gone off to the other end of the country?"

"Just outside London, but complicated and possibly exciting. He told me more than usual because he can't see any possible way I could get involved in the investigation."

"Do tell."

Daisy pondered for a moment. "I'd better not. Alec swore me to secrecy on some of it, and I can't be certain which bits he'd mind about. There's bound to be something in the evening papers, though."

"What if they don't name Alec as the man in charge? How will I know which is his case?"

"Unless the police really make an effort to hush up the details, it'll be the sensation of the day. Even if there's only a mention, you'll know because, as I said, it's just outside London. Northeast, to be more precise, and close enough for Alec to come home for the night."

"I shall buy a newspaper," Sakari vowed.

Alec had taken the *Chronicle* with him. Daisy had every intention of reading an evening paper, but she didn't get round to it. She was busy finishing off an article on the Crystal Palace for her American editor at *Abroad* magazine. She had told Elsie, the parlourmaid, not to disturb her, and to take a message if anyone rang up; unless it was Alec wanting to speak to her. At some point in the afternoon, Elsie crept in and left a cup of tea and a couple of digestive biscuits beside the typewriter, but the maid was far too proud of her mistress's literary attainments to interrupt by drawing her attention to the fact.

When Daisy typed the last full stop, leant back, and stretched, she discovered the empty cup and plate, so she must have eaten and drunk without noticing.

She rolled the sheets out of the typewriter, sorted the carbons from the wad, and distributed the typed pages between the three piles on the desk. The top copy was for her editor, the second for her files, and the smudged third for emergency salvage. Nana had been known to chew up articles carelessly left about, though not since she was a puppy. But the twins were reaching the age where tearing paper to shreds was lots of fun.

Alec came home at half past six. By then Daisy had visited the nursery, taken Nana out in the Circle garden, and was back at her typewriter dashing off a note to Mr. Thorwald to accompany the article.

"Hello, darling," said Daisy as Alec came into their shared office, and set his attaché-case on his own desk. "I'm glad you're home early—but you've brought work to do?"

He grimaced. "Medical reports. Spilsbury—Sir Bernard, the Home Office pathologist—has been working on our corpses all day. We can't start much in the way of an investigation until we've identified them, and we can't identify them without some idea of ages, appearances, and dates of death to match against missing persons lists."

"No, you can't very well go door-to-door asking people if they saw anything suspicious in the past year!"

"Especially as there aren't any doors within half a mile and thousands of people visit the Forest whenever the sun shines."

"There's not much to get your teeth into, is there."

"I can't help feeling that the bit of paper is significant and might help, if only we could decipher it. Any thoughts on the subject?"

"Only that it represents a target—that's obvious—and they were shot in revenge for what the killer perceives as an injustice."

"Or else the killer wants us to think that was his motive," Alec said gloomily.

"Oh, I hadn't thought of that. How difficult! I bet the local police were happy to pass on the case to the experts."

"As a matter of fact, no. The chief constable was, presumably, but the Essex inspector is about as resentful and uncooperative as a man can be."

"How silly of him. If you're finding it a hard slog, he probably wouldn't have the foggiest idea where to start."

"The hard slog has yet to come." Alec took a sheaf of papers out of the case.

"Has Sir Bernard done all three autopsies?"

"Not yet. The last, or rather the earliest, he'll do tomorrow. I haven't read the reports in detail yet, just skimmed them."

"Do you know what kind of gun they were shot with? Shouldn't you be able to trace it?"

"Sounds easy when you put it that way! They weren't shot from close enough range to be sure but Sir Bernard thinks the weapon was a pistol. There are plenty of those floating around since the War, issued and not turned in, or German guns acquired as souvenirs. Needless to say, they're mostly unregistered. Not many men brought home ammunition as well, but a few are bound to have picked up a full magazine. If we knew where they were shot, we might be able to find bullets that would help identify the make, at least."

"I'm sure reading medical reports would thoroughly put you off your meal. I hope you're going to leave that gruesome stuff till after dinner."

"You asked."

"Yes, sorry. I'm finished here except for sticking everything in an envelope. Come and have a drink."

Daisy's intention was to take his mind off the case for a while, but as she sipped her Cinzano and soda, she found herself wondering about something he had said. She tried to think of a way to phrase her question so that he wouldn't be able to accuse her of meddling.

No bright idea occurred to her.

Of course Alec noticed her abstraction. "What's on your mind? Have you come up with some sort of link?"

"Link?"

"Between the paper target and—oh, anything at all. I'm certain it has some meaning beyond the obvious."

" 'Fraid not. I was just thinking about something you said—"

"Don't ask me about the case. I've already told you far more than I ought."

"It's not specifically about this case. Just a sort of general question."

"Come off it, love. This case is all we've been talking about."

"No, honestly. It's a question arising out of what you said about the case but not specific to it. Just—I suppose you'd call it general procedure."

"Well, ask away, but—"

"—You don't promise to answer. I know. It's just that you said, or implied, that once you know when the victims were killed, you could consult the missing persons list and you'd know who they were. It can't be that simple. Nothing ever is. It seems to me, at best that would tell you who they might be."

"You're quite right. But once we have possible names and some idea where they might have come from, we can start checking dental records, laundry marks, that sort of thing."

"I take it none of them had any useful documents on them."

"Daisy, that is most definitely specific to this particular case! If you start interfering . . ."

"I don't see how I can, darling. I don't know the victims, let alone anyone who might be a suspect. But wouldn't it be strange if one of them turned out to be an acquaintance—"

"Daisy!" Alec swallowed the remains of his Scotch and soda, and set down the glass with a bit of a thump. "I'm going up to see the twins, who can be guaranteed not to be acquainted with anyone remotely concerned and not to start asking awkward questions."

"Not yet," said Daisy.

THREE

As Alec had expected, the most recently buried of the three bodies was the first to be identified.

"This looks like it, Chief," Tom reported. "Vincent Halliday, age forty-five. Eldest son and heir of Sir Daniel Halliday, Baronet, of Quigden Manor, Ayot St. Paul, Herts. He runs said Bart's estate. Generally popular with tenants—keeps a proper distance but no 'side' to him—and local gentry. Reported missing Sunday the sixth, by his teenaged daughter."

"Not his wife? Or is there no wife?"

Tom checked his notes. "There's a wife, and the missing man's mother is still alive as well as his father, the Bart. The sergeant who took the girl's report checked with the family, of course, and got the impression that they were all annoyed with her for making a fuss about his absence. They made out that he had gone off for the weekend on private business and forgotten to tell anyone where he could be reached."

Alec raised his eyebrows.

"He didn't see anything in that—Sergeant Lear, I mean. They're the stiff-upper-lip sort, he said, that wouldn't let on if something was wrong. He reckoned they were afraid

Mr. Halliday had gone off to have a bit of a fling, though by all accounts he was a pretty steady chap. Still, Lear went back a couple of days later. By then Halliday had been gone for four days, without a word, and the rest of the family were getting anxious."

"Though preserving the stiff upper lip?"

"He doesn't mention that, Chief."

"Well, I hope they manage to keep it in place if we have to go and tell them we've had his body since the sixteenth. Twelve days—Spilsbury said ten to fourteen. Circumstances of the disappearance?"

"He walked to the village pub for a drink before dinner, as was his habit on a Friday. Plenty of witnesses to his arrival, and to his departure about an hour later, but he never arrived home."

"And the family . . . ?"

"When the dinner gong rang and he hadn't yet come home to change his clothes, they agreed that it was tiresome of him to have lost track of the time and went ahead without him."

" 'Like a well-conducted person, went on cutting bread and butter,' " Alec muttered.

"What's that, Chief?" asked Ernie Piper.

"Oh, nothing. A poetic commentary on the sang-froid of the upper-classes in the face of disaster. But not really fair to the Hallidays, because they couldn't have known he was in trouble."

"From a poem, is it?" Tom said indulgently. "Must be catching."

"Catching?"

"That's what Mrs. Fletcher does. Things remind her of bits of poetry, and out they pop." He grinned. "Charming habit, I've always thought. Adds a bit of tone to the conversation, wouldn't you say, Ernie?"

"Couldn't have put it better myself, Sarge."

"This is gross insubordination! All right, I apologise, the office is no place for raising the tone of the conversation, however inadvertently. Back to business: what was Halliday wearing?"

"Fawn whipcord breeches and a tweed jacket with leather patches on the elbows. Shirt, tie, shoes, cap, all match what we've got."

"It's him," said Ernie.

"Not much room for doubt," Alec agreed.

"What you said, about the family couldn't know he was in trouble, Chief," said Tom, "you're counting them out, then?"

"Yes, I think so, don't you? If it was only Halliday, they'd top the list, of course."

"But with three corpses littering the case, this isn't a nice little domestic murder. I'd lay odds on that!"

"Much more complicated. That's why I'm going to have to leave Ernie here, to collate information as it comes in. We've got to find something in common between the three victims."

"The lad's got a good eye for details and patterns," Tom agreed.

"And you've got a way with barmaids, so you can deal with the pub end of things while I see what I can find out about him from the family. What was the name of the village?"

"Ayot St. Paul."

"There's an Ayot St. Peter and an Ayot Lawrence, too," Piper observed. "And Ayot Green." He had already consulted a gazetteer. "Nearest station Welwyn." He reached for Bradshaw.

"Can't wait to get rid of us, eh, lad?"

"We'll drive. If the murderer's got a little list, as seems probable, I don't want to be sitting in a train when he strikes again."

"Wouldn't look good on your report," Tom said, mock solemnly.

Alec grinned. "That aspect hadn't occurred to me, but you're right, it wouldn't. Though I should hope the questions in the House would concern insufficient provision of motor vehicles for the Metropolitan Police. Ernie, I can't leave you in charge here, you haven't the rank. But tell me who you'd like to work with—sergeant or inspector—and I'll see if I can get hold of him."

"DS Mackinnon got his transfer from S Division. If he's free . . ."

"Good choice." Alec himself, after working with Mackinnon several times at the divisional level, had recommended his transfer to the Yard. "I'll see what I can do. You'll have to brief him. Tom, I must see the super right away. He knows what we're working on so it shouldn't be a problem."

Before he finished speaking, Tom was on the telephone. A couple of minutes later, he reported, "The Super's with the AC, Chief, and they want to see you at once."

"Damn!"

Alec gave the Assistant Commissioner (Crime) a brief outline of the case and was congratulated on so quickly identifying one of the victims. The AC agreed to contact the Hertfordshire police immediately and arrange for their cooperation.

"I'll have the chief constable—Sir George Cheriton, if I'm not mistaken—inform the family that you'll be calling. Unless you'd prefer that he didn't give them warning?"

"No, thank you, sir, I'd rather they expected me, but I'd prefer that he not give them any further information, not even that the missing man is dead."

"I'll see what I can do," the AC said doubtfully, "but he may well know the family, so . . . I'll see what I can do. As regards the press," he went on, "I'll deal with them, but tell me what you'd like them to know. They've already got on to the triple burial, inevitably."

"If you'd tell them, sir, that we have the one identification—just to show we're progressing—but I'd rather you didn't give the name. They'll find out soon enough, no doubt. When we have all three, it'll be time to publish them and with any luck get helpful citizens suggesting connections between them."

"Good thinking, Fletcher, and I'm glad to hear 'when'

rather than 'if'. You'll be wanting a word with Mr. Crane now. Every facility, Crane. The public don't like mass murder. Thank you." He nodded dismissal.

They repaired to the superintendent's office, where Alec provided a little more detail, requested a car and driver, and asked for Mackinnon to work with DC Piper.

"Every facility," Crane repeated. "I'll see if he can be spared."

"We're relying on Piper for spotting the correlations we're going to need in this case, sir. I don't want him distracted by working under someone he doesn't know as well. He wanted Mackinnon."

"Bit of a prima donna, is he?"

"Not at all, sir. A very able young man whom I hope to see make sergeant soon. But this sort of detail work, spotting patterns, is his particular strength. I need his full attention on it as information comes in."

"He shall have Mackinnon, if I can possibly manage it."

"Thank you, sir."

"There's one blessing: Mrs. Fletcher can't possibly get herself mixed up in this one." A horrid possibility struck him. "These Hallidays aren't friends of hers, are they?"

"I sincerely hope not. I don't remember her ever mentioning them. She won't hear the name from me."

"When it comes out in the papers . . ." Crane said forebodingly.

"I doubt that will be before Saturday àt the earliest. She's going to be away for the weekend, so she won't be reading the papers."

"Good! So you're off to Hertfordshire immediately? Keep in touch and never mind the telephone charges. I don't need to tell you we've got to clear this one up quickly or the press are going to have a field day."

Ayot St. Paul did not boast its own resident constable, a single bobby with a bicycle serving for all the Ayots. They picked up

PC Pickett in Ayot Lawrence, a tiny village famous—or infamous, depending on one's political sympathies—for being home to the residence of George Bernard Shaw.

Ayot St. Paul turned out to be even smaller. It was scarcely a hamlet, with two or three pleasant "gentleman's residences"; two short rows of cottages, one brick, one white-washed, all tile-roofed; an ancient pub, the Goat and Compasses, that appeared to be crumbling into the ground; and a church so tiny it could surely never have aspired to being served by anyone more important than a neighbouring curate.

The driver stopped at the pub. At a little before noon, the June day was already growing warm, and the door stood hospitably open. An ancient rustic sat basking on a bench against the wall, a pewter half-pint in one gnarled hand.

"It's all yours, Sergeant," said Alec. "I expect you'd prefer to work alone?"

"Yes, sir, for a start anyway. Mr. Pickett, you said there's just the one bar?"

" 'Sright, and you'll not likely find many there at this hour, Sergeant. It mostly serves the farms, and this weather, this time o' day, they'll all be hard at work. Fred Wright, the landlord, he'll be happy to have someone to talk to 'sides the old geezers."

"Perfect."

Absent Pickett and the driver, DC Ledbetter, Alec would have chaffed Tom on the apparent lack of a barmaid to chat up. Instead, he said, "You'll probably be done before I will. Pickett, how far is it to Quigden Manor?"

"A mile or thereabouts by the lanes, sir, but there's a footpath cuts that by a third."

"I can see you know your district thoroughly. Tell Mr. Tring how to find the footpath."

Pickett obliged.

"Come along to the Manor, Sergeant, when you're finished here. All right, Ledbetter, let's go."

As they drove the short distance to the end of the village

and turned into a narrow lane, Alec explained what he expected of his two remaining men. "At present the family and staff are not under suspicion, and we have no reason to suppose they ever will be. I don't want any hint that we're interrogating them. You two will go to the kitchen with some excuse—a glass of water, perhaps—and the chances are they'll want to chat about the missing man."

"Can we let on he's been found dead, sir?" Ledbetter asked.

"Certainly. I'll be breaking the news to the family, though probably they've already guessed, when the chief constable rang up to tell them I was on my way. All you have to do is encourage the servants to talk about his character, friends and acquaintances, how he spends his time, in fact anything at all related to his life beyond this household. We've no idea what may be useful. Don't take notes. Or rather, only mental notes. I hope you've both got good memories."

Naturally both claimed excellent memories.

"The cook's my auntie," Pickett volunteered.

"Excellent. You'll know the best way to get her talking, then."

"It's stopping her'll be the problem. You don't know my Auntie Flo."

"All the better. DC Ledbetter is in charge, though."

"Yes, sir. Here's their drive, on the right there."

They passed between brick gateposts, devoid of gates and topped with simple stone balls rather than heraldic beasts. Ledbetter commented on this.

"The Hallidays have never been ones to make a display," said Pickett, rather severely.

Alec wondered whether, regardless of what Auntie Flo might reveal, it would be worthwhile turning to the constable for information about the family. As far as he knew, Sergeant Lear hadn't consulted the village bobby when Halliday was reported missing.

A couple of hundred yards of weed-free gravel drive brought them to the manor, a red brick Queen Anne house, not particularly large but attractive and well-kept amid smooth lawns. "Smugly prosperous" was the phrase that sprang to Alec's mind. So many small estates had been ravaged by high death duties since the War, but Quigden Manor seemed to have escaped. Of course, if the late Vincent Halliday had a teenaged daughter, his father, Sir Daniel must be getting on in years, so there had been no recent death of a title-holder.

Did Halliday leave a son as well as a daughter? If not, on the baronet's demise the title and estate would doubtless pass to a more distant relative, just as Daisy's father's viscountcy and her childhood home had gone to a cousin she barely knew. Could this be a family affair after all? Was the murderer the next heir, the other two victims nearer heirs, or even red herrings?

But he was theorising far ahead of his data. "Pickett, any other children?"

"Two boys, sir, but they'll be away at school. Miss Delia was sent home from school on account of an epidemic of scarlet fever."

So much for that!

Alec rang the doorbell, noting that the manor had been electrified. The door was opened by a stout elderly butler. His round, bland face did not reveal whether he knew—or cared—that "the young master" was missing, presumed dead. He looked Alec up and down, then glanced at the police car with the uniformed and plain-clothes officers sitting in it looking like policemen. One eyebrow twitched.

A second quick scrutiny of Alec apparently reassured him. At least, he didn't advise him to go round to the servants' entrance.

"May I be of assistance, sir?"

"Detective Chief Inspector Fletcher, Scotland Yard." He presented his official card, which the butler ignored. "I believe Sir Daniel is expecting me."

"Ah yes, the . . . gentleman from Scotland Yard. If you'll just step inside, sir, I'll see if it's convenient for Sir Daniel to see you now."

Alec had every intention of speaking to the baronet within the next ten minutes, convenient or not. However, arguing with butlers was not only a futile waste of time but set their backs up, reducing—even ending—their usefulness as sources of information. Meekly he stepped into the entrance hall.

As presaged by the exterior, everything was in discreet good taste, from the gleaming floorboards to the Chinese bowl of pink and yellow roses on the gleaming half-moon table.

The butler departed down a passage leading off to the left, but he returned in just a couple of minutes. "Sir Daniel will see you in the library, sir. This way, if you please."

The room was exactly as Alec expected. Walls of glass-fronted shelves held calf-bound volumes most of which had probably been there for at least a century. A long table, a large rosewood knee-hole desk, and leather armchairs completed the picture of a Victorian, even Georgian, gentleman's library. What he had seen of the house so far seemed frozen in time, no hint of the twentieth century intruding. What he had heard of the family sounded as if they—apart from the baronet's enterprising granddaughter—embraced Victorian domestic virtues as well as Victorian décor.

Keep a stiff upper lip and don't wash your dirty linen in public. How long would they have kept quiet about Vincent Halliday's disappearance if the girl had not taken the initiative?

The butler announced him. A tall, lean man who had been standing staring out of a window, came forward to greet him, walking with the aid of a stick. He moved stiffly, but his shoulders were unbowed by age, his steel-grey hair still thick. Observing his lined face and liver-spotted hands, knowing the age of his son, Alec reckoned he must be in his seventies.

"Chief Inspector, Cheriton did not inform me of the purport of your visit, but I can only assume you bring bad news."

"I'm afraid so, sir. Won't you sit down?"

Sir Daniel raised his chin with an impertinence-depressing stare, then thought better of it. With a sigh and a faint, ironic smile, he said, "We none of us want to admit the influence of anno domini, do we? Perhaps I will."

He moved to the table and took the seat at the end, motioning to Alec to join him. Alec was pulling out a chair when the door was flung open and a plump, fair girl-child burst in.

"Grandfather, they said there's a policeman—" She stopped dead on seeing Alec. "Oh!"

"You were not invited, Delia." The baronet's voice was icy. "I will not have you rushing about in this hoydenish manner."

"It's my daddy who's missing!" she cried. "You don't care."

"Of course I care."

"Then why didn't you—"

"Don't argue. Go back to your mother at once. You will be told what you need to know in due course."

He was unduly harsh, Alec thought, but it was none of his business and, in any case, nothing would make him relate the grim story in her presence. In fact, he was glad the girl's mother and grandmother were also apparently to be excluded.

Delia glared at her grandfather, then her face crumpled and she ran from the room, sobbing noisily.

"My apologies, Chief Inspector. I don't know what they teach at that school she goes to, but it's clearly not self-restraint."

The simple fact of his speaking thus to a stranger, and a mere policeman at that, showed him not half so cool and calm as he would have liked to appear. His face had taken on a greyish tinge Alec didn't like. He looked every minute of his age.

However, he continued abruptly, "Please go ahead. I assume your presence indicates that my son is dead."

Alec sat down. "Pending positive identification by a member of the family, sir, so we believe. All the evidence points that way. Have you a photograph?"

Sir Daniel was prepared. He handed over a studio portrait

in a silver frame of an army officer, a major—in his late thirties, at a guess—in dress uniform. "It's not very recent. We don't go in for family photography. Well?"

Army officers in uniform tend to look very alike, yet there was no doubt in Alec's mind. "I'm sorry, this strongly resembles the deceased. We're still required to have someone make a personal identification, I'm afraid."

He inclined his head in acceptance. "Regulations must be observed. I take it Scotland Yard would not be interested had Vincent died a natural death."

"Correct."

"May I know . . . what happened?"

After a brief internal debate, Alec said, "The information could materially affect our investigation, sir, but if you will give me your word—"

"You need not fear that I shall talk to the press," the baronet said with a touch of anger.

"I'm sure of that, sir, but I must have your assurance that you won't tell any of the family, even. No one at all."

"You have my word."

"Mr. Halliday was shot through the heart. Death must have been instantaneous."

There was silence while Sir Daniel absorbed this. Then he said, "May I at least tell the family that he didn't suffer?"

"If you wish." Alec didn't add that Spilsbury said Halliday had been bound hand and foot for several hours before death. He had undoubtedly suffered physical discomfort and considerable mental distress. "You don't want to wait until after formal identification of the deceased?"

"No. My wife and his are as capable of drawing conclusions from your arrival as I am. My daughter-in-law must decide what is to be told to the child, and when. But I wish to see . . . him as soon as possible. Can it be arranged?"

"Whenever you wish, sir. My driver can take you."

"I should prefer my own car and chauffeur."

"Then DC Ledbetter will accompany you."

"Am I—is the family under suspicion?" Sir Daniel asked harshly.

"No, sir. Circumstances are such that we can be fairly certain none of you is involved."

"*Fairly* certain!"

"I'm sure you understand, sir, that that's the best I can say until we're in a position to make an arrest."

"But for the present, at least, you'll be leaving us in peace."

"On the contrary, I'm afraid. You must see we can't possibly find your son's killer without knowing a great deal about him, his friends and associates, his history, every scrap of information we can pull together. In a case of murder, I don't need your permission to search his personal effects, including any papers, letters, and accounts. Strictly speaking, the body should be positively identified first. However, for reasons I can't go into, we strongly believe time is of the essence and I'd appreciate your allowing me to get on with it right away."

For a moment it was touch-and-go. The old man's eyes flashed beneath his bushy eyebrows. Then he sank back into a sort of apathy typical of many relatives of murder victims, when a sort of emotional anaesthesia set in. "Do what you must," he said listlessly. "Do you want to talk to me now, or after . . . ?"

"Better get it over with, sir. If you wouldn't mind arranging with Lady Halliday for her cooperation—"

"My wife will cooperate as she sees fit." So he wasn't the all-powerful paterfamilias! "I shall tell her I consider it the most sensible course. My butler will instruct the staff to offer every assistance. Now, if you would be so kind as to inform your sergeant I'll be ready to leave in twenty minutes?" Pushing on the table, he levered himself from his chair.

"Thank you, sir."

"Just one question: Would it have made any difference if we had notified the police sooner?"

"I very much doubt it."

"Thank you."

From his tone, he might have been thanking Alec for passing a cup of tea.

FOUR

"*I can't* get the hang of this chap at all," said Tom.

"A slippery character," suggested Ledbetter, behind the wheel again after his chauffeured jaunt to the mortuary. Having dropped PC Pickett off in Ayot Lawrence, they were on the road to London.

"Not that, exactly. At least, I don't think so, do you, Chief?"

"Not if you take that to mean someone adept at slipping through our fingers. I have no sense of his being involved in anything shady. Rather the reverse."

"Excessively law-abiding?" queried Tom dryly.

Alec laughed. "Hardly. Not from our point of view, anyway. But there's something excessive about that family. A sort of almost obsessive reticence, a reluctance to do anything whatsoever that could conceivably lead to people talking about them."

"I know what you mean, Chief. Conformity." Tom's vocabulary was occasionally surprising. He worked at it. "Not standing out in any way from what they consider the norm for people of their sort. They'll even do things that go against the grain because it's what they feel is expected of them. That came over very strongly from the people I talked to at the pub."

"Oh yes?"

"Vincent Halliday didn't drop in of a Friday for a nice relaxing pint. He went because he thought he ought. Never on a Saturday, when they have a piano and a sing, nor any other day of the week, come to that. Arrived at six and left at quarter to seven on the dot, to walk home to change for dinner. Broad daylight."

"Yes. He couldn't have been shot right away, but Sir Bernard said there's a big bruise on his head, easily enough to have knocked him out. Marks on ankles and wrists suggest he was tied hand and foot, with other, lesser, and so far inexplicable bruising all over the body. Impossible to tell with the earlier victims."

"The footpath's pretty isolated and goes through a wood. Wouldn't be difficult to lie in wait, seeing how regular he was in his habits."

"No. How did he get on with the locals at the pub?"

"Had an affable word for everyone, but he never relaxed, just didn't seem to be enjoying himself."

"No-bless obleedge," said Ledbetter unexpectedly.

"Did people resent being condescended to?" Alec asked.

"Not by what I was told. There weren't many there, mind, lunchtime on a Friday, like Pickett said. The way they talked, they appreciated him making the effort when it didn't come natural. Course, the estate's a good employer, the biggest hereabouts, and they're not going to bite the hand that feeds them. Besides, they knew he was missing and they knew I was a copper, so they wouldn't want to let on he was unpopular. All the same, it wasn't so much what they said as what came over without them putting it into words."

Ledbetter snorted—softly—but Alec said, "I trust your instinct, Tom. The estate's regarded as a good employer because they treat their employees well, or only because they employ a lot of people?"

"Fair wages, fair treatment, and they look after 'em when they're sick or old. The latter being what most of the patrons at the Goat and Compasses were."

"But it's noblesse oblige, as Ledbetter says, not because they really care about their welfare."

"Common sense, too, Chief. Treat people well, they work harder and you don't have any trouble finding and keeping workers."

"True. Still, it doesn't sound as if the locals have much cause for complaint, let alone murder."

Alec himself was not much wiser from his questioning of the family. It wasn't that anyone seemed secretive. In accordance with Sir Daniel's wishes, the residents of Quigden Manor had been willing to cooperate, even the old lady and the butler. Nothing anyone said gave the slightest hint of why Vincent Halliday's life should have ended with a bullet in his heart and a grave in Epping Forest.

There was no hint of dissension within the family, nor between family and servants. The staff were mostly old retainers, a number of them re-employed after their war service. A few younger maids yearned to leave service for the bright lights of London, but that was the influence of the picture papers they read, not of animosity towards their employers.

Though London was no more than thirty miles away, the Hallidays rarely went up to town and virtually never stayed overnight. They were on visiting, but not intimate, terms with the neighbouring gentry.

"What about the girl," Tom asked. "What did she have to say? She's got some spunk, going against the rest of the family to report her dad missing."

"I didn't manage to talk to her for very long. Floods of tears, as you can imagine. She wanted to see me alone, but I couldn't stop her mother sitting in. Daddy was a brick. Her grandfather wanted her to have a mouldy old governess and stay at home, but Daddy talked him into letting her go away to school. She didn't know how she was going to survive without him to take her side. Naturally, Mama came down pretty sharply on that and the interview was terminated pronto. Not at all the thing."

"The Bart was right, then, in his way."

"Yes, going away to school has reduced her willingness to conform to the family mores. Which, incidentally, her mother appears to have adopted wholesale. Perhaps she was chosen for the position because she comes from the same sort of set-up."

"Sounds as if the old man still has a firm grip on the reins. I mean, he let the girl go to school, but if he'd put his foot down, that would have been the end of that."

"I presume he controls the money."

"Expect so. A pretty fair tyrant. Now, if *he*'d been shot, we wouldn't have to look beyond the family for the murderer."

Ledbetter had been silent for some time, negotiating the increasing traffic as they reached the outskirts of the city. Now he commented, "What I don't get is, this family, they've got swarms of servants all over the place, what do they do all day?"

"An interesting question," Alec agreed, "but one which at present we need to answer only with regard to the victim. He seems to have kept himself harmlessly busy enough running the estate."

"Well, I don't mind admitting, Chief," said Tom, "I'm flummoxed. What would anyone want to do in a bloke like that for?"

"It beats me. We'll just have to hope we'll get enough information on the other two for Ernie to spot a correlation."

When they reached New Scotland Yard, the duty sergeant told them one of the larger rooms, with several tables and telephones, had been set aside for the investigation, and a number of officers, detectives and uniformed, had been seconded to work with Mackinnon. Alec sent Ledbetter to inform Mackinnon of their arrival.

"We're going to be here till midnight," he said to Tom. "I must ring home, and so must you. I don't want Mrs. Tring blaming me for keeping you out till all hours without notice. We'll go up to the office first."

Daisy wouldn't be surprised if he didn't ring her, but he always did if he was within reasonably easy reach of a telephone. Elsie answered the phone and went to fetch Daisy.

"Darling, you're going to be late," she greeted him.

"How did you guess?" Alec asked ironically.

"You know my methods, Watson. Very late?"

"Probably."

"I hope that means you're getting somewhere, not completely stymied. I suppose you're not going to tell me."

"Let's say, we've got enough information to keep us busy."

"But not enough to make it likely that you'll be able to come to Saffron Walden."

"Not tomorrow, certainly. And we'd have to be extraordinarily lucky for me to make it on Sunday."

Daisy sighed. "Poor Bel. Oh well, she's been a copper's daughter for thirteen years now. She's used to it. And that's not counting your daring days as a pilot in the RFC, when I expect she saw even less of you. All right, darling, thanks for letting me know. I'll give the twins a kiss from you and I'll see you when I see you."

If Belinda was used to being a copper's daughter, Alec reflected, ringing off, Daisy had adjusted admirably to being a copper's wife. It was one of the prospective problems that had worried him when he first realised that, come what might, he was going to ask the daughter of a viscount to marry him. He was fortunate that she had her own profession to occupy her. It was not really luck, though. He might never have been attracted to her in the first place, or even have met her, but for her determination to make a career for herself.

In fact, in spite of the irregularity of his hours—and her occasional solo forays into the country in pursuit of material for her articles—they probably spent more time together than many society couples, who often seemed to go their separate ways. Few families presented as united a face to the world as the Hallidays.

United and claustrophobic. Had Vincent Halliday some-how managed to conceal a secret life elsewhere?

Suppose he had had a mistress, another man's wife. Was it not entirely possible that this hypothetical woman had had previous lovers? And that the cuckolded husband made a habit of bumping off his rivals? A promising scenario.

At the very least, it gave them somewhere to start thinking about the triple murder.

They went downstairs to find that Ernie Piper had a prob-able identification for the second victim and a couple of pos-sibles for the first.

"Good work!" said Alec, draping his jacket over the back of his chair and loosening his tie. "All right, Mackinnon, what have we got?"

"The second body, sir, in chronological order by apparent date of burial," the the tall, lean redhead reported, his Scots accent in abeyance apart from a slight roll to the *R*s, "would appear to be a Martin Devine, of Guildford, Surrey. The right height, hair colour, and general build, age thirty-three, which accords with Sir Bernard's opeenion, as does the date on which he was last seen: the twenty-first of November."

"Sounds like a fit. And the other?"

"Two possibles. Edwin Surtees and Lieutenant-Colonel William Pelham, retired. Both in their late fifties and the right height. Surtees resided in Kent, near Maidstone, and the colonel in Tunbridge Wells. We've checked only the Home Counties reports, as you instructed."

"It's a place to start. It seems unlikely that anyone, however mad, would move a murdered corpse very far just for the sake of burying it in Epping Forest, especially if his only transport is a horse-cart."

"Verra true, sir." The Scots was creeping in as he became involved in what was being said and stopped worrying about the impression he was making on his fellow officers. "There were a few matches for age and height who disappeared in

41

London and the suburbs and were never accounted for, but none that wad hae been wearing handmade shoes."

"Handmade shoes?"

"Mr. Piper?" Mackinnon deferred to his junior's command of the details rather than grabbing all the credit, Alec noted with approval. The Scot might be as ready for promotion to inspector as Piper was to sergeant.

"It's one of the links, Chief," said Ernie eagerly. "All three were wearing good shoes and tailored clothes. There wasn't all that much left of the clothes on the first body, but the shoes survived pretty well. Buttons, too, only you can't be sure with buttons. They could be on second-hand clothes."

"Both the colonel and the other chap—"

"Surtees, sir."

"They wore the same size shoes?"

"Yes, Chief, with the left foot half a size larger."

"No maker's name?"

"Unreadable," Piper said regretfully.

"We're leaning towards yon colonel, wad ye no agree, Mr. Piper?"

"On what grounds?"

"It's another link, Chief, which applies to Halliday, Devine, and Colonel Pelham, but not to Surtees. All three of them vanished after leaving their local public house, which they visited regularly. Surtees left home for London, where he intended to stay a couple of days on business. He never turned up for his various appointments, nor at his club, where he was expected to stay."

Alec considered this for a moment. "It's a rather tenuous link," he said, "and probably sheer coincidence. Worth following up, though. Still, I presume we have dental information by now. It's a good job dentists aren't half so secretive about their patients as doctors are. With the names, we should be able to find the dentists concerned and get definite answers."

"Och, sir," said Mackinnon reproachfully, "hae I no had DC Burton working on yon already?"

"Burton?"

"I've rung up all the dentists in Guildford, Maidstone, and Tunbridge Wells, sir. Found Devine's and Surtees'. They both agreed to take the charts home with them and wait for a copper to show up with the information to compare."

"I didna care tae send anyone out wi'out asking you first, sir."

"Good work. We'll send a uniform on a motorbike, I think." He scanned the listening group and called on the most senior uniformed officer among them, "Sergeant Vane, get the information from Burton and set it in motion, please. Tell the rider to go to Maidstone first and send a wire with the dentist's answer. A discreet wire, no names."

"What if there's no motorcyclist available, sir?"

"Then call a man in. This case has a very high priority, as you can tell by the number of you in here. Are you all listening? The Great White Chief is going to get all hot and bothered if we don't clear this up quickly, and more important, so is the Great British Public."

A murmur of amusement ran round the room but they'd take it seriously all the same.

"Yes, sir." Vane consulted Burton, and hurried from the room with a sheaf of notes.

While all this was going on, phones had occasionally rung and been answered. Now a constable announced, "Sir, it's for you. Superintendent Crane."

Alec hoped no one heard his groan. He nodded, and the man switched the call through to the telephone on his desk. Mackinnon had them all working surprisingly smoothly.

"Fletcher here."

"One moment, sir."

"Fletcher? I hope I'm not interrupting . . . ?"

"Actually, sir . . ."

"I've got the AC on my back. Unfortunately the Home Sec read about the murders in the evening paper and wants to know what's being done about it."

"Ten minutes, sir? No, make that fifteen."

"I'll be here. Fletcher, your good lady's still not . . . ?"

"Absolutely not, sir. I'll be with you shortly."

Crane grunted. "Do what you need to do. And while you're about it, think about which inspector you'd like under you."

"DS Mackinnon is doing a good job, sir."

"I dare say, but we need not only to do a good job but to be seen to be doing a good job, and that requires someone of higher rank backing you up."

Damn politics! Alec thought. Mackinnon's nose was going to be out of joint. But the super hadn't specified a detective inspector. If Alec requested a uniformed man, he could be left to run the Yard end of things. Then Mackinnon would be free to join Alec and Tom in the field.

"Yes, sir. I'll be with you shortly," he repeated.

"Right you are." Crane rang off.

Alec returned his attention to the dental question. "So, we haven't found the dentist of one of the possible victims?"

"The colonel, sir," said Mackinnon. "Colonel Pelham. Tunbridge Wells."

"I talked to two dentists in Tunbridge Wells, sir," said Burton. "One of them said he thought the colonel went to a London man. Sounded a bit disgruntled about it."

"And how many dentists are there in London?" Alec queried rhetorically.

"Lots," said Ernie, waving a directory.

"Let's hope we get a positive from Surtees's dentist, even if it spoils your pub link, Piper. Otherwise, we're going to have to trouble Pelham's family even though we have virtually no evidence that he might be the first victim. We don't even know for certain that the body originated in the Home Counties."

"Could have been someone from elsewhere visiting London," Tom suggested.

"It's going to take some doing to persuade Mr. Crane to allow us to disturb the Pelham household, so Piper, you'd better try to convince me there's a good chance we've got the right man."

"One of two possibles," Piper reminded him. "Could be the pub angle is just coincidence and it's Surtees."

"Yes." Alec sighed. It was beginning to look, against considerable odds, as if they might to be able to identify all the bodies. As yet, he had no idea how they were to set about finding the killer. He hoped this case was not going to end up as a blot on his record.

"All right," he went on, "let's go over everything we know, quickly, before I go to see the super. Oh, by the way, he wants an inspector in charge here—no reflection on your capability, Mackinnon, just a matter of being seen to be doing everything possible. Besides, I can make better use of you elsewhere. I'm going to ask for Cavett."

"A uniform?" said Tom. "Good idea, Chief. He won't get any fancy notions about really being in charge of the case and he's a good solid man."

"Not half as solid as you, Sarge."

"I'll take that as a compliment, laddie, or you'd be for it!"

FIVE

Daisy ate dinner in solitary splendour. It was all very well popping into the kitchen for elevenses, or even afternoon tea on Elsie's day off, but the servants would not appreciate her presence in the evening. At least it left her free to read the *Evening Standard* in peace—or rather the article in the *Standard* about the "Epping Forest Massacre," as they'd decided to call it. A leader on the subject focussed on fact that one body had been there for many months.

Daisy wondered how the reporter had found out that particular detail. She was sure Alec would not have willingly released it. The writer demanded to know why the police had not discovered the burial ground sooner.

Did they really expect that a permanently undermanned force would run a weekly bloodhound patrol through the Forest on the off chance that someone had been burying bodies somewhere in its thousands of acres?

To her disappointment, the paper didn't actually seem to know any more than Alec had already told her, cagey as he had been.

Right at the very end of the article, came a brief mention

that Scotland Yard had put one of their best detectives, DCI Fletcher, on the case. Alec had said the top brass promised to try to keep his name out of it. Perhaps the Essex police had been less reticent.

One *of their best!* she thought indignantly. He was absolutely *the* best.

She reluctantly refused a second helping of gooseberry fool. "I'll have coffee in the small sitting room, please, Elsie." The room at the southwest corner of the house, with corners on two sides, caught the last light at this time of year. Having already packed for the weekend, she could watch the sunset at leisure.

As she stepped out of the dining room, the telephone rang. "I'll get it," she told the parlourmaid. "With any luck, it's Mr. Fletcher to say he won't be late after all."

"I'm sure I hope so, madam, if it means the master's caught the nasty crook that did in three people!"

But it was Sakari, or rather her butler.

"Oh dear," said Daisy, when Sakari came on the line, "don't tell me you're not able to go to Saffron Walden after all?"

"By no means, my dear Daisy. I have read in the newspaper about the case you mentioned, and I am expecting that Alec is busy elsewhere this evening. I thought you might be lonely."

Daisy laughed. "So you want to pick my brains."

"Such a horrid expression! But yes, I am nosy. I hope you may be able to tell me more of this terrible crime."

"Not really. But if you'd like to come round for coffee—"

"That will be delightful. Even if you can provide no news, we shall study the guidebook to Saffron Walden that I bought today and decide what we want to do with the children."

"In that case, why don't you ring Mel and see if she's free to come with you?"

"An excellent idea. Twenty minutes if I come alone, half an hour if I pick up Melanie on the way."

Daisy told Elsie to bring a Thermos flask of coffee with all the doings.

"Oh no, madam, I couldn't. If you've got guests coming, I'll bring the proper coffee pot and all when they arrive."

"It's time for you to go off duty and eat your dinner."

"Don't you worry, madam, I'll eat before they come. I'm sure I don't know what Mrs. Dobson would say if I was to ask for a flask when you've got guests coming, specially if it's that Mrs. Prasad that's so grand."

Admitting that it was indeed the grand Mrs. Prasad, Daisy gave up. Sakari's chauffeur, Kesin, would undoubtedly visit the kitchen and he and Mrs. Dobson were quite friendly. She wouldn't want to let the side down in front of him.

"Thank you, Elsie, that will be very nice. Oh, and put out the Drambuie, too, and liqueur glasses of course. I think there's half a bottle left."

Daisy went to the sitting room to write down everything she could remember that Alec had told her about the triple murder. She had to work out which bits were strictly in confidence and try to find a few snippets she could safely pass on to satisfy Sakari's insatiable thirst for knowledge.

He hadn't sworn her to secrecy till Thursday morning, when he asked her to ponder the paper targets with *Justice! Revenge!* pasted to them. She had been too busy all day to give them much thought. If her subconscious had been working on the question, it hadn't yet come up with an answer.

Presumably everything he had said on Wednesday evening was fair game. Daisy knew from experience that neither Sakari nor Melanie would tattle to anyone else if she asked them not to. So what could she tell them?

About the uncooperative Essex police, for a start. What was the inspector's name? Something short but unusual—it would come to her. Doubtless Alec had been unwise to name him, but Daisy could see no harm in passing it on. It wouldn't mean anything to either of her friends.

By the time Elsie announced Mrs. Prasad, Daisy had realised how little, in fact, Alec had let drop. He really was maddeningly discreet.

"Sakari, that was quick. Melanie couldn't come?"

"You know our Melanie, Daisy," said Sakari indulgently, kissing her cheek. "She claims she is not interested."

"To be fair, darling, I don't think she is."

"Also, she must pack for our journey tomorrow."

Melanie Germond was the wife of a bank manager. Like Daisy but unlike Sakari, she had no personal maid. Sakari had once confided that both she and her husband came from rich and influential families, without whose influence they would not have been in London. Daisy, who had obtained her first writing commission because of her family background, had no quibble with that. Some things were the same the world over.

She was sorry that Mel hadn't come, however. Though unable to deter Sakari's outspoken curiosity, her mild protests would have acted as a reminder to Daisy to mind her tongue.

The parlourmaid brought in coffee and the liqueur and set out everything on a table. Among the rest was a folded sheet of paper with Daisy's name printed on the outside. She reached for it.

"What's this, Elsie?"

"Enid brought it, madam, just a couple of minutes ago." Elsie's sister was the next-door neighbours' parlourmaid. "She's waiting for an answer."

"Do you mind?" Daisy asked Sakari.

"But of course not. I can guess what it says, however. The Jessup ladies are as eager as I to hear as much as you are permitted to tell."

Skimming the note, Daisy laughed. "You're right, of course. They want me to pop over for coffee. Elsie, tell Enid I have a guest but if Mrs. Jessup and Mrs. Aidan would like to join us, they'll be very welcome."

The Jessups could play the part she had intended for Melanie. Their more restrained interest would help her parry Sakari's questions. She hoped.

They arrived a few minutes later, just as Elsie brought in more cups and glasses and a fresh supply of coffee. Having met

Sakari before at the Fletchers', they were not discomposed to find a dark-skinned lady there before them. Mrs. Jessup was a small, silver-haired woman, elegantly dressed and made up, with alert blue eyes and the slightest hint of an Irish accent. Her daughter-in-law, Audrey, in her late twenties like Daisy, was equally elegant as to her evening frock. Flaxen-haired, she rejoiced in a perfect complexion that required no cosmetics, not to mention—in spite of two children—a slender figure perfectly suited to the hipless fashions of the past few years.

Daisy, constantly battling the assault of excess poundage, usually felt an involuntary pang of envy at the very sight of her. Daisy was a sylph, however, in comparison with the generously endowed Sakari, who was quite oblivious of such matters.

"Oh, what a beautiful sari, Mrs. Prasad!" said Audrey. "That's the right word, isn't it?"

Daisy, her mind running on murder, hadn't even noticed the green and gold splendour. Besides, she was more accustomed than the Jessups to Sakari's spectacular embroidered silks. Now she joined in the admiration and the exchange of civilities.

Sakari's mind, however, was also running on murder. It wasn't long before, setting down her empty cup and taking a sip of Drambuie, she said, "I hope you have come on the same errand as I, to extract as much information as possible from Daisy about this alarming crime?"

Audrey smiled, leaving it to Mrs. Jessup to say, "Naturally. You must forgive our inquisitiveness, Daisy. Neither of us took the slightest interest in crime before you came to live next door."

"So I'm to blame, am I? Alec's been very close-mouthed, so I doubt I can tell you much you haven't read in the papers. I don't think you need be alarmed, Sakari. I dare say it's just some East End gang feud."

"I doubt it," said Audrey. "Didn't they say, Mama Moira, that the victims, or at least one of them, was wearing expensively tailored clothes? It doesn't sound like East-Enders, does it?"

"Where did you read that? It wasn't in my *Evening Standard*."

"Aidan came home from work late and brought the latest edition of the *Evening News*."

"Mine was the afternoon edition. I wonder what else you know that I don't?"

They compared notes, but the clothes seemed to be the only tidbit Daisy had missed.

"Alec did not tell you this?" Sakari enquired. "I hope he has told you something we did not find out from the newshounds." She produced this colloquialism with her usual enjoyment of her mastery of vernacular English or the occasional Americanism. "What have you to relate, or did you bring us here on false pretences?"

"I warned you Alec hasn't been very forthcoming. Not that he ever is, but he seems particularly anxious in this case that some of the details shouldn't get out."

"I expect having three bodies adds complications we can't imagine," Mrs. Jessup proposed.

"It wouldn't surprise me. More coffee, anyone? Drambuie?" Everyone had had sufficient of the sweet liqueur. Daisy refilled coffee cups before she continued, "I suppose they have to work out how the three are connected."

"Apart from being buried close together," said Sakari, "and wearing good clothes."

"I bet Alec's furious that that got about. I wonder if Inspector Gant is trying to sabotage his investigation!" That was the name she'd been trying to recall. It reminded her of John of Gaunt.

"Inspector Gant? Who is this man?"

"Oh dear, I shouldn't have mentioned him without asking you all to promise not to breathe a word."

"I promise!" they chorussed, leaning closer.

"Thanks. Alec didn't tell me not to talk about this bit, but I'm sure he'd be as angry with me as with Gant if word spread. That's Detective Inspector Gant, of the Essex police."

"But why should he do such a thing, Daisy? Do not the police cooperate with each other?"

"Not always. You see, the local police are the first to be called in, of course, and sometimes they resent it when the chief constable of the county decides to ask Scotland Yard to take over a case. Apparently Gant was so furious he didn't even stay at the site to pass on to Alec whatever information he had already found. That's very bad form, not to mention exceedingly unhelpful."

"I should rather think so!" said Audrey. "My old nanny had to leave last year to go and take care of her aged father. Just imagine if she had refused to stay long enough to tell the new one all about the children!" Audrey saw most things in terms of her children.

"Nanny James was quite at liberty to leave, though, my dear," said her mother-in-law. "I'd have thought the police would have a rule, or a regulation, or something of the sort. Surely it was his duty to stay, Daisy, not just his choice?"

"Well, I'm no expert, but I expect so. Alec has no authority over Gant, but he had to send to the Yard for men with spades—"

"Detective Inspector Gant took everything with him?" Sakari asked.

"And everyone. At least, that's the impression I got. The local constable was still there, I think, and one other officer. Anyway, Alec's boss, Superintendent Crane, must have had to authorise the extra people, and I'm sure he'd take it up with the chief constable of Essex. If I'm not mistaken, they—the Metropolitan Police—bill the counties for their services, so Gant will probably get into trouble. And that's really about all I can tell you."

"This is very interesting," announced Sakari. "I shall see if I can find a lecture on the organisation of the British police force."

"Forces, darling. The Met, and one for each county, and big cities have their own, too, including the City of London. And the Scots are quite different, as well. It had better be a series of lectures."

Sakari chuckled. "In India, it is very difficult for a woman to obtain education," she explained to the Jessups, "so while I am here, I do the best I can for myself and my daughter. Deva is at boarding school with Daisy's Belinda. Perhaps you have heard that we are to visit them this weekend?"

"Yes, Daisy mentioned it," said Audrey. "Somewhere in Essex, isn't it?"

"An odd coincidence!" said Daisy. "I hope we don't run into DI Gant. The girls are in Saffron Walden. Do you know it?"

"I stayed the night there once," said Mrs. Jessup. "Maurice sometimes does business with Lord Braybrooke at Audley End House." Mr. Jessup was a very superior purveyor of wines and spirits. "In those days, I used to go with him when he wasn't travelling too far from town and it was an easy train journey."

"Did you explore the town?" Sakari asked.

"A little. I remember a very large and beautiful church."

"Perhaps you are able to advise us," said Sakari. "We have visited the girls at school before, of course, but never for more than a few hours. This time we must keep them amused for longer. I have brought a guidebook—always the quest for knowledge, you see!—so that Daisy and I may make plans. I left it on the hall table, Daisy, so that it would not distract you from telling me about the murders. But you have told us very little." She sighed.

"Sorry! If he says any more tonight or in the morning, anything not desperately secret, I'll tell you tomorrow."

"Please, go ahead and make your plans. I'll see if I can remember anything helpful."

The rest of the evening was spent discussing the rival merits of the Saffron Walden Museum and Bridge End Garden, with detours to the mediaeval maze on the common and the castle ruins.

"Let them run about in the gardens till they're tired," suggested Audrey, "then take them to the museum."

"Tired!" Sakari exclaimed. "I shall be exhausted."

"There are plenty of benches in the gardens," Mrs. Jessup assured her.

"We're assuming the weather will hold," said Daisy. "The forecast's good, so let's hope, but if it rains they'll have to make do with the museum."

When her friends left, Daisy's thoughts returned to Alec's case and the possible connections between the three bodies. They were all buried in close proximity—not that she actually knew how close. A few feet, she assumed. All three were well-dressed, which did indeed seem to dispose of the East-End gang theory. And then there was the paper target, the three targets.

Somewhere in the back of her mind, the targets rang a very faint bell. For some obscure reason, they made her think of Michael, her erstwhile fiancé, killed in the War while working with a Friends' Ambulance Unit.

It was because Michael had been a Quaker that the notion of sending Belinda to a Quaker school had not seemed utterly outlandish to her, when Bel begged to go with her friends. She was happy there, and doing well at her lessons, so what more could one ask for?

SIX

Alec didn't get home till midnight. When he let himself in, Daisy was in the front room reading, in her dressing-gown. Elsie had closed the curtains but left the windows open to the soft night air.

"Darling?"

He came into the room and slumped into a chair. "Whew! What a day!"

"You look more in need of a whisky than cocoa. Mrs. D left out veal-and-ham pie and gooseberry fool, too, if you're hungry."

"Ravenous! I've been running all over the Home Counties all day. I can't even remember when I last had a bite to eat."

"You stay there. I'll bring the tray. If it's not enough, I can always get you some bread and cheese to fill in the chinks."

"When did Mrs. D ever not provide enough? Ta, love. And whisky sounds like an excellent idea."

Daisy bustled about, and soon, jacket and tie discarded, he was wolfing his belated dinner.

She let him eat in peace, took away the tray and topped up

the whisky glass, then, as he leant back with a satisfied sigh, she asked, "I hope all your running about was productive?"

"Yes, thank heaven. And I can tell you some of it as we've notified the papers. We've reached the point where we need tips from the public. All three victims have been identified."

"Already? That's pretty good going, isn't it?"

Alec grinned. "The super's happy. He went so far as to ring up the AC at home to tell him."

"Mr. Crane's happy, all's well with the world. Who are—were they?"

"As you might expect, the most recent was the easiest. Vincent Halliday, son and heir of Sir Daniel Halliday, Baronet, of Hertfordshire. You're not acquainted with the Hallidays, are you?"

"No," Daisy said in surprise. "I've never heard of them, as far as I can remember. Why?"

"Oh, the super's got a bee in his bonnet about you, that's all."

"I know that." Indignantly, she added, "I don't see how he can possibly accuse me of meddling in *this* case!"

"He's not accusing you, just faintly nervous that you may turn out to be somehow involved."

"I call that a bit much! I've a good mind to try and dig up some mutual acquaintance who can introduce me to the Hallidays."

"This is not exactly a good time to meet them," Alec said dryly. "In any case, they seem to be a rather reclusive family. The old couple appear to disapprove thoroughly of the modern world and to do their best to keep the family from contamination. Lady Halliday's mouth is all pursed up as though it's set in an expression of disapproval."

"I know exactly what you mean!" Daisy forebore to remind him that his mother's mouth was much the same.

"Very strong on the Victorian virtues. Not much hope with the youngest generation, of course. Two boys at a public school—well, heaven knows, those are old-fashioned enough—

but the granddaughter is going to be a thorn in their flesh, if she isn't already."

"Good for her! Old couple? How old?"

"In their early seventies, at a guess. Vincent was forty-five. His daughter's about Bel's age, a year or two older. As far as we can find out, he was a quiet, harmless farmer, running the Halliday estate to the satisfaction of all concerned. He wasn't in the habit of going off to London for an occasional spree, or anything suggestive like that. We're still completely stumped for motive."

"What about the second victim?"

"Martin Devine, a Surrey man. He was the youngest, at thirty-three. Junior partner in a very prosperous firm of solicitors in Guildford. Unmarried. Father deceased, lived with his mother. I haven't had time to talk to her yet, or anyone else who knew him, come to that. That's on tomorrow's agenda. The local police are supposed to have informed her of his death this evening, so that his name in tomorrow's news won't come as a shock."

"Poor woman! Even if he's been missing for months, she must still have hoped he'd turn up. Alive, I mean."

"Yes. That doesn't seem to hold true for the last man, however. Or rather, the first."

"Oh?"

"William Pelham. His widow seemed more relieved than anything else that he wasn't coming back. She immediately started talking about repainting the house, and having seen it, I can't blame her! I had to call on her briefly tonight. We couldn't be sure of the identification without talking to her."

"How on earth did you identify him? You said there wasn't much left."

"Feeling ghoulish now, are you? We recovered two toe bones that had been broken and badly set. Not bad enough to make walking difficult, but his toes would have been misshapen and his wife could hardly help but know."

"And his doctor, presumably."

57

"Yes, but it's hopeless approaching doctors until you can assure them their patient is dead, which, of course, we couldn't. It's ticklish even then. They're extremely reluctant to part with information, as bad as—or worse than—solicitors and banks."

"So you had to see Mrs. Pelham, who was not over distressed to hear her vanished hubby had vanished for good."

"Rather to the contrary. I didn't have time to talk to her for long, nor, of course, to anyone else who knew Colonel Pelham. Have to go back tomorrow—"

"Later today," said Daisy, glancing at the clock on the mantelpiece.

This innocent remark prompted a vast yawn from Alec. "Later today," he agreed, standing up. "And if I don't go to bed now, it'll be time to get up. Come on. Oh, I managed to find a moment to buy some chocolate peppermint creams for Bel. I put them on the hall table. Don't forget to take them to her."

"I won't. She'd rather have you, but I don't suppose she'll reject them."

A wholly insufficient number of hours later, Daisy, again in her dressing-gown, joined Alec at the breakfast table. She wasn't awake enough to eat, and intended to go back to bed the minute he left. Nursing a cup of tea, she waited until he had finished with his bacon and eggs, poured him a second cup of coffee, and said:

"I woke up with an idea."

"An idea?"

"Well, it's not really enough to qualify as an idea. Call it a wonder. The first victim was Colonel Pelham, so I presume he's a soldier?"

"Retired. Territorials during the War, I think. I'm sure Ernie knows."

"I just wondered if you knew what the other two did in the War."

"No," he said thoughtfully. "I don't suppose Ernie does, either. It's long enough ago that I never considered a possible connection there. Even if they served together at some point, it seems unlikely that it could have anything to do with their murders eight years after the Armistice. As tenuous as the pub link."

"Pub link?"

"I shouldn't have mentioned that. Definitely not to be passed on."

"I won't."

"Nor your idea about their war service, just in case. But I will find out about it. I must run." He gulped the rest of his coffee. " 'Bye, love, and give Belinda my apologies and my love, won't you."

"Of course, darling. And the peppermint creams. Good luck."

He kissed her cheek and was gone.

"Oh well, it was an idea," she said to the empty air, and went back to bed.

On time to the minute, the Prasads' dark red Sunbeam tourer pulled up in front of the house. It was another gorgeous June day, so Kesin had let down the hood. Knowing Sakari, though, she would probably have it put up as soon as they got out of town. She wasn't one to put up with the inconvenience of wind in her face at thirty or forty miles an hour.

Melanie, in her typical self-effacing way, had moved to the passenger seat in front as soon as the car stopped in Constable Circle. Daisy joined Sakari in the back. Kesin hopped back in, and they proceeded in a stately manner round the circle and out into Well Walk.

"Kesin tells me," said Sakari, her tone dramatic, "that the most direct route runs through Epping Forest! I told him on no account to go that way, so we shall make a circuit. He says we shall not go far out of our way. Daisy, have you any further information from Alec?"

"Oh no!" Melanie protested, looking back. "Can't we let that subject rest for today?"

"You need not listen, Melanie."

"Short of putting my fingers in my ears, which would look very odd, I can hardly help it."

"I shan't talk about gruesome details," Daisy assured her, "if that's what you're worried about. In any case, Alec didn't tell me much beyond what was to be given to the papers, so you've probably read everything already."

"I never read about murders," said Melanie, somewhat self-righteously. "I hardly ever read the papers at all."

"I do," Sakari declared, "but this morning I had not time enough even to open the *Times*. Tell all, Daisy."

"It's mostly that all three victims have been identified, and their names. Alec's hoping for tips from the public about any connections between them."

"What sort of connections?"

"Any sort. As long as they're three discrete individuals—"

"My dear Daisy, being dead, they cannot help but be discreet!"

"Discrete spelt *e-t-e*."

"This is a word I do not know. Perhaps I should stay home from classes and lectures for a while and study the English dictionary instead."

"I don't know it, either, Sakari," said Melanie, proving she had been listening closely. "Remember Daisy is a writer. Words are her business."

"I wouldn't use that *discrete* in an article. It would go over the heads of too many of the sort of readers I write for."

"But you expected us to be better educated," said Sakari mournfully.

"English was always my best—my favourite—subject."

Sakari laughed. "Do not apologise, Daisy. We cannot hold you to blame for our ignorance, can we, Melanie?"

"Of course not, Daisy dear. It must mean something like separate, does it?"

"Yes, more or less, though in that context . . . But I'm not going to try and define it more precisely!"

"These are so far three separate individuals," said Sakari, "and Alec must discover what is the connection between them that explains why they were all murdered by the same person."

"Very well put."

"This is praise indeed from a professional writer!" Sakari laughed again. " 'Well put' I understand, though it is a rather odd idiom, is it not? I can see it is time for me to take another course in the English language that I think I know so well."

"You do know—and speak—it very well, Sakari," Melanie assured her.

"Well enough for most occasions, but always I strive to learn. I have not yet learnt the names of the victims, Daisy. Perhaps I shall be the one to supply the missing link."

"That *would* be an unexpected development! I can just imagine what Superintendent Crane would say. He'd be certain to find a reason to blame me, though for what, I can't imagine. Luckily, it seems extremely unlikely. Let's see, there's Vincent Halliday, son of Sir Something Halliday. A friend of yours?"

"No, alas. I have never heard the name. Nor do I recall ever meeting a Mrs. Halliday, nor a Lady Halliday, and as a diplomat's wife I have cultivated an excellent memory for names."

"Colonel—what was it?—Pelham, that's it. If Alec told me his given name, I've forgotten it."

"I have met a gentleman by this name, who works in the India Office, but he is not a colonel."

"A retired colonel at that. How old is your Pelham?"

"I find it difficult to judge with Europeans, but I should guess, about my own age."

"And how old is that?"

"Daisy, Daisy, have you not heard that one should never ask a woman her age?" Sakari shook her head in mock reproof.

"I want to know his age, not yours," Daisy retorted. Late thirties or fortyish, she thought, ten or twelve years older than herself. "In any case, you're not nearly old enough to be a retired colonel. It can't be the same man. What about Martin Devine?"

"Oh!" exclaimed Melanie.

"Mel, don't tell me you know him?"

"It must be a different person. Surely it's not such an uncommon name."

"Martin isn't, but I wouldn't say Devine is particularly common, and the two combined . . . Alec told me where they all lived. Devine was Guildford, I think. A solicitor."

"Oh!"

"It *is* the same man?"

"It must be. Daisy, how awful!" Melanie's face, turned back towards them, was pale with distress.

"Oh dear, was he a good friend?"

"No, thank heaven. Robert's parents live in Guildford, you know. We met Mr. Devine when we were visiting them. At a tennis party, I think, and a sherry morning. Bridge, perhaps. That sort of occasion."

"What was he like?" Sakari asked.

"I don't remember him particularly. Quite ordinary, I suppose. Agreeable."

"Agreeable?" said Daisy. "Not someone you'd expect to get involved in a quarrel?"

"Not at all. He was friendly but quite diffident. The kind of person who always falls in with other people's proposals even if he's just made a contrary suggestion."

"You see how much you can remember if you try?" Daisy was terribly tempted to ask whether Mel knew what Devine had done in the War. She resisted. Mel might not draw any inference, but it would most certainly dawn on Sakari that the question was relevant to Alec's case.

"Mr. Devine sounds like a most improbable person to be murdered," Sakari observed. "Was he married?"

"N-no, I don't think so. I didn't meet a wife. And that's really all I know, and I'm getting a crick in my neck, so can we please stop talking about it?"

"Of course. Shall I tell you about our researches, Daisy's and mine, into the interesting places to take the children in Saffron Walden? You need not turn your head to listen. I shall not take offence at speaking to the back of your neck."

Melanie agreed. Whether she listened or not, Daisy was not aware. Her own thoughts were puzzling over what motive anyone could possibly have for murdering an agreeable, diffident solicitor. Perhaps he knew about a will someone wanted kept secret?

Suppose Colonel Pelham had for some reason left all his worldly wealth to Vincent Halliday, instead of to his own offspring. In such a case, he might very well have decided to keep the will secret. And he might very well have let the information slip, including the name of his lawyer—in a fit of temper, perhaps.

His widow had seemed to Alec to be relieved that he was gone for good, which might be explained by a filthy temper.

Could Sakari's acquaintance at the India Office be his son and have killed him? It would be too neat a dénouement for words, guaranteed to infuriate Mr. Crane if he found out the connection with two of Daisy's friends!

But having decided, for whatever reason, to disinherit his son, why should Pelham make Halliday his heir? The only answer Daisy could think of was that Halliday had saved the colonel's life in the War. And an excellent answer it was, bringing everything back to her suggestion that the victims' war service might usefully be investigated.

She considered her structure with satisfaction, then suddenly realised its fatal flaw. Pelham had died first. Devine would have produced his will . . .

No, he wouldn't! No one but the murderer knew the colonel was dead. When someone disappeared, didn't one have to wait several years for a legal presumption of death? She rather thought so.

It was awfully risky for young Pelham to have waited several months to kill Devine. And even when he was safely out of the way, someone at his firm would take over his clients. Sooner or later, the will would come to light.

Blast! said Daisy to herself, as her house of cards came tumbling down. All the same, she'd mention her construction to Alec next time she saw him, if he hadn't solved the case by then. Perhaps it might put him on the right track.

SEVEN

Mrs. Devine lived in a small Georgian house on the outskirts of Guildford, down a lane with high hedges concealing
the houses of her neighbours. Behind a beech hedge, her front
garden was a mass of bearded irises. Their sweet, rather heavy
scent, brought out by the already warm sun, overwhelmed Alec
as he stepped out of the car.

"Monomaniacal gardener?" said Tom, joining him on the
pavement in front of the gate.

"She may do the garden herself. It doesn't look as if there'll
be much in the way of servants for you to talk to. When you're
finished with them, hie thee down to the pub."

"The Cricketers," put in Ernie. "That's the one he used to
frequent."

"Been at the dictionary again, have you, laddie?"

Alec opened the white-painted gate with its black-painted
legend: *Larches*. Looking up, he saw that there was indeed a pair
of larch trees in the back garden, their pale green spires tower-
ing above the red tile roof.

The three men trod single-file up the brick-paved path.

Before Alec reached the dark-green front door, it was opened by a short, plump, grey-haired woman in a black dress.

"Mrs. Devine?"

"No, I'm her sister, Mrs. Webb. You're the police?"

Presenting his warrant card, Alec admitted, "Yes, I'm—"

"Oh, good. Come in, do. Iris was afraid you might be more reporters, but I said, no, look at the way they walk, they're policemen. She doesn't really want to talk to *anyone*, but I told her she really must answer your questions if she wants justice for poor Martin. It's a sin and a shame that anyone would harm my poor nephew, who never harmed a fly. In a manner of speaking; if nasty flies get into the house, well, of course one gets the swatter, doesn't one?" Mrs. Webb nattered on as she led them to an open door on one side of the hall, at the front of the house. "I won't have flypapers in my house. They're deadly poison, you know, and what if one dropped in the soup, I ask you?"

It was obviously a rhetorical question, and Alec didn't attempt to answer. He nodded Tom towards a door at the back, at the end of a passage, beside the stairs going up to the first floor. At a guess, the door gave access to the kitchen area. He didn't want to interrupt Mrs. Webb by asking. She might yet say something relevant.

Following her, still chatting, into a sitting room overpoweringly decorated in iris-print chintzes, he thanked his lucky star that Daisy didn't insist on dressing up their house in an excess of daisies. Someone must once have told Mrs. Devine that she was as beautiful, or elegant, or sweet perhaps, as her namesake and she had taken it to heart. However, he had often noticed that an abundance of chintz tended to indicate an abundant volubility. He hoped, in spite of Mrs. Webb's statement, the two sisters might be alike in this.

They were alike in appearance, at least, the chief difference being that Mrs. Devine's eyes were red and swollen with weeping in a pale face. She sat in a low armchair, twisting a handkerchief (embroidered—wonder of wonders—with lilies) between restless fingers.

Before Mrs. Webb had finished introducing him, Mrs. Devine jumped up, clasped his hand in both hers, and burst into speech.

"I'm so glad you've come at last, Inspector! When they told me last night—such a pleasant policeman—they say it's better to know, not to wonder, but there's always hope, isn't there? Until they tell you—You're quite, quite certain it's my Martin?" She looked up at him with a pitiful remnant of hope.

"Quite certain, I'm afraid, Mrs. Devine. May I offer my sincere condolences?"

She burst into fresh sobs. He led her back to her chair and pressed one of his usual supply of fresh handkerchiefs into her hand.

"Now, now, Iris, calm yourself! You know you'll give your-self another headache. See what you've done, Inspector? I don't know what the world's coming to."

"Tea, perhaps, Mrs. Webb? Good and strong and sweet?"

"I'll ring for—"

"I don't want any more tea—I don't like sugar in it, anyway—I'm swimming in tea, already. I want a brandy."

"It'll only make your headache worse, Iris. Strong drink—"

"Mrs. Webb," Alec intervened forcefully, "I think this is the moment for a little brandy if ever there was one. I take it you know where your sister keeps it."

"Naturally," she said huffily. "It's in the buffet in the dining room. But—"

"Be so good as to show DC Piper if you please." He gave Piper a shadow of a wink, and Piper returned a shadow of a nod.

He would keep the woman talking in the dining room—about the evils of strong drink, if necessary—as long as he could. He herded her out, chattering as she went.

Alec sat down uninvited in the matching chair next to Mrs. Devine's. It was too low, so that his knees rose at a sharp angle. He wondered whether Martin Devine, of somewhat above av-erage height according to the autopsy, had constantly strug-gled with his mother's taste in furniture.

"Thank you, Inspector," she said, her sobs stilling. "Lily is an Abstainer—I've been longing for a brandy—just a drop—it *helps* my head—she wouldn't let me—Martin and I used to have a—he called it a tot—my late husband, too—after dinner on Sundays."

"There's no harm in a drop of brandy. I hope it will make you feel better. Do you feel able to talk to me now?"

"Whatever Lily may say, I'm sure I have always been ready to talk to the police about—the first policeman—he was a Guildford man—Lily did say you're from Scotland Yard, didn't she?"

"I am. Detective Chief Inspector Fletcher."

"I thought so, but she—*chief* inspector? I'm so glad someone is taking his disappearance *seriously* at—But it isn't just a disappearance now. He's dead, isn't he? They came last night and told—I just can't accustom my mind to—The first policeman said young men, even the steadiest—Martin was *very* steady. He always told me where he was going and when he'd come—so it was nonsense to say he'd probably gone off to have a fling!"

"Martin was very steady, was he? You must miss him terribly. Tell me about him, Mrs. Devine."

"He wanted to be a clergyman, you see. Then the War started, just as he finished school. He volunteered at once, of course—the Territorials—they didn't take volunteers into the regular army yet, not till—I'm not quite—sometime in 1915, I think, or was it '16? As soon as they did, he—and then he was sent to France. Or he volunteered to go. Must you know exactly?"

"That's all right, it doesn't matter." And, if necessary, could be looked up in the records. "Don't worry about the date. Do you know which regiment, or battalion, of the Territorials he was in?"

"Regiment—no. Did they have regiments, like the proper army? Does it matter? I thought they were all—But they didn't all go to France. Mesopotamia and India—but he transferred to the army in France. I wish he hadn't! When he came back, he said he couldn't be a clergyman because the Bible says, 'Thou shalt not kill,' and he had killed two men. Or three—he wasn't sure. It was the third—For some reason, that one worried him most but he never really—"

Alec decided not to press her about which unit her son had joined in France. Not unless they couldn't work it out from the records. "Never really . . . ?"

"Explained. So he articled as a solicitor in my brother-in-law's firm—Lily's husband—very good to him."

"He lived with you all this time, Mrs. Devine? Since he was demobbed, I mean."

"Yes. He never seemed interested in—We lead—led a quiet life—bridge, tennis—I don't play tennis but he was quite keen, though he didn't care for golf, though I encouraged—and cricket. I know what they say about widowed mothers but I *wasn't* clinging! I wasn't! I just wanted him to be happy." She broke down again, and Alec fished for another hankie.

Mrs. Webb bustled in, her face a study in outrage. "Have you been bullying my sister, Inspector? I shall—"

"No, no, Lily. The chief inspector has been all that is kind, only—If I could just have—"

Piper, having followed the sister, pressed a glass tumbler with half an inch of amber liquid into Mrs. Devine's shaking hand, then guided her hand as she attempted to raise it to her lips.

"There you go, madam," he said soothingly.

She sipped, and a little colour came into her cheeks. She bestowed a grateful glance on Piper. "Thank you."

"Just a few more questions, Mrs. Devine," said Alec, "if you're feeling better."

"Of course. I want to give you all the help I can." A telephone bell rang somewhere, but she ignored it, as did her sister. It stopped after a couple of rings, presumably answered by a domestic. "What else do you want to know?"

"Did Mr. Devine play tennis at a club, or with friends?"

"With friends, at private—I can give you their names," she

said doubtfully, "but they're very nice people. Perfectly respectable. Not at all the sort who—"

Nice and respectable or not, Alec wanted names. Piper took them down, and those of the Devines' bridge partners. Concentrating on these details further calmed the bereaved mother.

"Any others he associated with regularly?" Alec asked, "besides at the office." Mackinnon was at the solicitors' now. The senior partner, telephoned at home, had promised to go in, though he usually spent his Saturday mornings at the golf course, leaving any urgent business to underlings.

Mrs. Devine frowned in thought. "I don't—I can't think of—"

"The public house!" Mrs. Webb's mouth managed to remain a thin line even as she pronounced these condemnatory words. "My nephew frequented a public house. Goodness only knows what sort of low company he kept there."

"Frequented! Martin went for an hour or two, once or twice a—at most three times—and it's a perfectly—he went to the private bar, not—Sometimes he'd tell me he had met Dr. Darlington there, and even the Rector of St. Nicholas's occasionally—"

"I do not consider that a recommendation for either the place or the rector. Or the doctor come to that."

The doctor must be talked to, Alec thought, and the rector, too, especially in view of the victim's abandoned ambition to be ordained.

"Perfectly respectable," Mrs. Devine responded to her sister. "And he *never* came home inebriated! But that's where he had gone when he—" Once more, tears threatened.

Piper had had the forethought to bring the brandy bottle. He added a quarter-inch to her glass and she took an automatic sip.

Mrs. Webb glared at him. "These policemen seem intent on making *you* inebriated, Iris. Have a care!"

"Nonsense. I'm not at all inebriated." Judging by the way

she uttered the word, without stumbling or over-preciseness, she spoke the truth. "It just gives me a little courage. In any case, I have nothing to hide. If you're going to be so—so *negative*, Lily, I wish you would go away."

"I shall leave when Delphine arrives."

"Delphine?" Alec asked.

"Iris's daughter, Delphine Arbuthnot."

Alec met Piper's eyes and knew exactly what he was thinking: *At least the poor woman wasn't christened Delphinium!*

"Delphine lives up north, in—She's on her way, but she had to take the children to her in-laws' before—Such little dears! I wish Martin would—had—"

"Have you any other children, Mrs. Devine?"

"Just my younger daughter, Christine. She and her husband went to Australia as soon as he was demobbed after the—I can never remember the name of the place—*not* Billabong, that's from the song, but something like—I have the address in my book—"

"Never mind, I doubt if we'll need to get in touch with her." Christine wasn't likely to know anything useful about her brother, and unless the case dragged on endlessly, communication would take too long to help. One couldn't ask intimate questions by wireless telegraph. "I'd be glad, though, if you'd ring up the local police station when Mrs. Arbuthnot arrives, just in case we should want a word with her."

"I will. I promise."

"Then I believe that's all for now." There wasn't enough left of Devine to require a relative to make a formal identification. "I'm afraid we may have to get back to you later."

Mrs. Webb promptly rang the bell to summon a maid to show them out. It didn't seem to have crossed her mind that there might be questions for her, also. Alec gave her a considering look and decided she probably knew little and understood less of her nephew. And what she knew, she'd put the worst possible construction on, though she *had* said he wouldn't harm a fly. . . . Still, that was the sort of thing many people automatically said of murder victims. He wouldn't attempt to question her unless and until he was desperate.

"Thank you very much for your cooperation, Mrs. Devine. Once again, I apologise for the intrusion."

As Alec and Piper left the room, Mrs. Webb had already begun to pour a stream of words into her defenceless sister's ears.

The parlourmaid closed the sitting-room door firmly behind them. "Enough to try the patience of a saint!" she exclaimed. "As if the mistress hadn't got enough to bear! Sergeant Tring said to tell you, sir, as he's already left and he'll be waiting for further instructions. Ooh, he's a one! Begging your pardon, sir."

Piper waited till the front door was shut and they were halfway down the garden path before he remarked, half-admiring, half-disapproving, "I dunno how the sarge does it!"

"Does what?"

"Loosens their tongues. That girl, I bet she doesn't usually talk like that about Mrs. Devine and her sister, not to anyone but her fellow servants."

"Perhaps she considers you and me on a level with her fellow servants. What I'd like to know, is how you got Mrs. Webb to shut up for long enough for me to ask Mrs. Devine a few questions!"

Piper grinned. "I just told her, when we went for the brandy, that she didn't have to say anything, but it was my duty to write down everything she chose to say and it might be produced in evidence in a court of law."

"Ernie, you didn't! Talk about a stroke of genius. All right, we'll go and pick up Mackinnon—he's surely had long enough at Devine's office. You and he can see the doctor. I'll tackle the Rev."

The rector, a tall, thin man in a High Church soutane, was a disappointment. When Alec asked whether Martin Devine had confided in him, he shook his head gravely.

"I'm afraid he rarely attended church services, and never

took communion. On the rare occasions when he did come, Christmas and Easter for the most part, one had the impression that he did so to please his mother. Mrs. Devine is a regular communicant."

"Did you know him before the War, sir?"

"No. I came to St. Nicholas's during the War. Mrs. Devine told me Martin had once wanted to embrace a clerical life, but I put it down to the enthusiasm of youth. It rarely lasts long enough to bear fruit, alas." He sighed.

"Mrs. Devine mentioned that Martin had occasionally encountered you at the Cricketers' Arms."

"Yes, indeed. I try to visit all the public houses in my parish now and then. You would be surprised what confidences may be shared over a modest half-pint. But not by Martin Devine. Of course, if he had, naturally I should be unable to pass on anything he said."

"But you would pass on the fact that he had."

The Rector inclined his head. "Certainly." He hesitated, and Alec held his breath. "I can only say, since no words on the subject were ever uttered, that he presented a cheerful and contented façade, but I sensed in him—read in his eyes, perhaps—a deep bewilderment, verging on unhappiness. A troubled soul. I cannot express it otherwise. But such is of no use to a policeman, I suppose."

"On the contrary, sir. I dare say you'd be surprised at how much we rely on our impressions of people and on the obscure workings of intuition. I shan't lightly dismiss the insight of a clergyman. Thank you for your time."

Alec met the others at the Cricketers. Tom had already arranged with the landlord for the use of his snuggery, a tiny room with a desk where he did up his accounts. Two extra chairs had been squeezed in.

Entering last, Tom was barely able to close the door behind his huge bulk. He took out a large white handkerchief and wiped his endless forehead—merging as it did with the bald dome of his head, Daisy had once described it as continuing to the nape of his neck. "Won't that window open any wider, laddie?" he said to Piper, gesturing at the small square of glass high on the wall. "We'll all suffocate."

"I'll try." By main force, Ernie opened the stiff casement another two inches. The air that wafted in was distinctly warmer, but at least it was also fresher.

He was at the small desk, as he had to take notes whereas the others had only to report. Alec took the sagging armchair, while Tom and Mackinnon had the wooden chairs brought in from the bar. Four plates of limp-looking sandwiches, each adorned with a single gherkin, were spread out on the desk along with Ernie's papers.

"Don't know how the landlord can stand to do his book-keeping in here," Tom grumbled, wiping his neck. "And he does plenty, he says, this being a free house. It's easier to run a pub owned by a brewery, but they're looking over your shoulder all the time. He likes his freedom."

"You said in your report, Sarge, the pub in Ayot St. Paul was a free house, too," Ernie mentioned.

"He seeks them here, he seeks them there, he seeks connections everywhere," said Alec, in parody of *The Scarlet Pimpernel*.

"You never know," Ernie insisted.

"Very true. Right, you go first, Mackinnon."

"I talked to everybody at Devine's office, sir, from the senior partner, who was his uncle by marriage, down to the office boy. Hard-working, good tempered, polite—he sounds like a nice chap. That's what it all amounts to, though yon Mr. Webb put it in fifty words when ane would hae sufficed."

"Not really? The senior partner? The uncle?"

"Aye. I wonder that any of his clients ever manages to explain his business."

Alec and Ernie exchanged a glance and laughed.

"We had the dubious pleasure of meeting Mrs. Webb," Alec explained. "Ernie had to resort to underhanded methods to get her to shut up so that I could talk to her sister. How on earth do they manage at home?"

"Either one of 'em talks a lot elsewhere," Tom suggested, "because he or she can't get a word in edgewise at home, or else neither listens to t'other. Wasn't there any grain among the chaff, Mr. Mackinnon?"

"Plenty of names. Everyone he ever knew Devine to associate with. I kept a separate list, which I've already gi'en to Piper."

"A lot of 'em Mrs. Devine told us, too."

"How many total, Ernie?" Alec asked with deep misgiving.

"Maybe fifty, Chief."

An upheaval beneath Tom's moustache indicated a broad grin. "I can add a couple of dozen from the landlord, though some may be the same. No strangers about that evening."

Alec groaned. "Now how are we going to work out which of his acquaintances are significant and worth interviewing? Well, that can wait. We can't spend a lot more time here or we'll never make it to Tunbridge Wells today. Any lady friends, Mackinnon?"

"Plenty of ladies he played tennis or bridge with, and a few clients, but none he squired about, sir."

"The Devines' servants didn't know of any, either, Chief," said Tom.

"Hmm. We'll get to the servants in a minute. If that's the lot for the office, Mackinnon, did you have any better luck with the doctor?"

"Just a wee scrap. I'd say the guid doctor puts away a fair bit and wouldn't likely have noticed if Devine had bared his soul. Devine was never ill, but he did once ask for a prescription for sleeping powders."

"Ah!" said Tom, stroking his moustache.

"Tom?"

"The live-in servants, two maids and the cook, say Devine occasionally suffered from nightmares. They'd hear him crying out in his sleep. Mrs. Devine always wears earplugs because the least little sound wakes her, so she wouldn't know."

"The third man?" Alec wondered.

"Devine was the second," said Ernie with his usual precision.

"No, you missed that bit when you went to get the brandy for Mrs. Devine. The third man was the one Devine killed in the War, or may have killed. She thought it was what made him resolve not to become a clergyman. We'll never know for sure, but it wouldn't surprise me if that's what gave him nightmares. I don't suppose anyone found out which regiment or brigade of the Territorials he was in? Or the regular army?"

They all shook their heads.

"Colonel Pelham was in the Territorials," Ernie reminded him, "but I don't know which regiment. We should be able to find out this afternoon, and then we can go to their records and find out if Devine was in the same branch. D'you reckon it could be an important link, Chief?"

Alec sighed. "Who knows? But Daisy suggested it might be," he confessed.

EIGHT

Kesin turned off the High Street at the Cross Keys, an ancient half-timbered building with an overhanging first floor, where Daisy had often taken Belinda for lunch or high tea.

She would have liked to stay there, but Sakari preferred the larger and grander Rose and Crown, in the Market Place. As far as age was concerned there wasn't much between them, the Cross Keys being fourteenth century and the Rose and Crown fifteenth. The latter's flat three-story façade was plastered over and painted white, however. To Daisy's eye, it might be grander but it lacked the older inn's charm.

King Street was brightened by window boxes overflowing—inevitably—with red geraniums and blue lobelia. The Rose and Crown was straight ahead, half hidden by the projecting upper stories of another half-timbered building, these a fake frontage added by the Victorians, for inscrutable Victorian reasons, to the Georgian Town Hall—or so Sakari's guidebook had informed them.

The Market Place opened out on their left. It was a market day, the square full of stalls selling farm produce and all sorts of second-hand goods. Crowds of shoppers swirled about the Victorian drinking fountain in the centre.

Kesin edged the car forwards, saying something in Hindi. Sakari answered in the same language.

There was no room to park in front of the hotel, but the chauffeur paused for long enough to let the ladies out. As they went up the steps to the entrance, he turned into a narrow alley, running along the side of the building, with a sign pointing to the Rose and Crown Yard.

"He will unload our bags," said Sakari, "and then go to the school to await the girls." She pushed through the door.

The interior of the hotel had been modernised—just as well when it came to bathrooms, Daisy admitted—but the bedroom to which she was shown had an uneven floor to proclaim its age. Her window looked over the market. After unpacking and putting away her clothes in the wardrobe, she washed her face and hands and brushed her shingled curls. Then she leant against the sill, watching the bustle below, until she heard a knock on the door.

"Come in!"

Sakari came in, with Melanie following. "It is nearly one o'clock. Kesin will arrive with the children at any moment. Are you ready to go downstairs?"

They met the girls in the lobby. Belinda, skinny as ever but pink-cheeked and healthy, appeared to have grown at least an inch in the six weeks since Daisy last saw her. She gave Daisy a hug, but after politely greeting Sakari and Melanie, her first words were: "Daddy couldn't come?"

"No, darling. He came home very late last night and went off again very early this morning."

"Poor Daddy! But you're staying till tomorrow?"

"Yes. We're all staying to take you out to tea tomorrow. We'll have lunch together and the whole afternoon."

"Wizard!"

"Daddy sent you some chocolate peppermint creams."

"Oh, goody!"

"They're up in my room, and they'd better stay there until you've finished with your racing. You can have them after tea."

"All right. How are the twins? I miss them."

Daisy told her about her brother and sister's latest brilliant feats as they all went into the hotel restaurant.

All too soon, it was time to drive up the hill to the school, so that the girls could change into gym bloomers for their races. Daisy had always disliked participating in sports at school, and she was not much keener on watching them, but she did her best to share Bel's enthusiasm.

At the top of the High Street, they passed the War Memorial. It reminded Daisy of her vague hunch that Alec's case might somehow be connected with the War. A faded wreath was propped against the base. Next to it, a sad little bunch of drooping scarlet poppies, half their petals already fallen, was proof that the pain of loss was still acute.

But . . . murder? Three murders? More particularly, those three murders? Which of the doubtless myriad injustices of wartime could have led to such brutal revenge after so many years?

Daisy wondered whether Alec was following up the possibility, then dismissed the thought as the car turned into the school drive.

A few other motor-cars were parked at the side, and a couple of station taxis were disgorging passengers near the main entrance, at the foot of the central tower. The red brick building was massive, but its varied façade and roofline, many windows, and a few trees prevented an oppressive, institutional appearance. The gravel drive curved round a close-mown lawn. Between the lawn and the street grew a copper-beech hedge and a belt of trees, fresh spring-green leaves contrasting with dark evergreens, including a huge pine. A bed of crimson peonies, now fading to pink, dropped petals on the dark earth beneath—reminiscent of the poppies at the War Memorial.

"I wrote a poem about the peonies for English, Mummy,"

Belinda announced. "Mr. Pencote said it wasn't bad, for my age. I got an A."

"Well done. You must read it to me sometime."

"It's quite short. I can recite it."

"Not now, Bel," said Deva firmly, as Kesin pulled up behind the taxis. "We must run."

"We have to run to put on running togs so that we can run races," Lizzie said. She was the quietest of the trio but she wasn't going to turn out half such a prim and proper lady as her mother, Daisy thought with a smile.

All three giggled as they bounced out of the car and dashed off towards the pupils' entrance at the girls' end.

The visitors' entrance stood open. On the doorstep, parents were greeted by a senior boy in a school blazer and tie. He directed one of a cluster of juniors to escort each group of new arrivals to the playing fields.

Folding chairs had been set out in a row along the first hundred yards of the quarter-mile circular track. In the middle of the circle was the cricket pitch.

"Thank goodness we don't have to sit through a game of cricket!" Daisy exclaimed as they sat down. "It was bad enough having to play it at school."

"Robert took me to Lords' once," confessed Melanie. "I fell asleep right there in the stands and disgraced him. Never again!"

"The Marylebone Cricket Club is to tour India in the autumn," said Sakari. "I shall keep an eye on the scores in the newspaper, but I must admit that I have never understood the finer points of the game."

"I'm sure you can find a lecture course to enlighten you," Daisy suggested, laughing, "if you're sufficiently interested."

"I am not," Sakari affirmed. "Now, explain to me what we are to see today. I have never attended a sports day before."

Daisy and Melanie explained—or tried to explain—sprints versus long-distance races and hurdles, laps and heats and relays, and the house system, which pitted Lister, Mennell, and

Tuke against one another. Since the three "houses" were purely hypothetical, with no relation to bricks and mortar, Sakari wore a slightly befuddled look when the headmistress, Miss Priestman, came over to say hello. She introduced the games mistress, Miss Bascombe, whom none of them had met before as she had joined the staff at the beginning of the summer term, when her predecessor left to get married.

Miss Priestman moved on. Miss Bascombe was a hefty but pretty-faced young woman in a tennis dress, clutching a sheaf of papers. She said a few encouraging words in a doubtful tone about Belinda and Deva's athletic abilities. With more enthusiasm, she turned to Melanie, but Lizzie's prowess was destined to remain unsung.

"Miss Bascombe!" The man who hailed her was even heftier, with overdeveloped muscles and a stentorian voice to match. Dressed in shorts and singlet, he had a toothbrush moustache and hair clipped so short it bristled like a nailbrush. "I want a word with you about the ridiculous way you've scheduled the races. I can't have my chaps sitting about getting chilled while your little girls toddle along the track." He waved a matching sheaf of papers at her.

"If he'd helped me work out the schedule . . ." Miss Bascombe muttered resentfully. "Excuse me, Mrs. Germond. Coming, Mr. Harriman." She stalked off.

"A mistake, I fear," said a soft voice behind Daisy. Glancing back, she recognised the headmaster, Mr. Rowntree.

"The Committee had little choice," the man with him pointed out, sounding harassed. "Since the War we've had few applicants to be games master, and as you know very well, none of the Quaker applicants has been fit enough to fill the position adequately."

"I know. But still, an ex-sergeant major! I hate to say it, but Harriman has turned out to be something of a bully. It's a great pity . . ." They moved on and Daisy heard no more.

The girls came up just then. They had changed their shoes for canvas plimsolls, but they were wearing heavy, baggy serge bloomers and blouses with sailor collars and floppy bows. It was definitely not a convenient costume for running, though better than skirts. At least all the girls were at the same disadvantage, but it was just as well they didn't have to compete against the boys, who wore shorts and singlets like Mr. Harriman's. They sat down on the grass.

Kesin turned up bearing three large green silk umbrellas. Bowing, he handed one each to Daisy and Melanie, and then opened the third and stood behind his mistress, holding it over her head to shade her from the sun. The day was growing quite warm, but so far Daisy was enjoying it. The brim of her hat kept the direct rays off her nose, reducing—she hoped—the threat of freckles.

"I hope the children won't suffer from sun-stroke, running on a day like this," said Melanie anxiously.

"Oh, Mummy!" Lizzie protested. "We'll be perfectly all right. It's running in the cold and wet that's horrid."

"You should see our knees after a game of hockey in the winter," said Bel. "They're all blue and purple and red, not even counting the bruises."

"Mine aren't," Deva pointed out with a trace of smugness. "It gets much hotter in India, doesn't it, Mummy?"

"Yes, indeed," Sakari agreed, smiling, "but in India, young ladies do not run races."

"You're not going to stop me?" her daughter asked in alarm.

"No, no! Have I not come today especially to watch you?"

Harriman blew a whistle and started issuing orders through a megaphone. The girls jumped up and scampered off to the start line, and sports day proceeded on its scheduled—or possibly rescheduled—way. Belinda, all flying legs and pigtails, managed to come in second in her heat of the under-fifteen-hundred yards, thus winning two points for Lister.

"Only because Vanessa got a cramp in her leg halfway," she said dismissively when Daisy congratulated her. "And Jane didn't even start. She's in the San with an upset tummy."

"Well, it's jolly good, all the same," Daisy insisted. "I'm proud of you, and Daddy will be, too, when he hears."

"I wish he was here. Do you think he might come tomorrow?"

"How can I guess, darling? You know how it is."

Bel heaved a sigh. "Yes. I'm not making a fuss, honestly. Some people's fathers are in Africa, and Deva's and Lizzie's didn't come even though they're just in London, not off catching criminals."

Lizzie ended the day with four points for her house, and somehow Deva scraped up one, so three happy children dashed back to the school buildings later that afternoon. With the prospect of high tea in the town ahead, they were in a hurry to change. Their mothers followed more slowly.

"I'm quite worn out from watching so much energetic activity," Sakari declared.

Daisy saw two of Belinda's favourite teachers sitting together near the end of the row of seats. She had met them on a previous visit. Talking seriously, they seemed oblivious of the end of the athletic programme and the older boys now folding and removing the chairs. As their conversation was about to be interrupted anyway, Daisy stopped to have a word with them while Sakari and Melanie went on.

"Mrs. Fletcher!" Mr. Tesler, the science master, stood up. Daisy refrained from offering to shake hands as he had a crippled right hand.

Mr. Pencote reached for his crutches.

"Don't get up, Mr. Pencote," Daisy said quickly. The English teacher was also crippled, having lost both legs in the War. Belinda had told Daisy and Alec that often he wore two artificial legs and walked with only a cane, but sometimes he managed to get about on one leg and crutches. Bel being Bel, she worried about it. Alec had explained that sometimes a stump healed badly and made a prosthesis too uncomfortable to use all the time.

Not that understanding made Belinda stop worrying.

"I just wanted to tell both of you," Daisy continued, "how much Belinda enjoys your classes. At present she's torn between becoming a writer or a career as a scientist."

"You're a writer, aren't you, Mrs. Fletcher," said Pencote. "Belinda's very proud of you. She once brought a copy of *Town and Country* to school at the beginning of term, to show me. It's not a magazine I see regularly but I enjoyed your article."

Sitting down on the vacant chair beside him, Daisy went on chatting with him about her work and Belinda's studies, while Tesler turned aside to talk to another parent who approached him.

The boys clearing chairs came nearer. "We're going to have to move," said Pencote, once again reaching for his crutches.

Daisy leant down to pick up the one nearest her and handed it to him. As she straightened, Harriman paused as he strode past.

"Lending a hand to our hero here?" he said. "That's the ticket."

Pencote turned red. "Hero?" he shouted. "I'm not a hero, I'm a bloody victim! A victim of imperialist warmongers." With furious impotence, he swung one crutch at Harriman's back.

The games master, unheeding, had already gone on to bellow orders at the boys.

"Oh dear," said Daisy, unable to think of anything more pertinent to utter.

"Sorry, Mrs. Fletcher. I try to watch my language, in accordance with Quaker principles, but that b—that . . . that . . ."

"Bully," she suggested.

"He gets my goat, and what's more, he knows it. If I'd discovered Quakerism sooner," he said bitterly, "I wouldn't have been so keen to join up and I might . . . But that's water under the bridge. The real hero is Tesler. He stuck to his pacifist principles and was sent to Dartmoor." He lowered his voice.

"That's where he lost the use of his hand, you know. An accident in the quarries."

"The man I was engaged to was a Quaker." Daisy seldom spoke of Michael, but, much as she loved Alec, her throat still ached with tears when she thought of him. "He volunteered for the Friends' Ambulance Unit and was blown up in France."

"That's real heroism." Tesler had returned to them. Helping his friend stand up, he went on, "Dartmoor wasn't so bad, old chap. You shouldn't take any notice of what that fat-head says. He doesn't know what he's talking about. He's as lacking in brains as in nerves."

Pencote was obviously still seething, but he managed to chuckle. "That of God in every man?" he said, giving the Quaker principle an ironic inflection.

"Yes," Tesler said serenely. "Even Harriman, though he hides it well. Mrs. Fletcher, you say Belinda's talking of a career in science? I wish I could encourage her. She's one of the few pupils who truly grasp that science is not just about learning rules but about discovery. However, there are few—if any—opportunities for women in the sciences."

"Marie Curie!" Miss Bascombe joined them, as they moved slowly towards the school buildings.

"All right, few." Tesler gave her a fond smile, which was returned, Daisy noted.

"That child has determination. She'll be good at sports, too, Mrs. Fletcher, once she stops growing so fast. If she wants to be a scientist, don't discourage her."

"I wouldn't dream of it," Daisy assured the earnest young woman. "But she's only in the second form. She'll change her mind a dozen times, I dare say, before she has to decide."

At that moment, Harriman caught up with them, with a group of boys carrying chairs. As they passed, he swung round and said, "Look what I found on the field."

He handed something to Tesler, who automatically took it.

He strode on. Daisy and the three teachers stared down at the small object in Tesler's hand.

A white feather.

"A gull, I should think." Tesler seemed unmoved by the obvious implication that he was a coward. But Pencote and Miss Bascombe stared after Harriman with loathing.

NINE

By the time Alec and his team reached Tunbridge Wells, the day was still hotter, more like August than June. Colonel Pelham had lived on the north side of the common. His favourite public house, the Duke of York, was in the Pantiles on the south side, one of the old buildings surrounding the hot springs, a fashionable spa since the seventeenth century.

When they stopped to drop off Tom, he looked at the common, dropping into a valley then rising again, and groaned. "Why can't these people live closer to their locals?" he demanded.

"It would have made things more difficult for our murderer," Alec pointed out. "The common's well wooded, with plenty of lurking places, and roads as well as footpaths cutting across so he could have left a vehicle not too far from his chosen spot."

"Bloody lucky murderer," Tom grunted. "If one of 'em had lived in a busy street—"

"He'd have found a way. It seems to me he must have been obsessed with these three, and might well have been studying their habits and movements for some time."

"That means you think the pub connection's valid, Chief?" Piper asked eagerly.

"Hold on, Ernie! It's still only speculation. You're going too fast. The landlords of both the Cricketers and the Goat and Compasses said no strangers were about on the evenings Devine and Halliday disappeared."

Mackinnon nodded. "He canna hae been a local resident in both Guildford and Ayot St. Paul."

"No," Piper had to agree, somewhat crestfallen. "It must have been the army, then."

"I'm not ready to give up either possibility," Alec said firmly. "Let's hope Tom will find enlightenment at the Duke of York."

Tom cast another sour look at the common.

"Dunno about enlightenment but you'll find a pint, Sarge," Piper consoled him. "It's ten minutes to closing time."

"Ten minutes? Ta, laddie. I'm on my way." Always light on his feet for such a big man, Tom rapidly disappeared into the arcade.

"Happy thought, Ernie," said Alec. "Let's go."

Colonel Pelham had lived in a stuccoed post-war bungalow, painted a bilious shade of mustard yellow with a dreary olive-green front door. The contrast with the typical Kentish red-tile roof was particularly distressing.

The front garden was laid out with military precision. A rectangular patch of lawn on each side of the brick path had rectangular flowerbeds centred in each lawn, edged with low, rectangular box hedges, as was the path. The beds were planted with rigid rows of magenta rose-campion and sternly staked red-hot pokers.

The overall effect was sufficiently hideous to draw a "Blimey!" from Piper, who had not seen it the night before.

Alec sent Mackinnon to talk to the neighbours. The Kent police had done so when Mrs. Pelham first reported her husband missing, but without any great sense of urgency. After the passage of ten months, the likelihood of any remembering much about the late August evening he'd disappeared was slim. The possibility couldn't be ignored, though. The subsequent enquiries might have fixed some oddment in someone's memory that they hadn't bothered to bring up earlier but would recall now that it was a matter of murder.

As Alec and Piper walked up the garden path, their ears were assailed by a well-bred but determined female voice floating out through an open window.

"Everything," it insisted. "The lawn, the box, the campion—hideous colour!—the lot. I'm putting in a forsythia, and rambler roses, and . . . What else sprawls all over the place?"

"But madam—"

"What else?"

"Well, buddleia, madam, an' . . . But they be mortal untidy, madam!"

"Just what I want, a bit of untidiness in my life. Nasturtiums! Trailing geraniums! You can start digging everything up, Johnson, and I'll get a book to help me decide what to plant."

"Yes, madam," came the mournful, resigned voice of—presumably—the gardener.

Alec knocked on the front door.

"Oh good, that must be the painter. I wonder why he's come to the front door? But never mind, the sooner he gets busy the better. You, too, Johnson. Off you go and get rid of the whole lot."

"If 'ee sez so, madam."

"I do." Mrs. Pelham, a stout woman in her sixties, of commanding aspect, appeared at the window of the room to the right. "Oh, it's the police. Good afternoon, Mr. Fletcher. You haven't come to tell me there's been a mistake and the colonel's been found alive and well after all, have you?"

"I'm afraid not, Mrs. Pelham."

"Thank goodness! Come in, come in, do. Now I remember, you said you'd be back today. I hope you don't imagine *I* murdered William, though I can't say I didn't sometimes consider it!" She giggled, a sound so incongruous with her appearance and inappropriate to the occasion that Alec couldn't think of anything to say.

He opened the door, which was not locked, and stepped into a narrow hall. A man in gardener's clothes was tramping away towards the back of the house, muttering, "Mortal maggotty she be!"

As Piper was closing the front door behind him, Mrs. Pelham came to the sitting-room door. "Leave it open, young man," she commanded. "The colonel insisted on having it closed, even in the hottest weather, but at last I'm free of his tyranny. Leave it open, wide open!"

They followed her into the sitting room where Alec, last night, had posed delicate questions about her husband's toes. It was all dark wood, leather upholstery, and crimson curtains, in accordance, he assumed, with Colonel Pelham's taste. He wondered what she'd replace it with. She didn't seem the sort of woman who'd cover everything in chintz, but the girlish giggle proved her unpredictable. For all he knew, she'd always longed for a room decked in multiple shades of pink frills.

"Sit down," she commanded, and, as a maid came in, added, "will you take tea or coffee? Or—no—lemonade! William didn't care for lemonade. Have we any lemons, Bella? He didn't approve of calling servants by their given names, either."

"I'll ask Cook, ma'am," said Bella, and departed.

Mrs. Pelham turned to the men with an expectant air. Alec introduced Piper, who took out his notebook and one of his ever-ready well-sharpened pencils.

"All I want at present," said Alec, "is an idea of Colonel Pelham's character and as many names as you can come up with of his relatives, friends, and other people he associated with."

"Anyone he could buttonhole. He was a monumental bore, telling the same army stories over and over again. Very few of them were even remotely interesting the first time. He did have one friend of sorts, a junior officer who had served under him, a captain he was. Now what was his name?"

Alec could see that Piper was all agog, the name "Devine" hovering on his lips. He shook his head slightly at the eager young man. He didn't want his witness prompted.

"Beresford," said Mrs. Pelham, and Piper's shoulders sagged in disappointment. "Bernard Beresford, that's it. His family's local. We only came here after the War, you know. I'm not saying Captain Beresford would have chosen to be William's closest friend, but he was the sort who can't say boo to a goose, and my husband, as you may have gathered, was a tyrant and a bully."

Obviously Beresford could have held a grudge against the colonel for having been forced into intimacy with him. Could the constant repetition of pointless stories, like a variation on the Chinese water torture, have driven him in the end to murder? Was it possible he had also known Halliday and Devine in the army and found in their behaviour towards him a cause for bitter resentment? Devine hadn't sounded like someone who would take advantage of another's meekness.

"How on earth did Beresford rise to the rank of captain if he was so timid?" Alec asked.

"Sheer longevity! He was shoved into the army by his family—one of those ridiculous traditions. William said it was bad for morale to have a lieutenant in his late forties, so he was promoted, but there was simply no justification for making him a major."

"Where did they serve together?"

"In the Buffs, the East Kent Regiment. They were always dashing off to Africa to fight one war or another. They both retired before the Great War, of course, and Captain Beresford— who preferred, incidentally, to be addressed as plain Mister— Where was I? Oh, yes, he was too old for the Territorials, a dozen years older than William. He died just two years ago at nearly eighty. He joined the Local Defence Volunteers, though what use he'd have been boggles the imagination. But there, luckily we weren't invaded."

Alec and Piper had lost interest in Beresford as soon as they heard he'd been dead for two years.

"Which branch of the Territorial Army was your husband in, Mrs. Pelham?"

"One of the TA battalions of the Buffs, in the Home Counties Division. Once they started taking volunteers in the regular army, they let him go in spite of his age. They needed experienced officers, of course, even if they were mess-room bores. But I don't suppose they had much of a mess-room for him to bore people in, most of the time."

"You don't happen to know which battalion he ended up in?"

"Why on earth . . . ? Well, never mind, yes, as it happens, I do. If something's repeated often enough, it sinks in even if you're not listening. He was in the Eighth Battalion. They went all over the place, Ypres, Loos, the Somme, and who knows where else. Wherever there were trenches. William didn't approve of trenches. He said the Buffs had fought without in Napoleon's war and the Boer War and they ought to be out attacking, not cowering in holes in the ground. I must say, it seems to me that if someone is shooting at you, a hole in the ground is quite a sensible place to be."

Alec couldn't help smiling. "An eminently practical point of view," he agreed. "Was there anyone else your husband saw regularly, besides his elderly military friend?"

"Not if they saw him coming! I don't know whom he bored at the Duke of York—the barman if he couldn't catch anyone else, I feel sure."

"He walked to the Duke of York?"

"Yes, always, across the common whatever the weather. He had always seen worse somewhere—Africa, or the Himalaya mostly. He was determined to keep fit, but no one would play golf with him after he laid down the law once too often. He decided it was a footling game. No one invited us for bridge, for the same reason. We didn't go to church because he held a low opinion of army chaplains he'd known. As a matter of fact," she said simply, "I've felt very isolated for years, and now I'm going to join everything I can find. But I didn't kill him."

"We have no reason to suppose you did, Mrs. Pelham. What about relatives?"

"We never had children. I have quite a few relatives that I shall see more often now, but on his side there's only a nephew, with whom he quarrelled several years ago."

"How long ago?"

"Oh, just after the War."

Not much hope there, then, Alec thought, but he asked, "His name?"

"Reginald Pelham. A civil servant. The last I heard of him, he worked at the India Office, but I don't know if he's still there."

"Never mind, we'll find him." He asked a few more questions, thanked her, and warned her that he or one of his men might have to return in search of further information. He and Piper stood to leave.

"Oh, but you haven't had any lemonade, and it's such a hot day! Do stay a little longer. I don't know what can be taking Cook such an age." She went to the door and called, "Bella! Bella?" before going out into the hall.

"No sense in leaving before Mr. Tring arrives, Chief," Piper pointed out in a low voice. "Like as not we'd miss him on his way across the common, and Mr. Mackinnon, too."

"True. Very well, you can go to the kitchen and have a chat with Bella and Cook, and I'll let Mrs. Pelham entertain me."

"She's given us some good stuff. Maybe there's more to come. You never know your luck."

"It's about the first bit of luck we've had in this case! If any of it actually turns out to be useful."

Mrs. Pelham returned, followed by Bella with a tray. Ernie gallantly took the tray from the maid and deposited it on a table, then left the room with her.

The widow looked after them knowingly. "Your assistant's gone to interrogate my servants, I suppose," she said, pouring lemonade from a cut-glass pitcher.

"Just to chat with them. Thank you." Alec took the glass she offered and drank deeply. "Perfect."

"A little too much sugar, and she didn't have time to pour boiling water over the lemons and let them steep, but one can't blame her for that. Are you going to tell me what happened to William, and why?"

"As I told you last night, Mrs. Pelham, he was shot, and buried in Epping Forest alongside two others. As to the how and why, we have very little to go on."

"You don't think of someone being killed because they're boring," she mused, "more that they'll bore someone to death. Three victims murdered for that same reason seems even more unlikely. So it must have been his martinet side that did for him. Had the others any connection with Africa? Those Boers hold a long grudge."

"None. They were considerably younger than the colonel. Both lived all their lives in England, and neither had any connection with the army before the Great War. Nor was either of a tyrannical disposition, as far as we can judge."

"Hmm. Well, unless William kicked someone's dog while crossing the common, I can't think of anything he might have done or anyone he might have seriously offended since he retired for the second time, in '19. Do you want me to identify his body?"

Alec winced. "I'm sorry, there's . . . not enough left to make that necessary—or indeed, possible."

"Pity. It would have been a pleasure. What is it, Bella?" she asked, as the maid returned once more.

"It's the painter, madam, and two more policemen. Detectives, I should say. All come at once."

"That will be my sergeants," said Alec, standing up. "I'd better be off. You've been extremely helpful, Mrs. Pelham, and thank you for the lemonade. Just one more question, if I may: What colour are you going to paint the house?"

"White, with a medium blue front door and window-frames," Mrs. Pelham said firmly.

"It sounds most attractive."

"I never could abide mustard yellow. You may show the painter in, Bella, as long as his boots are clean."

Following the maid to the kitchen, Alec said, "A decisive lady, your mistress."

"And precious little she was let to decide till *he* vanished! Middling rousey, he were."

"Er . . . would you mind translating *middling rousey?*"

She laughed. "*Middling* means very, ever so, though it don't sound like it, to be sure. *Rousey*, that's bad-tempered. Never allowed as anyone else's opinion was worth a groat and he'd bite her head off was she to disagree. Me, I was ready to look for another place if he hadn't've gone. Not that I'd wish him murdered, mind. It's a nasty way to go, even for the likes of him."

The kitchen was crowded, with one medium, one large, and one very large policeman, a bulky cook, and a small, wiry painter. Tom Tring and Mackinnon each had a glass of lemonade. Bella summoned the painter to the door, examined his boots, and took him away. Piper slipped out of the back door. The detective sergeants swigged down their drinks, thanked the cook, and followed him. Apologising to Cook for the invasion as he passed through, Alec went to join his men outside.

"Back to town. We'll talk on the way. We may have something to go on at last."

TEN

The stalls in the Market Place were being dismantled when the ladies returned to the Rose and Crown. The girls were disappointed. They had hoped to hunt for bargains while their mothers went upstairs to tidy themselves. Instead, they went up, too.

"This is nice!" said Belinda, going over to Daisy's window. "You've got a bird's-eye view."

"Yes. I was watching earlier, before you came. I think I'll change into a skirt and blouse."

"Do you mind if I stay, Mummy? I'll keep looking out of the window."

"First tell me which top to wear with my blue pleated skirt."

Bel carefully considered the flowery top and the plain blue with two zigzags of braid down the front, laid out on the bed. Both were straight, hip-length tunics, which Daisy hoped gave the illusion that she had a fashionable figure—at first glance, at least.

"I like the flowers best," said Bel, and returned to contemplation of the demise of the market.

Hot, sticky, and dusty, Daisy stripped off her frock and

washed before putting on her clean clothes. As she dressed, she said, "I had a chat with a couple of your teachers after the races, after you girls left."

"Who?"

"Mr. Tesler and Mr. Pencote. They're both very happy with your work."

"Mr. Tesler's really nice. He never gets angry when your experiments don't come out right."

"And Mr. Pencote?"

"I like him. He's nice most of the time, but sometimes he gets in a terrific bate when people haven't read what they were supposed to, or they write stupid stuff, so some people don't like him. I think when he's impatient, it's because his legs hurt. The stumps, I mean. It must be awful to have no legs, don't you think?"

"Awful."

"And people always being sorry for you. That annoys him, too. It's so sad that they're both crippled, but they're still good teachers. It's lucky they don't have to teach games."

"Very. I had a word with Miss Bascombe this afternoon, too."

"Oh," Bel said doubtfully, "I'm not very good at games."

"Darling, you got two points for Lister today! Who could ask for more? I'm proud of you, and Daddy will be, too. Besides, Miss Bascombe thinks you'll do better when you stop growing so fast."

"I don't really care that much, Mummy, actually. It's sometimes fun but there's so many rules you have to worry about. I like swimming, though. At least Miss Bascombe isn't like Mr. Harriman."

"Oh?"

"He's the boys' games master. Most of the boys hate him. He's always shouting at them for the least little thing and he picks on the ones who aren't good at games. He says they ought to get 'six of the best' to encourage them. That means beating them! Isn't it awful? But they don't allow beating here, so he gives them Changing Practices."

"Changing Practices? What on earth is that?"

"They have to keep changing from sports clothes to every-day clothes and back, over and over again however many times Mr. Harriman says. They have to go to the changing room, then go and find the master on duty to show him, then back to change again, all afternoon sometimes."

"It sounds like a bore, but better than a beating." Daisy remembered her brother Gervaise's tales of caning at his school. He'd usually made a joke of it, but it had sounded pretty brutal to her.

"It's not fair, though," Bel protested. "They can't help not being good at games, can they? Anyway, he's horrible to everyone. He teases people, not in fun, being nasty. I'm glad Miss Bascombe's not like that. D'you know what, Mummy? She's sweet on Mr. Tesler!"

"Miss Bascombe? Is she, indeed," Daisy said noncommittally.

"She makes sheep's eyes at him when she thinks no one's looking. And we think he's sweet on her, too. So's Mr. Harriman, but she doesn't like him."

"Goodness, what gossips you children are! Come on, I'm ready. Let's go and see if the others are waiting for us. Oh, here are the peppermint creams. Not to be opened until after tea. I'd better just stick them in my handbag."

"Yes, please, Mummy. I won't forget to remind you to give them to me after tea. You will thank Daddy for me, won't you?"

"Of course, darling."

"I'll write to him next week, too." In spite of the distraction of the chocolates, Bel's thoughts were still on Miss Bascombe and Mr. Tesler. "I think it's nice that she doesn't mind about his hand. Don't you? I wonder if they'll get married."

When they all met downstairs, food became the only topic of interest. The girls were ravenous after the day's exertions and needed a proper meal, which would be their last of the day, before returning to school. Sakari wanted to stay at the Rose and Crown, but they had just finished serving afternoon tea and wouldn't reopen the dining room for dinner till half past seven.

"We could go to that place you took us once, Mrs. Fletcher," Deva proposed. "The very old hotel you were staying at, remember?"

"The Cross Keys," said Belinda.

"Oh yes!" Lizzie agreed enthusiastically. "We had a wonderful high tea there."

"It's just down the street, Mummy," Deva coaxed. "We drove past it. But if you don't want to walk, Kesin could take you in the car."

"How far?" Sakari asked, her misgivings obvious. "There are too many hills in this town."

Daisy laughed. "All of two minutes' walk, even for you, darling, and no hill. It really is very nice."

"It's in your guidebook, Sakari," said Melanie. "You read about it to me on the way from home."

Sakari sighed. "Then I suppose I must see it, for my education. How is it that I have missed it on previous visits to Deva?"

"Because when you come, Mummy, we've never gone anywhere except here and school. Now you've got a guidebook, we'll have to see everything."

"Not on one short visit!" Sakari exclaimed in horror, and everyone laughed.

They walked along King Street, the girls behind their mothers. Melanie and Sakari were talking about the history of the Cross Keys, Mel remembering every word the guidebook had said about it. Daisy heard Belinda say to her friends in a low voice, "I told Mummy about Miss Bascombe and Mr. Tesler."

"What did she say?" Deva asked.

"Just that we're gossips."

"Did you tell her Sally saw them together in Bridge End Garden? And Mr. Harriman creeping about spying on them?"

99

"That would be even worse gossip," said Lizzie with a hint of self-righteousness that reminded Daisy of Melanie.

"Why?" Deva wanted to know.

"Because we didn't see them ourselves. We'd just be repeating what Sally said, not knowing if it's true or not."

"Prob'ly not," Deva conceded. "She's a day brat. She could have made it up to make herself important."

"Then she'd have said she saw them kissing," Belinda argued, "or cuddling or something. I think it's true. Sally lives near the Garden. Besides, there's nothing wrong with going for a walk."

"Alone, just the two of them?"

"Mr. Pencote's Mr. Tesler's best friend. He couldn't walk that far."

"They didn't have to go so far," Lizzie pointed out.

Melanie turned. "Yes, they did, to escape from horrid little gossips like you."

"I didn't start it, Mummy!"

"I've told you before, Elizabeth, that's no excuse. I don't want to hear another word on the subject."

"Yes, Mummy."

Abashed, the other two also fell silent for the last few steps to the Cross Keys. They all revived once inside the dark-beamed, panelled restaurant. The girls discussed vigorously the items on the menu before opting unanimously for the mixed grill. Daisy, Melanie, and Sakari all decided a cup of tea was sufficient for the moment. They would dine later, after Kesin drove the children back up the hill to school.

All too soon for the girls, it was time to go, though the grumbles were quieted when Daisy handed over the peppermint chocolates. While they were waiting for Kesin to bring the car round, Belinda said to her, "Mummy, will you come to Meeting in the morning?"

Daisy was in a bit of a quandary. The question hadn't arisen before as she had always visited on a Saturday or Sunday afternoon. She wasn't much of a church-goer. She had always seen that Bel went to Sunday School at the parish church, more to placate her mother and mother-in-law than from any great sense of conviction. Otherwise, christenings, weddings, funerals, and Christmas carol services were about the limit of her observance.

But she had sent Belinda to a Quaker school, and it would hardly set a good example to refuse to attend the service. More to the point, Bel was looking at her hopefully, and it was hard to refuse the child, especially when her father wasn't able to be there.

"What time is it?"

"Ten o'clock. And it practically always finishes at eleven, unless someone starts to speak at the last minute, but they hardly ever do, because the little children come in for the last ten minutes and they get restless."

She wouldn't have to get up early, and she could survive an hour. "All right, darling, I'll be there."

"I'll go with you," said Melanie.

Five pairs of eyes turned to Sakari. She sighed. "Very well, I shall go as well. It will be educational."

Later, when they met in the Rose and Crown dining room, Sakari said, "Daisy, do you think it is true about Mr. Tesler and the games teacher?"

"It wouldn't surprise me if they're fond of each other. About the walk in the Paradise Garden—"

"Bridge End Garden, is it not?"

"Yes, I was being frivolous. *The Walk to the Paradise Garden* is a piece by Delius. The Paradise Garden is actually the name of a pub—but you don't want to hear about that. I have no idea whether Tesler and Miss Bascombe are 'walking out' seriously."

"I hope not. It is a bad example for the children."

"Sakari, we're in England in the 1920s, not India and not the Victorian era! Taking long walks together is about the only way they can escape the prying eyes and rumourmongering of several hundred children, even if that dreadful man Harriman is still able to spy on them."

"You two are as bad as the children," said Melanie. "May we please change the subject?"

"Yes, indeed," Sakari said promptly. "Let us talk about the murders."

"Sakari!"

"Have you received any messages from Alec, Daisy? You would assuredly have told us if he were able to join you tomorrow."

"I haven't heard from him. There's still time, but even if he makes an arrest tonight, he'll still have endless paperwork to complete. It seems to be an incredibly complicated case. As I told you, the three victims don't have anything obvious in common."

"Except that I have met a Mr. Pelham who may be a relative of one, and Melanie has met a Mr. Devine who almost certainly *is* another."

"Yes, well, we don't need to tell Alec. Not yet, at any rate. If your Pelham is a close relative, Sakari, Alec's bound to find him."

"I didn't know Martin Devine well enough to have anything to contribute to the investigation," Melanie said thankfully.

"And I don't know anyone by the name of Halliday. So not one of us has any helpful information."

"Nevertheless, I am quite certain that you have a theory, if not several. Tell us," Sakari urged.

"Nothing I haven't already picked holes in myself," Daisy admitted sadly. "Alec hasn't told me enough to base a sound theory on. It may seem to you as if I'm constantly getting involved in his cases, but most of them I don't know any more than you can read in the papers, and this is one of those."

"Thank goodness!" said Melanie. "It's bad enough being distantly acquainted with a murder victim, without having you mixed up in it. That dreadful business at the Tower of London!

And I'll never get over the dead dentist case you inveigled Sakari and me into."

"You may have been inveigled," said Sakari, "but I joined in willingly. Is it not our duty to aid the police in discovering a criminal if we are able?"

"Aiding is one thing. Meddling is another."

"You sound just like Alec, Mel," Daisy said, laughing. "Not to mention Superintendent Crane. I'm going to have the rhubarb tart with custard, which could probably be classified as a crime against my hips. What about you?"

ELEVEN

As they drove back to London, Mackinnon at the wheel, Ernie Piper taking notes, Alec told them about his interview with the widow.

"Ah," said Tom, ruminating, "it don't sound as if she's grief-stricken."

"No, but we'll talk about that when everyone's reported. Go ahead."

Tom's report from the Duke of York for the most part merely confirmed what Mrs. Pelham had said: The colonel was a monumental bore. In fact, the landlord, Chas. Watson, said a group of elderly regulars had concocted a defence, a rota of whose turn it was to take Colonel Pelham off into a corner and bear with him for a few hours, leaving the rest free for the evening. Tom had all their names, but considered it unlikely that they'd have anything to add.

"Watson can't remember specifically whether there were strangers in the saloon bar that evening, but he says more than likely. August they get a lot of visitors to the spa, and they're the kind that drink in the saloon, not the public. For what it's worth, laddie, the place is a free house. I had a nice pint of Mc-Mullen's bitter."

"I can't see what it means, if anything," Ernie admitted, "but you never know."

"Is that it, Tom?" Alec asked.

"Just about. Seems the colonel was pretty regular in his habits. He didn't go in every night, but when he came, he always arrived at a little after nine, after his dinner, and stayed till closing. Late August, it would have been dark when he left. Easy to waylay him on the common. Like you said, Chief, there's plenty of hiding places near the path he would've taken, the most direct route to his house."

"All three victims walked a lonesome road home from the pub," Mackinnon observed. "Pelham across yon common, Halliday across the fields, and Devine along a high-hedged lane. Did the killer choose them for that reason, or was it a fortunate coincidence for him?"

"A good question," said Alec. "We won't know the answer until we find a motive."

"But, as far as we know, nane o' the three showed any sign of concern that such might put them in danger?"

"Not as far as *I* know," Piper told him. "No one's mentioned it in any report."

"We ought to have asked," Alec acknowledged, "and will have to when we get to follow-up interviews. They were all vulnerable every time they walked home. It would appear that they didn't feel threatened, weren't conscious that someone might be gunning for them, or they would have taken precautions. Mackinnon, any luck with the neighbours?"

"Not what I'd call luck, sir. They all avoided the auld man like the plague, considered his hoose a blot on the landscape, and were sorry for his wife. I didna get any feeling of serious animosity. One young woman said she'd called one day when the colonel was out to give Mrs. Pelham a pamphlet on feminism. Mrs. Pelham returned it next day, saying she was all in favour, but you can't teach an old dog new tricks."

"She's certainly blossomed out, though, in the short time since I told her he won't be coming back!"

"Some of them are a wee bit shocked at how lightly she took his disappearance, and now his death, however much they disliked him."

"Some people want to be shocked," Tom observed tartly. "Good luck to her, I say."

"I rather liked her," said Alec. "She has considerable force of character. The colonel must have been a real tartar to keep her subdued."

"Ah," said Tom, "he'd have got the upper hand when she was young and unsure of herself, I dare say. Then he went off soldiering and she discovered her own strength, but, like she said, the habit of kowtowing was too strong for her."

"That sounds a lot like what you usually call psycho-rubbish, Sarge."

"You watch your cheek, laddie. Common sense, that's what it is."

"Common sense or psycho-rubbish, given her obvious feeling of liberation, would any of you consider her a suspect in his death?"

"No," Ernie said promptly. "For one thing, the servants swear she never went out the evening he didn't come home. She was knitting and listening to the wireless. And then, why would she want to murder Devine and Halliday? Doesn't seem likely she even knew of their existence."

"Unless he talked about them. She told me, if something's repeated often enough, it sinks in even if you're not listening."

"I can't see it, Chief," said Tom. "All the plotting and planning it must've taken to bag the other two. And what for? What could he have said about them that'd make her want them dead?"

"I ought to have asked the neighbours if she'd been away from home when Devine and Halliday were killed."

"I wouldn't worry about it, Mackinnon. Even if she was responsible, for some unfathomable reason, I can't imagine her carrying out the kidnapping and killing herself. Nor can I see her hiring someone, or even beginning to have any idea of where to look for a hired killer. The whole thing strikes me as extremely unlikely."

"Me, too," Tom agreed.

"I asked the servants," Ernie said smugly, "and Mrs. Pelham hasn't spent more than a few hours away from home in years. The colonel had enough of travel in the army and wouldn't stand for any more."

Alec laughed. "That looks like that, then. Now that we have the colonel's army service information, someone'll have to go and check the records to find out if Halliday and Devine were in the same unit."

"Saturday, Chief," Piper reminded him.

"Damn! It'll mean sending a request up the chain: the super, the AC, the commissioner, the home secretary, and, assuming they can all be got hold of tonight, hoping Joynson-Hicks will agree to talk some brass hat in the army into getting a clerk in to find the bumf for us."

"Shouldn't think we've got a hope, Chief," Tom said.

"I wadna be so sure, Mr. Tring. Whilst I was in charge at the Yard, Jix telephoned the AC twice to find out what was going on. There's nae doot he's verra consairned. A fourth murder wad be a blot on his record."

"And mine," said Alec grimly. "The trouble is, it may take a fourth to provide us with a useful connection."

"At the rate he's been bumping them off," Piper pointed out, "it could be months before he does another."

"Nor is he likely to bury the body in the same area," said Mackinnon. "It might never be found."

"There's always the possibility that he's come to the end of his list. Even if not, unless he's stupid enough to do the target trick again, we might never connect a fourth with the first three. Then the case would eventually be written off as unsolved, bad, but not quite so bad for our reputations."

"Only if we don't solve it, Chief," said Tom. "I'm betting we will, though it may take a while."

Piper was thoughtful. "I'm betting the *Justice! Revenge!* target is too important to him to leave off. Otherwise, why would he do it? Unless he's a madman."

"In which case, all bets are off," said Alec. "Catching a madman who appears sane under most circumstances is a matter of sheer luck. Of course, we have no evidence that there were three identical targets. The first and second safety-pins could have been something quite different for all we know. What I would like is some bit of tangible proof of something!"

"Let's hope we get something to go on from the army records," said Tom, "even if we have to wait till tomorrow."

"Or Monday! Yes, if we knew they were all together during the War, we could look for other veterans of the same battalion, or regiment. Someone might know of a particular incident the three were involved in. It must have been something out of the ordinary to incite such a desire for vengeance. Also, we might be able to find out if anyone else was mixed up in whatever it was, in time to protect him."

"Tell that to Sir William Joynson-Hicks and he'll fall over himself to help."

"I'll make sure Mr. Crane passes it on. One thing we haven't done—I admit it slipped my mind—is a thorough search of the burial area for bullets. Knowing what kind of gun was used might be useful."

"We did a pretty thorough search, Chief," Tom protested.

"In the rain, in the twilight. And I don't recall anyone checking the trunks of trees. The way the victims were tied up, he might have put them up against a tree to shoot them. Don't worry, Tom, I shan't send you, any of you three. It's a job for a couple of DCs. You're needed at the Yard this evening. What I'm betting on, is that we'll be faced with a lot of tips from the public, since the papers printed the names this morning. I assume Cavett's done some preliminary sorting, but it's up to us to decide which are worth following up."

The big room set aside for their use at Scotland Yard looked as if a multicoloured snowstorm had floated through. On every desk and table were drifts of official memo slips with telephone messages; blue, beige, and even violet notepaper; pink telegram forms; and scribbled scraps of all sizes and shapes. Over these pored Inspector Cavett and his men. A couple moved about the room, transferring sorted piles from one place to another.

Cavett looked up as Alec, Tom, Mackinnon, and Piper entered.

"Bloody impossible, sir," he said bluntly. "Three men, each of them apparently known to half the population of southern England and every newspaper-reading nut in the whole country. Plus a whole year since the first disappearance for people to let their imaginations run riot in, if they can't actually remember anything about last week."

A messenger brought in a new stack. "Who gets this lot?"

A man with a nearly clear space on the table in front of him raised a weary arm. "I'll take 'em."

Alec sat gingerly on the corner of his desk. "It looks as if you have everything under control, Inspector, but it must be about time you went home. I'll want you here for a meeting at ten thirty tomorrow. If you'd be so kind as to explain what's going on and your sorting system to DS Mackinnon, he'll take over."

"The CID never sleeps," said Piper.

"To start with, give your 'most likely' pile to Piper here. He can get started on it. I've got to talk to Superintendent Crane."

"He's gone home, sir."

"So they told me downstairs. Can't be helped, I'll try to get him on the phone. Tom, you'd better come with me."

They went up another floor to Alec's office, where Tom had his own desk and phone.

"Mind if I ring me old dutch, Chief?"

"That's what I brought you up for. You know I live in terror of Mrs. Tring's displeasure. As the super's at home, it's best if I call him direct." He slid his telephone towards him and unhooked the receiver. Connected to the switchboard, he asked for Crane's home number.

"Mr. Crane left word he's dining out, sir—"

"Great Scott!" What he meant was "Bloody hell!" but he spared the ears of the switchboard girl.

"—But he gave a telephone number where he can be reached in an emergency. Would you classify your call as an emergency, Chief Inspector?"

Did he? He wouldn't have been talking earlier about rousting out the home secretary on a Saturday evening if he didn't consider the matter urgent. The possible army connection was their only real lead, and the sooner they found out whether it actually led anywhere, the better. It would take time to dig through the mounds of paper below, to cross-check tips and contact tippers.

"Urgent enough to risk interrupting his evening, miss." And then the super could decide whether it was urgent enough to disturb the AC. "I'll stay on the line."

"Very well, sir."

He listened in as she spoke to a very hoity-toity butler. A few minutes passed before Crane came on the line.

"Fletcher? News?"

"Not exactly, sir. I need some information." He explained.

A long, windy sigh blew down the wire. "I'll see what I can do, but you realise that even getting hold of these people on a Saturday evening may be impossible, let alone getting their cooperation."

"I'm aware of that, sir. I wouldn't ask if—"

"I know you wouldn't. I'll get right to it. With my hostess's permission . . ."

"I'm sorry, sir."

"Never mind. Er, Fletcher, Mrs. Fletcher still well out of the way, is she?"

"Yes, she's in Saffron Walden. *North* Essex."

"Not far enough," Crane said gloomily.

Alec didn't consider it the right moment to inform him that it was Daisy who had first suggested the possibility of a military connection.

TWELVE

By the time Alec and Tom returned to the big room, Mackinnon had sent off a couple of detective constables to hunt for bullets at the scene of the burials while daylight lasted. He had arranged for the local bobby, PC Elliott, to show them the way. A stenographer was typing up the reports of the day's interviews, while a somewhat reduced crew continued to sort the thinning stream of incoming paper. Mackinnon was now skimming through the pile of tips that Cavett had classified as unlikely to be of use but not impossible.

"Good work. Keep at it." Alec went over to Ernie Piper.

Piper had divided about half of his "most likely" pile into three and was puzzling over the scribble on what appeared to be the back of a betting slip.

"If you ask me, Chief," he grumbled, "this one ended up getting passed on because no one could tell what it says so they didn't dare to discard it."

"Give it to Tom and get on with the ones you can read."

"I'm no handwriting expert, Chief!" Tom protested.

"If after five minutes you still don't know whether it's worth keeping, we'll set it aside in case we reach the point where we're desperate enough to take it to the experts. Ernie, which of these is the lot we need to get in touch with?"

"Dunno that we need to get in touch with all the writers, but this lot's worth following up one way or another." He pushed the smallest pile across the desk, then pointed at the other two in turn. "This lot maybe, these prob'ly not."

Alec sat on the corner of the desk and started reading. The first was a three-page diatribe, unsigned, from a man who had served under Pelham in the Boer War. Full of venom and a sense of bitter injustice, the writer wished he had met his well-deserved fate much sooner. He did not, however, mention what Pelham had done to earn such opprobium. The shaky hand-writing suggested an elderly man, and he didn't mention either Devine or Halliday, so the lack of either name or address wasn't important. Alec wondered why Piper had set it aside.

Then he noticed that at the bottom of the third sheet of ivory notepaper, upside down, was the reverse side of an em-bossed address. The old man had presumably not noticed it. His large writing also suggested poor eyesight. Turning the page over, Alec saw that the address was that of a residential hotel in Hounslow. Easy to find him—and he might shed light on Pel-ham's conduct in the army, on the sort of action that could have led to enmity enduring long enough to result in murder years later.

Tom came over with the letter he had been trying to deci-pher.

"Greek, or maybe Russian," he announced.

"What!" Alec took it from him.

"Well, it's some kind of foreign alphabet. I'd recognise Chi-nese, having seen plenty of it in Limehouse, and Arabian's all sort of twirly—"

"How on earth do you know that? We don't have an Arab colony in London, do we?"

Tom's face and head turned a rosy pink, an impressive sight. "The missus saw that film, *The Sheik*, with Rudolph Valentino. Very keen on it, she was. So when she read about an exhibition of Arabian stuff at the V and A, she talked me into taking her. There was that squirly-twirly writing all over the place."

"All right, so it's not Arabic. But you're right, it's not the Roman alphabet. It's hard to credit that anyone would write to us in Russian or Greek—if he doesn't know English, how did he find out we're asking for information?—but I suppose we'd better get it translated. Next week, if we're not getting anywhere."

"File and forget, laddie," Tom advised Piper as Alec laid the paper, which was indeed a betting slip, on the desk.

"I never forget anything, Sarge," Ernie retorted.

"Right now, Tom, I want you to read this, and go down to Hounslow for a chat with the chap who wrote it. See if you can find out what he's still all steamed up about a quarter of a century later."

"No peace for the wicked."

"You'd rather help with this lot?" Alec gestured at the room full of coppers reading and writing reports.

"Not bloody likely." Tom preferred—and was much better at—dealing with people than paperwork. "I'm on my way."

"Ring up after you've talked to him, just in case there's something else to be done out that way."

"Not in that lot you've got, Chief, there isn't," said Piper.

"Too much to hope for. The next little job'll be in Harrow or Clapham, one of those 'you can't get there from here' places as far as Hounslow is concerned, if it's not out of town altogether."

As far as Tom was concerned, "out of town" meant not on the tube, and "can't get there from here" meant having to go into central London to change tube lines. He carried a map of the underground railway system in his head.

So did Ernie. "Cheer up, Sarge," he said. "Hounslow's on the District Line, a straight run from Westminster. As long as you don't hop on the wrong train."

"Go teach your grandmother to suck eggs," Tom growled. "I'm not quite in my dotage." He went out, walking with less than his customary lightness of foot.

Not in his dotage by a long chalk, Alec thought, watching him with concern, *but no longer able to take a run of late nights in his stride.* If nothing further had come up in southwest London by the time he phoned, he could go home for the night.

A constable brought over a chair. Gratefully, Alec sat down. He wasn't growing any younger himself. He used to be able to perch comfortably on the corner of a desk for as long as he chose, but now he could feel a distinct ache in his lower back. It had been another long day, and it wasn't finished yet.

He turned to the next missive in his handful. Paperclipped to it was a note that it had been handed in at a police station in Southwark—M Division—just across the river. Written in an uneducated hand on a sheet of lined paper that looked as if it had been carefully cut from a school exercise-book, it was mercifully brief. The writer had served for a few weeks under a Lieutenant Devine and a Captain Halliday, though he didn't know "nobody" by the name of Pelham. He'd always been a law-abiding man, and if the police was to want to talk to him, he was their "obdt. servant, Robt. Thomson." The signature was followed by an address, also in Southwark.

"Devine and Halliday served together!"

"Pelham, too, Chief. You've got a couple there that was with all three in France. Sorry, I didn't get round to sorting in order of importance."

Damn! thought Alec. With a little patience, he could have avoided requesting immediate access to War Office records and thereby disturbing a number of important people. On the other hand, he could make a persuasive case for needing official confirmation of whatever these witnesses had to say. What was more, reports from the battlefields might reveal whatever it was the three officers did that had eventually led to their murders, not to mention who else had been involved and could now be in danger.

After all, a fourth murder was the nightmare of everyone from the man in the street to the home secretary.

While these considerations passed through his head, Alec

had flipped through the rest of his collection and found the two messages Piper referred to. The three names jumped out at him at a glance.

One of the tips was a letter. The other, unfortunately, came in a telegram from Newcastle upon Tyne. Unless the investigation dragged on to unthinkable lengths, in which case he'd probably be taken off it, he couldn't send someone up there. No telephone number was given. If a number to match the name could be found in the relevant directory, he'd have to make an expensive trunk call to interview Mr. Peter Chivers, who had served in Colonel Pelham's regiment with Halliday and Devine. If not, he'd have to ask the Newcastle police to help, not only ringing them up at equally vast expense to explain what he needed, but more than likely finding himself on the other end of the line from someone with an absolutely impenetrable accent.

No, surely they must have men on the force who spoke the King's English! The case was getting him down. He had to stop worrying about beating the killer to the next victim and concentrate on catching him.

"Ernie, get hold of a telephone number for Peter Chivers, Newcastle, if there is one. And train timetable for Gerrards Cross."

"No phone number, Chief." Ernie continued sorting as he spoke. "Fast trains every half hour from Marylebone, quarter to and quarter past, till eleven fifteen. It takes twenty-six minutes."

"I should have known you'd have checked already."

Gerrards Cross, in Buckinghamshire, was where the letter came from. Brief and businesslike, it stated that the writer, Stanley West, a captain at the time, had been posted close to Pelham's regiment at Loos. As liaison officer, he had made the colonel's acquaintance, but did not claim to know him well, except through what his junior officers had said of him. He had shared a mess with Halliday, Devine, and other officers of the regiment fairly regularly for several weeks.

An outsider's view—Alec would have liked to go himself to talk to West, but he decided he was the only person who could deal with the Newcastle police. Besides, he ought to stay in case something more urgent turned up. He went over to Mackinnon and dropped the letter on the desk in front of him.

"All yours," he said. "You know the case thoroughly and I trust you to ask the right questions. You've got things ticking over smoothly here. Delegate whomever you choose to keep it running while you're gone."

Mackinnon read the letter. "Ye think he'll bide at home this evening, sir?"

"One can only hope so. He gives a phone number, so ring beforehand, but if you're told he's out and will be coming home later, I want you to go out there anyway."

"Och, aye. And if there's no answer, I'll get the Gerrards Cross coppers to try and find out when he'll be back."

"I'll leave it to you. Piper has the train times. If it's after midnight when you finish there, you can go straight home. But before you go, get the switchboard to put through a call to the main police station in Newcastle upon Tyne, would you? When it comes through, I'll take it up in my office. After that, I'm going to pop over to Southwark." Alec could have sent a detective constable to interview his "obdt. servant, Robt. Thomson," but he had a feeling, illogical and inexplicable, that as he couldn't send Tom Tring, he ought to go himself, even though Thomson had not known Pelham.

"Southwark, sir? Better take a constable."

"I'll call in at the local coppers' and see what they say about the address I'm bound for. If it's in a respectable area, as I expect, I don't want to embarrass the man I'm going to see by turning up with a uniform in tow."

"Nor his guidwife, if any," Mackinnon agreed with a rare grin.

"Especially not his good wife, if any. I'll see you in the morning, if not before."

Upstairs, while waiting for the trunk call to come through,

Alec tried to analyse his feeling that Thomson might be important. There was a whiff about the crime of a lower-class, other-ranks grudge against superior officers. Perhaps he was letting himself be influenced by the choice of burial-place. Epping Forest was, after all, the traditional spot for the concealment of homicide victims originating in the East End, from illegitimate babies to those who fell afoul of gangs.

Was that the only indication? Unable to come up with anything more convincing to support the hypothesis, Alec decided a better use of his time would be going through the rest of the few papers Piper considered worthy of investigation.

None seemed as likely to yield results as the four he was already dealing with. *They could wait for the morning,* he thought, pushing them aside as the telephone bell rang.

After all the usual pauses, pings, crackles, and exhortations from operators, he was connected with DS Miniver, the senior detective on duty in Newcastle. Miniver's Geordie accent was quite strong but comprehensible. What was more, he had read about the case in the papers and was pleased to be asked to help in such a notorious affair. He quickly grasped what Alec wanted of Peter Chivers.

"Ah'll go to his hoose reet away, an if he's not in, Ah'll see if Ah can find him. Shall Ah ring back the neet?"

Alec blinked. *The neet?* Oh, tonight, presumably. "If you manage to see him, yes, please, and send a written report by first post. If you can't find him, a telegram to that effect will do. Then one of your day officers can try again tomorrow."

"Reet ye are, sir."

Thanking him, Alec rang off. He went over to the window and looked out over the Thames towards Southwark. The sun, already sinking in the west, glinted pinkly off the glass roof of Waterloo Station. It would be near dark before he reached the humble abode of Robert Thomson. Better get moving. Doubtless Ernie Piper would know which bus he should take across Westminster Bridge.

Ernie had the route number at his fingertips, along with three more letters.

"I'll read them on the bus. This shouldn't take long, I hope. I'll be back."

It was early enough for buses to be frequent, late enough for them not to be over-full. Alec spared a glance from his seat upstairs for the famous view from the bridge. Though Wordsworth's "All bright and glittering in the smokeless air" had ceased to apply long ago, on a warm June evening the permanent haze over the great city was at its minimum. In spite of familiarity, the vista was still majestic.

He took the new letters from his pocket. One was a stiff note from Pelham's nephew, who assumed the police would be in touch at their convenience. Alec had been too preoccupied with the immediate families of the victims and the search for links between the three to spare him a second thought. It was always possible he might be able to shed some light on his uncle's past. Tom or Mackinnon would have to see him tomorrow.

According to Mrs. Pelham, Reginald Pelham was, or had been, at the India Office. So was the husband of Daisy's close friend, Mrs. Prasad. Prasad and Pelham more than likely knew each other. *Perish the thought!* Did it bring Daisy close enough to the colonel to give the super ammunition for one of his diatribes? He must never find out.

The next letter Alec looked at was from an elderly gentleman who had been a lieutenant under then Captain Pelham in the Zulu war of 1879. He also had the pleasure of the acquaintance of Sir Daniel Halliday. He was not aware of any relationship—other than through himself—between the two families. However, if the police desired to speak to him, they could find him at his club, address above, where he resided.

Possibly interesting, Alec thought, *but hardly urgent.* Everett Davis-Slocumbe, Esq., could wait.

The last of the papers Ernie had thrust into his hands was a Yard memo slip reporting a telephone call from the police in

H Division—Stepney. A man had come into the station who claimed to know someone who knew who had committed the Epping Forest murders. He had refused to stay or to give his name, but said he would return on Sunday at noon. If the chief inspector he'd read about in the papers was there, he would pass on the information; if not, not.

Noon! Alec had planned a gathering at the Yard at half past ten. The man could be making up the story to get someone else into trouble, or he could just be a crank. He might or might not turn up. The message gave no indication as to whether the Stepney police considered him a credible witness.

The stroke of luck they needed, or a complete waste of time? Descending the steps as the bus pulled up at his stop, Alec decided to ring the Stepney inspector from the Southwark station.

Much of Southwark, though a more salubrious area than Stepney, was a grimy district of narrow streets, tenements, and long rows of terrace houses opening directly onto the pavement. Neither inspired much confidence in any effort of an inhabitant to aid the police. But Alec still had that lurking sense that the murderer was not to be sought in the same class as the victims.

He went into the police station. The sergeant at the desk told him he'd be better off not taking a uniformed constable with him to the address he was bound for.

"Give the neighbours something to talk about!" he said with a grin. "This bloke you're going to see, he and his missus wouldn't live it down for a month of Sundays, and he'd know it. Might be enough to make him keep his mouth shut. That street, they scrub their doorsteps every day and polish the aspidistra. It's not somewhere they're used to seeing us haul off a villain or two every couple of days."

Alec thanked him and requested the use of a telephone. He got through quickly to the H Division inspector on duty.

"I didn't see the man myself," the inspector said. "Hadn't come in yet, and the sergeant who talked to him's gone home.

But seeing it's to do with a big case, he reported to me in detail. Let me find my notes. What exactly did you want to know, sir?"

"Whether it's going to be worth my time to come and meet him. I realise you can't give me any certainty, but did the sergeant get the impression that the man was reliable?"

"What Sergeant Jones told me is, he was reluctant to have anything to do with the police—that's why he was willing to talk to you, sir, reckoning you wouldn't be interested in small fry—but he didn't hold with murder. Little ratty chap, sneak-thief type, not a smash-and-grabber."

"Not known to you, though, I take it."

"No, but could just be he operates on someone else's manor. He wasn't too sure, Jones said, that this other chap was telling the truth. Could be he was just boasting, talking through his hat. Same applies to him, of course, the one who came in, though Jones got the impression he was serious. That's about it, sir."

"Right, thanks." Alec sighed. "It sounds as if I'd better turn up. I'll be there at noon tomorrow." He rang off and went to pay a call on Robt. Thomson.

It was dusk when he turned into Balaclava Row. The Victorian terraces of tiny, soot-stained brick houses were no different from those he had walked between on his way here. Lights shone in lace curtained windows, the soft glow of gas. The street lamps at both crossroads were electric, but landlords in these parts had not yet caught up with the changing times.

Alec walked along to number 45 and knocked on the door. It was opened by a wiry man of about thirty, in his shirt-sleeves, with a cigarette in one corner of his mouth.

Removing it, he said, "Copper? I was wond'rin' if you'd show up. Come on in. The missus is gettin' the nippers to bed."

"Detective Chief Inspector Fletcher," Alec introduced himself, stepping into the tiny entrance hall. A Southern Railways porter's cap and jacket hung on a hook on the wall, announcing Thomson's job. "I appreciate your willingness to talk to us."

"Ain't got much to say," he grunted, "but you're welcome

to what I got. Come through to the kitchen, if you don't mind. The missus loikes her Ovaltine at bedtime, and I'm watchin' the milk."

"Through" to the kitchen was a couple of paces. Thomson stepped over to the stove and turned down the gas under a pan of milk. Alec sat down at the well-scrubbed table, noting faded but neat gingham curtains, pots and pans and crockery neatly stacked on a couple of shelves. The worn, green linoleum floor was polished to a gleam. A house-proud housewife, who definitely wouldn't have appreciated the arrival of a uniformed constable; he was glad he had taken the sergeant's advice.

"Fag?" offered his host, joining him at the table.

"No, thanks, I'm a pipe-man. Well, what can you tell me about Halliday and Devine?"

"Captain and lieutenant they was back then. Me and me mates'd just shipped out to France, see, and they was two of the officers we landed up with. You want to know where we was, and all?"

"No, that's not necessary. I'm trying to understand the sort of men they were, and what they might have done that led to murder."

Thomson shook his head slowly. "Nasty business, all right. But the fact is, guv, I can't see neither of 'em doing nuffing that'd get 'em snuffed out. 'Cepting by the Boche, nacherly, but they made it through the War, di'n' they?"

"Yes, they died quite recently."

"They was the same in some ways and diff'rent in others. They was gentlemen. Both of 'em treated you like a human being, even us Tommies. But the captain was kind of standoffish wiv it, like he was polite acos it was beneath him to be anyfing else. Lieutenant Devine, you got the feeling he reelly knew we was real people and he was sorry he couldn' do anyfing about us being stuck in them gawdforsaken trenches."

"You're an acute observer of character, Mr. Thomson."

"Yes, werl, you got to be to make a living as a porter, guv. Got to take a dekko at a passenger and know this lady'll give you a smile and a half-crown, even if you can't find her a window seat facing the engine, and that gentleman'll make a big fuss about whatever seat you bag him and give you sixpence for your trouble."

"I see what you mean!" said Alec, amused.

"And I do well enough." Thomson looked with satisfaction round the tiny but comfortable kitchen, then sprang to his feet to rescue the milk just in time to stop it boiling over. "Whew!" Wiping his forehead with his sleeve, he mimed relief. "She'd've 'ad me guts for garters!" He sat down again and lit another Woodbine. "Captain Halliday, now, he was going to do his duty, come what may. The lieutenant'd do what he was told."

"And you didn't see anything of Colonel Pelham?"

"There was talk that some old fossil was going to come out of retirement and take over the regiment, but I never heard his name. Then me and me mates, we was transferred to another unit. But what I reckon is, if them three, the colonel, Captain Halliday, and Lieutenant Devine, did summat as made someone want to murder the lot of 'em, it must've been the colonel as started it. The captain made up his mind it was his duty to go along, and the lieutenant just followed orders."

THIRTEEN

As Daisy, Sakari, and Melanie reached the Meeting House, they saw a crocodile of schoolchildren approaching, halfway down the hill. They had arrived a few minutes early, hoping they wouldn't have to walk into a room full of silent people.

Belinda had told Daisy about Quaker Meetings, so she had a rough idea of what to expect. She was surprised, though, when she entered the room with Sakari and Melanie, to see the pews arranged in a square facing a central table with a vase of pink roses. Beside the flowers lay a bible and another book, but there was nothing remotely resembling an altar! Several people were already there, sitting quietly with their hands folded in their laps. Most wore subdued colours, but one woman had a bright red hat, so Sakari, who didn't own anything subdued, wasn't too far out of line in her peacock sari.

A soft-voiced elderly lady in grey greeted them. "Welcome to our Meeting," she said. "The seats facing this way are reserved for the children from the school, but please sit anywhere else."

Sakari chose the nearest pew, closest to the door. "You two go first," she whispered, "in case I want to escape."

They left space between them for the girls, who had said they were allowed to sit with parents, when present. Several more people came in, and then the children arrived, remarkably quiet, the boys ushered by Mr. Tesler, the girls by Miss Bascombe. Bel, Lizzie, and Deva had no difficulty finding their mothers, given the beacon of Sakari's vivid turquoise.

With a big smile, Belinda kissed Daisy's cheek, but she didn't say anything.

Quite a few of their fellow-pupils also joined parents, while the rest filed into the reserved pews opposite. Tesler and Miss Bascombe stood at the back, on the outer edge of the boys' and girls' sections respectively, where they could keep an eye on their flocks. They waited till everyone was settled before they sat down. Daisy thought they both looked harassed and ill at ease. Twitchy was the word that came to mind. She wondered whether they had quarrelled, or perhaps that wretched Harriman had been making trouble for them.

Would the Committee that oversaw the school frown on their romance? Perhaps they were not sufficiently discreet about it, given that the children were apparently well aware of it.

Or perhaps just being in charge of keeping all those teen-aged children quiet for an hour was enough to explain their anxiety.

More people had come in while Daisy's thoughts were wandering. Now the woman who had greeted and directed them, closed the door and went to take her seat in a space obviously saved for her on the front bench at right-angles to the school pews. The hushed room took on a deeper stillness. Though the loud, slow tick of the clock on the wall intruded, clearly it was time to turn one's mind to higher things.

Despite her best intentions, Daisy's continued to wander. She soon ceased to notice the clock and started to wonder what Alec was doing. Was he any nearer to solving the triple murder? Perhaps he had already arrested someone and would join them in Saffron Walden for the afternoon. They had better go back to the hotel after Meeting to see if there was a message from him. If he didn't know by then, it would be too late to make the journey worthwhile. He might as well stay at home with the twins.

A man in front of her stood up and prayed for Mahatma Gandhi's success in his path to peaceful reform. From the corner of her eye, Daisy saw Sakari's shoulders relax their tautness. She hadn't realised her friend was feeling uncomfortable in these surroundings, unsure of her welcome.

Tesler, also, regained his characteristic serenity in the course of the Meeting, absorbed in meditation. Daisy wondered whether he would notice his charges misbehaving, as long as they didn't make a lot of noise.

In the next half-hour, several people stood and spoke. Some had an overtly Christian message, others talked about an act of kindness they had witnessed, or something inspiring they had read. One ancient woman rambled on for several minutes in a mumble Daisy couldn't make out at all, but on the whole, she found plenty of food for reflection during the periods of silence. Then the small children thundered down the stairs from Sunday School. They were very well-behaved, but inevitably a bit restless, as Bel had foretold.

A short, stout, balding man rose and said gloomily: "'Suffer little children, and forbid them not to come unto me, for of such is the kingdom of heaven.'" As he sat down, Daisy wondered whether he did the same every week, just to remind himself.

A couple of minutes later, the woman who had greeted them at the door turned to first one then the other of her neighbours and shook hands, as they did in turn with others on the bench. Apparently that was a signal.

"Those are the elders," Bel whispered. "That's the end."

People began to stir and to talk together. Daisy had survived her first Meeting. Several people came over to speak to her and her friends, seeming particularly anxious to make sure Sakari was welcomed. By the time they extricated themselves and reached the street, Sakari was beaming, her usual effervescence restored.

"You were lucky, Mummy," said Belinda. "Sometimes no one speaks at all and it seems to go on forever. Are we going to the Bridge End Garden now, before lunch?"

"I shall drive there," Sakari said firmly. "The walk up here from the Rose and Crown to the Meeting House was enough for me. This town has too many hills."

"It can't be much more than a quarter of a mile to the Garden," Melanie protested, "going by your guidebook, Sakari."

"I've got to go back to the hotel anyway," said Daisy, "to see if there's a message from Alec."

Belinda's face lit up. "Oh, Mummy, do you think Daddy may come after all?"

"Don't get your hopes up, darling. I rather doubt it, but I'd hate him to arrive and find us not there."

No message awaited them at the Rose and Crown. Daisy asked the receptionist how long it would take to walk to the Bridge End Garden.

"About ten minutes, madam, if you cut through the church yard."

"You see, Sakari," said Melanie, "it's no distance."

"Is it uphill?" Sakari asked suspiciously.

The receptionist admitted that there was indeed an uphill slope from the Market Place to the church. Sakari promptly sent for Kesin, but the others all decided to walk.

The day was still pleasantly cool, and Daisy enjoyed the walk. They passed the Sun Inn, another fourteenth-century building, with its fantastic plasterwork. Most was typical pargetting in repeated patterns, to be found on many local walls, but birds and fruit also appeared, in bas-relief, and one gable-end boasted two figures. The guidebook named them as the giants Gog and Magog, or possibly the Wisbech giant and Tom Hickathrift, whoever he might be. The controversy was unlikely ever to be resolved.

They came to the parish church, from which wafted the strains of organ and choral music. Though its spire was visible from most of the town, Daisy hadn't realised how big it was. According to the guidebook it was a "wool" church, built with the enormous profits of the mediaeval wool trade.

She started to wonder whether her American editor would be interested in an article about the ancient town.

Crossing Castle Street, they looked for the narrow passage between two houses that the receptionist had described. Sakari drove up just as they found it.

"You'll have to walk from here, Mummy," Deva told her, "but it looks as if it's downhill."

The girls ran ahead, their elders following at a pace suited to Sakari. They passed between several houses accessible only by the footpath, before a meadow opened out to their right. On the far side was a low, decorative stone wall. Beyond it, topiary shrubs were visible.

"Nearly there, darling," Daisy assured Sakari.

"If there is no bench near the entrance, I shall sit down on the grass!"

The entrance was between two brick pillars topped by stone eagles. One had its wings spread, and the other appeared to be giving it a quizzical look. Wrought iron gates decorated with scrollery stood open, and just beyond was an iron bench. Sakari promptly sat down on it, and Daisy and Melanie joined her. It faced a formal garden, yews trimmed in geometrical shapes and low box hedges forming an asymmetrical pattern of flowerbeds, divided by gravel paths. In the centre was a circular lawn, with a small pool and a fountain. The children were already racing about in a game of tag.

"Well, if this is the maze," said Melanie with a sigh of relief, "they can't possibly get lost in it."

"This is not the maze." Sakari dug in her handbag for the guidebook. "It is the Dutch Garden, if I am not mistaken. Yes, look. The maze has high hedges, like the one at Hampton Court."

They all studied the book for a few minutes. The Garden as a whole was layed out in various sections, including a walled kitchen garden (called the "Walled Garden"), a rose garden, and a wilderness (called the "Wilderness"). There was plenty of space for poor Miss Bascombe and Mr. Tesler to wander at leisure.

Then Mel looked up and exclaimed, "They've disappeared!"

There was no sign of the girls.

"They're probably playing hide and seek now," said Daisy, "behind those tall topiaries."

"I hope they haven't gone into the maze by themselves and got lost. Or in the Wilderness."

"No, look!" Daisy pointed. Bel, Deva, and Lizzie appeared to be standing about eight feet above the ground, waist-deep in a hedge. They were waving and calling. "What on earth . . . ? Let's go and see what they're up to."

They walked along the central path, round the fountain—three fish with intertwined tails supporting a small boy with curly hair and no clothes—and came to the base of the yew hedge supporting three giggling girls (fully clothed).

"There's steps, Mummy," Lizzie explained, "inside the hedge."

"Do be careful!" Melanie was ever the worrier.

"There's a railing, Mrs. Germond," said Deva. "We won't fall."

"Come up and see," Bel invited them. "You get a good view of the Garden from here. We'll come down first, though. There isn't room for everyone."

Was the dreadful Harriman in the habit of lurking up there to spy on Tesler and his sweetheart? Daisy wondered.

Even Sakari climbed the iron steps. From the platform at the top, the pattern of the Dutch Garden spread out below, each box-hedged shape filled in with colourful flowers. In the opposite direction, Daisy was glad to see a gardener scything grass under the trees in the so-called Wilderness, which was more like a copse. She had been afraid that, as it was Sunday, there would be no staff present to retrieve the girls from the maze if they did manage to get themselves lost.

By the time they descended the steps, the girls were impatient to explore the maze. All Sakari wanted, of course, was another bench. They found one, shaded by a spreading tree, on a wide lawn on the way to the maze. Daisy offered to go with the girls so that Melanie could keep Sakari company.

To get to the maze, they passed a statue of a peacock, went up several steps between grinning gargoyles, and passed through another elaborately scrolled iron gate. On one side was the brick wall of the Walled Garden. The high yew hedges of the maze itself were surrounded by a lawn, trees, and shrubs. No one else was visible, though of course there might be someone in the maze. It wasn't exactly the sort of thing one did by oneself, though, and Daisy couldn't hear anyone talking.

The girls, still full of energy, rushed to the nearby gap in the hedge. Deva and Lizzie disappeared. Belinda looked back.

"Aren't you coming, Mummy?"

"I'll wait here, in case you have to be rescued."

"We won't!" Bel vanished after the others.

Irritatingly, now that Daisy really wanted one, there was no bench. She strolled round the outer edge of the maze, hearing the girls voices:

"This way!"

"No, this way!"

"I'm going that way!"

"Lizzie, Bel, where are you?"

"I'm just the other side of the hedge."

"How did you get there?"

"Here's a bench."

Inside, not outside, Daisy thought with indignation.

"Oh, this is another dead end. Bother!"

"I've found a sort of a stone vase."

"I think I've gone round in a circle!"

Then one of them began to scream.

FOURTEEN

Daisy's instinct on hearing a child scream was to rush to the child. She ran round the outside of the maze towards the entrance and had nearly reached it when she realised how idiotic it would be to go in.

The only result would be another person lost. Why had she not gone into the maze with the children and insisted that they stay together?

Through the sound of the screams, she heard Belinda and Deva shouting in fearful voices.

"What's happened?"

"Where are you, Lizzie?"

A futile question if ever there was one, though Daisy had been tempted to do the same. Instead, she stuck her forefingers in her mouth and uttered the piercing whistle Gervaise had taught her. As she had hoped, all three girls were surprised into silence.

"Lizzie, can you hear me? What's wrong? Are you hurt?"

"No." Her voice was barely audible, muffled by a sob, not to mention the thick hedges. "Oh, Mrs. Fletcher, it's Mr. Harriman, and I think he's dead!"

Harriman? Dead? This couldn't be happening! Daisy had a nightmare feeling that if she could only stop and think she would know what to do. But the children were wailing, panic-stricken. She had to say something at once.

"Deva, Bel, be quiet, and stay where you are. Lizzie, are you still looking at him?" Harriman? Dead? "Turn your back!"

"But he might—"

"If he's dead, he's not going to do anything. Move farther away from him. What makes you think he's dead?" Suppose he was hurt and needed help?

"He's lying so still! On his back, with his eyes shut and his arms by his sides. And his face is white as . . . as anything. He's not moving. I'm sure he's not breathing!"

"Is he bleeding?"

"N-no. I don't think so. I'm pretty sure not. Oh, Mrs. Fletcher, can't you come—?"

"I don't know how to get to you, darling. Lizzie, can you be very brave?"

"I—I don't know." Her voice quavered. "What . . . ?"

"I want you to look at him more closely. Can you bear to? I need to be sure he's not bleeding."

"Do I have to . . . touch him?"

"No, darling." *Fingerprints*, she thought, *and footprints . . .* but she had to be sure he wasn't bleeding to death. "Just look. Take a deep breath, then turn round. If you start to feel funny, sit down quickly and take another deep breath, all right?"

"All right. I'll try."

"I think you're awfully brave, Lizzie," called Belinda.

"I wouldn't look at him," said Deva, unhelpfully. "I want to get out of here!"

"Be quiet, Deva. I'll get you out as soon as I can. Lizzie?"

"I can't see any blood on him, Mrs. Fletcher. Not on the ground, either. May I stop looking?"

"Yes, darling. And—this is a bit complicated—move away from him to a place where you can't see him but you know exactly where he is, so that you can tell us how to find him."

There must be a viewing platform somewhere, so that lost visitors could be directed out of the maze, but a man flat on the ground might not be visible. "Can you do that?"

"Y-yes. It's a dead-end. I'll just go past the first corner. It doesn't branch or anything."

"Good girl. Now, all of you, I'm going to fetch a gardener to get you out. Stay where you are. There's no point running all over the place."

"We might be able to find Lizzie, Mummy," said Belinda. "Then we could wait with her."

"Oh yes, please try! It's scary on my own."

"All right, I suppose you might as well try. I'm off. I'll be as quick as I can, I promise."

Daisy sped back through the fanciful gates, past the oblivious stone peacock, towards the bench where Sakari and Melanie sat. Mel saw her coming and jumped up in alarm.

"What's wrong? Is someone hurt?"

"No, the girls are lost in the maze, as was to be expected, but no one's hurt. Not exactly. . . ."

"Daisy, what do you mean, *not exactly*?"

Realisation and reaction hit Daisy. She flopped down on the bench. "They've found a body. Harriman. The games master."

"*Dead?*" Mel and Sakari demanded with one startled, incredulous voice.

"That's what it sounds like. In the maze. I didn't see him."

"We must get them out of there!" Melanie started across the lawn towards the peacock.

"No, Mel, wait!" Daisy pulled herself together. "You'd only get lost with them. I'm going to fetch the gardener I saw in the Wilderness. If he can't direct them out, he'll have tools to cut through the hedges. What you've got to do is go for the police. Quickly. Go back to the car. If you can't find a telephone at once, Kesin will drive you to the police station."

"But—"

"Please, Mel, go at once. The police and a doctor, just in case. . . . Sakari will stay here so that we have a rallying place."

"You can go much faster than I, Melanie," Sakari pointed out.

"All right." Reluctantly, but walking fast, Melanie set off for the main gates.

Daisy had deliberately not told her friend it was Lizzie who actually found the body and was the only one to have seen it. Melanie would have refused point-blank to leave. Not only did Daisy feel she herself was better able to get the gardener moving, she didn't want to have anything more to do with the police than she absolutely had to. Melanie was so obviously a respectable, sensible citizen that they were bound to take her report seriously. Sakari had a more commanding presence, but the colour of her skin was all too likely to be counted against her.

"You don't mind staying put, Sakari?"

"*Staying put*," Sakari mused, "another odd idiom. I am happy to stay put. Daisy, are you sure the children are not making up stories?"

"If you'd heard the screams, you wouldn't ask. I'm going to look for that gardener." Standing up, she turned towards the Wilderness. "Oh, here he comes."

A flat cap covered his hair, if any, and the weather-beaten face gave no clue to the age of the man trudging across the lawn, his scythe over his shoulder. His demeanour gave no clue that he had noticed the presence of the ladies. Daisy thought he'd have passed without so much as a glance in their direction if she hadn't accosted him.

"Excuse me, I need your help."

"It do be me dinnertime." He continued walking.

At least he was heading in the right direction. She walked alongside. "There are three young girls lost in the maze."

"They can woit."

"No they can't. There's a dead body in there with them."

He stopped and looked at her without speaking, his bright blue eyes assessing but incurious.

"Really! My friend has gone to fetch the police."

Turning his head away from her, he spat, then set off again, still without speaking and at the same steady pace. However, his course altered slightly so that instead of aiming at the door to the Walled Garden, he was making a bee-line for the gates to the maze.

"Thank you!" said Daisy with heartfelt relief. She went on beside him for a few yards, then realising that nothing would speed him up, she hurried ahead. Up the steps, through the trees: "I'm back! You'll be out of there in no time."

"I found Lizzie, Mummy. She can't stop crying."

"I don't blame her. Stay with her, darling."

"I found the middle, Mrs. Fletcher," Deva called, sounding pleased with herself. "There's a sort of thing here you can climb, but I'm not tall enough to see much from the top. I can't see Bel and Lizzie."

"Stay there, Deva." Daisy turned to the gardener as he caught up with her, now without his scythe. "Do we really have to go all the way to the middle to see where they are? To tell them how to get out?"

"Aye."

Surely it would have been more practical to build a platform outside! What would it matter if some people succumbed to temptation and tried to work out a route to the centre before they started?

The gardener trudged on into the thicket, his heavy footsteps crunching on the gravel path. Daisy followed.

Start with a right turn. She was determined to remember the way. Right, then wind about for a bit. Left—no, that didn't count as there was no alternative. Left here. That was *right*, *left*, another left, left again—*right, three lefts*—Round a curve, straight ahead, but there was a left turn possible, so did straight ahead count as a keep right?

She heard Lizzie crying just the other side of the hedge and promptly forgot the lot.

"Lizzie! Bel! We're coming!" She wanted to stop and offer words of comfort, but the gardener had already disappeared.

She hurried after him, just in time to see him make another left turn, then immediately right.

Without him, she would have been hopelessly lost already.

There was a long straight stretch, with an obligatory right turn at the end. On her left was the entrance to a small open space, with a bench shaded by a wooden shelter. Daisy could have done with a sit-down in the shade, but she plodded on, determined to keep the gardener in sight. It would be too humiliating to have to be rescued herself!

Turn followed turn. Then she heard Deva's voice, behind and above her:

"Mrs. Fletcher, I can see your hat!"

She scarcely dared look back in case the gardener vanished again. "I hope that means we're nearly there," she called back over her shoulder.

Left curve—again she heard Lizzie, whimpering now, just the other side of the thick, impassable yew—left turn, and a long open space lay before her.

It was mostly lawn, the gravel path continuing all round the edge. A pair of iron benches faced each other across the grass. In the middle stood a sort of menhir, an odd-shaped stone. At the far end rose a wrought iron structure, a steep ladder leading up to a railed platform on stilts. From the platform, Deva waved excitedly.

Daisy had found one of her charges.

The gardener, going straight to the platform, hooked a thumb at Deva in an easily interpreted gesture.

"But I want to stay up here!"

"Come down now, Deva," Daisy said quickly, afraid the man might just turn and leave if his instructions were not followed. All the same, when he went up the ladder, she followed him.

The platform was quite small, crowded with the two of them. They both turned, scanning the maze. It was an irregular shape, Daisy saw. She could make out the gap at one end where they had entered and the wooden shelter over the bench at the other, but otherwise nothing but hedge, hedge, and more hedge.

"Don't see nobody," the gardener grunted.

"Belinda, we can't see you! Are you sitting down? Stand up and wave. Jump up and down."

Not far from the entrance, a small hand, waving madly, appeared and disappeared, then a second as Lizzie joined in. "We're here, Mummy. How do we get out?"

"Wait a minute, darling, while we work it out."

It only took a moment for her to work out that it would take her hours, with paper and pencil, to work out how to get to the children, let alone how to escape the maze.

"'S easy," said the gardener. "I'll tell 'em which way to turn." He raised cupped hands to his mouth to shout.

"Hold on." She ought to see the body for herself, Daisy decided reluctantly, to make sure Harriman was really dead and there was nothing she could do for him. "Could you lead me there, and then lead us all out?"

He gave her that assessing look again. "Course."

She didn't warn him that he would then have to show the police the way to the body. She'd never be able to explain how to find it. At best, the gardener was not an enthusiastic collaborator, and she remembered his spitting when she told him the police were on their way. Or would soon be on their way, she hoped.

"Bel, Lizzie, we're coming!"

Carefully—*a broken leg would really throw a spanner in the works!*—she descended the ladder. The gardener followed her down and set off towards the exit.

Deva had been studying the menhir. Joining Daisy, she said, "It's strange. It's got wavy-line patterns carved on it, like water, and a shape that looks sort of as if it could be a mermaid. Why do we have to walk all the way to Lizzie and Bel and all the way back, Mrs. Fletcher? Couldn't that man tell them which way to go then lead us out?"

The gardener turned and gave her his look. "Don't make

much difference," he said indifferently. "C'n leave you at the turn t'wait for us."

"No! Don't leave me alone!" Deva clutched Daisy's arm.

"Do stop fussing and come along," said Daisy, hurrying after their guide.

It seemed as if they went right round the maze again, following the silent gardener, before he paused at a corner and muttered to himself, "Roight here? Reckon so." Daisy guessed they must be turning off the direct route to the way out—if anything in here could be described as direct.

A few more twists and turns: there were Bel and Lizzie. Lizzie's face was tear-stained, and Belinda started crying as they both rushed into Daisy's arms. She held them both tight.

"Let's go." The gardener was impatient for his dinner.

"Give me two minutes. I can't leave without making sure the . . . the man really is dead, not just ill or injured and in need of help."

"Listen, lady, I—"

"You wouldn't want his death on your conscience, would you? He's just round the next corner, Lizzie?"

"Yes, it's not far." Lizzie shuddered.

"Do you have to, Mummy?" Bel looked frightened.

"Yes." Daisy certainly wasn't going to look at Harriman because she *wanted* to, whether he was dead or alive. She approached the corner with trepidation. Which would be worse, to find him dead or to find him alive and not know what to do for him?

At first glance, he looked remarkably dead. She felt a momentary surge of relief, and realised she had still not been absolutely sure that Lizzie was not romancing. His face was not white, as the child had described it—he was too much of an outdoorsman for that. It was a ghastly, drained, sallow colour. He was dressed in slacks and a short-sleeved shirt, with no jacket, but Daisy could detect no movement of his chest.

She forced herself to move closer, keeping right to the side of the path, brushing against the yew. Alec would be livid if she destroyed any clues. Much as she might wish to keep the affair from him, she had never succeeded yet and didn't expect to this time.

Afraid she might faint if she stooped over the body, she crouched and reached for his wrist. No pulse that she could feel. Should she try his neck? She simply couldn't bring herself to touch it. The limp, chill heaviness of his arm told her all she needed, and more than she wanted, to know.

In glancing towards his neck, she noticed a discoloured area on the side of his head. Had he not kept his hair cropped so short, it would have been invisible. To steady herself, she shut her eyes and swallowed, her mouth dry, before she looked again, more closely. The skin was not broken, as far as she could make out, but was the skull dented?

Enough was enough! She straightened and moved back, keeping her back against the unyielding hedge. A quick survey revealed nothing on which he could have knocked his head.

There was something else odd about the scene. What was it?

It was too neat. It dawned on Daisy that Harriman was laid out as carefully as if he was just waiting for a coffin.

FIFTEEN

"*What I* don't get, Chief," Tom rumbled, back in fine form after his early night, "is why you reckon it wasn't another toff, one of their own kind, that did for 'em."

"Instinct, at least to start with. I dare say you could call my reasoning since then rationalisation. Mackinnon, Ernie, any thoughts on the subject?"

"I keep coming back to the same question, sir," said Mackinnon. He seemed to have got over his disappointment that his brief exeat from the Yard, to Gerrards Cross, had merely confirmed their existing impressions of Halliday's and Devine's characters. "Why did he wait sae lang? The only link we've found between them is the War—"

"And the pubs," Ernie muttered.

"We'll come back to the pubs in a minute," Alec promised. "Go on, Mackinnon."

"The Armistice was nearly eight years ago, and the records the War Office sent over show that all three victims were demobbed early in 1919. The colonel died a year sin'. Yon murtherer had nae less than six years to lay his plans. This suggests to me that he didna find it simple. A gentleman should hae had little difficulty discovering the whereabouts of the three. E'en allowing for a delay until circumstances were just right, it doesna make sense."

"The colonel could have died in the meantime," Tom observed, "and he'd have lost his chance."

"Verra true."

"My own thinking exactly," Alec agreed. "A working man, on the other hand, might well have had considerable difficulty running them to earth, especially as he'd presumably have only his one day off a week to look and to make his arrangements. What's your opinion, Cavett?"

The inspector shook his head. "That's detective stuff, sir. I'm just a plain copper."

"An excellent organiser. Don't think your efforts go unappreciated. Any other suggestions? Hold the pubs, Ernie!"

"Just, where they were buried," said Tom. "You don't get many nobs picnicking there on a Sunday. Queen Victoria may've called it 'The People's Forest,' but she was talking about East Enders, not West Enders."

"Dabbling in History now, are you, Sarge?"

"That's right, laddie. Seems to me my vocabulary is currently as extensive as is requisite for my profession."

"Cor blimey!" said Ernie with mock admiration.

"Anything else?" Alec said impatiently. "If we're agreed, more or less, that the murderer probably is not a member of high society, I've got to get moving or I'll miss our volunteer at the Stepney station. Don't worry, Ernie, we'll consider the significance of the pubs when I get back."

A Yard car, driven by a uniformed constable, delivered him to the Stepney police station at five to twelve. He told the man to wait. If the informant showed up and if his information seemed worth following up, then the sooner the better.

He was shown to a small, dingy room with a scratched battered table and two equally hard-used chairs.

"Tea, please," he requested. "For two." It would be disgusting, stewed and probably with milk and sugar included as a matter of course, but it might help set the man he'd come to see at ease.

"Ratty" was an apt word for both the face and the clothes of the small man who sidled in, preceding the PC with the mugs of tea.

"Sit down," Alec invited.

"I ain't gonna stay but a minute."

"Sit down," Alec ordered.

He sat. The constable deposited one mug in front of him with a slight thud, slopping some on the table. The other he set more carefully before Alec.

"Anything else, sir? I'll be right outside the door, sir."

"Don't bother." Hardly a necessary precaution! Outweighed two to one, the worst the rat could do to Alec was throw the tea at him. A guard at the door was quite likely to make him more reluctant to speak, not less.

"I appreciate your coming forward to help us, Mr. . . . ?"

"No names, no pack-drill."

"As you will. But you came to give me a name, didn't you."

"That's different, innit. If you arst me, 'e oughter 'ave come to you 'imself. I ain't no coppers' nark but three stiffs, that's going a bit far, that is. 'Ere, you're that detective chief inspector, aren't you? Mr. Fletcher? I ain't talking to no one else."

"I'm DCI Fletcher. Would you like to see my card?"

"Nah, that's all right. I believe you; thousands wouldn't." This was obviously a catch-phrase, not a serious comment. "What I want to know is, what's in it for me?"

"Come, come, I thought you were being public-spirited, because you disapprove of murder. Triple murder, at any rate."

"That's all very well for them as can afford it. I fought in the War, same as the next man, di'n' I? But I'm down on me luck now, see?"

Alec had expected something of the sort. He took a ten-shilling note from the breast pocket of his jacket, laid it on the table, and put his hand on it.

"Blimey, guv, it's worf a fiver at least!" the man whined.

"Ten bob down, and ten bob if your information turns out to be useful."

"But how—?"

"You don't have to give me your name. *If* you tell me something worth knowing, you can collect it here. They know your face now."

His jaw dropped in alarm. "I ain't done nuffing!" he protested.

"Nothing to earn a quid, certainly. Come on, let's have it. I haven't got all day. You'll be down to a couple of half-crowns in a minute." He picked up the note and reached for his pocket.

"Orright, orright, keep your 'air on! It's this bloke in Tottenham, see, the landlord of the Barley Mow."

The pub connection! Perhaps Piper had been right to keep harping on it.

Alec knew from long experience that his face didn't show his sudden alertness. The anonymous rat was twitching with anxiety.

"That's enough, innit? You can find him wivout me telling you his name? That way, if he asks, you can say you never 'eard it from me."

Staring at him, Alec asked, "Just why would the landlord of a pub, even a crummy pot-house in Tottenham, confide in you, of all people?"

"'Ere, you mind what you're saying! The Barley Mow's a respectable place."

Alec raised sceptical eyebrows. "Which makes it the more surprising that he'd talk to you. Or that you'd be there in the first place, come to that."

"As it 'appens, a friend of mine was treating me to a pint yes'day midday. Just pulled off—come into some money, he had. Some other mates of his come in and he went to talk to them. Didn't know 'em, did I, so while I was waiting for him, I pass the time of day with Mr. Sh—with the landlord, like anyone might."

Alec nodded. It all sounded like "corroborative detail

intended to give artistic verisimilitude to an otherwise bald and unconvincing narrative." However, the man was obviously not a good liar, so it might be true. Most of it.

"And this other bloke, he comes up just then to get a refill, like, and he passes a remark about them bodies in the Forest, them being just the other side of the Lea, which he just read about in the *Standard*. 'Buried in a foxhole,' he says, 'just like the War.'"

The army connection, as well!

"Mr. Shadd, he draws the bloke a couple of pints of Hertford's bitter and he goes off, and I says, a mate of mine got buried in a fox'ole in France. Up to his neck in mud, he was. And Mr.—the landlord says so was he, and whaddaya know, turns out him and me mate was stuck in the same bloody trench! So then we was all pally, and he gives me a half on the house. I says, me mate ain't got over it to this day. Them bodies in the Forest, at least they was dead when they was buried. Then he says, all mysterious like, 'And I got a pretty good idea who croaked 'em.'"

"'A pretty good idea!'" Alec said in disgust, closing his hand over the ten-shilling note. "That's not what you told them here yesterday."

"Fat lot of notice they'd've taken if I had!" The rat's shifty gaze was fixed anxiously on the money. "I'd've never've got to see you, would I, so I told 'em he said he knows. But I'm not gonna give no guff to the Yard. 'A pretty good idea,' that's what he said, and that's God's truth." He shrugged thin shoulders. "So maybe he'll tell you he don't know nuffing and never said he did. You can't blame me."

Sighing, Alec pushed the ten shillings across the table. Were it not for the double link with information they already possessed, he would have been inclined to dismiss the whole story. As it was, he'd have to follow up.

"All right, we'll see what he has to say. You can go." Sarcastically, he added, "Thank you for being a public-spirited citizen."

"You won't forget to give this lot here the other ten bob?"

"I won't. If your tip is worth it. Now get out, before I have you arrested for extortion!"

The rat scuttled out.

Alec regarded with distaste the untouched mugs of tea, with milk scumming on top. Had the stuff been even remotely drinkable, he would have liked to wash the taste of the interview out of his mouth. Some coppers were not fussy about using paid informants, but he had always tried to avoid them.

Just how respectable was the Barley Mow? he wondered. Would it be better to turn up on his own, or was a show of force indicated? If the latter, plain-clothes or uniforms? He could ring up and ask. . . .

He glanced at his watch. No time to set up anything complicated if he was to talk to the landlord before closing time. After that, Mr. Shadd might go out, or he might settle down for a nap, in which case waking him would not be the best way to encourage him to cooperate. Alec didn't want to have to wait until seven, opening hour on a Sunday evening.

Tom and Ernie would suit all occasions, he decided. Tom was big and Ernie, despite his lack of inches, could handle his fists. Both of them were also good at blending with their surroundings if they chose, rather than being immediately picked out as coppers.

He went out to the front desk and rang the Yard, asking for Mackinnon. After quickly explaining the situation, he said, "You stay there and hold the fort, with due deference to Inspector Cavett, of course. I want Piper to find out how to get to the Barley Mow, in Tottenham. Then he and Mr. Tring are to meet me. We'll pick them up on the Embankment. Got it?"

"Aye, sir. The Barley Mow, Tottenham, and the Embankment entrance."

"Anything new at your end?"

"Nothing that canna wait, sir."

"Good. I'm on my way."

Sunday traffic was light. The police car stopped at the

Embankment entrance to New Scotland Yard a couple of minutes before the others appeared. Ernie, in his dark suit, looked like a City clerk on his day off. Tom was wearing one of his more subdued checks, blue and green, and could have been anything from a bookie to a commercial traveller to a country squire. He could change his speech to suit any witness, a big advantage in a case like this that involved people of all classes.

Alec thought of dismissing the driver. However, a uniformed officer might come in handy if the informant's notion of a respectable pub turned out to be a haunt of shady characters like the rat himself and the mate who had "pulled off" something remunerative—and probably illegal.

Also, if Ernie drove, he'd be less able to concentrate on discussing the case. He and Tom must hear the story Alec had just been told, and they hadn't had time before he left the Yard for Stepney for more than the briefest report from Tom on his interviews in Hounslow last night and with Pelham's nephew this morning.

Ernie hopped into the front of the car beside the driver and started to give him directions to the Barley Mow. Tom climbed in beside Alec in the back. The police vehicle was larger and sturdier than Alec's Austin Chummy, their usual transport before the Yard had acquired its present fleet, but the springs still dipped a bit as Tom's bulk settled on the seat. They headed north on the Victoria Embankment.

Turning to look backwards, Ernie grinned at Alec. "So, Chief, what did I say about pubs?"

"You may be right. Or we may be on a pointless errand. My informant did not, in himself, inspire confidence."

"Then why are we on our way to Tottenham?" Tom asked.

"Because, besides the pub, the War also came into his tale."

"Ah." Tom was capable of expressing a wealth of meaning with his favourite monosyllable. This one meant he was interested.

"Aha!" said Ernie, his grin broadening. He took out his

notebook and one of his ever-ready supply of pencils. "What did this unreliable chap have to say for himself, then?"

Alec told them. He included much of the "corroborative detail," still far from certain whether it enhanced or detracted from the credibility of the narrative.

When he finished, Tom said "Ah" again, this time signifying satisfaction.

"You're our pub expert, Tom. You find it believable that the landlord would confide such a thing to a scruffy stranger?"

"In those circumstances, yes. The chance conjunction—"

"Whew!" said Ernie.

"The conjunction"—Tom repeated with a severe look— "of talk of the murders and the War, on top of an uneasy conscience because he wasn't rushing to the police with his information . . . Well, I can understand him blurting out what was at the top of his mind. He probably regretted it right away. But he's probably not too worried because, by the sound of it, Chief, the laddie he told doesn't exactly look like the sort who's likely to seek out the company of coppers."

"Would it be a good idea, do you think, to make him worried?"

"Well now." Tom stroked his moustache thoughtfully. "That I couldn't rightly say without talking to him first."

"And so you shall." Alec had intended to talk to Shadd himself, but Tom was obviously a better choice. "I'll see what the place looks like before I decide whether Ernie and I should come in with you. Now, let's go back over Pelham the nephew and this chap you saw in Hounslow last night."

"Peter Wensley, Major, retired. Pelham the uncle was his superior officer in South Africa, when he had just attained the rank of colonel and was feeling his oats. Major Wensley had married a Boer woman in Pretoria after our troops took the city. She was expecting his child. He assumed she was safe there, but he received a message that she had gone to visit relations in the veld. The whole family ended up in one of our concentration camps and were in dire straits. To cut a long story short, Pelham refused to let Wensley go to his wife's rescue. She died."

No one spoke for an interminable half-minute. Then Alec said softly, "No wonder he had it in for Pelham."

"He's an old man, Chief. His legs are as shaky as his handwriting."

"Pelham really liked to throw his weight about, didn't he!" said Ernie. "He sounds like a real bastard who had it coming to him. Can't have been the major that gave it to him, though. Not just his weakness, but he didn't know Devine or Halliday, did he, Sarge?"

"No, he was already in dodgy health before the Great War—wounded in the Boer War—and didn't rejoin the army. He's been living in pretty straitened circumstances in that residential hotel for years. Didn't seem like he knew anyone much except the other residents."

"So much for him. What about Pelham the nephew, Tom?" Alec asked.

"He spent the War with the Indian Army in Mesopotamia, Chief. That's one reason he ended up at the India Office. He was actually out in India last autumn, went out in September, back just in time for Christmas. Which knocks him out as far as Devine is concerned."

"November, Devine disappeared." Ernie had the detail at his fingertips, as usual. "The twenty-first."

"He swears he'd never heard of Devine or Halliday. I couldn't see any reason to disbelieve him."

"What did he say about his quarrel with his uncle?"

"The colonel tried to tell him what to do one time too many. The final straw was in '21 or '22. He's not absolutely sure what that particular spat was about, the one that finished off relations between them, because they had so many over the years."

"Such as?"

"The colonel disapproved of him going into the civil service rather than the army—that was the most frequent trouble. They disagreed on politics. The nephew dared to protest a couple of times about the way the colonel bullied his wife. All in all, he never expected to inherit anything and knew nothing about his uncle's will, but presumed that Mrs. Pelham would scoop the pool."

"What did you make of him, Tom? Was he worried about being suspected of doing away with the colonel?"

"Not him. A very ordinary gentleman who was more worried about whether he ought to send his condolences to his aunt, or call on her, or would she maybe not want anything to do with him, in accordance with his uncle's wishes. After what you said about her, Chief, I ventured to advise getting in touch."

"She certainly had no qualms about not observing her husband's wishes!"

"That's what I thought. What about that bloke you went to see in Southwark? Get anything from him?"

Alec told them about the porter who had served briefly under Halliday and Devine, and his summing up of their characters. "Halliday would obey orders because it was his duty. Devine would go along because he was easily led."

"You reckon he read them right, this porter?"

"He seemed a pretty astute fellow. It appears more and more likely that Halliday and Devine were dragged willy-nilly into some mischief started by Colonel Pelham. The urgent question is, was anyone else equally involved in whatever it was? Is there another unwitting target waiting out there?"

Tom shook his head. "If he's read the papers, Chief, he's not unwitting. Seeing nobody's asked us for protection, it looks like that's the lot."

"Or else he doesn't read the papers," Ernie pointed out. "Some don't. Lots only read the racing pages of *The Pink 'Un*."

"Very true, laddie. We better find out if the *Sporting Times* reported the names of the victims."

Ernie made a note.

By this time they were in the Tottenham High Road. The

driver asked Ernie for more precise directions to the Barley Mow. He turned off the High Road.

"Drive past the pub," said Alec, "then stop round the nearest corner."

The Barley Mow, despite its old-fashioned name, was a post-war hostelry in the middle of a row of newish shops. The exterior gave the impression of aspiring to serve a better class of clientèle than would probably ever find their way thither. Hoping to attract the superior sort of commercial traveller, it was surrounded by the dwellings of petty clerks. Either Tom or Ernie would fit in to a nicety.

"All yours, Tom. We'll wait here."

The car uttered a grateful sigh as the detective sergeant got out. As he closed the door and walked back towards the corner, Ernie said in a significant tone, "Free house."

"You think that's important?"

"We-ell . . ."

"You've got a theory."

"Well, I do, Chief. But I could be all wrong. I don't want to talk about it till we hear what Mr. Tring finds out."

"All right. What do you think of Major Wensley and the younger Pelham?"

They were in agreement that, given Tom's opinions of their respective characters, neither could seriously be considered a suspect. They had hardly reached this conclusion when Tom reappeared.

"No luck, Chief. The barman says Shadd's taken the missus and kiddies to the seaside—Clacton—for the day. But they get pretty busy Sunday evenings, so he's supposed to be back by seven to run the saloon bar."

Alec sighed. "Then we'll just have to wait, won't we?"

SIXTEEN

"*I'm off* for me dinner," announced the gardener as he led Daisy and her flock through the gap in the hedge, emerging into the wide world at last.

Daisy tipped him. The girls thanked him politely, then ran off towards the gate, chattering. The gardener turned in the opposite direction.

Daisy walked beside him, pleading. "You'll be needed to show the police how to get to him. And out again." She hadn't even attempted to memorise the turns between the body and the exit, after her previous failure.

"'T's past me dinnertime."

He didn't seem to care whether he inconvenienced the police, and he regarded the presence of a corpse in the maze as none of his business. Time to employ more persuasive means: "If you don't help, they'll probably have to cut through the hedges to get to the body."

For a moment she was sure he was going to give an indifferent shrug and walk on. It was not his maze after all, she presumed. But he turned to subject her once again to that bright, unsettling stare and said, "Tell 'em to look for me in the tool-shed in the Walled Garden."

Either he didn't want to annoy his employer or, like most gardeners, he took pride in his work and didn't want to see it damaged. Ten-foot yews, cut down, would take a long time to regrow.

He made for a door in the brick wall and disappeared through it. Daisy followed the girls down the steps, between the grinning gargoyles and past the peacock. Lizzie and Deva were sitting on the bench on either side of Sakari. She had her arm round Lizzie, who had started crying again. Belinda stood in front of them, she and Deva talking nineteen to the dozen.

Sakari greeted Daisy with relief. "I cannot understand one word in ten that these children are uttering. You will tell me all."

Daisy gave her a tiny shake of the head. She wasn't about to describe the body in the children's presence, though she knew Sakari would want to hear about it. "There isn't much to tell. The gardener took me to the centre, where there's a viewing platform. Deva was already there."

"I'm the only one who found it, Mummy."

"He and I went up and spotted Lizzie and Bel. He led the way to them and then brought us all out."

"Mummy went round the corner and looked at Mr. Harriman's body," said Belinda.

So much for discretion. "I had to make sure it was really there. Not that I didn't believe you, Lizzie darling, but the police are bound to want to know whether a grown-up actually saw it with her own eyes."

"I want *my* mummy," Lizzie wept.

"I'm sure she'll be back soon, darling, with a policeman. We were in there for ages."

Sakari looked at her wrist-watch. "Not very long. It is ten minutes past noon."

"It seemed forever. Bel, Deva, why don't the two of you go with Lizzie up to the street to wait for her mother?"

"An excellent idea," said Sakari, as the three went off and Daisy sat down. "Now you can tell me everything."

"I'm pretty sure Harriman was murdered."

"But of course."

"What do you mean, *of course*?"

"Daisy, in this life your *karma* is to discover the victims of murder and bring their killers to justice. Perhaps in your previous life you were a murderer."

"Darling, honestly!"

"I am not saying this is so. Who can tell? Perhaps you failed to avenge a killing."

"Perhaps I was murdered! Now I'm trying to avenge myself."

Sakari frowned. "Possibly. The workings of karma are inscrutable. That is not quite the right word, but it will do. What is evident is that this is the purpose of your present incarnation. How many murder victims have you found?"

"I prefer not to count," Daisy said, with what dignity she could muster.

"Many. What makes you think this Harriman was murdered?"

"He was a bully and a brute." She didn't want to dwell on the injury she had noted.

"Most bullies and brutes do not meet with unnatural death."

"No." Daisy sighed. "It looked to me as if he'd been hit on the head, and there was nothing nearby that he could have hit it on in falling. Also, he was laid out as if ready for burial. Enough?"

"Enough. He was murdered. Now we must find out who did it."

"We?"

"But naturally. My karma is to be your friend. Besides, it will be much more interesting than taking the children to a museum."

"I thought you liked museums."

"Not as escort to three giggling schoolgirls. Where shall we start? With those whom Harriman bullied, I dare say. You must know some of them, at least, or you would not be aware that he is a brute."

Daisy hesitated. She didn't want to get Pencote, Tesler, and Miss Bascombe into trouble, but they were the only three she had personal knowledge of. "There must be many I don't know," she hedged. "I heard Mr. Rowntree himself acknowledge that Harriman is a bully."

"We cannot investigate those who are as yet unknown. We must start somewhere. It is someone you like, is it not?"

"You're a mind-reader!"

"Not I. But I know you, Daisy. You need not fear I shall peach to the police."

The occasional unexpected colloquialism in the midst of Sakari's formal English always delighted Daisy, but she was too worried to appreciate it properly. "I'm sure you won't, darling, but not so sure of Mel."

"Perhaps it is best that we do not speak freely before Melanie," Sakari agreed judiciously. "She is in general a very conventional person, though always exceedingly kind to me. However, I think she will in any case not wish to discuss such a subject."

"No, she won't, that's true."

"Nor have we any facts to lay before the police. We have only your suspicions, which are not evidence, are they?"

"Absolutely not. And now I come to think of it, none of them could have done it anyway."

"None of whom? And why not? You are being abominably reticent!"

Daisy laughed. "Darling, you're beginning to sound like my American editor, who never uses a two-syllable word when three or four will do! All right, then. I've heard Harriman being perfectly beastly to Mr. Pencote, Mr. Tesler, and Miss Bascombe."

"Mr. Pencote has no legs; Mr. Tesler has but one useful hand; Miss Bascombe is a woman. You are right, we must look elsewhere."

"Belinda told me Harriman bullied the boys who aren't any good at games. He threatened to beat them, though as the school doesn't allow caning, he found other ways to harass and intimidate them. But an unathletic child isn't much more likely than a cripple to have manhandled a grown man into the maze."

"Deva said Harriman spied on Miss Bascombe and Mr. Tesler. Of what else was he guilty?"

"He also called Tesler a coward, because he went to prison as a conchie—a conscientious objector—rather than fight."

"Gandhiji would approve. How did he offend against Mr. Pencote?"

"What does it matter, since Pencote can't possibly have had anything to do with the murder?"

"Comprehending the way Harriman chose to express his malice may help us to understand who else would be vulnerable, and thus whom he might have mortally offended."

"You've been to too many lectures on psychology! Not to mention grammar. He keeps—kept calling Pencote a hero."

"This does not seem objectionable!"

"To Pencote it is. He sees himself as a victim, not a hero."

"So Harriman specialises—specialised in both humiliation and harassment."

"If he threatened to physically abuse those boys, he may have actually—Oh, here comes a policeman!"

A single stout, sweating, harried constable hove into view. He was harried not by Harriman or his ghost but by the three girls, who clustered about him, impeding his progress as they all talked at once. Lizzie appeared to have recovered from her unpleasant experience. Melanie walked alongside, looking weary. Daisy felt guilty for having sent her to deal with the police and hoped they hadn't given her too hard a time.

She also hoped the bobby was too befuddled by the girls'

chatter to have gathered that Lizzie was the one who had found the body. She wished she had warned them to leave it to her to decide what information the police really needed.

Behind the group came Kesin, bearing the umbrella-sunshades and a large picnic hamper.

"Excellent!" said Sakari. "I am more than ready for lunch."

"You'll be lucky. The order of the day's going to be talk, not eat. Oh, but I can send him off after the gardener, and then he'll be occupied in the maze for a bit. We'll have to eat quickly while he's gone."

"You will have to eat quickly, Daisy. I have nothing to contribute in the way of information and I intend to eat at leisure. Melanie, my dear, come and sit down. You are exhausted!"

The constable stood before them, red face portentous beneath his helmet, legs planted apart, notebook at the ready. "Well, now," he said, "what's a-going on of here?"

"You'd better take a look for yourself, Constable," Daisy said firmly. She pointed. "You see that brick wall? If you go through the gate over there, the left-hand one, not the right, you'll see a garden shed, and in or near it you'll find the gardener. He can lead you to the body Mrs. Germond reported."

Pencil poised, he asked, "And you'll be . . . ?"

"I'm Mrs. Fletcher. I can assure you that there really is a dead man in the maze, and I can assure you equally that I can't possibly find my way back to it."

He nodded and, surprisingly, grinned. "Used t'get lost in that maze reg'lar when I was a nipper. Thank you, madam. I shall pursue my enquiries as you suggest."

He trudged off towards the Walled Garden.

"Quick," said Daisy the moment his back was turned, "lunch!"

Kesin had already started unpacking the hamper. The girls rushed to give him a hand. But Melanie said, "How can you even think of food? When Kesin opened the boot and took out the picnic Sakari had ordered from the hotel, I nearly told him to put it back."

"You will feel better after something to eat, Melanie."

"I couldn't swallow a mouthful."

"Then why don't you tell us about your encounter with the police," Daisy suggested. "I've got to eat fast, because I'm sure I'm going to have to talk to the bobby as soon as he's seen Harriman. Have a drink, though. You look hot and parched."

"Here's some lemonade, Mrs. Germond," Belinda offered, holding out a pewter tankard. Apparently the Rose and Crown didn't trust picnickers with their glassware.

"Thank you, dear." Melanie sipped, then gulped, and looked much better for it. "I must say, Daisy, I do think you might have told me it was Lizzie who found the body!"

"She doesn't seem any the worse for it, darling. Would you have gone to report it if I had?"

"Certainly not! I would have gone straight to the maze to comfort her."

"Well, there you are. What was needed was the gardener to get her out. A fat lot of good it would've done if you'd got lost in there, too, while I was running off to the police station. Tell us about it."

While Daisy devoured a leg of cold chicken, a hard-boiled egg, a buttered roll, and an orange, peeled for her by Belinda, Mel talked.

"I've never been in a police station before, let alone reported a dead body! It's quite an impressive building for a small town, brick, with inlaid patterns, and bigger than you'd expect."

"It could have living quarters for an officer or two," Daisy said.

"Oh, I hadn't thought of that. I—I was a bit nervous, so I had Kesin come in with me."

The Indian chauffeur smiled and nodded.

"The man I talked to was a sergeant in uniform, Sergeant Weaver. You didn't say, Daisy, whether I ought to ask for a detective."

Her mouth full of a rather chewy roll, Daisy shook her head.

Sakari laughed. "*No*, you did not say, or *no*, Melanie did not need to ask for a detective?"

Daisy, still chewing, nodded agreement to both alternatives, then shook her head to indicate that Mel had not needed to speak to a detective at that point, then seeing the others look confused, nodded again.

"Well, it's too late to change," said Melanie with a touch of asperity. "Sergeant Weaver was very polite, but I decided not to tell him it was a child who found the body."

Nodding vigorously, Daisy managed to swallow at last. "Quite right. The police are sceptical by nature. It wouldn't have done at all to tell them no adult had actually seen him."

"I hope you didn't expect me to claim I'd seen it myself."

"Of course not, Mel. It's much better to tell the police the truth—though not always *all* of the truth."

"I said I thought he was dead but I wasn't absolutely sure. He rang up the hospital at once and asked the matron to send along any doctor she happened to have about the place, or to dig one up elsewhere. That's exactly how he put it. I must have looked surprised, because he explained that she's his cousin."

"Here he comes now," said Deva.

A short, tubby man carrying a black bag was approaching them across the lawn at a near trot. Suddenly he altered course. The constable and the gardener had just come out of the Walled Garden and he hurried to join them. All three disappeared through the gate to the maze.

"Would you like some cherries, Mummy?" Belinda delved into the hamper.

"Yes, please, darling. I'm afraid it's much too late for a doctor to help Harriman. I hope he realises he has to be careful not to disturb things before the detectives arrive."

"Was Mr. Harriman murdered, Mummy?" Bel asked, wide-eyed. Lizzie's face lost the colour it had regained.

Daisy wished her words unuttered. "That's not what I said. When someone dies unexpectedly, the police always have to find out how it happened, even if they died of illness or an accident. That's what detectives do, find out what happened. You know that, darling. Daddy doesn't spend all his time hunting murderers."

"Mr. Harriman didn't come to breakfast, remember?" said Deva. "Perhaps he felt ill and thought some fresh air would make him feel better. He was always going on about fresh air."

"Apparently there aren't any detectives in Saffron Walden," said Melanie. "Sergeant Weaver was going to telephone the county headquarters, so that they'd be ready to send a detective if necessary, depending on the constable's and the doctor's reports. I offered to bring the constable back here in your car, Sakari."

"Very proper, Melanie. The quicker the better."

"The sergeant was grateful. So was the constable."

"Look, they're coming back already." Deva seemed to have appointed herself as look-out. "The gardener's closed the gate to the maze. I think he locked it."

They all looked that way. The gardener stumped off back into the Walled Garden, to resume his dinner-break, presumably. The policeman and the doctor exchanged a few words, then the doctor departed towards the entrance gates and the bobby came towards the picnickers.

"Here goes!" said Daisy. She swallowed a last gulp of lemonade and went to meet him. "I'm the one who saw the body, Constable." An accurate statement if slightly misleading. She hoped the taciturn gardener hadn't already reported that she had seen it only after he had led her to Lizzie and Belinda.

"But it wasn't you as reported it, madam."

"No. I was rather upset."

"Very understandable," he said soothingly. "It's a nasty shock finding a dead body."

"Especially when it's someone you know."

She could almost see his ears prick up. The notebook came out.

"Friend of yours, was he, madam?"

"Heavens no! He's—he was a teacher at the Friends' School.

159

The girls are all boarders there, and we three adults are their mothers."

"His name, madam?"

"Harriman. I've no idea what his given name was. He was the games master, so the girls didn't have much to do with him."

"But you knew him?"

"I don't believe I've ever actually spoken to him. I've seen him about, particularly yesterday, which was sports day, and I've heard him addressed as Harriman."

"Ah, that would explain it. You ladies are visiting for the school sports day."

"That's right." Daisy gave him an encouraging smile. "We've come down from London. We're staying at the Rose and Crown."

"You won't know much about the deceased, then. I don't suppose either of the other ladies has a son at the school?"

"No, or he'd be picnicking with us."

"The young ladies'd likely know more than you do, though."

She put as much doubt into her voice as she could. "A little bit more, I dare say, but I'm afraid it would upset them frightfully to be questioned by the police. Once young girls start crying, it's awfully difficult to turn them off. Besides, you'd find out much more by talking to the other teachers at the school, and even the boys he taught."

"To be sure. That won't be up to me to decide. The doctor's going to ring up the station, and Sergeant Weaver's sure to call in the detectives from county headquarters."

"Detectives from headquarters? Oh dear, does that mean you think Mr. Harriman was murdered?"

"That's for the coroner's jury to decide. All I know is, we agree, me and the doctor, that it looks very fishy! No doubt about it, there'll be a detective inspector coming over from Chelmsford."

"From Chelmsford!"

The constable gave her a rather odd look.

Oh blast! Daisy thought, *wasn't that where the detective came from who had behaved so abominably to Alec?* Suppose they should happen to send DI Gant? He was probably still seething at having the triple murder investigation taken out of his hands. He would not have forgotten the name of the man who took it from him.

If Gant took charge, he was bound to ferret out Daisy's connection with Scotland Yard. And in that case, she wouldn't have a hope in Hades of concealing from Alec her involvement in the murder in the maze.

SEVENTEEN

Detective Inspector Gant stared suspiciously at Daisy, smoothing the strands of hair carefully, if ineffectively, draped across his balding pate. In his late forties, at a guess, he had an incongruous round, babyish face, with a ridiculous little toothbrush moustache. "Fletcher?"

"It's not an uncommon name." Daisy had her fingers crossed in her lap.

In vain. He wasn't going to be satisfied with "Daisy Fletcher."

"*Mrs.* Fletcher. As you say, madam, it's not an uncommon name. I'll need it in full."

Seeking a brainwave, Daisy let her gaze wander round the hotel writing room, commandeered by Gant for his interviews. It was rather shabby, crammed with heavy Victorian furniture unwanted elsewhere. In a corner, half hidden in an enormous armchair, lurked a stolid detective constable with a notebook.

She looked from Sakari to Melanie and back, but neither was inspired to interrupt with a timely comment or question. Did she dare tell the inspector her husband's name was James, or William, or . . . No, the truth, if not the whole truth, as she had advised Mel.

"Mrs. Alec Fletcher."

Gant stiffened. His baby-face reddened. "And you're visiting from London?"

"All of us, just for the weekend."

"We shall drive back to town tonight." Too late, Sakari drew his fire.

"Oh no you won't! I'll have to ask you not to leave Saffron Walden for the present, until I'm satisfied that none of you had anything to do with the death of Harriman."

"Inspector, you've obviously realised that my husband is DCI Fletcher of Scotland Yard. I wish you'd admit that he had no say in taking charge of the Epping Forest affair. He goes where he's sent."

"How do you know I had anything to do with that case? He must have told you!"

"Why on earth should he do that? I suppose I read it in the newspapers."

"I don't recall seeing my name in any newspaper."

"It must have been." Daisy appealed to her friends. "You two both knew Mr. Gant was on that case before I mentioned it just now, didn't you?"

Of course they did. She had told them earlier. Both agreed, Melanie hesitantly, Sakari with a twinkle in her eye. She was enjoying the battle of wits.

Daisy turned back to Gant. "You see? You can't possibly imagine that the wives of a chief inspector of the CID, a banker, and a high official in the civil service conspired to murder a schoolmaster!"

"Stranger things have happened," he insisted. "From all I've heard, there's some nasty business going on at some of these boarding schools."

"I suspect you're thinking of boys' Public Schools. We all have daughters at the school. We're talking about a school for both boys and girls—"

"If shutting 'em up together isn't asking for trouble, I don't know what is!"

Daisy, who had had her own qualms when the idea was first broached, ignored this. "And Harriman taught only the boys. What's more, it's run by the Quakers."

"Some of these peculiar religious sects are downright dangerous. They ought to be banned. Quakers—I've heard of them. They're pacifists, aren't they? Encouraging war resisters! The lot of 'em should be in prison, or shot!"

"That's beside the point, except that it shows they're against violence and the least likely people to commit murder."

"So if they didn't kill this schoolmaster, who did?" Gant said sarcastically.

"That's for you to find out, isn't it. It wasn't we three."

The inspector eyed them with increasing doubt. He could hardly deny that Daisy and Melanie looked like thoroughly ordinary, respectable middle-class matrons, as was indeed true of Melanie. Daisy did her best to look just as middle-class and respectable. Gant was the sort who very likely considered the aristocracy just as untrustworthy as the dregs of society. However, as he already disliked her for being Alec's wife, if he found out her father had been a lord it wouldn't make much difference.

Inevitably, he singled out Sakari. "What's this native woman doing here with you?" he demanded of Daisy.

"Mrs. Prasad is not a native," she said coldly. "Here in England, you and I are natives. She is a British citizen, however. She is our friend, Mrs. Germond's and mine. Her daughter, like ours, is a boarder at the school. Her husband is in the upper ranks of the British civil service, a much more important gentleman than mine."

"And mine," added Melanie.

So put that in your pipe and smoke it, Daisy thought, smiling at Mel.

She could see calculations racing through Gant's mind. If Sakari's husband was more important than a detective chief inspector of the Yard, where did that leave a mere county detective inspector? Certainly not in a position to insult the *lady*.

"No offence, madam." He did at least attempt to sound conciliatory.

"None taken," Sakari assured him, beaming—another English idiom mastered. She was not easily offended. Daisy noted that the twinkle had not vanished from her dark eyes. To her, Gant's insult was doubtless just part of his amusing conflict with Daisy.

"All the same, you'll all have to stay. At the very least, the coroner will want you as witnesses to the discovery of the victim's body."

"Mrs. Prasad and Mrs. Germond didn't discover the body." Nor did Daisy, but she wasn't going to let that stop her, nor allow this dreadful man to pester poor Lizzie. Thank goodness the constable had allowed Kesin to take all three girls back to school, with strict instructions to tell no one what had happened.

If Gant had gathered the impression that Daisy was the one who had stumbled upon Harriman, that was his look-out. She continued, "They never even saw the body. They didn't go anywhere near the maze. They're of no conceivable use as witnesses."

Gant glanced at his notes. "It was Mrs. Germond who reported the discovery to the local police station," he pointed out accusingly.

Melanie looked apprehensive, but left it to Daisy to respond.

"Because I asked her to. The children were still lost in the maze. I had promised them I'd go back and help them find the way out."

Once again, all depended upon the taciturnity of the gardener. Daisy couldn't imagine him actually volunteering any information.

The inspector glared at her. "Very well," he snapped, "Mrs. Prasad and Mrs. Germond can leave. After I've questioned—"

He glanced at Sakari and changed his choice of words. "After I've talked to them. But you'll have to stay, Mrs. Fletcher."

"I shall stay with you, Daisy," said Sakari, "to support you in this ordeal."

"Oh, Daisy," Melanie cried, distressed, "you won't think I'm deserting you and Elizabeth if I go home? It's just that Robert, and the younger children . . . Robert expects me back. He'll be quite upset if . . . My housekeeper gets in such a muddle, you see, if I'm not there to keep things running smoothly."

"Of course you must go, Mel. I'm sure Sakari will be a more than adequate support for me, and we'll both make sure the girls are all right."

Judging by his face, Gant had changed his mind and would much prefer Sakari's departure to her presence at—and on— Daisy's side.

"Kesin shall drive you home, Melanie."

"Oh, but, you don't like to walk. . . ."

"If it is necessary to go any distance, I shall summon a taxi. Besides, my husband may have need of the motor-car during the week."

"All the same, it's very kind of—"

"If you've quite finished?" Gant interrupted Melanie's thanks. He asked for her address, apparently not trusting the local constable's notes. "Mrs. Germond, did you ever talk to the deceased?"

"Talk to Mr. Harriman? Oh no. I had no reason to. As Mrs. Fletcher explained, he taught only boys. My eldest son is at a different school. All boys."

He glowered at her, as if he suspected she was being ironic at his expense because of his exchange with Daisy about boys' schools. Mel looked dismayed, recognising his animosity but not understanding the reason for it. Daisy, who knew her friend incapable of irony, was about to jump to her defence when she realised her intervention was more likely to foment trouble than to help.

"You would have recognised Harriman, though," Gant barked at Melanie.

"Certainly. I had seen him about the school, on previous visits but especially yesterday."

"Why yesterday?"

"He's—he was the games master, so he was organising the sports, as Mrs. Fletcher explained."

This time he glowered at Daisy. She wished she could warn Mel not to mention her name if she could possibly help it.

"Did you see or hear him quarrelling with anyone?"

"I wasn't watching him, Inspector. I was watching my daughter and chatting with Mrs. Prasad and Mrs. Fletcher. I had no interest whatsoever in Mr. Harriman."

"I suppose you couldn't know he was going to be murdered," Gant admitted grudgingly.

"It *was* murder, then?" Sakari asked.

Her turn to be on the receiving end of the glower. "I'm asking the questions," he reminded her, then as an afterthought added, "madam."

Daisy had heard the phrase more than once before. She had come to the conclusion that it was often a sign of a detective who had lost control of an interview and didn't know where he was going.

"Mrs. Germond, you were familiar enough with Harriman, I take it, to recognise him when you saw his body."

"I didn't see it," Melanie explained patiently. "Of the three of us, only Mrs. Fletcher saw it."

Gant gritted his teeth. "When was the last time you saw him alive?"

"Yesterday afternoon. It was impossible to miss him, because he was shouting through a megaphone, starting the races. I suppose the last time I actually noticed him was when the last race began. We left when it ended. I'm afraid I don't know what time that was, but I dare say someone at the school will be able to tell you."

"How did you spend the rest of the afternoon and evening?"

She told him about taking the girls out for an early meal, sending them back to school in time for their curfew, and dining at the Rose and Crown. "And then we had coffee in the residents' lounge. We stayed there chatting until we retired for the night."

"Did you, for any reason, leave the hotel again after that?"

"Certainly not!" Melanie exclaimed, astonished. "What reason could I possibly have for wandering about in the dark?"

"Perhaps, Melanie, the inspector suspects you of having a secret tryst with Mr. Harriman."

"Really, Sakari, that's not in the least funny!"

"It's not a joke, Mel," said Daisy, frowning at Sakari. "It's his job to suspect everyone."

Melanie turned her outrage on Gant. "You suspect *me* of arranging a secret tryst with a man? You must be mad!"

"Th-that isn't what I said, madam!"

"It isn't, darling. He suspects all of us of murder. Along with everyone else who's ever come into contact with Harriman. Recently, at least. Hundreds of people. He just doesn't know their names yet, and he has us close to hand."

"Hundreds?" said the inspector, appalled.

"There are nearly two hundred pupils at the school, I believe, not to mention the other teachers. Yesterday scores of parents attended sports day. I haven't the faintest idea whether he's married or not, or what other family he might have. For all I know he goes to pubs, where he quarrels with other patrons, or barmen, or insults barmaids. Perhaps he gambles and owes a lot of money to a bookmaker. Quakers frown on drinking and gambling, but Harriman wasn't the shy, retiring sort. Don't worry, Mel. We've got plenty of company."

"Hundreds!" Gant repeated despairingly. "Er . . . You're free to go, Mrs. Germond."

"Do you wish to leave at once, Melanie?"

"Yes, please. If you're quite sure you don't mind, Daisy?"

"Absolutely certain. You'd better go and pack."

"Yes. Sakari, would it be all right if Kesin took me up to the school first, to say good-bye to Lizzie?"

"I shall instruct him to do so. Be so kind as to ring the bell, Inspector," said Sakari regally. "It is over there, by the mantelpiece, I see. I will answer your questions when I have given my chauffeur his orders."

Meekly, Gant obeyed. He was obviously out of his depth. No wonder he had been taken off the "Epping Forest Massacre"; the wonder was that he had ever risen to the rank of inspector.

In answer to the bell, the Rose and Crown's manager came in. Sakari asked him to send Kesin to her. As he started to leave, the inspector stopped him to question him about night porters and what time the hotel's exterior doors were locked.

"Naturally we have a porter on duty all night," the manager said stiffly. "However, he is not expected to watch any comings and goings. He has a cubbyhole near the front door and the door-bell is switched to ring in there, as well as all the room bells. Even if he dozes off, they cannot help but wake him. He locks the front and back doors at eleven—there is not a great deal of activity in Saffron Walden late at night, nor any trains arriving. He unlocks them at six in the morning."

"What about keys? Do you issue front-door keys to residents?"

"Upon request. None of these ladies has asked for one. Now you must excuse me, Inspector. Mrs. Prasad is waiting for her chauffeur." He marched out, his back eloquent of his disdain for anyone who dared to doubt the uprightness of guests at his hotel.

Gant was disconsolate. Daisy didn't think he honestly suspected her of having murdered Harriman, but he would dearly have liked to catch her wrong-footed in some way, to justify persecuting her. She wouldn't have minded half so much if he had any real cause for resentment against her. It wasn't fair to vent his spleen on her innocent—fairly innocent—head because he was angry with Alec, especially as Alec himself was innocent of any desire to be landed with a triple murder.

"Sakari, I must let Alec know what's going on. I don't want to send a cable, that anyone can read, or telephone from the lobby. Could Kesin deliver a note to my house?"

"But of course, Daisy. I, too, ought to write to my husband."

They took a couple of sheets of the hotel note-paper and retrieved their fountain pens from their handbags. At that point, Sakari started writing. Daisy, after dating the sheet and opening with "Darling . . ." came to a halt.

Alec was not going to be pleased that she was once again mixed up in murder. Nor would he take it kindly that her opponent—or rather, the investigating officer—was the ghastly Gant. How was she to phrase her letter so as to vex him least? Would it be best to omit Gant's name altogether?

"What are you telling him?" she asked Sakari.

"Only that you must stay in Saffron Walden, so I shall stay with you. I see no need to trouble him with details." Calmly, Sakari signed her note, sealed it in an envelope, and wrote her husband's name on the front, in both English and Hindi. Kesin came in. She gave him the envelope and his orders.

Rushed, Daisy hastily scribbled that the police were investigating the unexpected death of Harriman, the games master at Belinda's school. They wanted to talk to visitors to the school. Though she had never exchanged a word with Harriman (true enough, though he had spoken to her), the detectives had requested that she stay on for a day or two. Adding lots of love, and hugs and kisses for the twins, she folded it, stuck it in an envelope, wrote Alec's name on the front, and handed it to Kesin.

Kesin bowed. "I shall deliver it to your house today, madam."

In spite of his excellent—though strongly accented—English, Inspector Gant showed no sign of wanting to question him. He had been looking on with strong disapproval as Daisy and Sakari wrote, but he could hardly object to their notifying their husbands, both outranking him, that they would not be home when expected.

"When you're quite ready, madam," he said as Kesin went out.

Sakari smiled at him. "I am quite ready, Inspector. Fire away!"

He consulted his notes. "You and Mrs. Germond stayed behind when Mrs. Fletcher took your girls to the maze. Why was that?"

"As Mrs. Germond mentioned, I do not enjoy walking. Many English ladies take pleasure in exercise, to a most fatiguing excess. I never developed the habit, because in India, ladies of high caste do not walk when they can be carried."

The "high caste" rocked Gant. He became almost obsequious. "I understand, madam. So, when Mrs. Fletcher came back and told you about the dead body in the maze, you stayed sitting on the bench, while Mrs. Germond reported to the police and Mrs. Fletcher returned to the maze with the gardener."

"I should certainly have moved had there been anything useful for me to do."

"Of course, madam."

"Mrs. Fletcher suggested that I stay to provide a meeting place where all might find me and each other."

"Very sensi—" The inspector stopped himself just in time, before he uttered a word in praise of Daisy. He fell back on: "Of course, madam."

"I stayed put until that charming bobby gave us leave to leave. English is a very strange language at times. Do you not find it so, Inspector?"

"I—er—well, I . . ."

"Perhaps you do not, as speaking it is natural to you. But only consider the idiom, 'Fire away.' Anyone might have reasonably assumed I was inviting you to shoot with a gun, whereas I merely gave you leave, or permission, to ask me questions. Very odd!"

"Yes, madam. I—Just one more question, if you please, madam. Did you see Harriman alive at any time after the end of the events at the school?"

"I did not. Nor dead. In India, only Untouchables have any contact with the dead. Now, before you have your little chat with Mrs. Fletcher, she and I will drink tea. You will join us, perhaps, Inspector? Will you be so kind as to ring the bell?"

With a hopeless shrug, Gant went to ring the bell.

While his back was turned, Daisy met Sakari's eyes. They were brimful with wicked mirth. She had routed the inspector. Which was all very well, but it wouldn't leave him any more kindly disposed towards Daisy.

EIGHTEEN

The manager came. The manager went away again, slightly irritable, promising to send a waiter. Next time the bell rang, Daisy thought, the manager would not turn up in person, anxious to help the police.

Gant rubbed his hands together. "We can get down to business while we're waiting."

"Mrs. Fletcher and I are going to wash our hands." Majestically, Sakari surged to her feet. "In India it is the custom among people of high caste to wash before eating and drinking. No doubt it is a habit you have not developed. You may order the full afternoon tea. Our luncheon was interrupted."

Jumping up, Gant stammered, "Y-yes, madam. I'll wash, of course, as soon as I've passed on your order to the waiter."

Daisy closed the door firmly behind them. "Sakari, you are abominable! I'm almost beginning to feel sorry for the poor little man."

"I badly need to spend a penny, Daisy. I hope there is no one in the cloakroom. I thought I might as well take the opportunity to put the inspector in his place."

"You'd already done that, darling. Thoroughly." She pushed

open the door to the ladies' room across the lobby. "*Vacant.* You're in luck."

Sakari disappeared behind the heavy wooden door with frosted glass panes. Daisy regarded herself in the looking-glass over the basin and decided she had survived the harrowing day without too much overt damage. She powdered her nose, refreshed her lipstick, and poked at her shingled curls, somewhat flattened by heat and hat. A *clank*, a *whoosh* of water, and Sakari reemerged.

"Ah, I feel much better now. I am ready for another bout with Mr. Gant."

"It's my turn, both for the lav and for Gant. Wait for me."

"But of course."

A couple of minutes later, washing her hands and drying them on the roller towel, Daisy said, "I mean it, Sakari. My turn. Let me tackle the inspector, or he's just going to get more and more irritable."

"He is not a pleasant person."

"No, and he's pretty incompetent, too. If he had the least notion how to question a witness, he'd have found out long ago that it was Lizzie who discovered Harriman's body. It's not as if any of us has lied about it. He had his own preconceived notions and put words into our mouths."

"I think it is good that he does not know about Lizzie. Shall you tell him?"

"Heavens, no, not unless he asks me a direct question. On present form, that's unlikely."

"If he does, I shall distract him."

"No! Please don't interrupt. If he asks I must tell him. Any more distractions and he'll start to smell something fishy."

"Do you prefer that I am not present, Daisy?"

"Not at all, darling. I need a high caste protector! But a silent one, if you can possibly manage it."

"I shall do my best to keep my lip buttoned. Should it not be 'lips'?"

"Singular is usual, though I can't imagine why. Where do

you find these expressions?" Daisy laughed. "His face when you started talking about the peculiarities of the English language!"

Sakari smiled. "I keep my ears open, that is all."

"And I've never known you to wave India like a flag before."

"It is a diversionary tactic, Daisy, as well as a lesson to the ignorant that 'natives' are not all savages. But no more diversions. I will be silent."

"Just sit there looking like the wife of a very important high official. . . ."

". . . Enjoying her afternoon tea," added Sakari, as a waiter with a laden tray crossed the lobby ahead of them.

Daisy sighed. "I suppose I'll have to snatch bites and sips between questions."

A gleam entered Sakari's eyes. "Just one more little diversion," she pleaded, "to allow you, too, to enjoy your tea."

"Oh, Sakari, you are incorrigible. All right."

They entered the writing room on the waiter's heels. The inspector stood up, looking relieved, as if he had half-expected them to do a bunk.

"All right," he said, rubbing his hands again, "*now* we can get down to business."

"My dear Inspector, have you never heard of the Tea Ceremony?"

His face went red and his moustache bristled, but he had been too thoroughly cowed to completely regain his uppitiness during their absence. "No, madam," he said sullenly.

"It is unheard of to discuss business during the Tea Ceremony," she assured him.

"Will that be all, madam?" asked the waiter, having emptied his tray at one end of the big writing table. Besides the tea things, there were plates of bread and butter, watercress sandwiches, a variety of biscuits, and cherry and Dundee cakes. The Rose and Crown did an excellent afternoon tea.

"I trust they have remembered to give us the Darjeeling."

"But of course, madam."

"Do you like Indian tea, Inspector, or shall I send for China?"

"No, no, Indian will do nicely, thank you, ma'am."

"Then that is all, thank you," Sakari said to the waiter. "Daisy, will you pour?"

Pouring, Daisy recalled hearing mention of a Tea Ceremony. But it was Chinese, or Japanese, she thought, not Indian. Of course, an English afternoon tea was something of a ceremony in itself, and polite conversation was the order of the day, definitely not business. "Milk and sugar, Inspector? Splendid weather we're having, aren't we, for the time of year."

"Forecast says rain tonight," he told her grumpily.

"Constable," Sakari invited, "you will join us, won't you? Luckily they have brought four cups, so I shall not have to send for another. They cannot have realised in the kitchen that Mrs. Germond has left us."

The detective constable, whose silent presence Daisy had completely forgotten, looked hopefully at his superior, who glared at him, then sighed and nodded.

Neither of the men contributed to the polite conversation. Sakari and Daisy, trying to avoid all mention of the school and Bridge End Garden, quickly exhausted the weather, past, present, and future, and even in India. They went on to the latest vagaries of Paris fashion, in which Sakari was much more interested than Daisy although she never wore anything but a sari. Daisy soon found she couldn't think of anything *but* the school and the happenings in the Garden, and the obvious connections between them.

However, her efforts not to think of them prevented any constructive speculation. She was suddenly very tired.

Sakari kept up the chatter without much encouragement for a while, but the strain began to tell. When the only sound for a noticeable period was the constable's munching, she gave up. "Daisy, unless you would care for another cup of tea, I shall have the table cleared."

"No, thanks, darling. That was just what I needed to perk me up no end."

"Then, if you would be so kind as to ring the bell, Inspector?"

Gant jerked his head at the constable, who washed down a mouthful of cherry cake with a gulp of tea and obeyed, before retreating to his corner.

The two detectives had accounted for more than their share of the meal. As the waiter loaded his tray, Daisy hoped the refreshments had not refreshed Gant's brain cells. There were any number of awkward questions he might ask. If he phrased them unambiguously and put them to her directly, she would have to answer.

She had no more desire to reveal Harriman's sadistic tormenting of Tesler, Pencote, and Miss Bascombe than to bring Lizzie into the foreground of the picture.

All too soon, the crumbs had been whisked from the table and the tray carried off.

"Thank you, ma'am," the inspector said grudgingly. "Very kind of you."

"Thanks," echoed a mumble from the corner.

Sakari gave them a gracious nod.

Turning to Daisy with a sneer, Gant said, "Well, Mrs. Fletcher, I expect you're an expert in murder investigations."

Daisy widened her blue eyes, which Alec had so often described as "misleadingly guileless." "Why, no, Inspector. Even if my husband wanted my assistance, it would be most improper for me to interfere." As Alec was not slow to remind her, even when he actually did admit to needing her help.

"I'm glad you realise that. It's a serious offence to interfere with the police in the discharge of their duties. Yesterday afternoon, you stayed with the other ladies to watch the races?"

"I did. Harriman was busy with his megaphone from the first race to the last. I wasn't watching him all the time, but I didn't see him speak to anyone other than the runners." Though, come to think of it, Miss Bascombe had been with him during the girls' races, so he had probably ordered her about a bit.

However Daisy hadn't heard him so it was pure speculation and not to be reported.

"Did you see him alive after you left the school?"

"No. What time did he die?"

"Asking questions is my job. Yours is answering them. This morning, you—the three of you—motored with your daughters to the public garden. You took the girls to the maze while the other two stayed behind. Why was that?"

"As a matter of fact, only Mrs. Prasad motored. The rest of us walked. We spent quite a time in the Dutch Garden—"

"Dutch Garden? What's that?"

"You must have passed it to get to the maze. You have been to the maze, haven't you? To see the body where it was found?"

"Naturally," he said stiffly. "I *am* a trained detective. It's the first section of the garden after the entrance, I take it."

Daisy was tempted to applaud his deduction, but decided it wouldn't go down well. "That's it. We walked about for some time, and as you know, one has to walk some distance from the street to reach the Garden. By the time the girls wanted to go on to the maze, Mrs. Prasad had had enough of walking. Mrs. Germond offered to stay with her, so I took the children."

"While you were in the Dutch Garden, did you see anyone about?"

"Only the gardener. I never did get his name. Obviously they have to have someone there on Sundays if they're going to open the place to the public."

"So, after the discovery of the body in the maze, you returned to the other ladies, asked Mrs. Germond to report to the police, and then had the gardener go with you to guide the girls out."

"Exactly." Daisy tried not to breathe a sigh of relief. He apparently accepted without doubt that she had been the one to find the body, and he didn't seem to care how she had found her own way out of the maze. What was more, by referring to "*the* discovery" rather than "*your* discovery," he allowed her to evade the issue. He wasn't finished yet, though.

"When you saw the body, did you touch it?"

"Of course. I had to know whether he was in urgent need of medical care. I felt for a pulse. I couldn't find one, and his arm was . . ." She started to feel rather sick. "I'd really rather not talk about it."

"Was what, Mrs. Fletcher?" he persisted.

"It was limp, and cold, and sort of heavy. . . ." She shuddered.

"You lifted it?"

He was obviously dying to be able to accuse her of interfering with the scene. "Certainly not. That's the impression I got just from holding his wrist."

"You didn't move the body?"

"I didn't move it, and I did my best to keep to the very side of the path so as not to make confusing marks. My husband may not want my help, but I do know that much. Besides, anyone who reads detective stories can tell you all about footprints and fingerprints and so on."

He looked sour. "Did you notice anything else about the body?"

"Yes." Daisy hesitated. "If his hair wasn't cut so short, I wouldn't have noticed. It looked to me as if he had a bruise on the side of his head and possibly . . . possibly even a dent in his skull."

"Brandy!" exclaimed Sakari. "You are as pale as a ghost, Daisy." She rose and went herself to ring the bell.

"No, darling, truly, I don't want any. I'll be all right in a minute. I . . . It was just so vivid for a moment, but I'll stop thinking about it."

Sakari, hands on ample hips, glared at Gant. "You will not badger Mrs. Fletcher any further on that subject," she commanded.

The inspector glared back. "You can't tell me what to say. I'll ask what questions I choose. As it happens," he added sulkily, "that's all I wanted to know about that."

"How fortunate," said Sakari, "for you."

179

The interruption allowed Daisy time to recover. It also distracted Gant from asking how she had found her way out of the maze after seeing the horrid sight. If he ever started wondering, Lizzie's part in the affair was bound to come out. As it was, he didn't even realise he was confused about the order of events.

He was chasing another hare. "Mrs. Fletcher, when you spoke to the gardener, requesting his help to get the children out, was he reluctant to enter the maze?"

"Very."

"Aha!"

He suspected the gardener! If he pressed him hard enough, he might manage to squeeze a coherent account out of him.

Daisy said quickly, "Don't let that mislead you, Inspector. He would have been equally reluctant to show me the way to the . . ." She racked her brains for the other attractions of the Garden, as detailed in the guidebook. "To the Poet's Corner, or the Rose Garden. All he wanted was his dinner. In his opinion, it wouldn't hurt the girls to wait till he was ready to return to work."

"By that time, they'd probably have found their own way out, so he wouldn't have to go near the scene of the crime."

"I wasn't about to allow any delay! If they'd gone on wandering . . . Just imagine the shock for a young girl of stumbling upon the corpse of someone she knew!"

"I suppose you offered a big enough tip to change his mind, made it worth his while to risk—"

"I didn't offer him a penny, though naturally I tipped him afterwards. I just told him about the body."

"You hadn't told him right away?" Gant asked sceptically.

"I thought the fewer people knew about it the better. But it was more important to get the girls out quickly and I hoped he'd understand, realise they mustn't wander about at random in there. And he did."

"Did he seem surprised to hear about the body? What did he say?"

"Nothing. He was walking towards the Walled Garden as I

spoke and he just changed direction, towards the maze, without opening his mouth. I'm sure you've discovered he's a man of few words."

"That's one way of putting it!"

"He also has a remarkably inexpressive face. I can only hazard a guess as to what he was thinking by his actions. He didn't hesitate before heading for the maze, when I told him there was a body in there with them. Oh, wait a minute! That's not quite right."

"Hah!"

"I'd forgotten. He stopped walking and looked at me as if he wasn't sure whether to believe me or not. So I told him my friend had gone for the police. At that, he—well, he spat—on the grass, not at me—"

"He doesn't like the police!" Gant said triumphantly.

"Plenty of people don't," Daisy pointed out. "It doesn't mean they're criminals, let alone murderers. I can say that as the wife of a policeman." She immediately wished she hadn't reminded him.

"Is it not possible," Sakari said, having forgotten or abandoned her resolve to keep her lip buttoned, "that the man expectorated simply because he needed to clear his throat?"

"Either way," said Daisy, "I don't believe any conclusions can be drawn from it. Certainly not that he had anything to do with Harriman's death."

"You leave the conclusions to me!"

"Sorry, Inspector! I hate to think he might get into trouble because of anything I said, after he was so helpful."

"In the end," muttered Sakari.

"He won't get into trouble if he didn't do anything. Well, I can't waste any more time here. You may have found the body, Mrs. Fletcher, but it's obvious you can't tell me anything useful. The school's the place where I'm going to find out what's been going on."

He bustled out importantly, the silent constable following in his wake.

Daisy leant back in her chair. "Whew, I am properly put in my place! What a—"

"Sshhh!"

The constable reappeared. "Mr. Gant was wondering," he said diffidently, "who's the best person to ask for at the school. I mean, seeing it's this funny religion and all, he doesn't want to take any chances. What's that, sir?" He turned his head to look backwards. "Oh, sorry, sir. What I meant to say is," he said, turning back, "you've got to be careful not to offend people."

"Very true," said Daisy. "He'd better ask for . . . the headmaster, Mr. Rowntree."

"Thank you, madam." He disappeared again, closing the door.

Sakari snorted. "I would wager a good deal that the inspector did not instruct him to thank you."

"Probably not. Oh, Sakari, you've no idea how tempted I was to advise him to ask for the Great Panjandrum himself!"

NINETEEN

When Alec got back to the Yard from the abortive visit to the Barley Mow, a few new tips had come in.

"None of them looks promising," Mackinnon reported.

"Let Piper have a look. Have we heard from Newcastle yet?"

"DS Miniver rang up just after you left, sir. Peter Chivers was dining out when he went round last night, so he tried again this morning, although it was his day off—"

"I hope you thanked him appropriately."

"Och, aye. Wanted to be able to say he had his finger in the Epping pie, if you ask me. He caught Mr. Chivers after church. Chivers served as a lieutenant under Pelham, in Flanders, but only briefly. He was wounded badly enough—which means he could neither stand nor shoot—that the colonel had no choice but to send him back to a field hospital. When he had recovered enough to return to the front, he wangled a transfer."

"Wise man."

"Pelham was a tyrant, Halliday went by the rule book, and Devine did what he was told, just what we've already heard about the three. Chivers did add that Halliday would remonstrate wi' Pelham if he strayed too far from the regulations governing the men's welfare."

"There wasn't much welfare available in the trenches under the best of officers," Alec commented. "Anything else?"

"The officers who went back to the burial site didn't come up with anything last night so they returned this morning. They found a tree nearby wi' three bullets in it. Same side, different heights, but all about heart-high. The bark shows signs of having been rubbed by tight ropes, more or less ankle-, waist-, and armpit-high."

"Nasty," said Tom.

"Aye. Looks as if the murderer waited for them to come round before shooting them."

"The bullets are being analysed?"

"Aye, sir. The preliminary report is that they're all from the same 9 mm Luger."

"Not a hope of tracing it, then. Tom, tell Mackinnon what's going on in Tottenham, will you? I must have a word with Inspector Cavett."

The room was thinly staffed now. Cavett was shuffling papers, his bored expression suggesting that he was making work for himself. As Alec approached his desk, he sort of half-stood and half-saluted, saying eagerly, "What's up, sir?"

Alec gestured to him to sit, and pulled up a chair for himself. "No luck. The man we want to talk to wasn't there. They say he'll be back this evening at seven though, when his pub opens."

"I'm supposed to go off at five, sir. Inspector Lowe will be taking over. I could stay on, if—"

"No, that's all right. But I'll rely on you to brief Lowe thoroughly. I'm going to take a few hours off, and so are my chaps, before we go back to Tottenham. Now, let me make sure you have all the information you'll need to explain the situation to Lowe."

Half an hour later, he was rattling homeward underground. The Hampstead tube platforms were *very* underground, the deepest of the entire system. Once, soon after the Fletchers had moved to Hampstead, Alec got fed up with waiting for the lift and decided to take the emergency stairs. Three hundred steps later, legs aching and knees wobbling, he had decided to save his energy for better things in future. The lift had beaten him to the top, anyway.

He took the lift. Walking from the station, he hoped Oliver and Miranda were not napping. Absolutely nothing would make Nurse Gilpin permit them to be awoken until the allotted time had elapsed. He wanted to take them out on the Heath while it was fine. The sky had hazed over but though rain was probably on the way, the afternoon was still warm.

He was in luck. Mrs. Gilpin was actually preparing to take the twins out. She was even—grudgingly—pleased to delegate the outing to their father, provided, of course, he took Bertha, the nurserymaid, with them.

"She wants to put her feet up," Bertha confided. She trotted alongside, holding Nana's lead, as he pushed the double push-chair along the unmade lane connecting Constable Circle with Hampstead Heath. "Her bones are telling her it's going to rain."

"Bones," said Miranda with ghoulish glee. "Out, Daddy. Mirrie get down!"

"Down, down, down," chanted Oliver.

"When we get to the Heath," Alec promised.

The children had such a wonderful time rolling down a slope, in spite of having to climb back up each time, that Alec was almost tempted to have a go himself. It was probably just as well that far too many people were about, taking the air on this fine Sunday afternoon, for him to risk it. He exchanged greetings with several neighbours. What gossip he'd start if they saw a detective chief inspector indulging in so undignified a pastime! Though they might never mention it to him, Daisy would never hear the last of it.

When it was time to go home for nursery tea if they were not to earn Nurse's displeasure, Nana came at the first call but the twins were very reluctant to climb back into the pushchair. To Alec's chagrin, in the end they obeyed Bertha rather than their father. At the Yard, he could command legions, but his own children were beyond his control.

He really must make more effort to spend time with them, even if it meant battling Mrs. Gilpin and her rules. Kissing them good-night in their sleep when he came home late was not good enough.

Mrs. Gilpin had dozed off during their absence. Alec helped Bertha with nursery tea, a messy occasion. He even wiped Oliver's and Miranda's jammy hands and faces clean afterwards, while the nurserymaid cleared the table and took the crockery and debris down to the kitchen. Then he helped them build towers of wooden blocks to knock down and, when they tired of that, read them a story. By the time Elsie called him for his own early meal, he was both exhausted and exhilarated.

Yes, he must spend more time with the twins, but all the same he was very glad to be able to leave them to Nurse Gilpin's care.

Mrs. Dobson, accustomed to odd hours and short notice, provided an excellent dinner. Much refreshed, he was picked up at half past six by a car from the Yard. After seeing the Barley Mow and hearing Tom's description of the interior, he had concluded that they would do better without a uniformed presence, so Ernie was at the wheel. Tom sat beside him. Alec joined Mackinnon in the back.

"You want me to tackle Shadd?" Tom asked.

"No, I'm going to talk to him myself. To all appearances, he's a respectable householder with a wife and children, so if he bolted we'd find him in the end, but we can't afford any more delay."

"Always supposing he hasn't already scarpered, after the barman told him I was asking for him."

"We can only hope not. I want you guarding the back door. We'll give you ten minutes after we arrive to find it."

"Right, Chief. I noticed there's an alley behind the row, wide enough for lorries."

"With any luck they haven't got a yard at the back, then. If they do, the gates may be locked, in which case you'll have to wait outside them. If not, well, that's a private part of the premises, so you'll have to wait outside in any case, unfortunately." He hated to leave Tom outside when the dark sky presaged rain, but he was capable of handling just about anyone single-handed, whereas Alec wasn't familiar with Mackinnon's abilities in that capacity. "There's glass in the doors between the front entrance and the two bar-rooms, you said?"

"That's right. And they're connected by a swing-door behind the two bar counters. It was propped open at lunchtime, as they only had the one barman serving both."

"Good. Mackinnon, you'll hang about just inside the saloon bar door, looking like a plain-clothes copper."

Mackinnon grinned. "Aye, sir."

"We don't want to scare off any customers, but if it happens it can't be helped. If Shadd makes a move towards the public, dodge back out so you can watch for him heading either way. Ernie, you'll come with me, notebook very much in evidence. If all goes well, Shadd will take us to a private room, at which point I'll send you to fetch the others. Not, of course, that I have any intention of trying to intimidate the man, but I do want him to think twice before refusing to answer all my questions fully, should he be so inclined."

"D'you think he won't want to talk, Chief?" Piper asked.

"He hasn't come forward of his own accord, laddie," said Tom. "That's a bad sign."

"Maybe he was putting it off till tomorrow, so's not to spoil his day at the seaside. He could've told us he didn't find out the names of the victims till then, if it wasn't for the bloke who snitched on him."

"If it wasn't for the snitch, we might even have believed him, if he wasn't a barman. What with the bodies being found just a few miles away, he'd've had a hard time making me believe the murders hadn't already been talked to death—if you see what I mean—in the bar."

Alec laughed. "Very true. All the same, Ernie's got a point. He could have just put it off. We don't get so many fine weekends anyone can afford to waste one."

As he spoke, the first drops of rain hit the windscreen.

"Except coppers," said Tom gloomily.

"Sorry, Tom. You're the best man for that job."

Ernie turned on the windscreen wipers.

They reached the pub just as the doors opened to a flood of thirsty customers. As they drove past it, Tom counted shops. Ernie parked round the corner, in the same place as earlier. The street lamps at the crossroads illuminated the entrance to the asphalted alley, just ahead.

"Five minutes, Chief," said Tom. "I'll find the place, easy."

"No, wait here for a few minutes. We'll let him serve the first rush before we go in. I'm going to look like a proper fool if we're on a wild-goose chase, so the less we disrupt trade, the better."

"If you reckon the snitch was telling the truth, Chief," said Ernie, "you wouldn't catch me betting against you."

"Instinct honed by experience," Tom said profoundly.

"Blimey, Sarge, you've said a mouthful!"

They all laughed.

"I won't ask whether you'd bet *on* me, Ernie, or how much. I'm just certain enough to put a bit of pressure on if Shadd makes difficulties."

"Which is why we're all here," said Mackinnon, "wi' orders to look like plain-clothes coppers."

That was good for another laugh.

A couple of minutes later, Alec said, "All right, Tom, off you go, or the boozers will be ready for their second rounds. Five minutes."

They both checked the time. Tom got out into the rain, now coming down in a steady drizzle, then leant back into the car. "Don't leave me out in this any longer than you have to, Chief!" He disappeared into the alley.

The second hand of Alec's watch moved with agonising slowness. Both the others also kept their eyes on the time.

"Four minutes, Chief," Ernie reported at last. "It'll take us a minute to get round there. Save Mr. Tring sixty seconds in the wet."

"Let's go."

Alec entered the tiny lobby first. Two inner doors faced him, separated by a cigarette machine. The upper halves were glazed with small panes, none too clean. The one on the right was marked PUBLIC. Peering through, he saw a tall, thin man behind the bar, presumably the hired barman, whom Tom had described as a beanpole. Through the left-hand door he made out a shorter, burlier red-faced citizen serving at the saloon bar. He looked to be in his late forties, thinning hair, a bit of a paunch but beefy with it. He was laughing at something a customer was saying, but when he stopped laughing, his face settled into an anxious expression and he glanced at the door.

Shadd.

Pushing through the door, Alec felt like the sheriff in a Wild West film, entering a saloon with his posse to round up the outlaws. At least the likelihood of a gun-fight was nil; neither he nor his deputies owned—far less carried—a trusty Colt six-shooter.

So strong was the impression that it took an effort not to adopt a Wild West lawman's swagger as he walked up to the bar.

"Mr. Shadd? I'd like a word with you. Somewhere quiet."

He nodded, resigned. "It'll have to be the stockroom. The wife and kids are upstairs. Just let me tell Alf he'll have to take care of this side, too."

"I'll tell him, sir." Ernie had already rounded the end of the counter, opened the flap, and gone through.

Shadd stood back to let him get to the swinging door

connecting the two bars. Then he indicated another door, in the back wall. "In here," he said to Alec.

Alec followed him into a room dimly lit by a dangling, unshaded bulb and crammed with crates and boxes. Ernie stood in the doorway.

"D'you want me to fetch Mr. Mackinnon, Chief?"

Considering the lack of space and Shadd's apparent docility, Alec said, "No, that's all right. Just tell him he can get himself a pint as long as he keeps his eyes open."

"Have a heart, guv," Shadd protested. "You'll be chasing all me customers orf, leaving a bloody rozzer out there, sticking out like a bloody sore thumb."

"If that's the way you want it. Go ahead, Piper."

Ernie went back into the bar, closing the door behind him. Looking round in the dimness, Alec saw that the aisle between the crates led to a wide door at the rear.

He pointed. "To the alley, Mr. Shadd? Is it locked?"

"Wouldn't have any stock left if it wasn't, would I."

"The key, please." He held out his hand. "I've another man out there, and he might as well come in out of the rain."

"Blimey, brought half the bloody force, did you?" The landlord took a bunch of keys from his pocket, sorted through them, picked out one and made for the back door.

Alec let him go. If he had any thoughts of escape, Tom would change his mind, but as he hadn't already scarpered he probably wouldn't try.

He opened the door. "Come and join the party, mate," he invited sardonically. "Make yerself at home."

"Thank you. Mr. Shadd, I presume." Tom came in, large and damp, keeping his eyes on Shadd in case he tried to dodge past.

He didn't. He swung the heavy door shut against a spatter of rain, turning as Mackinnon and Piper entered from the bar. "Take a seat, gents. Might as well make ourselves cosy."

The only seats available were on the crates, so that was where they perched.

"I appreciate your cooperation, Mr. Shadd," said Alec. "I'm—as I expect you've worked out—Detective Chief Inspector Fletcher, in charge of the Epping Forest case." He introduced the others. "Could we start with your full name, please, and your address—you live above the pub?—for the record."

"Victor Shadd. I live upstairs, me and the family, like I said. You found me, so you know the bloody address. As for cooperating, we'll see about that. Alf told me the rozzers was asking for me, but I dunno what for. I'm a law-abiding citizen and I got me rights."

In the dimness, his expression was unreadable, but he didn't sound indignant, as he surely would if he really had no idea what they wanted. Alec's spirits rose. The anonymous rat had not been talking through his disreputable hat. He might have earned his quid, possibly even a bonus.

"You'll get your rights, Mr. Shadd. We're acting on information received. Our informant claims you told him you have a very good idea of who committed the Epping Forest murders."

After a long silence, Shadd said cautiously, "Well, I may've, mayn't I."

"Is it true, or not?" Alec insisted.

"Kind of."

"What exactly do you mean by that?"

"That's what I told him, all right. Ferrety bloke I never seen before and don't never want to set eyes on again. I dunno what come over me, and that's the truth. It was his mate and me being stuck in the same trench, that's what it was. Took me back a bit, I'm telling you. And that other bloke—he's a regular—talking about the bodies you found in the Forest. Made me think." He stopped.

"And what you thought was that you knew who had killed them."

"I wouldn't put it as strong as that, guv! I'd read their names in the paper, see, and I put two and two together, but—"

"But why in heaven's name didn't you come to us?"

"Because I'm only guessing, aren't I," Shadd said uneasily. "Two and two don't always add up to four, and I wouldn't want to get a pal in trouble over nothing. I bet you lot at the Yard aren't that keen on people that come running to you with guesses."

"It depends on the person and what led him to that conclusion." And, to be honest, on how desperate they were for any little scrap of information. "You're a respectable business man. We would have listened. We'll listen now."

"I dunno—"

"Mr. Shadd, this 'pal' of yours may be a multiple murderer!"

"But it's not like he's picking off targets at random. If he was, I'd've never've guessed."

"Explain. Now."

"Well, I hope you're comf'table, then," the landlord said with a sigh, "because it's a long story."

TWENTY

When the ghastly Gant left the Rose and Crown, and Daisy and Sakari had discussed how ghastly he was, they found themselves at a loose end.

"I wonder if we also ought to go up to the school," said Sakari.

"Just what I was thinking. It's all very well to tell the girls not to talk about Harriman's death. I'm sure they must be more upset about it than they seemed. Someone's bound to notice and ask what's the matter."

"You told Ghastly Gant to see the headmaster. Perhaps we ought to inform the headmistress of what has occurred."

"Good idea—so that she'll understand if the girls, Lizzie especially, behave oddly. Miss Priestman frightens me rather, though."

"Nonsense, Daisy."

"She does. She reminds me of my own headmistress, who was a real Tartar."

"You were a pupil then, no doubt an erring pupil."

"Well, sometimes," Daisy admitted.

Sakari laughed. "As I thought. It is not like you to quail when action is necessary."

"My friends and I did used to get into mischief. I remember when Lucy and I climbed out of the bathroom window onto the roof of the kitchen. . . ."

"But why, Daisy?"

"It seemed like a good idea at the time."

"You English are all mad," Sakari said with conviction. "Now you are a parent, a worried parent. I assure you, Miss Priestman is very kind. She could not have been more reassuring when I first talked to her about sending Deva here."

"All the same, I wish I'd thought to give Belinda a note to take to her."

"Had you done so, the constable might have been suspicious. I am certain it is as well that you did not. Come, you have faced any number of murders—"

"Not all that many!"

"Any number," Sakari repeated, "without turning tail. *And* climbed out of upstairs windows. You are quite brave enough to face Miss Priestman. I shall send for a taxi. Ring the bell, dear Daisy. I have been bouncing up and down all afternoon like a rubber ball."

"No you haven't. Somehow you induced Gant to do it for you."

Daisy rang the bell. A short time later they were jouncing up the hill in a pre-War Vauxhall, hoping they would make it to the school before the rain started. Ahead, at the top, a fleeting glimpse of sun made the red-brick water tower stand out against dark clouds. The taxi's hood was up, but it looked as if it probably leaked in a dozen places.

Gant's police car was parked in the school drive, near the central tower beneath which the headmaster's office was located.

"Stop here," Daisy told the driver. To Sakari she said, "We don't want to run into the inspector. Let's go straight in at the girls' end."

Miss Priestman's quarters were at the west end of the long

building. The girls' entrance, not intended for visitors, led them into uncharted byways, clean but rather utilitarian, with concrete floors. Daisy's school, for young ladies of the aristocracy, had been far more inviting—unless her memory painted it in rosy colours, as seemed quite likely.

Neither of them had previously penetrated thus far without a guide. Looking round the big room, with its rows of battered wooden tuck-boxes and the corner dedicated to weekly shoe-cleaning, and not a soul in sight, Sakari said plaintively, "Where is everyone?"

"Bel said they all go out for walks on Sunday afternoons."

"Again this unnatural passion for walking! If they do not come in soon, they will all be soaked to the skin. Do you know how to get from here to Miss Priestman's apartments?"

"Haven't a clue."

"I could show you the way, if you like," said a hesitant voice. From a hitherto unnoticed corner a girl appeared, her finger marking her place in a book. "But you'll have to promise not to tell on me."

"Tell what?" Sakari asked.

"I'm supposed to be out getting fresh air and exercise, but I'd rather read."

"I have every sympathy."

"So have I," Daisy agreed. For all her derring-do where window-climbing was concerned, she had always resented being chased outside when all she wanted was to read in peace. "We won't say a word."

Their guide escorted them as far as Miss Priestman's door. "Wait just a minute before you knock, if you don't mind," she said, "so that I can get out of sight." She disappeared as quickly and thoroughly as she had appeared.

"You see," said Daisy, raising her hand to knock, "headmistresses are inherently scary."

"When you are disobeying rules. So are policemen when you are disobeying laws. I do not speak from experience, naturally."

Daisy laughed. "Naturally. All the same, I hope she won't be too annoyed at our interrupting her day of rest."

Miss Priestman opened the door. "The teacher on duty can—Oh, Mrs. Fletcher, isn't it? And Mrs. Prasad." She frowned, but even to Daisy it looked like a frown of concern, not disapproval. "Is something the matter? Do come in. It's a little untidy, I'm afraid."

"We're sorry to disturb you on a Sunday afternoon," said Daisy, "but we do feel you ought to be warned. Quite apart from the girls, that is."

"Warned?" Miss Priestman said in alarm. "Your daughters? You'd better sit down and tell me all about it."

The small sitting room, was furnished with a flap-top desk, many bookcases, and several slightly shabby but comfortable armchairs. They all sat, and Daisy looked at Sakari.

"It is your story, Daisy," she said unhelpfully.

So Daisy plunged in. She explained about taking the girls, including Elizabeth Germond, to Bridge End Garden after Meeting. She told how they had gone into the maze on their own, and how she had heard Lizzie start to scream.

"Good gracious! Not one of those men who . . . like Noah?"

"Noah?" asked Daisy, confused.

"When he was drunk," Miss Priestman explained. "Though the Bible says he was within his tent and only his sons saw him, so it seems to me no great sin. But there are men who . . . er . . ."

"I know what you mean," Daisy said hurriedly. "No, nothing like that. Much worse."

"Worse? Good gracious!"

"A body. A corpse. Of someone she knew. One of the teachers, in fact."

"Howard Harriman."

"Good gracious, how did you guess?"

"He didn't take breakfast. He was a rigid stickler for discipline, and he would never have shirked it for anything far short of death. In the *maze*? What on earth was he doing in the maze? Oh, but of course you wouldn't know."

Daisy had no intention of revealing Harriman's spying on Tesler and Miss Bascombe, which was in any case at best a rumour. But she felt a sudden qualm: Tesler and Miss Bascombe, between them, would they have been capable of a deadly attack on their tormentor?

"Heart failure, I suppose," Miss Priestman continued. "I'm surprised. He kept himself very fit. How dreadful that Elizabeth should have discovered the body! I quite understand your concern."

"Unfortunately Melanie—Mrs. Germond—had to return to London, so we said we'd make sure poor Lizzie is all right. It was a shock to Deva and Belinda, too, though they didn't see him. But what I haven't made clear is that Mr. Harriman's death doesn't appear to have been natural."

"Good gracious!"

"The police are investigating. They're talking to Mr. Rowntree now. Mrs. Prasad and I thought you ought to know what's going on . . . and we're hoping the girls won't be drawn into the investigation and further upset." Daisy hesitated. Whatever she said, it would be obvious she had misled, if not outright lied to the police. How would the upright Quaker react to her deception? She ploughed on: "You see, somehow the police seem to have got the impression that I found him."

"Indeed!" said Miss Priestman, adding dryly, "I wonder how that happened. Your husband is a policeman, is he not, Mrs. Fletcher? A detective, I believe."

"Alec has nothing whatsoever to do with this case. And I hope to keep it that way."

"Well, that is your business. My concern is Elizabeth and your daughters. Where are they at present?"

"They seemed to be all right, so we sent them back to school, while we were interviewed by the detective in charge. The constable who was first to arrive on the scene told them not to talk about it."

"Which they probably have not, so far, or I would have heard sooner. Nonetheless, they must be in a state of shock, however normal they may appear. It seems to me they would benefit from a few days in the San, where Sister could keep an eye on them."

"The Sanatorium?" said Sakari. "An excellent idea."

"Perfect," Daisy agreed. The school nurse could keep an eye on them, and Gant couldn't. Nor would they be tempted to tell their friends the whole story.

"They ought to be outside." Miss Priestman glanced at the window. "But it's nearly four o'clock and beginning to rain, so everyone will be coming in. You'll want to talk to the girls, I expect?"

"Yes." *But not*, Daisy thought, *in this room under the headmistress's eye.* "Could we meet them at the San?"

"Certainly. Let me see, Miss Bascombe and Mr. Tesler took the children down to Meeting, so they'll go off duty at four. Let me see who's taking over." She went to her desk and consulted a list. "Yes. If you wouldn't mind waiting here for a short time, I'll go and make the necessary arrangements."

She left. Sakari said, "You see, Daisy, she is very kind."

"And discreet. For an awful moment, I was afraid she'd ask me whether Alec would approve of my letting Gant misinterpret what happened."

"I assume he would not."

"Probably not. Definitely not. But considering how uncooperative Gant was, and the fact that I'm protecting Bel as well as Lizzie, I don't think he'd be as furious as he would in other circumstances. Still, I hope he never finds out."

"It is most fortunate that Melanie decided her presence was more necessary at home than here. She was not at all happy at leaving the inspector in ignorance, it seemed to me, yet she did not want him to be troubling Lizzie. She might have given us away inadvertently."

"She was glad to escape, if you ask me. She hates to be caught up in such murky affairs."

"And never was before she met you, Daisy! Have you already decided what happened? Who killed Harriman and moved the body to the maze?"

"Heavens no. There are too many suspects. I wasn't misleading Ghastly Gant when I told him that. Harriman was too nasty to too many people to . . ." She stopped as the door opened.

Miss Bascombe came in. She looked very much under the weather, her face pale, her voice uncertain. "Miss Priestman asked me to take you to the San? It's only a three minute walk. . . ."

"I hope you have umbrellas," said Sakari. "I dislike walking in the rain even more than when it is fine."

"There should be some in the stand by the door. Have Deva and Belinda been taken ill? I'm so sorry! I've been on duty and I ought to have known."

Daisy, seeing Sakari open her mouth to answer, laid a hand on her arm. She didn't really think Miss Bascombe had had anything to do with Harriman's death, but nor did she think this was the moment to broach the subject, if that was what Sakari had been about to do.

"Nothing serious," she said, as they followed the games mistress from the room.

"That usually means a rash that might be catching," said Miss Bascombe with a sigh. "I hope we're not in for an epidemic. Miss Priestman sent her apologies for not saying goodbye. She was on her way to see Mr. Rowntree."

She led them out by a side door, collecting three umbrellas on the way.

"Miserable weather," said Daisy, as raindrops pattered on the black oiled silk. "I don't know why, but whatever it's doing, sun or shine, I'm always sure it will go on forever. I didn't even bring an umbrella or a mac."

"I'm glad it held off till now," said Miss Bascombe. "Taking the children down to Meeting in the rain involves such a fuss and bother."

"It is fortunate," said Sakari, "that we decided not to wait until this afternoon to take the girls to the Bridge End Gardens."

Miss Bascombe gasped audibly.

"Are you all right?" Daisy asked, mentally castigating Sakari. She was apt sometimes to rush in where angels feared to tread—which admittedly was pretty much what Alec had been known to say of Daisy.

"Yes! Oh yes! I—I turned my ankle a little but it's nothing. You know how sometimes one is afraid for a moment that—that one has ricked it or even sprained it, but it turns out to be nothing. There must have been a larger stone among the gravel, and I happened to step on it. I'm quite all right, really. We were really very lucky that the fine weather held for sports day, weren't we? If anything is worse than running races in mud, I don't know. . . ." Her voice trailed away.

She did *know what was worse*, Daisy thought.

Was it possible that Tesler, with his crippled hand, could have delivered the blow that killed Harriman? He had surely developed the strength of his left arm and hand to compensate. He might even be left-handed—Daisy realised she didn't know. But wouldn't it have taken a two-handed swing to create that horrible dent in the victim's skull? Besides, what she had heard and observed of Tesler's character argued against his having attacked the bully even verbally, let alone physically.

Miss Bascombe herself was a sportswoman. She was probably quite strong enough to do the damage. Tennis, rounders, hockey, netball, gymnastics, swimming, she taught all of them. A hockey stick would make a good weapon, or a rounders bat, more likely close to hand at this time of year. Had she swung out at Harriman in a fury when he taunted Tesler once too often?

Tesler's principles might prevent his resorting to violence, but that didn't mean he wouldn't help his sweetheart conceal her crime.

Supposing they had the means to transport Harriman's

body to the Garden at the other end of town, they'd still have quite a job to carry it into the Garden, even with two of them. They would have had to do it after the place was closed to the public, which presumably would involve climbing over the wall. Would Tesler be able to manage that, even without the deadweight of a body to contend with?

Then, why all the way to the maze? To delay discovery of the body, Daisy supposed. It might not have been found till it started to smell. Her nose wrinkled at the thought.

All the same, they would have risked getting lost in the maze—unless they'd visited it so often they knew every twist and turn. Perhaps they'd even drawn up a plan of it, so as to find their way easily to the privacy of the central space. Tesler was a scientist, after all, and scientists were always drawing diagrams, weren't they?

Or the whole business might have taken place in Bridge End Garden in the first place. If Tesler and Miss Bascombe had lingered after closing time and seen Harriman spying on them. . . . No rounders bat available though. Daisy couldn't think of anything they might have found or taken with them that could be used as a weapon. It hadn't even been umbrella weather.

All sheer speculation, she thought with a mental sigh. She had built a house of cards on the couple's obvious inquietude at the beginning of Meeting and Miss Bascombe's present state of nervous tension. Doubtless they were on edge because of some minor disagreement.

While Daisy had been constructing her fragile edifice of wild theories, Miss Bascombe was babbling away rather feverishly to Sakari's sceptical ear about the importance of physical exercise. As Daisy's house collapsed under the weight of her own scepticism, they reached the Sanatorium.

Miss Bascombe opened the door and ushered them in. "Ring the bell," she said, "and Sister will come. I do hope the girls are all right. Are you staying in town? To make sure they . . . haven't caught anything really serious, I mean."

"We'll be staying on at the Rose and Crown for a couple of days at least."

"Oh. That will . . . be nice for them." She scurried away without giving them a chance to thank her for her guidance.

"I wonder why Miss Priestman sent a teacher to escort us," said Daisy, "rather than one of the children."

"Perhaps she feared that we might talk about Harriman. A teacher would be more discreet than a pupil about anything she overheard. Now, Daisy, you were very silent all the way here, and I bore with the young woman's chatter to allow you to think in peace. Have you at last worked out who killed Harriman?"

"Don't expect miracles! No, all I've done is demolish a theory or two."

"I knew it!" said Sakari triumphantly. "Later you will tell me, and we shall stick the shards back together. We cannot allow Inspector Gant to reach a solution before us."

Daisy laughed. "If I hadn't met Gant, I'd say you were being excessively optimistic. As it is, it seems as likely—or unlikely—that we'll solve it as that he will."

TWENTY-ONE

Against the wall stood a small table with a brass bell and a vase of stiff orange marigolds, their somewhat acrid smell faintly medicinal. Daisy tapped the bell.

Nothing happened.

After waiting for a few moments, Sakari sat down heavily on a chair, one of two on either side of the table. "I must take the weight off my feet. Perhaps the young woman is correct about the desirability of regular physical exercise."

"I'm sure she is." Daisy glanced about the entrance and spotted a door with a sign: SISTER. "Shall I ring again or knock on the door?"

"Patience, Daisy. Perhaps she is busy elsewhere and cannot hear the bell."

"In which case, I'll have to go and look for her. No, listen. I can hear voices in her room."

She was about to go over and knock when the door opened. A small woman appeared, dressed in the uniform of a nurse, a dark blue frock with white collar and cuffs and a white, starched headdress. "I'm sorry, I'm busy," she said. She looked worried and more than a little vexed. "Would you mind waiting just a— Oh, you must be Deva's mother?"

"I am."

"And I'm Belinda's."

"Thank goodness you're here. Your daughters, and Elizabeth Germond, arrived a couple of minutes ago, saying—"

"Mummy!" Bel dodged past Sister and flung herself at Daisy. "One of the prefects said Miss Priestman said we had to come here immediately and not wait to get our things and we don't know why because we're not ill, and Sister won't believe us!"

"I've *tried* to ring Miss Priestman but she doesn't seem to be in her room—"

"I wish Mummy had stayed," said a forlorn little voice, as Deva rushed to hang on Sakari's arm.

"Lizzie, darling, your mother knew we'd take care of you, Mrs. Prasad and I, and she felt she ought to go home to your little sister and brother."

"That's what she said. But all the same . . ." Lizzie bit her lip. "I expert my father would have been annoyed if she had stayed. He doesn't like it when she's away."

"Oh." Lizzie bit her lip. "I expect my father would have been annoyed if she had stayed. He doesn't like it when she's away."

Daisy and Sakari exchanged a glance. Both their husbands had given up trying to dictate their movements long ago.

Daisy gave Lizzie a hug.

"We shall stay in Saffron Walden for as long as you need us, Elizabeth," Sakari assured her.

"Would someone kindly explain to me just what's going on?" enquired Sister, with a touch of impatience. "Are these children ill or are they not?"

"Not," five voices assured her.

"Could we go into your office, Sister?" Daisy suggested. "I'll explain what I can, though I'd better leave it to Miss Priestman to give you what details she thinks appropriate."

Sister turned back into her room, her back as stiff as her headdress. She sat down behind her desk, while Daisy and Sakari took the other two chairs, Sakari with one arm round Deva, Daisy with both arms occupied.

Daisy continued, "The girls had a very disturbing experience this morning, especially Lizzie. We, including Miss Priestman, are concerned that they may suffer after-effects. Nightmares, and so on," she said rather vaguely. "Sort of like shell-shock. Also, Miss Priestman's naturally anxious that they shouldn't talk to the other children about what happened."

"Mummy, we wouldn't! The policeman said not to talk to *any*one."

"Policeman!" Sister exclaimed. "Very well, I'm sure I don't want to pry into police business. But the girls arrived without a note from Matron, or their night things, or a change of underwear, or their toothbrushes, or anything at all."

Deva piped up. "Bella Sadler told us Miss Priestman said to run down right away. She's a prefect, so we did, even though it was beginning to rain and we didn't have our coats."

"You'll all be coming down with colds next!"

"It wasn't raining hard," said Lizzie. She felt her shoulders. "I'm not even damp anymore. Mrs. Fletcher, do you really think I'm going to have nightmares?"

"I shouldn't think so," Daisy said cheerfully. She felt that expecting nightmares would probably ensure having them. Perhaps she ought to have talked to the nurse without the girls present, but then they'd have been worrying about what was being said behind their backs.

Sister was still worrying about practicalities, such as obtaining the girls' clothes, ordering their tea—the hour for which was fast approaching—and whether she could squeeze all three into the two-bed isolation ward upstairs. "Because I have four in the main girls' ward already, two asthmatics, an upset tummy—"

"You need not concern yourself with tea, Sister," Sakari interrupted. "We shall take our three into the town to eat. Such was our original intention and so we informed the school before coming for the weekend. May I use your telephone to ring for a taxi?"

With obvious relief, Sister agreed. "That would give me time to get everything organised," she said. "I really must have a word with the headmistress. . . ." She started making a list.

The girls voted for the Cross Keys again for high tea. Their appetites didn't appear to have suffered from their disturbing experience, nor from the picnic lunch they had avidly consumed immediately thereafter. Daisy and Sakari kept the conversation turned away from the Bridge End Garden and what had happened there.

Afterwards, Sakari had a taxi summoned to take the trio back to the San, though they would have been quite happy to walk up the hill. Even Lizzie was cheerful, looking forward to missing classes for a day or two.

Waving good-bye as the taxi drove off, Daisy said, "I'd be surprised if their teachers don't set them work to do. At my school, one had to be at death's door to avoid lessons. I didn't want to depress their high spirits by warning them."

"I am glad Miss Priestman thought to send them to the Sanatorium, and that Sister will arrange for all three to share a room. It is better not to wake alone from a nightmare."

"Much. And speaking of nightmares, I really don't want to go back to the Rose and Crown yet, in case Gant is lying in wait. I was thinking of strolling over to the church for Evensong. When we passed by this morning, it sounded as if they have good music. Will you come with me? You survived Meeting, and if we sit at the back, you needn't worry about all the goings-on, the kneeling and standing and so on. It's no farther to walk than back to the Rose and Crown."

"But it is uphill, Daisy. In the rain! And I would like to discuss your theories. We can instruct the hotel people not to tell anyone we have come in, and go up to one of our rooms."

"Gant's a policeman. They might feel obliged to tell him."

"This is true. Not everyone possesses your blithe insouciance when it comes to concealing information from the police."

"Blithe insouciance? I'd have you know I quake in my shoes every time—"

"Every time! You are hardened in deceit, do not deny it. Come, if we are to walk uphill to the church, we had better get going. I am glad Miss Bascombe forgot to take the umbrellas with her, so that we were able to borrow them."

"She was in no state to remember them. It's odd. . . . But we'll talk about that later."

The interior of St. Mary's—*Perpendicular,* Daisy thought, though she was a little vague about architecture—and the music were well worth dragging Sakari up the hill. Daisy decided she would definitely propose an article on Saffron Walden to Mr. Thorwald, her American editor.

They returned to the Rose and Crown for dinner. DI Gant was not lying in wait, but as they reached the pudding course, a message was brought to them: He had arrived and wanted to see Daisy.

Daisy was speechless. She had thought herself safe for the day, though she should have considered the irregular hours worked by detectives. Somehow she hadn't expected Gant to stay on the job late. After all, he had abandoned the triple burial site before Alec even arrived there.

Sakari spoke for her. "Tell the inspector that Mrs. Fletcher will receive him when she has finished her dinner."

"I've lost my appetite," said Daisy, pushing away her enormous slice of sponge cake layered with fresh strawberries and whipped cream.

"Nonsense, Daisy. It will do him good to wait. If you let him spoil your meal, you give him a victory."

"We can't have that." Daisy took another look at the cake and decided it was still irresistible—worth lingering over, in fact. She savoured every bite.

After a twenty-minute wait, Detective Inspector Gant was even more irritable than earlier in the day. When Daisy and Sakari joined him and his silent acolyte in the writing room, he said rudely, "I don't need Mrs. Prasad."

"But I do," said Daisy. "I'd be extremely uncomfortable shut up alone in here with two men who are virtual strangers."

"But we're police officers, madam!"

"So is my husband. Perhaps I should send for him to come and—"

"That won't be necessary," Gant conceded with a martyred air. "Mrs. Prasad may stay."

As Sakari had already sat down and looked singularly immoveable, he had little choice, short of arresting her for obstruction. It was a near thing, though, when a waiter brought in the ladies' coffee, and Sakari decided she wanted a liqueur with it. Daisy was sure she was just being awkward, and she guessed Gant realised it, too. His face turned an interesting shade of mauve.

"Daisy, will you have something? A Drambuie? I know it's your favourite."

"Lovely, thank you." Might as well be hanged for a sheep as a lamb. She could do with a bracer.

So Gant had to wait for the waiter to go off and return before he could start the interview. He paced round and round the writing table till Sakari said, "Do take a seat, Inspector. You are making me quite dizzy. If you insist on disturbing us at this hour, you must take us as you find us."

"It's only nine o'clock! And may I point out, I'd no intention of disturbing *you*." He sat down. "*You're* at liberty to leave!"

"Do you imagine I could rest easy," Sakari said soulfully, "while you interrogate my dearest friend?"

Daisy frowned at her irrepressible friend. Sakari sighed and fell silent. The waiter came in with the liqueurs and poured out their coffee.

"Anything else, madam?"

Sakari opened her mouth. Daisy and Gant waited on tenterhooks, but all she said was, "No, thank you. That will be all. For now."

Gant pursed his lips but managed to contain himself in the face of the final provocation. "Mrs. Fletcher, all I want is for you to go over again exactly what you saw and did when you found the body."

"If you're hoping I'll remember some clue I didn't mention before, I'm afraid you'll be disappointed. But here goes."

Once again, the way he had worded his request allowed her to leave the girls out of her story. She began with the moment when she had turned the corner and seen Harriman lying there. As far as she was aware, she didn't add or alter any significant details. Gant, checking her recital against the constable's report and the notes his subordinate had taken first time round, was obviously as disappointed as Daisy had predicted. Had he expected she would suddenly remember having come across a cudgel, nicely adorned with fingerprints, and tidied it out of the way, into the hedge?

"As soon as I'd made sure he was past needing help, I left. I'm afraid I didn't notice any footprints or cigarette ends, or helpful scraps of cloth caught in the hedges as the gardener guided me out of the maze."

"Ah yes, the gardener: Did he look at the body, examine it, touch it?"

"No, he refused to go round the corner. He couldn't see it from where he was." Daisy hardly dared to breathe. Surely he must be wondering about the sequence of events, just when the gardener had come upon the scene, how she had summoned him if she was lost in the maze, all the questions she didn't want him to ask.

Apparently not. "Fishy," said Gant. "He wouldn't look at it; he won't talk about it; what has he got to hide?"

"You suspect the gardener?"

"He's on the spot. His cottage is just off the footpath to the Garden, so he wouldn't have to be traipsing all over town. He can find his way about the maze. He's strong enough—all that digging. He has a shed full of tools, lots of 'em with handles that could have inflicted the blow. *Had*, I should say. We've taken them away to be examined."

"But what motive could he possibly have had?"

Gant laid his finger against his nose with a sly look. "From what I hear, the deceased had a nasty habit of insulting people. Bullying sort of a bloke, picked on them that couldn't fight back. The Garden's open late on Saturday evenings in the summer. Who's to say he didn't go there after this sports day affair and pick a quarrel with the gardener? Threatened to report him for sitting down on the job. Insulted his marrows, maybe!"

"That's awfully hard to believe." Daisy hoped she wasn't going to have to correct the inspector's misapprehensions in order to save the gardener's skin. Actually, though, nothing he had said or done contradicted the theory. He had been extremely unwilling to go to the maze, only agreeing when she told him the police had been sent for. "It seems so unlikely that Harriman would have gone there after a very busy day."

"He ended up there, didn't he?" said Gant irrefutably.

"Is the gardener your only suspect?" Daisy asked, not really expecting an answer.

But he was in a chatty mood. "Like you said, there's a lot of people we've got to sort out, what with teachers and visiting parents and the older boys. Half the parents don't live in Essex. That'd really make things difficult, except that hardly any of 'em stayed in the town overnight."

"Someone could have killed Harriman and then gone home. Do you know what time he died?"

"Not yet. Nor I wouldn't tell you if I did. Once I know, that'll narrow things down a lot, of course. No good asking people for alibis when you don't know the time of death."

"Very true," said Daisy.

Mistaking her ironic comment for approval, he preened. "Mind you, there's another one I've got my eyes on, besides the gardener. Good, solid motive. I just can't see how he could've done it. Got no legs, you see. One of the teachers, name of Pencote. D'you know him?"

"Yes, he teaches my daughter English." Cautiously, she

asked, "What makes you think he would have liked to murder Harriman?"

"He was witnessed shouting at him and threatening him with one of his crutches, on the school field yesterday. The trouble is, I can't for the life of me see how anybody as badly crippled as him could have managed it."

"I quite agree, Inspector. He couldn't possibly."

Gant looked gratified. "We have to consider every possibility," he said pompously, "but Mr. Pencote is an impossibility. If you happen to remember anything else, Mrs. Fletcher, anything at all, please telephone the local police station at any hour."

"Are you going to work all night, Inspector?" asked Sakari.

Flushing, he said pettishly, "You can't interview people in the middle of the night, madam. Besides, a man needs his sleep if he's to outwit villains. The local police will take messages for me."

"I'll ring them right away," Daisy said quickly, "if I think of anything I've forgotten to report."

"Thank you, madam. I'll say good-night, then."

He brought the silent acolyte to heel with a crooked finger and departed.

"Well!" said Sakari. "I can't believe he told you so much! Or anything at all. You must have learnt your interrogation technique from Alec."

"That's part of it. Mostly, it's just that you were so obnoxious, darling, that in comparison, I was charming!"

"You have pulled the wool over his eyes nicely so far. Little does he know he ought to be enquiring not as to what you have forgotten to report but what you have chosen not to report."

"We can but hope," said Daisy, holding up crossed fingers. "Is there any coffee left in the pot? My throat's dry after going through all that again."

Sakari felt the coffee pot. "It is barely lukewarm. I shall order another pot, and you deserve another Drambuie as a reward for brilliant obfuscation. I should have asked the inspector to ring the bell before he left."

"Shall we move to the lounge? It's much more comfortable."

"Privacy is more important at present than comfort. You have still to explain your theories, Daisy."

So Daisy rang the bell, and once they were provided with hot coffee and another tiny glass of liqueur each, she expounded her reasoning.

Sakari listened to her speculations with interest, but frowned when she unravelled the case against Tesler and Miss Bascombe. "Are you certain you do not dismiss your suspicions because you like Mr. Tesler and admire his character?"

"How can I tell?" said Daisy crossly. "It's true that I don't want to think they're guilty, but I truly don't believe it, either."

"What would Alec say?"

"That's easy. He'd tell me it's none of my business and I'm not to meddle in a police investigation."

"In spite of his unfortunate experience with Detective Inspector Gant?"

"He does have a low opinion of Gant."

"So perhaps he would not mind your meddling quite so much. However, this is not at all to the point. What would be his opinion of your basing your case, or your lack of a case, on your view of the suspect's character?"

Daisy pondered. "I think he'd say, character can be a guide but not a determining factor, and to what extent it guides one should be based on how well one knows the suspect. I suppose I can't claim to know Tesler well after talking to him a few times."

"And hearing about him from Belinda, I am sure."

"Yes," said Daisy, brightening. "She really likes him, and not just because she's keen on science. She loves English, too, but prefers Tesler to Pencote because unlike Pencote, who has quite a temper, he never gets 'in a bate,' as they say. Alec would take her opinion into account."

"Unfortunately, one cannot expect the same of Gant. Do not look so downcast, Daisy. Fortunately there are plenty of other suspects."

"With whom I'm even less familiar."

"Did you not hear the headmaster speaking of his dislike of Harriman? When we were sitting on those abominably uncomfortable chairs on the field?"

Daisy burst out laughing. "Darling, you can't suggest Mr. Rowntree might have killed Harriman because he was a rotten choice as a member of staff!"

"Suppose he cherishes the school as if it were his own child. What if Harriman were to ruin its reputation, so that parents no longer wish to entrust their children to it?"

"He'd give him the sack."

"Perhaps he cannot. Do not teachers belong to unions? Everyone else seems to. But never mind. As you told Gant, there are a great many possible suspects of whom we know little or nothing."

"Yes, and probably never will know much. My only reason for picking out Tesler and Miss Bascombe was that I do know them a little. But I must admit, I still wonder what they were so upset about today!"

TWENTY-TWO

Shadd had trouble finding the right way to start his long story. Thinking about it, he looked unseeingly round the dimly lit stock room. His roving gaze paused on the massive figure of Tom, uncomfortably perched on a crate of Gordon's gin. He started to sweat heavily and wiped his brow with the back of his sleeve.

"You gotta understand, guv, I didn't know what he was going to do. I couldn't've guessed, could I!"

"Let's start with his name," Alec suggested in his most soothing voice. He was afraid the landlord might decide silence was the better part of discretion before he'd given that essential bit of information.

"Clem—Clement Rosworth."

Not John Smith, thank goodness! Ernie wrote it down and kept his pencil poised.

"How did you come to know Rosworth, Mr. Shadd?"

"We grew up just round the corner from each other, right here in Tottenham. Went to school together, went to Spurs games, kicked a ball round, and dreamt of getting on the team. Fat chance! Me dad was a tapster, so I went in as pot-boy at fourteen. Clem, he had a yen to see the world and got took on by a carter. I didn't see much of him for a while, just when he'd come home to visit his mum."

"When was this?"

"In the '90s. Must've been roundabout 1898, '99, he met a girl somewheres not too far off—St. Albans, it was. Baby on the way, you know how it goes, so he married young. Well, being a travelling man, he was off on a job when she went into labour early. The baby survived but his wife died. He brought the boy back home and his mother took him in—still had a couple of her own at home."

"Is she still around? The mother?"

"Nah, she died a few years ago. Dunno where the rest of 'em went off to. There's none left hereabouts."

A pity, Alec thought. "Go on."

"Well, Clem, he worshipped that kid. Quit his long-distance carting because he wanted to stay nearby. I was a barman meself by then. Talked to some pals and found him a job as drayman with a local brewery."

Ernie looked up from his rapidly filling notebook with a triumphant expression. Here was additional evidence for his beloved pub link.

"What's the name of the brewery?" Alec asked.

"That won't help you. It went out of business years ago. Clem got taken on by McMullen's."

"Where are they based? Local?"

"Hertford. Not too far. McMullen's Hertford Brewery."

"Right. Go on."

"Then the War came along and Clem was called up in the first draft. So was I, but I ended up in France, and he got sent to Mess-pot."

"Rosworth never fought in France?" So what became of the military link?

"Nah. Learnt to drive a motor-lorry out East. Me, I ended up as a mess orderly."

"A nice easy billet."

"Don't make me laugh. Wasn't that fun in the trenches, trying to cater to a bunch of officers that like as not had been blowed up before you got there, and often as not ended up eating the same rations as the men! I can tell you, I carried a rifle more often than a soup-plate, and they drank their whisky straight from the bottle. Come to think of it, it was soup near as nothing done me in. Buried up to me neck in a trench I was, with a satchelful of thermos flasks of soup on me back. They pulled the other blokes out easy, even the two that was dead, but that satchel got in the way and weighed me down. Nearly drowned in mud, that's me."

"And Rosworth?"

"Sand, that was his trouble. Sand and dust."

"But he came through in one piece?"

"*He* did. It was his boy didn't." Shadd passed his hand across his face as if trying to hide the first real emotion he'd shown. "Very close they was, like I told you. He missed his dad something dreadful. Lied about his age, didn't he, thinking he'd get to go join him. And where does he end up? In bloody France, in my outfit, under Colonel bloody Pelham."

"Ah!" said Tom softly. The others held quite still. After a short, brooding silence, Shadd continued.

"Sixteen, should've been knee-high to a brussels sprout, but he put on his growth early, did Sammy Rosworth. All the same, that mud that came up to me neck, it was up to his nose, and I'm not a tall man. Half drowned he was before they got him out. The poor little bugger should've been sent back to base to recover. Lieutenant Devine—he wasn't a captain then, not till Captain Douglas bought it—he wanted to send Sammy back, I'll give him that. But Colonel bloody Pelham said he was fit to go right back into the next trench, which hadn't collapsed—yet." Again he fell silent. "Devine didn't argue. He wasn't the arguing sort."

"Sammy was caught in a second collapse and killed?" Alec asked.

"Nah. A shell did hit it that night—five men dead—but he

was gone by then. Absent without leave. Deserting his post. The Redcaps brought him back at dawn. My sergeant—I was a corporal then—he talked to them and they said they was just returning him to the battle line. But that wasn't enough for the bloody colonel. He convened a scratch court martial—no judge-advocate nor nothing, nobody to speak for the kid. He didn't have a hope in hell, and hell was where he was, and we all was, come to that. The bastard was bound and determined to convict him."

"The other two members of the court were . . . ?"

"Come off it, guv, them's who you're here about, aren't they? He picked 'em carefully, them that wouldn't go against him. Major Halliday, he was so set on discipline, used to quote Nelson at us, you know: 'England expects that every man will do his duty.' Well, there's this to say for him, he stuck to it himself. Everything by the rule book, he was, which don't always make the best officers, mind. And Sammy broke the rules, there's no arguing about that."

"And Devine?"

"Like I said before, he wasn't the arguing sort. Not a chance he'd go against that bastard Pelham and the major. Sammy hadn't got a hope. The sergeant rounding up the firing squad had a tough time of it. Everyone made themselves scarce at the sight of him—the Boche weren't pounding us for a change. But he was a bully like the colonel. Twin souls, they was. He found his 'twelve good men and true.' Not their fault, poor buggers, and I know for a fact most of 'em aimed to miss. But it only takes one."

For a moment the only sound in the gloom was a faint murmur from the bar. Then Alec heard the softest of sighs, as if Tom, Ernie, and Mackinnon were all letting out the breath they'd been holding.

"Sixteen, shell-shocked, executed." Enough motive for any father to contemplate murder. Unhappily, this father had carried through. "How did Rosworth find out? I didn't think they notified families."

"Nah. Killed in France was what they told him. He knew I was in the same outfit and came to me to ask. I didn't want to break it to him, but he was desp'rit to know how his boy died, and did he suffer much. So I told him. Then he had to know all the details. They didn't have too many deserters in the desert—nowhere to run to." Shadd shrugged. "Maybe I should've kept me mouth shut."

"Maybe you should have," Alec agreed grimly.

"How was I to know he'd go berserk? He just got quieter and quieter when I told him how they'd blindfolded the kid and tied him to a post. Didn't even turn pale—well, after a coupla years in the desert he couldn't've, I s'pose. They used to make 'em drunk first, I've heard, but that Sergeant Harris—Harrison—I've forgot his name, something like that—he didn't give him a drop. He pinned a bit of paper over his heart for a target. The squad had their backs turned. When the sergeant gave the order to fire, they had to turn round, aim, and shoot. Only a coupla shots hit the kid, but that did for him, all right. Only takes one."

There was a long silence before Alec could bring himself to say, "When was it—how long ago, that you told Rosworth the story?"

"Not long after we was demobbed. I got the job of barman here soon as I got home, and he got his old job back. Must've been the first time I seen him after the War."

"Obviously you told him the names of the officers involved. Did you mention Sergeant Harris by name?"

"Can't remember. That was a long time ago. Prob'ly."

"And the men on the firing squad?"

"Nah, not them. Didn't have any choice, did they."

"So it's Harris we have to worry about. Harris or Harrison?"

Shadd shook his head. "Dunno. Can't remember. He wasn't my sergeant and I think he got transferred not long after. There's ways of making even a sergeant uncomf'table. Like the thought of a nasty mistake when he's making the rounds at night, sentries nervous, took him for a Boche infiltrator. . . . It happened."

"I dare say. We've got to find him. Your sergeant would know his name."

"Dead."

They would have to go back to the army records. "What about Rosworth? Where does he live? You said he still works for the brewery in Hertford?"

"McMullen's. 'Sright. That's how come I seen quite a bit of him over the years. He delivers here."

"Regularly?"

"Nah. I let 'em know when I need a delivery. Sometimes it's him, sometimes one of the other blokes that drives for 'em."

"He drives a motor-lorry, you said?"

"Sometimes. Sometimes a horse dray. Depends what other deliveries they're making. We're one of the closest customers, and you don't have to drive through the Smoke to get here. They deliver right down to the south coast. Use the lorries for that, of course. They're switching over to all motors, but it takes a few quid to spare."

"Give DC Piper their address. The brewery's." He waited till Shadd had complied. "Are they on the telephone?"

"'Spect so, but I haven't got their number. Too bloody expensive by half, trunk calls. My owners won't stand for it."

"Anyone have any questions?" Alec asked his men.

"The motor-lorries have the brewery's name painted on the sides?" Tom asked.

"What d'you think? Not likely to pass up a chance for advertising, are they?"

"What does Rosworth look like?"

"We-ell, he's not that big. About my height, but he don't look brawny. Strong as an ox, though. You have to be to shift them casks about, even with a Spanish windlass. Mid-forties, like me. But he ain't nothing special to look at, just ordinary. Hair darkish, eyes—never noticed, to tell the truth. You wouldn't pick him out of a crowd, not even you lot."

"How big are these casks?" Mackinnon wanted to know. "The ones Rosworth delivers."

Shadd waved his hands vaguely, then pointed into the dim recesses of the room. "There's some over there."

"Just tell us this," said Ernie. "Could a man fit inside one?"

"They pickled Lord Nelson in a cask of rum, didn't they? After Trafalgar?"

A few minutes later, they returned to the car. Alec had given the landlord a severe warning about withholding evidence from the police. In view of his eventual cooperation, though, he wasn't going to charge him—unless Sergeant Harris was murdered because of the delay and it could be proved that earlier information might have saved him. It would be difficult, Alec thought, considering they were still unsure of his name, let alone his whereabouts.

"Ernie, I take it you've got all those details committed to memory?"

"Course, Chief."

"Then give your notebook to Mackinnon—you have a spare on you?"

"Course, Chief!"

"Mackinnon, we're going to drop you at the nearest tube station—"

"Wood Green, Chief." Ernie pressed the self-starter and they set off. Trust him, given a chance to glance at a map in advance, to know how to get from wherever they were to wherever they were going.

"Thank you. Mackinnon, you'll go to the Yard. You and the inspector on duty will put out an all-stations call, for both Rosworth and Sergeant Harris or Harrison, and a watch on all ports for Rosworth. Don't forget a warning that he's armed. Not that we have much hope of finding him, with the rotten description we've got, if he's had the sense to abandon his lorry. You'll also try to get the War Office records people back on the job, to find out what that damn sergeant's name is and if possible where he is now. I don't expect much success with that till the morning."

"Yes, sir."

"Failing immediate action from them, and I mean immediate, you're going to have to get in touch with all the people we've already spoken to about Pelham's regiment. Apart from laying our hands on Rosworth, it's of the first importance to find out the sergeant's name."

"I understand, sir."

"The rest of us will go straight to Hertford. You can get in touch through the station there. We'll go to the brewery. With any luck we'll find someone who can give us access to the office. Don't they have to keep an eye on the beer constantly?"

"Sunday evening . . ." Tom said doubtfully.

"Well, if not, we'll have to dig up—what's his name?—the owner." Alec had made no attempt to memorise the details, his mind busy planning the necessary moves even as he listened to Shadd.

"McMullen," Ernie supplied, pulling up in front of the Wood Green underground station.

"Any questions, Mackinnon?"

"Aye, sir: Will I no need permission from Superintendent Crane, or even the Assistant Commissioner, for setting a watch on ports and such?"

"Technically, yes. But, as Tom has pointed out, it's Sunday evening. If you can't get the super on the phone first try, go ahead in the name of the Yard and hope no one asks who's authorised it. I'll take responsibility, of course."

"Thank you, sir. Good luck."

"And good luck to you," Alec said as Mackinnon got out of the car.

They headed north towards Hertford. Most of the sparse traffic was moving in the opposite direction, returning to London after a day in the country. As the built-up area fell behind them, Ernie stepped on the accelerator.

"What did I say?" he crowed. "All three victims disappeared after visiting their local pub, and all the pubs were free houses. You even mentioned, Sarge, you'd had a pint of Hertford's bitter at the Duke of York in Tunbridge Wells. No, I tell a lie, McMullen's is what you said."

"One or t'other, so I did."

"Maybe Rosworth wouldn't have got them—wouldn't even have found them—if they'd stuck to tied pubs, or just pubs that didn't sell Hertford Brewery's ales."

"It's a sobering thought, laddie. The man had the patience of an ox. He must have been looking for them for years."

"And laying his plans, Sarge. He had it pretty well taped. Bagged all three before we caught on."

"The one we have to worry about now," Alec reminded them, "is the fourth potential victim, Harris."

"Maybe we just haven't found his body yet, Chief. Maybe he does go to a tied pub, or maybe he doesn't drink, or only at home. It'd make it hard for Rosworth to even find him, let alone give him an excuse to hang about long enough to come up with a different plan."

"You're full of theories, laddie. But I've got to admit, it makes sense."

"What about your original theory, Ernie?" Alec asked. "The one you weren't willing to propound without further evidence?"

"Stuffing them into empty barrels." His attempt to sound modest was no great success. "I mean, I thought maybe the murderer was a dray-man. That business of two of the landlords saying no strangers were there, that tipped me off. Who's not a stranger yet not a local resident? The dray-man, who delivers regularly. And if that's what the murderer was, he'd have a good way to move 'em."

"A horribly unpleasant way," Alec observed. "Tied up, crouching, or perhaps bent double, unable to stir. Probably not enough air, even with vent holes."

"They must've been unconscious to start with, Chief, or

he'd never have got them in. Good job none of them was as big as Mr. Tring."

"On the contrary, laddie," Tom said soberly. It might've saved their lives. But can you imagine what they felt like when they came round? Not only cramped and stuffy, and more than likely they had headaches, but not knowing what was going to happen to them."

"Can you imagine what the boy, Sammy Rosworth, felt like?" Alec said soberly. "Not to mention his father, when he heard. This is a murderer I can almost sympathise with." Then he remembered Halliday's daughter and Devine's mother. No, in spite of the results of Halliday's rigid code and Devine's weak character, they had not deserved such horrible deaths.

Nor had Sammy Rosworth.

TWENTY-THREE

None of them, not even Ernie, was familiar with Hertford. Alec hoped to find the brewery without calling first at the police station. Explaining the situation would be a waste of precious time. Better to set things in motion and then go and apologise.

"We'll stop at a pub on the outskirts and ask how to get there," he said. "They're bound to know."

As it happened, the first pub they came to had a Hertford Brewery sign in the window. Tom went in, to reappear with directions and the landlord's opinion that no one would be there.

"I got directions to the police station, too," he said. "They're not far apart, both in the town centre."

"We'll check the brewery," Alec decided.

The big, red-brick Victorian building was easy to find, looming on a corner with woodland visible beyond.

Sniffing the pervasive aroma of malt, yeast, and hops, Tom said, "Couldn't mistake it for anything but a brewery, could you!"

It rose from one story at the front, no doubt offices, to four or five behind, capped with a tower. The lower part boasted a frivolous little domed clock tower, its golden hands showing nearly nine o'clock. Considering the time, Alec wasn't surprised that the front entrance—an equally frivolous pillared, pedimented door—was locked.

The rain had let up a bit, but dark clouds hung overhead, bringing twilight early for the time of year. Darkness would make everything more difficult.

"They must have a night-watchman, at least," Alec said, and rang the electric bell. "You two split up, reconnoitre round the sides and back."

Tom and Ernie returned before anyone came to the door.

"There's a yard at the back where they keep the lorries," Tom reported. "The night-watchman there doesn't have access to the offices, only the brewery itself, the factory as you might say. It's kept locked but he does his rounds in there two or three times a shift. He's heard they don't keep much in the way of cash in the offices; they make daily deposits at the bank, and they have their own safe."

"Seems the only break-ins they've ever had have been people after beer," Ernie put in, grinning. "There's nobody else there now, and he doesn't know the McMullens' address."

"The police station it is, then. I just hope they don't insist on getting in touch with their chief constable," Alec sighed, "though we'll have to sooner or later. He did already give us permission to interview the Hallidays. I'd rather wait till tomorrow to involve him."

Copeland, the duty sergeant at the station had already received an alert from the Yard. He was cooperative about not reporting their arrival to the inspector on duty until they had departed.

"I'll give you Mr. McMullen's telephone number and directions to his house, sir," he said, "but if you ask me, you'd do better to ask his chief clerk. He's more likely to know where to find the information you need, drivers' addresses and schedules and such. I've got Kelly's directory here, of course, but if I was your man, I'd keep moving."

"I suspect he's the sort of loner who probably lives in a boarding house. The chief clerk sounds like a good idea. I take it you know his name."

"My brother-in-law, sir. He's not on the telephone, but he lives quite near. Tell him Jimmy sent you." He wrote down his brother-in-law's name—Frederick Hodder—his address, and directions to his house.

Alec handed the paper to Ernie. "Thank you. Give my apologies to Inspector—Yates, was it?—would you, please, Sergeant, for dashing in and out so unceremoniously. Remind him Rosworth's armed. We may well call for uniformed assistance to collar him. The inspector may want to ring his superintendent for authorisation."

"I wouldn't mind having a hand in collaring the Epping Executioner!" the sergeant exclaimed.

"Great Scott, is that what the papers are calling him now?"

"Ah," said Tom, "the fellows who write the headlines always fancy a bit of alliteration."

Ernie looked impressed. Next time he had a dictionary to hand, he'd be looking up Tom's latest addition to his remarkably extensive vocabulary.

They went out to the car.

"Executioner!" Alec was not amused. "Alliteration, my foot! It sounds to me as if the Essex police are as leaky as a sieve. The press were not supposed to be told how they were killed."

"Maybe they weren't, Chief," Tom said soothingly. "Could be chance, just the alliteration, like I said."

"I'd be more inclined to credit that if it weren't for the way Gant behaved when we took over. I wouldn't put it past him to try a bit of deliberate sabotage. Come on, let's get moving."

Hodder's modest brick villa was just a few minutes walk beyond the brewery. Ernie parked the police car a few doors down the street to avoid alerting nosy neighbours. Answering the door himself, in his carpet slippers, Hodder was at first alarmed to find Scotland Yard on his doorstep on a gloomy

Sunday evening. He was reassured on hearing Sergeant Jimmy Copeland had directed them to him.

"Come in, come in, Chief Inspector. The wife and I were just listening to the wireless."

"I'm afraid I'm hoping to drag you away from your programme. We need your help."

"Goodness me!" Behind strong spectacles, his eyes shone. "But come in out of the rain to tell me about it, do. Emmy, my dear, Scotland Yard needs my help!"

"Goodness me!" His wife, as plump as he was spare, turned off the wireless set. "I'll go and make some tea."

"I'm afraid we haven't time to stop for tea, Mrs. Hodder."

Blue eyes opened wide, making her look like a china doll. "Goodness me," she repeated placidly. "Well, I'll go and make tea anyway. I could do with a cup and you won't want me listening. Do sit down, gentlemen."

"Emmy is the soul of discretion." Hodder seemed earnestly reluctant to deprive his wife of a treat.

"No, Fred, it won't do. You know what Jimmy always says, 'Those that don't know, can't tell.' If you go out, don't forget your umbrella."

"No, dear."

At last they were all seated in comfortable armchairs covered with faded chintz. Alec explained that he was looking for information about an employee of the firm. When Hodder heard that one of the Hertford Brewery drivers might be the Epping Executioner, he was horrified, but also thrilled at the possibility of being involved in his capture.

"Naturally, I know where to find such records as there may be," he said doubtfully, "only I can't promise we have up-to-date addresses for all the drivers. They get their schedules at the yard, and they're paid in cash at the office, so we're not sending anything to them in the post. These fellows who can drive heavy lorries can always find work. They come and go."

"My information is that Clement Rosworth has been with the company for many years, since before the War, with a gap for military service."

"Oh, Rosworth. You didn't mention the name. Yes, he's been with us for a long time. Are you sure he's the man you're looking for? I rarely deal with the drivers myself, but I'd be prepared to say he's a very reliable employee, a quiet chap who keeps himself to himself. Not at all the sort you'd expect to be shooting people and burying the bodies."

"I dare say you'd be surprised at how many murderers are quiet chaps who keep themselves to themselves. We haven't absolute proof of Rosworth's guilt, but at the least we need to question him as soon as possible. If you're ready, Mr. Hodder, let's get going."

"I'll just fetch my keys. And my coat and umbrella."

"You might want to change your shoes, sir," Tom suggested.

Hodder looked down at his feet. "My goodness, I quite forgot I'm in my slippers. Thank you, Sergeant."

The clerk was thrilled all over again when he found he was to have a ride in a police car, even if it was just the half-mile to the brewery. He sat in the back with Alec.

Turning the car, Ernie said over his shoulder, "I was wondering, sir, if you can give us a good description of Rosworth. What we've got isn't much use."

"Oh dear, I don't believe I can help. I must have seen him now and then over all those years, but he didn't make much impression."

"Or a photograph, maybe? A company picnic, something like that?"

"Well, yes. We've got them on the walls in the office, going back to the turn of the century. But to tell the truth, I can barely recognise myself."

"We'll take a look," said Alec. "Blowing them up—enlarging them—might help. It may be more useful to talk to someone who knows him better than you do, Mr. Hodder. How about the yard boss? The foreman, or whoever's in charge."

"Mr. Garvey. Yes, Chief Inspector, I can tell you where he lives. If he's not at home at this time on a Sunday evening, you'll catch him when the pubs close. Not that he's a heavy drinker, I wouldn't want you to think that, but he likes his pint with his friends. I find daily contact with the odours of brewing quite put me off strong drink. My wife makes excellent tea."

"'The cup that cheers but not inebriates,'" Tom intoned. "I'm partial to a good cuppa myself, and sorry we didn't have time to accept Mrs. Hodder's offer."

"You must drop by, Sergeant, any time you're in Hertford. She'll be delighted to brew a pot for you."

Before the chitchat could get out of hand, they stopped outside the brewery. Leading them to a side door, Hodder took a ring of keys from his pocket, and opened it. Apart from the smell, the offices were no different from those of any middle-sized, reasonably prosperous business. Hodder went straight to a filing cabinet labelled EMPLOYEE RECORDS. Everything was grouped by job categories and neatly alphabetised. In no time, he pulled out a folder with Clement Rosworth's name on it.

"Here we are."

Alec gestured at Ernie, who took the folder, laid it on the nearest desk, and opened it.

"Clement Rosworth. Address is a local boarding house, Chief. Run by a Miss Florence Dill." He wrote down the address in his notebook. "But there's a bunch of others crossed out. Looks as if he's moved about a bit since the War."

"Doesn't surprise me. Quite apart from the discomforts of boarding-house life, assuming he's been planning this pretty much ever since he was told, he wouldn't want to get too close to anyone."

"Chief Inspector, may I ask . . . ?" Hodder said tentatively. He had a piece of paper in his hand, taken down from several drawing-pinned to a board on the wall.

"'Fraid not, Mr. Hodder. I will say that there would not appear to be any danger to anyone at the Hertford Brewery. Telephone number, Ernie?"

"No such luck. It's mostly pay and pension details. That the schedule you've got there, Mr. Hodder?"

"Yes, Rosworth's schedule for next week. I'm afraid it's a carbon copy. The master sheet will be in the yard office."

Ernie took it and cast a glance over it. "This'll do, thank you, sir."

Meanwhile, Tom had been wandering about the room, looking at the group portraits hanging on the walls. He took one down. "This one's the latest, Chief. Looks like it might blow up well. The names are printed underneath so he's definitely in it."

"Careless of him. May we borrow it, Mr. Hodder?"

"Of course, of course. Anything I can do to help."

Tom already had the photo out of its frame. He looked at the back. "Local photographer's stamp."

"Good! One more thing, Mr. Hodder, if it won't be trespassing on your kindness. You must be anxious to get home, but I would very much appreciate it if you would accompany DC Piper to see Mr. Garvey, just to reassure him that it's in order for him to assist us."

"By all means, Chief Inspector."

"Excellent." Alec turned to the door. "I'll drop you both off at his house. I'm going to the police station to sort things out there. I'll send someone to Garvey's to drive you home, Mr. Hodder."

"Oh, no, indeed." Hodder locked the door behind him. "That won't be necessary. We're quite a small town still, though growing, growing. The rain seems to have stopped. I can very well walk home."

"It's nearly dark. I'll send the car. Piper, if you're not finished with Garvey when the car arrives, have it come back for you. We can't waste any time."

When Alec and Tom arrived at the police station, the local

superintendent was already there and the chief constable of the county was on his way. Luckily the super was a reasonable man and understood the urgency of the case. Alec hoped the CC would be willing to admit they were still on the same case. If he decided to be awkward, or to take a personal hand in things, he could delay them considerably.

Best to get things started without him.

After arranging for enlargements of the photograph to be printed, he said to Superintendent Starke, "The first thing, sir, is to find out whether Rosworth is at home. If so, we should be able to get the job done without a fuss. But I'll need to post men all round the house, or front and back if it's a terrace—"

"It is," the local inspector confirmed.

"Good. What I propose is to send DS Tring here into the house. Depending on the suspect's presence or absence, he'll attempt an arrest or have a chat with the landlady."

"To find out whether she has any idea where the fellow's got to," said Starke intelligently. Of course, superintendents, who had worked for their rank, were often if not always more intelligent than chief constables appointed because of their connections.

"Exactly, sir."

The details were quickly worked out and they left the station before either the CC or Ernie Piper arrived. A very unhappy Sergeant Jimmy Copeland was left behind to hold the fort, which included explaining matters to the chief constable.

"Sir George can't hold you responsible, Sergeant," said Starke cheerfully. "You can blame it all on me." Which was kind of him, but didn't change the fact that the blame would all be Alec's if things went wrong.

It was completely dark by now, the street lamps islands of light, but at least the rain hadn't started again. The air was cool, but fresh and pleasant.

The boarding house was just a couple of minutes' walk away. The inspector and a constable who knew the beat well were to go round to the alley at the back. Though terraced, their target was taller than its neighbours, they agreed, and easy to recognise from behind.

"Er, if you don't mind me making a suggestion, Chief Inspector," said the inspector as they reached the corner of the street, "Miss Dill is what they call a 'gentlewoman in distressed circumstances.' She might take more kindly to you than to Mr. Tring."

Tom made an inarticulate sound of protest.

"Don't you worry about that, Inspector," said Alec. "DS Tring can do genteel with the best of them. Or jovial commercial, or tough customer. His size is intimidating, but he's quick on his feet. If Rosworth is there, he's much more likely to come quietly when he sees Tom at his door, and if he doesn't, Tom can cope with him."

"Spare my blushes, Chief!"

The inspector looked Tom up and down. "Don't say I wouldn't go quietly myself," he admitted.

They split up. Alec and Tom walked briskly along the near side of the street, while Starke and a couple of detective constables strolled down the opposite pavement, apparently chatting.

The terraced row had no front gardens, just fenced areas with steps down to semi-basements, suggesting more prosperous times. Though it wasn't really very late, Alec was relieved to see a light in the bay window at the front of the boarding house. Landladies, genteel or not, were not apt to be helpful if summoned unwillingly from their beds. Taking out his pipe, he made a great play of tapping out the dottle on the fence, blowing out the last scraps of ash, taking out his tobacco pouch, selecting a pinch of tobacco and stuffing it into the bowl. The process of lighting it could be spun out indefinitely.

Meanwhile the three on the far side had stopped one house along, apparently engaged in argument. There were trees on that side, and they were nearly invisible in the shadow. And

Tom had ascended the front steps to knock on Miss Dill's front door. As Alec lit his first match, the fanlight above the door lit up, and the door was opened on a chain.

Tom raised his hat. "I do beg your pardon for disturbing you, madam," he said in the voice he kept for witnesses not merely genteel but aristocratic. "May I enquire, is Mr. Rosworth at home?"

"I believe not," said a thin, elderly voice. "I didn't hear him come in, and he hasn't left his key on the hook. I do insist on that. Suppose there were a fire and I didn't know how many people were in the house?"

"Very sensible, madam." Behind his back, Tom showed a thumbs-down sign. Alec, in any case, could hear every word.

"I'm afraid Mr. Rosworth is not an educated person—one has to take whomever one can find these days—but he is extremely reliable, although as a travelling man he cannot always let me know in advance when he will return."

"Quite understandable, madam. May I ask—But perhaps you'd allow me to come in for a moment instead of keeping you standing at the door?"

The door closed. The chain rattled. The door reopened. Tom disappeared within. Alec allowed the fourth match to light his pipe and, puffing, strolled across the street to join the disputatious group on the other side.

"What did I tell you? Tring has a deuced smooth tongue. The old lady didn't even ask who he was or what he wanted. One can't help wondering whether she has to take in boarders because she lost her money to a con man."

"He didn't have a chance to show his warrant card?" Starke asked sharply. "He'll show it once he's inside?"

"Of course, sir. From what I heard, it seems probable, but not certain, that Rosworth isn't there. He may come home, and we're a bit conspicuous. We'd better split up. You two—" he indicated the constables "—cross over. Leisurely, don't rush. One of you can go down the area steps next door, as if you're visiting a maid or the occupant of the basement flat. Stay below street level. The other can walk back and forth, smoking and glancing at your watch from time to time, as if you're waiting for your pal. You can whistle if you want, as long as you can listen at the same time. Off you go. You and I, sir, will just move closer to this tree, where the shadow's deepest."

"Don't you think—Sorry, Chief Inspector! You're in charge."

Alec managed not to grind his teeth. Superior officers accustomed to desk jobs were a real menace when they insisted on standing obbo. They'd almost always forgotten that patience was the name of the game.

"We'll just watch and listen, if you don't mind, sir."

Across the way, lights went on in the windows above the front door, successively on the first and second floors. Tom was on his way upstairs to make sure Rosworth really wasn't in his room. A couple of minutes later, his silhouette appeared on the second-floor window blind. A few seconds of shadow-play clearly indicated a negative.

Alec released his held breath.

"Should have gone on the stage," Starke murmured appreciatively as the top light went out.

The lower light disappeared.

"Now he'll have a nice chat with Miss Dill. Knowing Tring, he'll be offered a cuppa and a slice of cake, too, lucky beggar."

"Peckish?"

"Dinner seems a long time ago. I ate at five."

"Ah, those were the days! Grab a bite when you can. One tends to remember the occasional excitement and forget the inconveniences. I expect they'll be able to exhume a few sandwiches for you when we get back to the station."

"By then, I might even be ready to eat them."

"You're expecting to be here for—"

"Hush! Someone's coming."

From the direction of the town centre, a man was walking towards them. His face, shadowed by his hat, was invisible. He was not noticeably tall, nor noticeably burly, but his brisk step suggested physical strength.

"Rosworth?" breathed the superintendent.

"Could be. What little description we have is pretty vague, but such as it is, he matches."

TWENTY-FOUR

Alec recognised the approaching figure by his walk when he was still several houses away on the opposite side of the street.

"It's my man, sir. DC Piper. The one I sent to interview the supervisor of the brewery's yard." He laid his hand on the super's arm as Starke started to move. "Don't worry, he'll find us."

"Sorry!" came a whispered apology. "I'm rustier than I thought. Must get out of the office more often. Of course, Rosworth may yet turn up."

Ernie walked up to the officer who was strolling back and forth smoking. "Got a light, mate?"

"Hang on." A book of matches appeared.

For no obvious reason, since the night was still, it took three strikes for Ernie's Woodbine to catch. "Blast!" and "Must be damp. This damn weather!" came to Alec's ears, but the scratch of the matches was louder than the exchange of information he knew was going on.

"Ta, mate."

Cigarette between his lips, Ernie came across the street

in the leisurely manner Alec had recommended earlier to the two local DCs. His dark mac blended into the shadow of the next tree, then he emerged briefly into comparative light before joining them in their own patch of shadow. He dropped the cigarette and ground out the remains with his heel.

"Sir." He nodded to Starke, having evidently been told who he was. "Bad news, Chief."

"Hell!" Alec swore softly but vehemently.

"Not that bad! We've got a good chance at him. You want it here?"

"He's not likely to turn up?"

"Shouldn't think so."

"We'll go back to the station. Your fag went out. Go back and get another light. Tell him he and his pal are on obbo till relieved. They don't have to stay where they are; probably better over here. When Tom comes out, he's to come to the station. You'd better keep straight on in the direction you were going, then head back through the alley behind the row. You'll recognise the house?"

"Chief!" said Ernie reproachfully.

"There's a local inspector and a constable back there. Tell 'em the same: Stay till relieved. Off you go."

Ernie shook another cigarette from his packet. He crossed back to the other pavement. "Sorry, mate, it went out. Definitely damp."

A further exchange of flame and information took place, then Ernie went briskly on his way. When he turned the corner, Alec and Starke sauntered out from their shelter and took the direct route back towards the station, their pace increasing as soon as they were out of sight of the house.

"Both your men are admirable," Starke observed.

"I rely on them a good deal. They both use their heads and usually know what I want without long explanations. DS Tring is extremely good at what he does. DC Piper is headed upwards, if I don't miss my guess. He's young yet."

"I wonder what he meant. . . . Well, no use speculating. We'll find out soon enough."

"Sir, is the chief constable going to be a problem? Whatever Piper has to report, we'll probably have to move fast. I won't ask you to tell tales, of course, but I'd prefer to know what I'm likely to face in the way of interference, so that I can plan a way round—"

"You leave Sir George to me. He'd like to have a finger in every pie, though he doesn't understand police business. Occasionally he needs to be reminded of it." Starke sighed. "Bursting though I am with curiosity, you and your men had better find an out-of-the-way corner to do whatever you need to do. My men and the telephones and so on are at your disposal, of course. In that case, I hope you'll let me know later what's what."

"Of course, sir. I'm very grateful—"

"Tush, man, as Sir George would say, we have a multiple murderer on the loose. Anything I can do to help."

Ernie was on their heels when they reached the station. A Bentley was parked outside, a chauffeur lounging at the wheel.

"Sir George's," said Starke gloomily. They went in.

Sergeant Copeland looked up from something he was writing with a very industrious air. "Sir! Thank goodness you're back! The CC is . . . a bit annoyed at finding nobody higher than a sergeant waiting for him. He went up to your office."

"Bloody furious, is he? Thanks, Sergeant, I'll deal with him. Find a room down here to hide Mr. Fletcher in, will you? And don't let anyone interrupt him except me or DS Tring." He made for the stairs.

"Unless there's a phone call or message from the Yard," Alec amended, "or if the blown-up photos arrive."

"A wire came just a minute ago, sir." Copeland held out a memo slip. "I was just logging it in. Very slowly, in case the CC came down again and found me with nothing to do."

Alec passed it to Ernie. "I suppose you've already logged the time you received this?" he asked the sergeant.

"Yes. Sorry, sir, it'd be as much as my job's worth to change it."

"Of course. Never mind, just don't log us or Mr. Starke into the station just yet, will you?"

"Right you are, sir. Luckily the CC don't concern himself with such petty details as log books. I take it you don't want me to get the Yard on the line for you!"

"No, but come to think of it, you'd better send a wire to DS Mackinnon: 'Urgent all morning dailies hold space front page photo,' signed, 'Fletcher.'"

"Will do. Now, where am I going to hide you? Short of the broom cupboard or the lock-up—"

"Any office will do. If Mr. Starke can't hold Sir George off, I don't want to look as if we're hiding from him. We wouldn't mind being interrupted by a cup of tea, if it's not too much trouble."

"No trouble at all, sir. Down the passage there, second door on the left, should suit. There's a telephone if you need it."

The room, with its drab paint and the well-worn furniture was just as Alec expected. He and Ernie sat down on either side of one of the two desks, Ernie already reporting before his trousers touched the seat.

"I know where Rosworth ought to be, Chief. Course, I don't know if he's there. If he is, there's a chance he may try a get-away to the Continent."

"Mackinnon says he's arranged for the watch on all ports."

"On passenger ferries, not freighters. Mr. Garvey says every few months the brewery ships a load over to Amsterdam and Rotterdam, via Harwich and The Hook. There's hotels over there that cater to English businessmen, and they want English beer. Rosworth's conscientious and reliable so it's generally him that drives the stuff to Harwich and sees it on board. He actually goes on board to see it properly stowed, so I reckon he could stow himself away easy enough."

"When?"

"He left midday yesterday, Mr. McMullen not expecting his drivers to work on Sundays. Union members, TGWU, means overtime pay. The ship's expected to load tomorrow morning and sail when the cargo's all aboard. The harbour's not tidal, it seems. But because it's a freighter, not a ferry, the schedule's erratic."

"All the same . . ." Alec reached for the telephone. "Garvey gave you the name of the ship?"

"SS *Mayfly*. May Line: *May Tree, May Queen*—"

"Sergeant Copeland here," said the phone.

"Copeland, it's DCI Fletcher. I must send an urgent wire to the Harbour Master at Harwich."

"Just dictate it, sir, and I'll phone it in. Ready when you are."

As soon as Alec picked up the phone, Ernie had started writing. Now he pushed his notebook across the desk. He had written a list of the essential facts, so that all Alec had to do was string them together in as few words as possible. With distaste, he began: "Epping Executioner . . ." He hated the phrase, but it would get attention.

He didn't want to waste time compressing his message into an absolute minimum number of words, so it came out rather lengthy. The Hertfordshire and Essex police could fight it out with the Met over who was to pay for it.

"Details photograph follow," he ended, and signed it in full, "Detective Chief Inspector Fletcher CID Scotland Yard."

"Got it, sir."

"Read it back, please."

Copeland obliged.

"Right, thanks, send it." Once the cable was winging its way towards Harwich, Alec felt his tension lessen slightly. "Surely we've got him. If he goes there."

"Let's hope. He left the brewery with the lorry on Saturday morning. If he went somewhere else with it, it'll be found."

"But whether he'll still be with it is another matter. Where's that damn photograph? If it's any good at all, we need to get it into the morning papers. The early editions will be going to press. . . . Great Scott, is it really half past ten?"

"Nearly. Chief, I think he probably will—" Ernie stopped as the door opened.

Tom came in, carrying a tray with three mugs of tea. "Not a sausage." He sat down, shaking his head. "Waste of bloody time. The old duck said she'd never had such an uncommunicative lodger—paying guest—before. That'd be why he kept changing lodgings, Chief. Didn't want to get too pally with anyone, considering what was on his mind. Mr. Copeland said we're looking at Harwich?"

"Explain, Ernie." Sipping tea, Alec listened closely to Ernie's exposition, hoping some helpful scrap of information might come out that had previously eluded him.

The story was substantially the same, until Ernie said, "And I was just about to tell you, Chief: The last two shipments to Holland were about the times of the disappearances of the first two victims. Mr. Garvey couldn't give me exact dates—we'd have to go back to Hodder for those—but there's always a couple of weeks' notice."

"Ah!" said Tom. "It looks as if Rosworth might have been planning all along to escape by sea."

"Possibly," Alec agreed cautiously. "More likely coincidence. He couldn't possibly know that the bodies would be found so soon after a fresh burial." Remembering the stench of Halliday's corpse, he amended his words, "Comparatively fresh. The dog might not have found it till a couple of weeks or even months later, long after the ship had sailed."

Tom nodded. "True."

"Still, with no alternative we'll have to concentrate on Harwich. I'd like to be there, but I'm going to have to return to the Yard to pacify the super and to make sure the photo gets to the papers pronto. I've a mind to send the two of you. You know everything there is to know. You can brief the Harbour Master, the Customs and Excise people, and the local police."

"You're not expecting us to take charge, Chief!" Tom protested.

"Great Scott, no! Neither of you has the rank. But that might be better—if any of them are touchy, I might get tied up in jurisdictional disputes. You two are more likely to be easily accepted in a purely advisory capacity. You'll take our car. You know how to get to Harwich, Ernie?"

Ernie had studied a road-map of Essex when they were first called in to the triple murder. With an abstracted air, he now consulted the map in his head. "Bishop's Stortford, Braintree, Colchester, I should think, Chief. It won't take a moment to check the map in the car. Sixty miles or so, I reckon, and good roads. Shouldn't be much traffic, so a couple of hours at most."

"Excellent. I'll ask Superintendent Starke to telephone ahead to tell them you're on your way with photos. He'll get me back to town as quickly as possible, I'm sure. Thank goodness he's cooperative, and seems able to cope with his CC."

The telephone bell rang. Ernie picked up the receiver. "DC Piper." He listened. "That was quick! Yes, please, Mr. Copeland, right away. The photos have come, Chief."

Copeland came in with a large manila envelope. Handing it over, he said, "The photographer's my cousin. He was in his dark-room printing up some christening photos from this morning, so he got onto it right away. He's put the negative in, in case you need more copies, but he'd like it back, please. And the print—he thought you might need the names."

"You have useful relatives, Sergeant." Alec took out the wad of prints and set it in the middle of the desk, face up. They all crowded round.

It was a good, clear photo, there was no denying that. Nor was it possible to deny the accuracy of Shadd's description:

darkish hair and nondescript features. The grim expression did not make the thin face more distinctive. Since the disastrous failure of the General Strike the previous month, the faces of many working-men bore the same look.

Alec sighed. "By the time that's been reproduced in the papers, it could be any one of millions. Might help in Harwich. Here you are, Tom." He returned half the pile to the envelope and handed it over. "Off you go, the two of you. If he's there, you'll find him."

Copeland wished them luck, then turned back to Alec. "What's next, sir?"

"I've got to get back to London as fast as possible, if not faster. Tell me how to find your super and the CC, and put these in an envelope for me, please. I'll pick it up at your desk as I leave."

As Alec took the stairs two at a time, a bold idea came to him. He knocked on the door Copeland had directed him to and went straight in. With Starke was a balding man in evening dress, sitting bolt upright and looking irritable.

"Here's DCI Fletcher now, Sir George," said the superintendent with relief.

"Chief Inspector, I really cannot put up with being kept in ignorance of what's going on in my county!"

"I've no desire or intention of keeping you in ignorance, sir. However, the investigation has moved out of your county for the present. My men are on their way to Harwich."

"That's no—"

"If you'll pardon me, sir, it's of the utmost urgency that I return to the Yard with the greatest possible speed. I wondered whether perhaps the motor-car you came here in would be able to get me there quickly. If you can spare the time, I could brief you on the way."

Sir George looked flabbergasted. "In *my* car?"

"My chaps have taken mine. Is yours a powerful vehicle?"

"Good God, yes, man. It's the latest Lancia. And my

chauffeur is an excellent driver. No nonsense about speed limits, eh? with you aboard on an urgent errand. What are we waiting for?"

The road from Hertford to Westminster passed in a blur. If any traffic policeman had the temerity to attempt to hold them up, Alec didn't see him. Sir George wanted every detail of the case to date. His enthusiasm made Alec suspect he was not as a rule provided with much information about what was going on in his county.

When the chauffeur pulled up at the Embankment entrance to New Scotland Yard, Sir George said wistfully, "I'd love to come in and look round, but my wife will be worrying."

"Another time, sir," said Alec, already half out of the car. "My thanks for the lift."

Hurrying in, he arranged with the sergeant on duty to have the photos sent immediately by motorcycle to the morning papers with the highest circulations. "Clement Rosworth, wanted for questioning in connection with . . . etc." The negative would go straight to the photography department for more enlargements to be made.

The most pressing business taken care of, Alec slowed down. He was in no rush to talk to the super, but at least his recital of the facts to Sir George had got everything straight in his mind.

"I don't suppose Mr. Crane is still in?"

"'Smatter of fact, he is, sir. In his office or in the Epping Executioner room." Smirking at Alec's wince, the sergeant reached for his phone. "You want me to find out—?"

"No, I'll find him. Get those photos moving."

"Yessir." The man glanced at the clock. "Too late for first edition, but most of those go to the North and Scotland anyway."

Alec hoped Rosworth had not taken off for the North or Scotland. Though his roots were in London and the Southeast, with his skills he wouldn't find it hard to get a licence to drive and a job under an assumed name anywhere in Britain. The Continent would be much more difficult.

Was it a mistake to concentrate on Harwich? No, the port was the only direct indication they had of Rosworth's possible movements. And Alec wasn't disregarding the rest of the country.

He entered the Epping Executioner room, as it had apparently been dubbed in his absence. He found Superintendent Crane presiding, and Mackinnon missing.

"Fletcher! At last! I've been expecting to hear from you."

"I'll tell you all about it, sir, but DS Mackinnon ought to hear this as well. Where is he?"

"He'd set everything going as you requested. I sent him to find a corner for a couple of hours sleep. Better if he's fresh tomorrow. I've taken over for the present, so get on with the story." With a raised finger, he summoned a stenographer. "We'll have it taken down and typed so that you can go home for a kip, too, instead of writing up your report."

Alec was sure his mind was too busy for sleep, but a rest wouldn't come amiss. He tried—and failed—to remember at what point in the saga he had last brought the super up to date. Crane had been extremely forbearing, not pestering him for constant reports. Though in part, no doubt, he had the weekend and his dashing hither and yon to thank for that small mercy.

He started at the beginning, skipping quickly over the bits that had turned out to be irrelevant, but mentioning the common opinion of the characters of the three victims. From the second visit to the Barley Mow onward, he went into more detail. Finally, he explained the urgency of his rush back to town, which had prevented his ringing Crane earlier.

"Good work, Fletcher. I can't see how you could have done better. Let's hope the man falls into your chaps' hands in Harwich, but if not, you'll tackle the job better tomorrow if you take a break now."

"You'll ring if I'm needed, though, sir?"

"Can you doubt it? One more thing: Mrs. Fletcher, she's not anywhere near Harwich, is she? You said she's somewhere in Essex."

"She was in north Essex, sir. Harwich is in the east. But in any case she'll be safe back at home by now."

"I hope so, Fletcher, I hope so."

TWENTY-FIVE

Back of sleep was catching up with Alec. On the doorstep, although Elsie had left the porch light on, he fumbled with his keys and dropped them. When he stooped to retrieve them, straightening seemed to take an inordinate effort.

Quietly, he let himself into the house, intent on a brief visit to the nursery to kiss the twins in their sleep, followed immediately by sinking into his own blissful bed.

On the hall table were a plate of wax-papered sandwiches and a flask, and yesterday's post. Suddenly hungry, he poured a cup of cocoa and started to unwrap the sandwiches. The post could wait till the morning.

Then he noticed that the top envelope had just his name on it, in Daisy's writing, obviously delivered by hand. What the deuce . . . ? Wasn't she supposed to have come home that evening, after taking Bel out for high tea? She ought to be fast asleep upstairs.

He ripped open the envelope.

The note was just a couple of scribbled sentences. Reading it, he groaned. "Unexpected death . . . detectives." What *was*

Daisy's extraordinary affinity with unnatural death? But perhaps the poor chap had merely had a heart attack. Harriman—

"Great Scott! Harriman!" *Harris? Or Harrison?* Or Harriman? It was too much of a coincidence to be ignored.

What the hell was he going to tell the super?

Wide-awake now, he needed time to consider his next move. He took a gulp of cocoa, in the process catching sight of himself in the looking-glass hanging over the table. First things first: a wash, a shave, and a clean shirt. Sandwich in hand, he hurried up the stairs.

His immediate impulse was to dash off to Saffron Walden to find out what Daisy was up to, not to mention whether Harriman was, in fact, the sergeant who had led the firing squad. But the man, whatever his identity, was dead. They were too late to save him—and wouldn't the press have a field day with that!

Unless, of course, the similar name was sheer coincidence. There was no sense in going off half-cocked. Yet the all-consuming desire for sleep had left him. He needed to be up and doing.

In terms of his investigation, rushing to Saffron Walden couldn't be justified without more details of Harriman's life and death. Alec could, however, make a case for joining the team in Harwich. If the local police and the Haven Authority failed to find Rosworth, or worse, found him and let him slip through their fingers, they would be all too happy to unload the blame on the absence of the detective in charge.

To Harwich he would go.

Despite his sense of urgency, he popped into the nursery before returning downstairs. Oliver slept with his knees drawn up under his chest, his rusty-bronze head sideways on the pillow, thumb in mouth. Miranda lay on her back, arms and legs flung outwards in abandon. Alec kissed their rosy cheeks, and ventured to ruffle Mirrie's dark curls, very gently so as not to wake her and rouse Mrs. Gilpin's wrath.

When this was over, he vowed, they'd all go away for a few

days, leaving no address or telephone number. In between catching up on sleep, he'd spend some waking hours with his children!

On his way downstairs, he prepared to justify to the super his decision to go to Harwich. Before phoning, though, he went into the office and dug out the Ordnance Survey map of Essex—he kept a full set of county maps at home. Hertford—Saffron Walden—Harwich, it was hardly any distance out of Rosworth's way, and he'd had a day and a half to get from the brewery to the port.

Back to the phone. "Whitehall 1212." At this time in the morning, the connection went through quickly.

"New Scotland Yard. May I help you?"

"DCI Fletcher. Put me through to Superintendent Crane."

"Mr. Crane went home a few minutes ago, sir. DS Mackinnon's taken over."

Alec breathed a sigh of relief. "Mackinnon then, please."

The Scot sounded alert, refreshed by his brief respite. "Sir, I was havering about whether to ring you. Just after Superintendent Crane left, Harwich telephoned."

"They've got him?"

"No, sir, but they've found the dray, Hertford's lorry."

"Fast work. Where?"

"Parked on the dock at Parkeston Quay, I gather, just where it ought to be, ready for transferring the cargo into the ship." Not such fast work. "He can't have twigged that we're after him."

"What about him? Rosworth?"

"Not a sign. They've made enquiries at all the usual doss-houses near the harbour. A lot of angry landladies, I gather. DC Piper suggested that he might be sleeping in the cab of the lorry. They haven't dared approach too closely for fear of alerting him before they're ready. They won't start loading the *Mayfly* in the dark, so there's no need to disturb him yet. They're getting boats on the Stour in case he jumps in and tries to swim for it, and a couple of armed men, as he's got a gun."

"I'm going. Send a car right away. Uniformed driver." Alec didn't want to be stopped by some officious local constable for driving over the speed limit.

"Sir." Mackinnon could be heard giving the order, then he came back on the line. "On its way, sir. Should I notify Mr. Crane?"

"He won't be home yet. No, best not to disturb his household. It can wait. Ring him at seven. With any luck it will all be over by then, and we'll have Rosworth in our hands. In the meantime, find out what's going on in Saffron Walden—police activity."

"Saffron Walden?"

"A man by the name of Harriman died unexpectedly in Saffron Walden—it's a small town in northern Essex—probably over the weekend."

Mackinnon made the connection instantly. "Harri*man*? 'Harris or Harrison'?"

"That's my thought. Since the super didn't mention it last night, I assume you weren't able to discover the name and whereabouts of the missing sergeant yesterday."

"No, sir. Impossible to get hold of anyone at the records office on a Sunday. We did talk again to two of those who served under Pelham but neither remembered a Sergeant Harris or Harrison. You'd think they would mention it if they recalled a name as similar as Harriman, particularly as we were uncertain."

"Try them again, as early as won't lead to major complaints, and those you couldn't reach yesterday, as well. Get those damn army records people moving. Clerks probably turn up at eight. Have a man on their doorstep. And I think we'd be justified in waking Shadd at seven or thereabouts to see if the name jogs his memory."

"Right you are, sir. You think the sergeant's in Saffron Walden?"

"I think he's *dead* in Saffron Walden. I hope I'm wrong. I may end up going on there from Harwich."

Alec debated whether to send Daisy a wire. But no, if he went, he'd be strictly on police business. She had been questioned by now and was no doubt out of the picture. He hoped. The thought of breaking to Crane that his wife had been caught up in yet another murder investigation—especially if it turned out to be linked to the Epping Forest burials, with which, he had assured the super, she had absolutely no connection . . . His mind boggled.

The car arrived a good five minutes before Alec expected it. The driver whisked them out of London by a route Alec would never have thought to take.

In answer to an enquiry, he explained that he had passed "The Knowledge," the rigorous exam for London taxi-drivers, before he decided to join the increasingly motorised Metropolitan Police.

"Don't 'ave to worry about passengers complaining you're running up the meter," he said with a grin. "Take the fastest route 'stead of the shortest. Course, it depends on the time of day. Right now, I guarantee you, sir, you'd get held up something awful on the main roads by heavy lorries crawling across the Smoke between the evening crush and the morning hullabaloo."

"I hope you're equally good at country roads."

"Not bad, sir, though I says it as shouldn't."

He was as good as his word. The sky ahead was barely beginning to lighten as they approached the coast. Then they started to encounter ribbons of mist writhing across the road. It wasn't enough to slow them, but, as the driver said pessimistically, "It's bound to be worse down by the waterfront."

How much worse? Enough to severely complicate or even wreck whatever plans had been made to take Rosworth?

Assuming he was in fact sleeping in his lorry, and hadn't abandoned it and skedaddled. If the latter were the case, they'd have to fall back on hoping someone, somewhere, would recognise the fugitive from the picture in the papers.

The mist thickened, hiding the sky, but not yet impeding

their course—at least in the opinion of Alec's enthusiastic driver. Alec hung onto the strap as they rounded a bend and a heavy-laden lorry loomed ahead. They overtook it and cleared a tractor coming the other way with inches to spare.

"I'd like to get there alive."

"You did say you're in a hurry, sir."

By the time they drove into the town, the mist qualified as fog, though nothing to compare to a London pea-souper. The grey beginnings of daylight seeped through, making it just possible to read the street signs to Parkeston Quay. Alec was of two minds whether to go straight there or call at the police station first. But it was growing lighter by the minute, and it seemed likely that daybreak would be the time chosen for the forces of law and order to swoop down upon the Hertford dray.

He wanted to be there, to speak to Rosworth before the system enveloped him and turned him into something he was not yet—because probable though it seemed that he was the murderer of three or four men, they had no proof that such was the case. The exchange of a few words, whether truth or lies, would allow Alec to be certain in his own mind of the man's guilt. Then the law could take its course.

The signs now offered a choice between passenger and freight. High wire fences ran along the roadside, with dim shapes lurking beyond. A moment later their way was barred by wide gates guarded by two men, one in unfamiliar uniform inside and a bobby outside. Alec leant over just in time to prevent the driver demanding admittance with a blast of the horn.

Alec got out and presented his warrant card to the constable.

"No vehicles allowed in, sir. There's a small gate at the side there. It's been a rush, and the fog didn't help," he added chattily, "but it's all set up. You'll be wanting the superintendent? He's in the Haven Authority building, over that way." He pointed.

A dawn breeze had suddenly arisen, breaking up the mist and flapping the flags on the big white building: the Union Jack, the Blue Ensign with crown of Customs and Excise, and the Harwich Haven Authority pennant. As Alec passed through the wicket gate, the wharf patchily emerged. He stopped to look.

A dark green freighter patched with orange rust dominated the scene, its superstructure grimy, smoke trickling from its two funnels. Cranes towered along the quay. To the left stood a row of lorries and a few horse-carts, waiting to move alongside for their loads to be transferred to the holds. The only signs of sound and movement were a flock of sparrows squabbling over a crust and seagulls crying as they wheeled overhead.

Alec scanned the line for the Hertford Brewery's motordray. He frowned. *Where the hell...?* Then he spotted the distinctive shape of barrels beneath a tarpaulin draped over the rear of the fifth vehicle, effectively hiding the company name painted on its low sides.

Clever, he thought. Nothing to arouse suspicion, just enough to delay identification of the lorry if the search for it had been less thorough and determined.

As the mist cleared further, he saw men crouched beside bollards, stacks of crates, the bases of the cranes, the other lorries. The dray was surrounded.

What were they waiting for?

The first rays of the rising sun glinted on windscreen glass. Within the cab of the dray, a figure sat up, stretching.

A whistle blew. Sparrows scattered in alarm as a dozen helmeted figures converged on the dray. Someone shouted an indistinct command to surrender in the name of the Law.

With a startling roar, a motor revved. The dray jerked forward—apparently no one had considered the possibility of its being able to start without being cranked, that it might have a self-starter. Swearing, Alec glanced behind him, at the fence. Though it looked sturdy, if Rosworth drove straight at the gates he might be able to break through. The two guards dithered, alarmed and uncertain, all too obviously unprepared for the situation.

But the front wheels of the dray turned towards the water.

The two men closest to it leapt for it. One failed to get a hold on the rope fastening down the tarpaulin. The other grabbed the door and hung on with one hand, the other arm reaching in to wrestle for control of the steering wheel.

Accelerating madly, the lorry sailed off the edge of the quay, out over the river, and disappeared.

Alec ran. He was in time to see a bubble of air break to the surface from the cab, and the tarpaulin belched out a series of smaller bubbles. A moment later, the dray was invisible in the murky harbour.

"Deep water," said a constable, shaking his head. "He's gone."

Alec took off his hat, but the time was not ripe for a moment of silent contemplation of the death of a man who, whatever his misdeeds, had deeply loved his son.

Two coppers floundered in the water. Already a pair of row-boats was pulling towards them. From the quay, men shouted encouragement and confused directions. In no doubt that they would be rescued, Alec trudged off to find the superintendent and arrange for divers to recover Rosworth's body.

That, of course, was the least of it. Over an hour passed before Alec was able to tear himself away from explanations, apologetic self-justifications, and, on his part, qualified congratulations. After all, they had found the man and hadn't exactly let him escape.

"I really must report to the Yard," he insisted at last. He escaped into a small office with a telephone, with Tom and Ernie, who had lain low in the background, in tow.

Alec dropped into the nearest chair, the sense of urgency he had lived with for days no longer making up for lost sleep.

"So it's all over, Chief," said Tom, slumping on the other chair, leaving Ernie to lean against the desk.

The youngest of the three, DC Piper was the least frayed at the edges. He reached for the telephone. "The Yard, Chief?"

"Yes, please," Alec said to him, and to Tom, "Not quite."

"Not quite?"

"Well, apart from at least another couple of hours sorting things out with the people here, we've got a lead on the firing squad sergeant. I'll explain in a minute. I'm hoping to get hold of Mackinnon before the super turns up."

"Before six in the morning? Come off it, Chief!"

"Not likely, but he was there till well after midnight last night. This case has had the brass worried stiff."

"Mr. Mackinnon, Chief." Ernie pushed the telephone to-wards Alec. "Operators got nothing better to do this time in the morning than put you right through."

"Mackinnon? You haven't rung Mr. Crane yet?"

"No, sir. Seven, you said. Hae ye collared Rosworth al-ready?"

"Not what you might call 'collared.'" Alec explained what had happened.

"Ye'll no be wanting me to break it to the super, sir!"

"'Fraid so. Think you can handle it?"

"Aye, sir." Mackinnon's tone suggested a squaring of the shoulders. "If I must, I must."

"Since there's no longer any urgency, you can let him sleep till eight. He'll ring me here, I expect, but with any luck he'll have to make do with his local counterpart. I hope to tie things up and be on my way before he gets through."

"To Saffron Walden? I rang the local station earlier and they confirmed that Harriman was a sergeant in the War. He was killed Saturday night, by a blow to the head. I didna talk to DI Gant himself, but—"

"Gant's in charge? Bloody hell! I'm off to Saffron Walden as soon as I can get away."

"I was just about to tell you, sir, there's word come through from DS Miniver in Newcastle. He rang up as soon as he came on duty, early shift. The inspector on duty yesterday sent a man over to see Mr. Chivers about the sergeant. He didn't think it was urgent so he left it for—"

"And?" Alec cut him short.

"Chivers remembered a Sergeant Harriman, sir."

"That confirms it, then." Alec sighed. "So Rosworth bagged his fourth victim. The AC, the home sec, and the Great British public are not going to be pleased. Be glad it's only Mr. Crane you have to report to."

Ringing off, Alec told Tring and Piper the bad news.

"Sounds like Rosworth hit him too hard," said Tom. "The shooting scene he liked to set up was superfluous."

"Or, knowing we were on his trail, he didn't have time for the fancy touches," Piper suggested. "He had to get here, too, to catch the ship. So we're going to Saffron Walden, Chief?"

"I am. I'll take Tom. If they haven't brought up the body yet, I'll have to leave you, Ernie, to deal with Rosworth's personal effects and so on. But Daisy's there, and involved in the business at least to the extent of being asked not to leave the town. I'm Gant's *bête noire* at the moment, after taking the Epping Executioner out of his hands. If the two get together, there's no knowing what might happen! I daren't even think what the Super's going to say . . ."

TWENTY-SIX

Daisy couldn't sleep. Or perhaps she did, she wasn't sure. Much of the night she was in that half-waking, half-sleeping state where thoughts and dreams are so interwoven one can't tell which is which.

The centre round which her musings meandered was the War.

People swirled past her inner eye: Tesler, the conscientious objector, crippled by the meaningless task set to punish him for refusing to kill people; Pencote, crippled by the War Tesler had refused to fight, no longer believing he had suffered for a just cause. How could either not be bitter? How could either not resent Harriman's brutal teasing, Tesler damned as a coward and Pencote a hero who saw himself as a victim?

Pencote, though, considered Tesler a hero for standing up for his principles to the point of going to prison.

Miss Bascombe, her hand on Tesler's arm. . . .

Michael came to Daisy, his face as clear as the day she heard of his death, blown up driving a Friends' Ambulance at the front. Awake, she could no longer picture her "conchie" fiancé with such clarity, and she had destroyed her photos of him out of loyalty to Alec.

"Blessed are the peacemakers." The vicar had spoken the phrase at Evensong that very afternoon. Yet most of the officers going like patriotic sheep to war must have been Anglicans. On the whole, one simply was.

Alec's Colonel Pelham, for instance—she would be extremely surprised to hear he hadn't considered himself a member of the Church of England, however rarely he attended services. It was the colonel who had first made Daisy's thoughts turned to war. She had said as much to Alec hadn't she? He was looking for connections, and she had wondered. . . .

Connections. Three bodies connected by burial close to one another in Epping Forest, connected by the manner of their death, connected by the paper targets pinned to their chests. Where had Daisy heard of such a thing before?

Gervaise, she thought. Her brother, patriotic, Anglican, an officer, and dead, hadn't he told her, on his one and only leave from France, that they pinned targets over the hearts of deserters when they were shot? Or had it been one of the officers in the military hospital where she had worked in the office? Too cowardly to be a VAD nurse tending their gruesome wounds, she had talked to them when they were safely bandaged. Those capable of speech.

Someone had told her only the rank and file were shot when they ran away. Patriotic Anglican officers were sent to special hospitals, whence, once deemed cured of cowardice, they were returned to the front.

Pencote—she didn't know whether he had been an officer, but if once he had been patriotic, he was no more, not as Gervaise would have understood it. Perhaps if he had been a coward, he'd have been sent to a hospital instead of having his legs blown off. Pencote, striking out in vain at his tormentor with his crutch. . . . Miss Bascombe with her hand on Tesler's arm. . . .

Tesler, attaining serenity in Meeting. . . . Miss Bascombe scared to death of something. . . .

Who the coward, who the hero, who the villain, who the fool?

Blessed are the peacemakers for they shall . . . Shall what? Trying to remember, Daisy drifted off to sleep at last.

In the morning, when a chambermaid came in with early-morning tea, Daisy awoke with jumbled, fading memories of last night's ideas, fancies, or dreams floating through her head. Just one image was still clear in her mind: Pencote flailing at Harriman with his crutch. Could Harriman, after long hours supervising sports day, have failed to move fast enough to get out of range?

She had to talk to Sakari. What time was it? She reached for her wrist-watch—nearly eight o'clock already. The hotel stopped serving breakfast at nine on weekdays, so they had agreed to meet in the dining room at half-past eight.

Daisy got up and washed, wishing she had brought more clothes. She was supposed to be at home by now. She had washed out her knickers and stockings last night, and they were dry enough to wear. It wasn't raining, thank goodness. Sun and cloud alternated, so her summer-weight costume would do, and the flowery blouse she had worn on Saturday evening was still presentable.

She knocked on Sakari's door.

"Daisy? I'll be with you in five minutes."

"All right. I'm going down."

Hardly anyone was about. The parents who had come for the weekend had apparently escaped Inspector Gant's clutches, presumably leaving their names and addresses behind them. The commercial travellers who made up most of the Rose and Crown's usual clientèle wouldn't arrive for a few hours. The dining room was empty but for a couple of professional-looking men sitting alone, who had an indefinable air of being bachelors who always breakfasted here, and a lounging waiter.

Daisy sat at a table by a window and ordered coffee and breakfast for two, knowing it wouldn't come for at least five minutes. Sakari arrived first.

"Good morning, Daisy. I hope you slept well?"

"Actually, no. I hardly slept a wink. Did you?"

"Oh yes. You suffered from indigestion—"

"I never get indigestion!"

"—from a surfeit of religion, perhaps, not to mention murder. I leave the worrying about murder to you."

"I am worried. You don't mind talking about it?"

"Not in the least. I am all agog to hear your latest theory."

"I don't like it."

They dropped the subject momentarily as breakfast arrived. The waiter poured coffee and removed the silver-plate dish covers. Milk and sugar; salt and pepper; toast, butter, and marmalade were passed.

Hungry as she was, Daisy scarcely noticed what was on her plate. As soon as the waiter was out of earshot, she said, "Sakari, I have an awful feeling that Mr. Pencote might have killed Harriman."

"Nonsense, Daisy, he is a cripple. Inspector Gant has already considered him and decided it would be impossible."

"That in itself is almost a good enough reason for thinking it's possible!"

Sakari chuckled. "This is true. But only *almost* a good enough reason. The man has no legs."

"I still think he could have done it. I saw him take a swipe at Harriman with one of his crutches. Harriman was already moving onwards so the crutch missed by a mile. I doubt whether he even noticed. But supposing he stopped to talk and was his usual offensive self. Like everyone else, he'd think of Pencote as harmless, defenceless. He wouldn't be watching out for an attack. And Pencote, having missed before, might have hit out again with no expectation of landing a blow."

"You do not believe he intended to kill Harriman?"

"Oh no, I'm sure he didn't mean to."

"Surely he cannot be strong enough to hit hard enough to kill!"

"Think about it, Sakari. Imagine how much effort it must

take to hang your whole weight from your arms, not just for a second or two, but for a long time."

"I could not do it for a second or two."

"I don't suppose I could, either. Pencote does. And on top of that, he has to move the crutches with his weight hanging from them, controlling them with his muscles so that he doesn't lose his balance. I'm sure his arms and shoulders must be very strong."

"I do not like this, Daisy."

"I told you, nor do I."

"Fortunately, even if he has the strength to kill Harriman, you cannot persuade me that he could then move the body to the Garden and hide it in the maze."

"No, I can't work out how he could do it. But I like the answer even less. Tesler and Miss Bascombe must have done that part. Pencote and Tesler are close friends, and Miss Bascombe is in love with Tesler. Knowing it was an accident, they would have helped him."

"Why are you so certain Mr. Pencote was involved? Is it not possible that the other two were responsible for everything? After all, Harriman's insult to Tesler was much more unpleasant than that he offered Pencote, which, indeed, he himself may not have intended as an insult. There are few men who would be angry at being called a hero."

"True, and of course it's physically possible. But psychologically—you're the one who goes to lectures on psychology. Can you imagine Mahatma Gandhi attacking someone who called him a coward?"

"No. He has been subject to worse insults."

"Tesler also suffered for his abhorrence of violence. What makes it still more improbable: If it was Tesler, it would have had to be a deliberate attack, not an unthinking striking out."

"This I like still less! I am exceedingly glad that we are merely speculating. You do not feel obliged to explain your theory to the inspector, I trust?"

"To Ghastly Gant? Certainly not! I doubt I'd even tell Alec, if it were his case. As you say, it's pure speculation." But if nothing of the sort had happened, why was Miss Bascombe so upset?

"If you intend to do nothing about it, you had best stop worrying about it," said Sakari practically. "What are your plans for today?"

"I thought I'd walk up to the San to see how the girls are doing. Will you come?"

"Walk!"

Daisy shook her head with a smile. "You take a taxi, if you prefer. I could do with the exercise. It'll clear my head, and it's a nice day, not too hot and not raining."

"Yet. I want to read the newspaper, and I have some letters I ought to write. I shall get on with those. Tell Deva I shall come and see her this afternoon. I dare say Sister will be happier if her Sanatorium is not overflowing with anxious mothers."

"All right. I'll be back by lunchtime."

Daisy went upstairs to fetch her hat and gloves. One of the school umbrellas leant against the wardrobe, where she had left it after returning from church. It ought to be returned, as should the one Sakari had borrowed, but Daisy refused to carry two umbrellas through the town and up the hill. Her shady straw cloche was adorned with a jaunty cockade, and she did wonder for a moment whether she should buy a black ribbon to substitute. However, it would be pure hypocrisy to don any sign of mourning for Harriman, she decided, besides looking very odd with her flowered blouse.

The Market Square, King Street, and the High Street were busy with Monday morning shoppers. Two or three women nodded to Daisy in a friendly way. They must be Friends, with a capital F, who had seen her in Meeting, she presumed.

Considering all Gant's bustling about, the news of Harriman's death must be widespread, even if it hadn't yet reached the national press, but the inspector might very well have kept quiet about Daisy's connection with it. The last thing he'd want was to have the name of Fletcher—Mrs. Alec Fletcher—associated with his murder case.

Daisy paused at the top of the High Street, where it forked, to look at the War Memorial. So many names, representing so much misery! She crossed the street to read the inscription: "For perpetual remembrance of the men of Saffron Walden who laid down their lives for their country in the Great War 1914–1919. The victor heroes rest in many lands but here the symbol of their glory stands."

What price glory? The glory faded but the misery dragged on and on.

Daisy crossed to the Debden Road and went on up the hill to the Sanatorium. A ping on the bell in the hall brought no response. She assumed Sister was dealing with a patient, so she sat down to wait.

Several minutes passed. Wondering whether to go in search of Sister, or even the girls, Daisy regretfully decided that the risk of walking in on some embarrassing nursing procedure was too great. Then the front door opened and Miss Bascombe came in.

"Oh, Mrs. Fletcher. I didn't . . . Sorry, I . . ." As she turned slightly to close the door behind her, Daisy saw that her face was very pale, her shoulders slumped.

"Come and sit down, Miss Bascombe. You don't look at all well. I'm not sure where Sister is. Shall I go and find her?"

"Oh no, I'll wait. I just . . ." She dropped limply onto a chair. "I have a simply awful headache. Matron gave me a powder last night, but it didn't really help. I hope Sister's got something stronger."

"I expect so," Daisy said, sympathetic and encouraging. "Headaches are miserable. One can ignore pain in a foot or an elbow, but when it's in one's head, it's impossible to get away from. I thought you looked not quite comfortable in Meeting yesterday."

"Yes, I . . . It was already coming on a bit. Oh dear, was it so obvious?"

"Not to people whose thoughts were where they should have been. I'm rather inclined to watch people, I'm afraid, as some people watch birds. Shepherding all those girls down the hill and back can't have helped."

"No. Though they're very good, really. Most of them, most of the time. You . . . watch people?"

"That sounds awful, doesn't it? As if I'm a terrible busybody! But I don't go poking into people's lives, let alone gossiping about them." Except, naturally, in the detection of murder, but that couldn't really be classified as gossip. "I'm interested in people and I just can't help observing."

"I know what you mean. I have to watch the girls, of course, mostly to help them with sports, but also to make sure they don't get hurt."

"You have training in first aid?"

"Oh yes. You have to to teach physical education—that's what we really prefer to 'games,' actually."

"I'll try to remember," Daisy promised absently, glad to think that Miss Bascombe would have checked that Harriman was dead before moving him at the risk of causing his death—if her speculations had any foundation in fact.

"It's a different kind of watching from when I'm Duty Mistress." Miss Bascombe had a little colour in her cheeks now, her headache apparently forgotten as she became interested in the conversation. "Then it's more a case of watching their behaviour. First you have to make sure they're obeying the rules, but sometimes you can tell that someone's upset about something, and then sometimes they'll talk to you about it, and sometimes you can help them. That's what I like best about this school. The school I went to, as long as you did your lessons and obeyed the rules, they didn't care much if you weren't happy."

"Mine, too. Sometimes it helps just to talk about what's worrying you, don't you find?"

"I . . . Yes, but . . . It's not . . . Other people are involved, you see. And it was all a dreadful accident in the first place! We couldn't refuse to help, could we?"

"If you're quite absolutely sure it was an accident . . . ?"

"Oh yes!"

"And your help didn't . . . um . . . didn't make things worse for . . . anyone else?"

"It was too late," Miss Bascombe said simply.

"Then what's done is done, and there's no point worrying about—" Daisy suddenly thought of a snag. "That is, as long as someone else isn't blamed for it."

Miss Bascombe looked horrified. "No, that would be terrible!"

"Well, yes, but on the other hand, it may not happen."

"It may, though. We ought to talk about it, decide what we'd do if . . ." She spoke with a new determination. "Thank you, Mrs. Fletcher, you've helped me see things straight. I was so muddled before. Now I know what to do, or at least what we have to discuss. Even that's better than just feeling completely lost. Do you know what time it is?"

"Ten to ten."

"I must run. I've got a class in ten minutes." She jumped up. "Oh, I do hope your daughter is all right."

"I haven't seen her yet, but I don't suppose there's anything much wrong."

"I hope not." With that she whisked away.

Daisy had heard that confession was good for the soul; also for headaches, it seemed—those caused by an uneasy conscience and no clear course of action, at least.

From Daisy's perspective, the best thing about it was that no one, not even Alec, could expect her to report anything so vague to the police. She understood because it fitted in with her favourite theory, but Miss Bascombe hadn't actually made any statement implicating anyone in anything criminal.

TWENTY-SEVEN

Where was Sister? Daisy decided she had waited quite long enough—though admittedly the time had not been wasted—to justify ringing the bell again.

Ping!

Just as her hand touched the bell, Sister looked out of the door next to her office. "Mrs. Fletcher, I thought I heard your voice. And someone else was here?"

"Yes, Miss Bascombe, but she felt better and went to take a class."

"I'm sorry you've been kept waiting. As you didn't ring again immediately, I assumed it wasn't urgent so I just finished up what I was doing."

"Not at all urgent, Sister. I'd like to have a word with the girls, if I may."

"Of course you—What's that, Mr. Pencote?"

Daisy heard Pencote's voice, though she couldn't make out what he was saying except for her own name.

"Are you sure?" Sister asked doubtfully. "You—"

A vigorous affirmative came to Daisy's ears.

"Very well, I'll ask. Mrs. Fletcher, Mr. Pencote would like to have a word with you." As she spoke, she came out of the room and closed the door. "I don't know what bee he's got in his bonnet," she said in a low voice. "He's in quite a bit of pain. His legs, you know, and his shoulders from the crutches. I've been putting a healing unguent on the sores. He overdid things on sports day and ought to have rested yesterday, but didn't. Men! But it can't hurt him to talk, if you don't mind, and it'll take his mind off the pain."

"I don't mind a bit." Daisy tried not to sound unnaturally eager. Look where soothing Miss Bascombe's headache had got her! Still, it was too much to hope that Pencote was anxious to confide, and in her, of all people. More likely he wanted to make sure she encouraged Belinda to keep up with her English lessons while she was in the San.

And did she really want him to confess to her, anyway? What on earth would she do about it?

"I'd better warn you," Sister continued, "I've managed to persuade him to take a dose of laudanum, so he may wander a bit. Not but what it doesn't usually take him that way, like it does some people. You never can tell." She opened the door. "Are we decent, Mr. Pencote?"

"*We* are," he growled.

"It's my surgery, Mrs. Fletcher, so it's not set up for visitors. I want him to lie down for a little while—No, don't get up, Mr. Pencote! I'm sure Mrs. Fletcher will excuse you—"

"No, you mustn't get up," Daisy interrupted.

"I'll tell the girls you'll be with them *very* soon," said Sister and went away at last, with a rustle of her starched apron.

Covered to the waist with a folded sheet, Pencote leant back on the chaise longue, which served as an examination couch. Beside it on the floor, within reach, lay his crutches. A pungent medicinal odour hung in the air.

"Excuse the smell, Mrs. Fletcher," Pencote said wryly. "I'm sorry to inflict it on you."

"That's all right. Just don't blame me if I sneeze."

"I shan't." The grin looked odd on his drawn face. It quickly faded. "I beg your pardon for taking up your time. I heard you say you were talking to Miss Bascombe and I wondered whether she . . . unburdened herself to you. I know . . . something was weighing on her mind, you see."

"She didn't name any names, Mr. Pencote. Nor deeds, come to that."

"Oh." He was silent for a few moments. Daisy waited. At last he went on: "My cursed temper! Belinda's father's a policeman, isn't he? Belinda talks about him. It's you she's especially proud of though, your writing. I've read a couple of your articles, as I think I told you, and they're very well written. But you're her stepmother, so I can't say she's inherited her writing ability. She shows real promise."

Cut the cackle and get to the 'osses, Daisy thought. Aloud, she said, "I'm glad. Perhaps she'll decide to teach English, like you."

"As long as that's the only way she imitates me! Mrs. Fletcher, you know about Harriman's death. In fact, there's a rumour that you found his body . . . ?"

"In a manner of speaking."

"The girls did," he guessed instantly. "You're trying to protect them. Perhaps you'll be able to understand my situation, then. I was too shocked—appalled!—at the time to see where the help of my friends would lead. Now I realise I ought to admit my guilt and take my medicine, hoping a jury will conclude that I had no expectation, no intention, of . . . such serious consequences. But no one would believe I'd be capable of moving him." He gestured at the place where his legs ought to be. "If I speak up, they'll be in almost as much trouble as I will. I can't do that to them."

"They must have foreseen the possibility."

"I don't know about that. Tes—One of them is rather unworldly, and the other perhaps a bit naïve. They thought only of me. I wish they hadn't been with me when it happened! Come to that, of course I wish it hadn't happened. But it did. What I wondered is, you being somewhat familiar with police procedures, I assume, you might be able to advise me. Is there any way I can confess without implicating them?"

"Not that I can see," Daisy said frankly. "The officer in charge is astoundingly incompetent and seems to have a genius for omitting to ask the right questions, but even he worked out quite quickly that you couldn't have done it. If you told him you did, even he would realise you must have had help."

"I could refuse to tell him who helped me."

"An awful lot of people know the three of you are good friends, Mr. Pencote."

"Yes."

"Well, on present form, I rather doubt Inspector Gant will solve the case. Solve it correctly, I mean. He may arrest someone who had nothing to do with it."

"That would solve *my* problem," Pencote said emphatically. "I couldn't stand by and let an innocent person suffer, and I'm quite sure Tesler wouldn't."

Daisy pretended she hadn't heard the name. "It's possible, however, that the other two people involved might continue to try to protect you. In fact, I'm pretty sure some such thought is in the mind of one of them."

"If you mean they'd take responsibility for the whole business, I couldn't allow that, either."

"No. The only alternative I can see is that Gant will admit he's beaten and Scotland Yard will be called in."

"*They'd* hardly fail to come up with a conspiracy theory! We might as well just confess at once and be finished with it."

"Don't do anything precipitate. You'll have to talk to the others first, anyway, and I wouldn't advise confessing to Gant if you can avoid it."

"Then I take it you don't intend to give us away?"

"What do I *know*? I've had a couple of decidedly ambiguous conversations. If they happen to accord with any theories I may have developed, I have no duty to present Gant with my theories. If he'd been a different sort of person . . . Well, I don't know what I might have done. Or if you three were different sorts of people. But that's the way it is. Besides, I doubt he'd be willing to listen to me. He happens to have a grudge against my husband."

That surprised a laugh from Pencote, a rather feeble one. "Somehow one thinks of the police as a united body of men. If your husband were in charge, would you tell him?"

"I can't be sure. Probably not. He tends to pooh-pooh my theories. In any case, I don't know how it all happened so I don't actually have any facts to offer."

"Would you like to know how it happened?"

"I can guess. What I can't quite picture is where. I may suffer from 'satiable curtiosity,' but that's no reason for you to tell me."

"It was on the school field, where you witnessed my inexcusable exhibition earlier. A beautiful evening—we were sitting on the bench against the wall of the swimming pool, after the children went to bed. Harriman was running laps, round and round the track. He altered course to come and offer his usual insults. I took it for granted he'd keep moving, as he usually did, but he stopped. I can't imagine why he should have wanted to prolong the 'conversation,' if such it can be called. In fact, he stooped—perhaps he had a stone in his plimsoll—"

"That's enough," Daisy said firmly. "You've satisfied my curiosity and I don't want to hear any more. It was an accident, as I presumed. Now I really must go and talk to the girls."

"Amidst all the rest, I'm extremely sorry that an action of mine should have troubled them."

"That's one apology I shan't be passing on! Good-bye, Mr. Pencote, and good luck."

Daisy found the three girls sitting in a row on the chairs in the hall, whispering to one another. Belinda jumped up and came to hug her, saying in a voice barely louder than a whisper, "Sister said if we make any noise she'll send us back upstairs to get on with our lessons. We're doing them sitting on our beds!"

The other two gathered round.

"Where's my mother, Mrs. Fletcher?" asked Deva.

"She had some letters that had to be written, darling. She'll come and see you later. Lizzie, my dear, how are you holding up?"

"All right, thank you, Mrs. Fletcher."

"She had a bad dream last night, though, Mummy. I woke her up."

"Oh, Lizzie, I *am* sorry." Daisy hugged her, and then had to hug Deva to make it fair. "Do you want to talk about it? Would it help?"

"I told Bel and Deva all about it, what he looked like and everything. I hope you don't mind."

"Of course not, darling, if it made you feel better."

"I didn't have any more nightmares afterwards."

"Bel and I didn't, either, Mrs. Fletcher."

"Hearing about it is not the same as seeing it," said Belinda. "I'm glad it wasn't a teacher we liked. It spoilt the Garden, though. Not what Lizzie said, just that it happened there. I don't ever want to go back into that maze."

"I wouldn't mind," said Deva. "It was fun, till . . . There are so many dead-ends, and all the hedges look just the same—you'd never know if you happened to go to the same place."

"That's what's so creepy." Lizzie shivered. "Not knowing."

"What about the other part of the Garden, the one with all the winding paths and the look-out?" Bel asked. "Would you—"

"Girls!" Sister popped out of her office. "Sorry, Mrs. Fletcher, but I can't have all this racket going on."

"Sorry, Sister. I didn't realise we were getting louder."

"Sorry, Sister," echoed the girls.

"Is there somewhere out of the way outside where we could sit and talk?"

"I think the girls ought to be getting back to their lessons," Sister said severely. "It's most irregular to have parents visiting on a Monday, specially during school hours. I only permitted it because of the unusual situation."

"My—" Deva stopped as Daisy put a finger to her lips. Forewarned, Sister might forbid Sakari's visit this afternoon, but if she turned up without advance notice, Daisy would bet on Sakari over Sister any day.

"Back to lessons you go," Daisy said. "You don't want to find you've fallen behind when you get back to school."

"Are you staying in Saffron Walden, Mummy?"

"Yes, darling. We won't go back to town without saying good-bye, I promise." She gave each of them a kiss.

Walking back down the hill, she thought about her conversations with Pencote and Miss Bascombe. Had she been out of her mind to tell Pencote she wouldn't report him to the police?

She repeated to herself the arguments she had offered him. She didn't actually have any facts to go on. Nothing specific had been said about any specific person committing a specific crime. As far as she was concerned, the stories were no better founded than idle rumour, even considering her sources. Rumour from third parties, thoroughly mixed with her own speculation: detectives in general objected vigorously and vociferously to the speculations of anyone but themselves, and heavily discounted rumours not backed by solid evidence.

Coppers weren't keen on confessions, either. All sorts of eccentrics were liable to confess to crimes for a variety of peculiar reasons, from a desire for notoriety to vague and general feelings of guilt. Weeding them out just wasted valuable police time. What they wanted was for criminals to confess *after* they had been arrested on good, solid evidence.

Daisy had no evidence whatsoever. Moreover, she wasn't a police officer, and a confession made to her had no value in the eyes of the law. Nor had there been any witnesses to back up her story.

She might have decided differently if Ghastly Gant were not in charge of the case. She couldn't possibly go to him with such a vague tale. If it had been Alec, or even the Hampshire policeman she had encountered a few months ago, who had at least been intelligent. . . . But no, she wouldn't have told either of them what she had heard from Miss Bascombe and Pencote.

The whole affair was all too likely to end in disaster for the two of them, and for Tesler, with or without her interference.

She reached the Rose and Crown in dire need of a cup of coffee.

"Do you know where Mrs. Prasad is?" she asked the receptionist.

"In the writing room, madam. With Inspector Gant."

"Not again!"

"I'm afraid so, madam. The management would be very happy to find a legal way of excluding the inspector from the premises, from troubling our guests. So far they have failed to find one." She gave Daisy an interrogative look.

Daisy sighed. "It's no good asking me."

"The inspector's instructions were to tell you to join him when you returned, madam. I said that I would convey his request. I'm extremely sorry that you should be inconvenienced. The management wishes me to convey their apologies—"

"Don't worry, I don't hold the hotel responsible."

"Such a thing has never happened on our premises before, I assure you, madam."

"And probably never will again. Just send lots of coffee and lots of cakes to the writing room, will you, please? Two cups will be sufficient."

"Very good, madam." The receptionist almost smiled. "Two cups. There will be no charge for any refreshments you or Mrs. Prasad choose to order for yourselves as long as the inspector is on the premises."

"Thank you." If that wasn't an invitation to overindulgence, Daisy didn't know what was.

She went to the cloakroom to powder her nose, comb her ruffled curls, and calm her ruffled temper. How many times was Gant going to make her repeat her story? Sooner or later, she'd slip and reveal that Lizzie had found the body. It had no relevance whatever to his enquiry but was bound to cause trouble all round.

Would Alec accept the excuse that Gant simply hadn't asked the right questions and hadn't given her a chance to tell him? Having himself suffered from Gant's incompetence, he might. Daisy began to feel more cheerful.

She met a waiter with the coffee in the passage and preceded him into the writing room.

"Sakari, darling, I've brought elevenses. I don't know about you, but I'm in need of sustenance."

"Excellent, Daisy." Casting a glance over the supplies the waiter unloaded from the tray on the table in front of her, Sakari tipped him. "I, too, am parched. I have been telling Inspector Gant for half an hour that I did not hear the gardener speak one single word."

"I didn't hear more than a dozen or so." Daisy chose a chocolate éclair from the plate of cakes. She had, after all, walked all the way up and back down the hill. Besides, each sticky bite, even eaten with a fork, would allow her time to think.

The inspector's silent acolyte looked hopefully at the table. His face fell as he saw there were only two cups and plates. Daisy felt guilty, but she was determined not to feed Gant.

"He must have said more than you've told me," Gant said peevishly.

"Why?"

"What do you mean, why?"

"Why must he have said more than I've told you?"

"Because . . . Because nobody says so little!"

"He's a very uncommunicative individual."

"I found that out for myself! But we'll go back over it all again and hope you remember something more."

Daisy quickly took a bite of éclair. Masticating the glutinous mouthful, she thought furiously. To "go back over it all" would be dangerous and might lead to questions she had avoided so far. She swallowed. "That would be an awful waste of your time, Inspector. You're a very busy man, I know. Suppose you read to me what I've already told you about the gardener and I'll see if I can add to it."

"All right," Gant said grudgingly, and he gestured at his acolyte, who flipped through his notebook then started reading in a monotone.

"Inspector Gant: 'When you spoke to the gardener requesting his help to get the children out was he reluctant to enter the maze.'

"Mrs. Fletcher: 'Very.'

"Inspector Gant: 'Aha.'"

"You can cut that out, Constable."

"What, sir?"

"The last remark of mine that you read. Erase it."

"I can't do that, sir. It'd show."

"Then cross it out," Gant snarled. "Get on with it!"

Daisy helped herself to another cup of coffee and a Bakewell tart as the monotone resumed. "Mrs. Fletcher: 'Don't let that mislead you Inspector he would have been equally reluctant to show me the way to the poet's corner or the rose garden all he wanted was his dinner in his opinion it wouldn't hurt the girls to wait till he was ready to return to work.'

"Inspector Gant: 'By that time, they'd probably have found their own way out so he wouldn't have to go near the scene of the crime.'

"Mrs. Fletcher: 'I wasn't about to allow any delay if they'd gone on wandering just imagine the shock for a young girl of stumbling upon the corpse of someone she knew.'

"Inspector Gant: 'I suppose you offered a big enough tip to change his mind made it worth his while to risk.'

"Mrs. Fletcher: 'I didn't offer him a penny though naturally I tipped him afterwards I just told him about the body.'

"Inspector Gant: 'You hadn't told him right away.'

"Mrs. Fletcher: 'I thought the fewer people knew about it the better but it was more important to get the girls out quickly and I hoped he'd understand realise they mustn't wander about at random in there as he did.'

"Inspector Gant: 'Did he seem surprised to hear about the body what did he say.'

"Mrs. Fletcher: 'Nothing he was walking towards the walled garden as I spoke and he just changed direction towards the maze without opening his mouth I'm sure you've discovered he's a man of few words.'

"Inspector Gant: 'That's one way of putting it.'"

"You can cross that out, too. And leave it out when you type your report."

"Yes, sir. Mrs. Fletcher: 'He also has a remarkably inexpressive face I can only hazard a guess as to what he was thinking by his actions he didn't hesitate before heading for the maze when I told him there was a body in there with them oh wait a minute that's not quite right.'

"Inspector Gant: 'Hah.' Do you want me to cross that out, sir?"

Gant just glared at him.

"Mrs. Fletcher: 'I'd forgotten he stopped walking and looked at me as if he wasn't sure whether to believe me or not so I told him my friend had gone for the police at that he well he spat on the grass not at me.'

"Inspector Gant: 'He doesn't like the police.' That's the end of the bit about the gardener, sir."

"After that," said Daisy, "after he spat when I mentioned the police, I don't recall his saying anything but 'Aye,' when I asked if he could lead them—you—back to the body."

"Must've reckoned you lot tramping about the place had wiped out any marks he'd left." He stood up and addressed the constable. "Right, we'll have to pull him into the station for questioning. Come along."

Daisy and Sakari looked at each other. It would take a better man than Inspector Gant to get the gardener to talk, Daisy was certain. But what really concerned her was what Pencote, Tesler, and Miss Bascombe would decide to do when they heard he'd been taken in for questioning.

His hand on the door handle, Gant turned. "I almost forgot. Mrs. Fletcher, I've been wondering how you managed to find your way out of the maze after discovering the deceased. I sent four men in to make a thorough search, and every single one of the fools got lost."

Oh help! Daisy thought. Unless she could come up with a viable explanation, the inspector was about to find out that she had misled him. Obstruction of an officer in the course of his duties, at the very least, but given Gant's animosity towards Alec, might he make a charge of accessory after the fact?

TWENTY-EIGHT

A knock on the door of the writing room was followed so abruptly by its opening that Inspector Gant scarcely had time to jump out of the way. His face irate, he swung round to blast the intruder. Daisy was ready to bless the waiter, come to clear away, for giving her time to think.

Instead of the expected waiter, Alec strolled in, followed by Tom Tring.

She exhaled a long breath. However furious Alec was with her, he wouldn't let her be arrested. Behind his back, Tom winked at her.

"Good morning, Mr. Fletcher," said Sakari composedly. "I shall send for more coffee."

"Not just now, thank you, Mrs. Prasad."

Gant stopped gaping and exploded. "Fletcher!"

"DCI Fletcher, CID." Alec eyed him with disdain. So this was the man who had deserted the scene of the burials and then departed for Chelmsford headquarters, leaving only a most inadequate report. "You, I think, must be Detective Inspector Gant?"

"What are you doing here?"

"I'm afraid I've come to relieve you of this case."

"The CC wouldn't . . . But I'm just about to make an arrest!"

"How lucky I've arrived in time to prevent your making a nasty mistake. As it turns out, the murder of Harriman is part of the Epping investigation. However, this is no place to discuss the matter. Shall we adjourn to the local station?"

"B-but . . . What . . . How . . . I don't . . ."

Daisy almost felt sorry for him.

"I'll explain." Alec stood aside.

"Sir." Tom, holding the door, gestured courteously for Gant to precede him. The inspector went out, moving like a sleepwalker stuck in a bad dream. Tom went after him.

"I'll see you later, Daisy," Alec said grimly. "And you, Mrs. Prasad." He smiled, at Sakari.

He departed. Gant's acolyte, wordless, shrugged with his eyes raised to heaven and followed, closing the door behind him.

"Whew!" Once again Daisy expelled a lungful of breath. "Talk about saved by the bell! I'm not the only one, either."

"The gardener. And the children, especially Elizabeth."

"They're the least of it!"

"What do you mean, Daisy? Do not tell me your theory proved correct?"

"'Proved' is just the word I want to avoid. I met both Miss Bascombe and Pencote at the San, quite fortuitously. *You* know I didn't arrange to meet them."

"Certainly."

"And both of them wanted to talk."

"People always want to talk to you."

"Excluding the gardener."

"To be sure. What did they say? They confirmed your theory? Are you not obliged to report this to Alec?"

"One question at a time, darling! They were both very cautious, fortunately. Well, call it wisely. If it weren't for my theory, I wouldn't have had a clue what they were talking about. As it was, both their stories fitted the theory perfectly."

"So nothing is proved."

"Exactly. I could tell Alec my speculations, but he hates it when I speculate about his cases. Now he's sure he's got the whole thing sewn up, he'd be even more upset. And if he's blaming it on the Epping Forest murderer, there's no one innocent going to suffer for it."

"What if the murderer confesses to burying the three bodies but denies responsibility for Harriman's death?"

"We'll just have to hope they won't believe him," Daisy said optimistically.

"You do not think Mr. Pencote might kill someone else if he is not caught?"

"No. I'm sure it was an accident. Well, he struck at Harriman, admittedly, but he never expected to hit him."

"I hope you are right, Daisy. I should greatly dislike to see any of Deva's teachers arrested, and one cannot help but pity Mr. Pencote. What are you going to say to Alec?"

"It depends, really, on what Ghastly Gant tells him. I can't see why he should mention the discrepancies in my story, but if he does, I don't mind explaining to Alec. After all, I was protecting Bel, and he can't very well disapprove of that. All the same, I'd like to put it off for a bit."

"He is likely to be occupied with police business for some time, is he not? Perhaps we should just take the first train back to London."

"Darling, you're a genius! Let's!"

"Daisy, I was not serious. The police have not given us leave to go."

"No, but it was Gant who told us to stay, not Alec, and Alec is not very fond of Gant." She thought for a moment, then sighed. "I expect you're right, though. Gant's going to be looking for any excuse to be awkward, and we don't want to provide him with one."

"Let us take a taxi to the Sanatorium and persuade Sister to allow the girls to go out to lunch with us. Thus we shall all be out of the way if for any reason any of the police come looking for us."

"Good idea!" said Daisy. If Pencote was still there, she'd make an opportunity to reassure him.

In fact, when the taxi pulled up in front of the San, Pencote was just coming out, swinging wearily along on his crutches.

"Poor man," said Sakari. "The taxi can take him round to the school while it is waiting for us. Tell him, Daisy, while I instruct the driver."

Daisy went to meet Pencote. "I have news that should relieve your worries somewhat. Scotland Yard has taken the case out of DI Gant's hands, and they seem quite certain it's tied to the Epping Forest case. They believe the same person was responsible for Harriman's death as well."

He looked at her in astonishment. "The *Epping* murders? How extraordinary! Have they caught the murderer?"

"I don't know."

"But when they do, he'll deny killing Harriman. Good morning, Mrs. Prasad."

Sakari sailed by with a nod and a smile.

"He'll deny killing all of them," said Daisy, "if he has any sense. Don't cross your bridges until you come to them. I don't want the three of you arrested—I don't think you really deserve it—but I do think you deserve to live with a little guilt and anxiety!"

"I do," he said humbly, "and worse, but I wish I could be sure the others are safe."

"If wishes were horses, beggars would ride. Oh dear, here I am talking to an English teacher in clichés!"

Pencote managed to summon up a smile. "You've been very kind, Mrs. Fletcher. I promise you, I've had a salutory shock. With Tesler's help, I'm going to work very hard at mastering my wicked temper."

"You couldn't find a better tutor. I must go. Mrs. Prasad is counting on my support. Good-bye for now. Oh, I almost forgot: She arranged for the taxi to take you round to the school while it's waiting for us."

She walked on quickly to escape his thanks, wondering whether she had made the right decision. *Time would tell*, she thought with a sigh.

And there went another cliché.

Between Sakari and Daisy, even the formidable Sister didn't stand a chance. They took the children out for lunch. Belinda was excited to hear her father was in Saffron Walden. Daisy said she would do her best to get him to come and see her.

"He's in the middle of a case, though, darling, so he may not be able to."

"Oh well, it's not too long till the summer hols."

"If he does come and see you, there's no need to worry him about Lizzie finding the body." Encouraging the child to keep secrets from her father—disgraceful! Daisy was going to be living with a good share of guilt herself. She passed hurriedly on. "Because he's arrived, the local police may soon allow Mrs. Prasad and me to go home. Would it upset you if we left? How about you, Lizzie?"

"I'm all right now, Mrs. Fletcher, honestly. It was sort of like our secret adventure, wasn't it? And Sister says Miss Priestman wants us to stay in the San for the rest of the week, so it'll be fun."

Sister, consulted, said the less fuss made, the sooner the children would get over the experience. The way she said it suggested that the absence of their mothers would be of great assistance.

"Assuming the police let us leave, Sister, we'll come back at once if we're needed. Here, I'll write down both our telephone numbers for you, though the school office has them, of course."

"I'm sure they won't be needed, Mrs. Fletcher. Between me and Miss Priestman, we'll be able to cope, so don't worry yourselves."

Their consciences somewhat assuaged, Daisy and Sakari left. Not that Daisy's conscience was entirely easy about other matters. On the way down the hill in the taxi, she expressed her qualms about having advised Belinda not to tell her father about Lizzie having been the one to stumble upon Harriman's corpse.

"Nonsense, Daisy. What good would it do Alec to know? It would only distract him from his work."

"But Bel will learn—"

"Belinda will learn that it is unnecessary and unwise for a woman to trouble her husband with all her little concerns."

Looked at from that perspective, it was indeed a valuable lesson!

When they reached the Rose and Crown, a message awaited them saying they were free to leave. Now that she was allowed to go, Daisy wanted to stay on for a while in hopes of seeing Alec, but Sakari said that would be tempting fate. So Daisy wrote a note to Alec, while Sakari telephoned the school and asked them to tell the children. They packed and caught the next train to town.

Once she had stopped worrying about Belinda, Daisy was consumed with curiosity about Alec's investigation and how he had worked out that the two cases were one.

The newspapers seemed to have lost interest, after reporting little more than that the Epping Forest Executioner had killed himself when about to be apprehended. As far as they were concerned, the case was over. There was always plenty of fresh news with which to titillate their readers.

Three days passed before Alec came home early enough for questions, and then it was touch and go whether he would be willing to tell her. She asked after dinner, when he dropped wearily into an armchair in the sitting room.

"It's left a nasty taste in my mouth, love. Can't we let it go at that?"

"I'm sure it's better to talk about it than to let it fester in your mind."

283

His lips quirked. "Is that what Mrs. Prasad's passed on to you from those psychology lectures she attends?"

"Well, yes, but sounds like common sense. Besides, think how it'll fester in my mind if I never find out."

"That I can believe!"

"I'll get you a whisky."

"You can't bribe a British policeman. Not often, anyway."

"This is one of those rare occasions. Water or soda?"

"Is there any Malvern water?"

"Yes, of course."

"Just a drop."

"There you go. Why is it this case disturbs you so much, darling? Because the man committed suicide before you could arrest him?"

"No, I'm glad he did. Much better than prison and hanging. You see, he really was after justice quite as much as revenge. His sixteen-year-old son was shot as a deserter. From all I've heard, if Colonel Pelham had sent him back to the medics, he'd have been diagnosed with shell-shock. But Pelham was a tyrant and a bully. He convened a drum-head court martial, a summary trial without a judge-advocate to speak for the prisoner, not at all according to military regulations. Your Sergeant Harriman volunteered to head the firing squad."

"*My* Sergeant Harriman? He was loathsome. I couldn't stick him at any price. And that was before I knew he offered his services to shoot a defenceless boy. The colonel sounds as if he got what was coming to him, too."

"He was a terror. So far, my sympathies are all with Rosworth. But his other two victims—the other officers Pelham coerced into supporting his verdict—Halliday might have been able to force the issue, if he'd tried harder, but he was constrained by his overwhelming sense of duty. Devine was a nice lad, not so much older than Sammy Rosworth, and without much force of character. I don't think he'd ever have made captain if the carnage among subaltern officers hadn't been so enormous. They didn't have much choice of lieutenants to promote. He didn't deserve to be murdered at the age of thirty-three."

"No."

"By all accounts, Devine seems to have been haunted by Sammy's death."

"You're right, it's all horrible. What put you on to it?"

"As a matter of fact, you were the first to suggest a military link."

"Alec, are you admitting I said something helpful?"

"A wild guess, on the basis of Pelham continuing to call himself colonel. But it stuck in my mind and we followed it up."

"You did tell Mr. Crane, didn't you, in mitigation of my being on the scene of the fourth murder? Was he furious?"

"I've seen him calmer," Alec admitted. "What particularly irked him was its being the fourth murder, the one we'd hoped to prevent. He seems to think your presence should have helped us prevent it, but in fact, we'd never have managed to link it to the others if not for the note you sent me from Saffron Walden."

"What? Explain!"

"We didn't know the name of the sergeant involved. Harris or Harrison, our informant said. Then you turn up with a dead Harriman—"

"Darling, I don't at all care for that way of putting it!" Daisy said indignantly.

He laughed, and went on, "In a town not very far from the direct route from Hertford to Harwich. A telephone call to the local police told us he'd been a sergeant in the War. Later we found out from the school that he had not turned out to be an asset for a peaceable Quaker community. Besides the bullying, he fell short in other directions."

"Do tell."

"He drank. Not to excess, as far as I know, but Quakers tend to frown on the use of alcohol."

"Yes, Bel says Miss Priestman doesn't even like the girls eating wine gums. Shall I refill your glass, by the way?"

"No, thanks, love. I can feel her disapproval from here. The thing is, because of that general disapproval, Harriman didn't go to pubs. He drank at home. The other three were all kidnapped on their way home from the pub. That was the obvious link between them. Ernie Piper insisted the pub connection was significant and important, and he turned out to be right."

"Good for Ernie!"

"Yes, and he got the kudos in my report."

"Unlike me, I assume," Daisy said mournfully. "Never mind, it really was a wild guess."

"Also, you are not officially a member of the force."

"I like 'officially.'"

"Daisy!"

"Don't worry, I won't push my luck."

"I wish I could believe that. Anyway, obviously Rosworth couldn't use the same method in killing Harriman as he had with the others. He must have had difficulty finding him in the first place. Harriman moved about a lot and hadn't been long in Saffron Walden—"

"He's only been at the school since last September."

"That's right, whereas Pelham, Halliday, and Devine were all settled. They all frequented free houses that served Hertford Brewery's products, which makes it tempting to believe the gods were on Rosworth's side! We'll probably never know how he tracked Harriman down, but apparently the sergeant had been seen more than once walking in Bridge End Garden. Presumably Rosworth followed him there from the school or his house and seized his chance."

"You're absolutely sure Rosworth was the murderer?"

"Oh yes. The landlords and the brewery confirmed the dates of deliveries to the respective pubs. The width of the wheel tracks in the Forest matches the brewery's horse-drays. And above all, Rosworth had a suicide note in his wallet that somehow survived being dunked in the River Stour. It must have been written before he set out on his last journey, because he exulted in having killed the three he buried in the Forest, but where Harriman was concerned he fulminated and hoped he'd get a chance at him before he died."

"It sounds as if he always intended to do away with himself once he'd completed his mission. He wasn't driven to it by the police catching up with him."

"No, he probably laid his final plans when he read in the papers that we'd identified the bodies. He wrote that the only thing he had left to live for was getting Harriman. You could say he struck it lucky again, at the last possible moment."

"What I can't really understand is why he then drove to Harwich, where he must have realised you'd look for him if you'd worked out who he was."

"Oh, everyone says he was a very reliable, conscientious, and honest employee. My guess is that he hoped to load the barrels into the ship before doing away with himself. It must have pained him to take the lot into the harbour with him."

"Poor man!" Daisy sighed. "I can't imagine what it would be like to lose your only child in such a horrible way. Let's go up and give Oliver and Miranda an extra kiss. I'm glad you got home in time to play with them before bedtime today."

"Mrs. Gilpin swore they'd never go to sleep after I'd over-excited them," Alec said with a grin, heaving himself out of his chair. "Luckily they dropped off right away. Are they too young to enjoy playing in sand?"

"No, they love the sandpit in the Jessups' back garden. Why?"

"I talked the super into giving me next week off. We're going somewhere where he can't find me. I thought we might take the twins to the Isle of Wight."

"Marvellous!"

Daisy wasn't thinking only about a week at the seaside with the babies—and Mrs. Gilpin, of course. She thought of Pencote, Tesler, and Miss Bascombe. She thought of the comparatively innocent victims: Sammy Rosworth; Halliday, slave to duty; Devine, living for so long with the boy's death on his conscience. She thought of Sammy's grieving father, and of the brutal Pelham and Harriman . . . On the whole, she considered, a kind of justice had been achieved, although, if they knew what she did, neither Alec nor his superintendent would agree.

She sighed. "Yes, marvellous idea," she said. "On an island, with any luck, we should be safe from Mr. Crane!"

HISTORICAL NOTE

During the First World War, 306 British and Common-
wealth troops were executed by firing squad in the field for
deserting their posts and for cowardice. Almost all were non-
commissioned soldiers. (Officers in the same situation were
diagnosed with shell-shock and sent to hospitals.) The youngest was sixteen years old. In 2006, all were granted pardons
by the secretary of defence.

Though Mr. Tesler is fictional, FSSW did have a history
teacher, Stanley King Beer, who was imprisoned as a Conscientious Objector during WWI. He was a vegetarian, and as
no allowance was made for this, he survived mostly on bread
and his health was seriously undermined.